RUNNI[illegible]

THE FREEDOM TRAP

Desmond Bagley was born in 1923 in Kendal, Westmorland, and brought up in Blackpool. He began his working life, aged 14, in the printing industry and then did a variety of jobs until going into an aircraft factory at the start of the Second World War.

When the war ended, he decided to travel to southern Africa, going overland through Europe and the Sahara. He worked en route, reaching South Africa in 1951.

Bagley became a freelance journalist in Johannesburg and wrote his first published novel, *The Golden Keel*, in 1962. In 1964 he returned to England and lived in Totnes, Devon, for twelve years. He and his wife Joan then moved to Guernsey in the Channel Islands. Here he found the ideal place for combining his writing and his other interests, which included computers, mathematics, military history, and entertaining friends from all over the world.

Desmond Bagley died in April 1983, having become one of the world's top-selling authors, with his 16 books – two of them published after his death – translated into more than 30 languages.

'I've read all Bagley's books and he's marvellous, the best.' ALISTAIR MACLEAN

By the same author

Flyaway AND *Windfall*

The Golden Keel AND *The Vivero Letter*

High Citadel AND *Landslide*

The Snow Tiger AND *Night of Error*

The Spoilers AND *Juggernaut*

The Tightrope Men AND *The Enemy*

Wyatt's Hurricane AND *Bahama Crisis*

DESMOND BAGLEY

Running Blind

AND

The Freedom Trap

HARPER

HARPER
an imprint of HarperCollins*Publishers*
77-85 Fulham Palace Road
Hammersmith, London W6 8JB
www.harpercollins.co.uk

This omnibus edition 2009
1

Running Blind first published in Great Britain by Collins 1970
The Freedom Trap first published in Great Britain by Collins 1971
A Matter of Months first published in *Winter's Crimes 8*,
edited by Hilary Watson, by Macmillan 1976

Desmond Bagley asserts the moral right to
be identified as the author of these works

ISBN 978 0 00 730474 5

Printed and bound in Great Britain by
Clays Ltd, St Ives plc

CONTENTS

RUNNING BLIND

To: Torfi, Gudjon, Helga, Gisli, Herdis
Valtýr, Gudmundur, Teitur, Siggi, and all
the other Icelanders.
Thanks for lending me your country.

ONE

To be encumbered with a corpse is to be in a difficult position, especially when the corpse is without benefit of death certificate. True, any doctor, even one just hatched from medical school, would have been able to diagnose the cause of death. The man had died of heart failure or what the medical boys pompously call cardiac arrest.

The proximate cause of his pumper having stopped pumping was that someone had slid a sharp sliver of steel between his ribs just far enough to penetrate the great muscle of the heart and to cause a serious and irreversible leakage of blood so that it stopped beating. Cardiac arrest, as I said.

I wasn't too anxious to find a doctor because the knife was mine and the hilt had been in my hand when the point pricked out his life. I stood on the open road with the body at my feet and I was scared, so scared that my bowels loosened and the nausea rose in my throat to choke me. I don't know which is the worse – to kill someone you know or to kill a stranger. This particular body had been a stranger – in fact, he still was – I had never seen him before in my life.

And this was the way it happened.

Less than two hours previously the airliner had slid beneath the clouds and I saw the familiar, grim landscape of Southern Iceland. The aircraft lost height over the Reykjanes Peninsula and landed dead on time at Keflavik

International Airport, where it was raining, a thin drizzle weeping from an iron grey sky.

I was unarmed, if you except the *sgian dubh.* Customs officers don't like guns so I didn't carry a pistol, and Slade said it wasn't necessary. The *sgian dubh* – the black knife of the Highlander – is a much underrated weapon if, these days, it is ever regarded as a weapon at all. One sees it in the stocking tops of sober Scotsmen when they are in the glory of national dress and it is just another piece of masculine costume jewellery.

Mine was more functional. It had been given to me by my grandfather who had it off his grandfather, so that made it at least a hundred and fifty years old. Like any good piece of killing equipment it had no unnecessary trimmings – even the apparent decorations had a function. The ebony haft was ribbed on one side in the classic Celtic basket-weave pattern to give a good grip when drawing, but smooth on the other side so it would draw clear without catching; the blade was less than four inches long, but long enough to reach a vital organ; even the gaudy cairngorm stone set in the pommel had its use – it balanced the knife so that it made a superlative throwing weapon.

It lived in a flat sheath in my left stocking top. Where else would you expect to keep a *sgian dubh*? The obvious way is often the best because most people don't see the obvious. The Customs officer didn't even look, not into my luggage and certainly not into the more intimate realms of my person. I had been in and out of the country so often that I am tolerably well known, and the fact I speak the language was a help – there are only 20,000 people who speak Icelandic and the Icelanders have a comical air of pleased surprise when they encounter a foreigner who has taken the trouble to learn it.

'Will you be fishing again, Mr Stewart?' asked the Customs officer.

I nodded. 'Yes, I hope to kill a few of your salmon. I've had my gear sterilized – here's the certificate.' The Icelanders are trying to keep out the salmon disease which has attacked the fish in British rivers.

He took the certificate and waved me through the barrier. 'The best of luck,' he said.

I smiled at him and passed through into the concourse and went into the coffee shop in accordance with the instructions Slade had given me. I ordered coffee and presently someone sat next to me and laid down a copy of the *New York Times*. 'Gee!' he said. 'It's colder here than in the States.'

'It's even colder in Birmingham,' I said solemnly, and then, the silly business of the passwords over, we got down to business.

'It's wrapped in the newspaper,' he said.

He was a short, balding man with the worried look of the ulcered executive. I tapped the newspaper. 'What is it?' I asked.

'I don't know. You know where to take it?'

'Akureyri,' I said. 'But why me? Why can't you take it?'

'Not me,' he said definitely. 'I take the next flight out to the States.' He seemed relieved at that simple fact.

'Let's be normal,' I said. 'I'll buy you a coffee.' I caught the eye of a waitress.

'Thanks,' he said, and laid down a key-ring. 'There's a car in the parking lot outside – the registration number is written alongside the masthead of *The Times* there.'

'Most obliging of you,' I said. 'I was going to take a taxi.'

'I don't do things to be obliging,' he said shortly. 'I do things because I'm told to do them, just like you – and right now I'm doing the telling and you're doing the doing. You don't drive along the main road to Reykjavik; you go by way of Krysuvik and Kleifavatn.'

I was sipping coffee when he said that and I spluttered. When I came to the surface and got my breath back I said,

'Why the hell should I do that? It's double the distance and along lousy roads.'

'I don't know,' he said. 'I'm just the guy who passes the word. But it was a last-minute instruction so maybe someone's got wind that maybe someone else is laying for you somewhere on the main road. I wouldn't know.'

'You don't know much, do you?' I said acidly, and tapped the newspaper. 'You don't know what's in here; you don't know why I should waste the afternoon in driving around the Reykjanes Peninsula. If I asked you the time of day I doubt if you'd tell me.'

He gave me a sly, sideways grin. 'I bet one thing,' he said. 'I bet I know more than you do.'

'That wouldn't be too difficult,' I said grumpily. It was all of a piece with everything Slade did; he worked on the 'need to know' principle and what you didn't know wouldn't hurt him.

He finished his coffee. 'That's it, buster – except for one thing. When you get to Reykjavik leave the car parked outside the Hotel Saga and just walk away from it. It'll be taken care of.'

He got up without another word and walked away, seemingly in a hurry to get away from me. All during our brief conversation he had seemed jittery, which worried me because it didn't square with Slade's description of the job. 'It'll be simple,' Slade had said. 'You're just a messenger boy.' The twist of his lips had added the implied sneer that it was all I was good for.

I stood and jammed the newspaper under my arm. The concealed package was moderately heavy but not obtrusive. I picked up my gear and went outside to look for the car; it proved to be a Ford Cortina, and minutes later I was on my way out of Keflavik and going south – away from Reykjavik. I wished I knew the idiot who said, 'The longest way round is the shortest way there.'

When I found a quiet piece of road I pulled on to the shoulder and picked up the newspaper from the seat where I had tossed it. The package was as Slade had described it – small and heavier than one would have expected. It was covered in brown hessian, neatly stitched up, and looked completely anonymous. Careful tapping seemed to indicate that under the hessian was a metal box, and there were no rattles when it was shaken.

I regarded it thoughtfully but that didn't give me any clue, so I wrapped it in the newspaper again, dropped it on the back seat, and drove on. It had stopped raining and driving conditions weren't too bad – for Iceland. The average Icelandic road makes an English farm track look like a super-highway. Where there are roads, that is. In the interior, which Icelanders know as the *Óbyggdir*, there are no roads and in winter the *Óbyggdir* is pretty near as inaccessible as the moon unless you're the hearty explorer type. It looks very much like the moon, too; Neil Armstrong practised his moon-walk there.

I drove on and, at Krysuvik, I turned inland, past the distant vapour-covered slopes where super-heated steam boils from the guts of the earth. Not far short of the lake of Kleifavatn I saw a car ahead, pulled off the road, and a man waving the universally recognized distress signal of the stranded motorist.

We were both damned fools; I because I stopped and he because he was alone. He spoke to me in bad Danish and then in good Swedish, both of which I understand. It turned out, quite naturally, that there was something wrong with his car and he couldn't get it to move.

I got out of the Cortina. 'Lindholm,' he said in the formal Swedish manner, and stuck out his hand which I pumped up and down once in the way which protocol dictates.

'I'm Stewart,' I said, and walked over to his Volkswagen and peered at the exposed rear engine.

I don't think he wanted to kill me at first or he would have used the gun straight away. As it was he took a swipe at me with a very professionally designed lead-loaded cosh. I think it was when he got behind me that I realized I was being a flaming idiot – that's a result of being out of practice. I turned my head and saw his upraised arm and dodged sideways. If the cosh had connected with my skull it would have jarred my brains loose; instead it hit my shoulder and my whole arm went numb.

I gave him the boot in the shin, raking down from knee to ankle, and he yelped and hopped back, which gave me time to put the car between us, and groped for the *sgian dubh* as I went. Fortunately it's a left-handed weapon which was just as well because my right arm wasn't going to be of use.

He came for me again but when he saw the knife he hesitated, his lips curling away from his teeth. He dropped the cosh and dipped his hand beneath his jacket and it was my turn to hesitate. But his cosh was *too* well designed; it had a leather wrist loop and the dangling weapon impeded his draw and I jumped him just as the pistol came out.

I didn't stab him. He swung around and ran straight into the blade. There was a gush of blood over my hand and he sagged against me with a ludicrous look of surprise on his face. Then he went down at my feet and the knife came free and blood pulsed from his chest into the lava dust.

So there I was on a lonely road in Southern Iceland with a newly created corpse at my feet and a bloody knife in my hand, the taste of raw bile in my throat and a frozen brain. From the time I had got out of the Cortina to the moment of death had been less than two minutes.

I don't think I consciously thought of what I did next; I think that rigorous training took over. I jumped for the Cortina and ran it forward a little so that it covered the body. Lonely though the road might be that didn't mean a car couldn't pass at any time and a body in plain sight would take a hell of a lot of explaining away.

Then I took the *New York Times* which, its other virtues apart, contains more newsprint than practically any other newspaper in the world, and used it to line the boot of the car. That done, I reversed again, picked up the body and dumped it into the boot and slammed the lid down quickly. Lindholm – if that was his name – was now out of sight if not out of mind.

He had bled like a cow in a Moslem slaughter-house and there was a great pool of blood by the side of the road. My jacket and trousers were also liberally bedaubed. I couldn't do much about my clothing right then but I covered the blood pool with handfuls of lava dust. I closed the engine compartment of the Volkswagen, got behind the wheel and switched on. Lindholm had not only been an attempted murderer – he had also been a liar because the engine caught immediately. I reversed the car over the bloody bit of ground and left it there. It was too much to hope that the blood wouldn't be noticed when the car was taken away but I had to do what I could.

I got back into the Cortina after one last look at the scene of the crime and drove away, and it was then I began to think consciously. First I thought of Slade and damned his soul to hell and then I moved into more practicable channels of thought such as how to get rid of Lindholm. You'd think that in a country four-fifths the size of England with a population less than half of, say Plymouth, there'd be wide open spaces with enough nooks and crannies to hide an inconvenient body. True enough, but this particular bit of Iceland – the south-west – was also the most heavily populated and it wasn't going to be particularly easy.

Still, I knew the country and, after a little while, I began to get ideas. I checked the petrol gauge and settled down for a long drive, hoping that the car was in good trim. To stop and be found with a blood-smeared jacket would cause the asking of pointed questions. I had another outfit in my suitcase but all at once there were too many cars about and I preferred to change discreetly.

Most of Iceland is volcanic and the south-west is particularly so with bleak vistas of lava fields, ash cones and shield volcanoes, some of them extinct, some not. In my travels I had once come across a gas vent which now seemed an ideal place for the last repose of Lindholm, and it was there I was heading.

It was a two-hour drive and, towards the end, I had to leave the road and take to the open country, bouncing across a waste of volcanic ash and scoria which did the Cortina no good. The last time I had been that way I had driven my Land-Rover which is made for that sort of country.

The place was exactly as I remembered it. There was an extinct crater with a riven side so that one could drive right into the caldera and in the middle was a rocky pustule with a hole in it through which the hot volcanic gases had driven in some long-gone eruption. The only sign that any other human being had been there since the creation of the world was the mark of tyre tracks driving up towards the lip of the crater. The Icelanders have their own peculiar form of motor sport; they drive into a crater and try to get out the hard way. I've never known anyone break his neck at this hazardous game but it's not for want of trying.

I drove the car as near to the gas vent as I could and then went forward on foot until I could look into the impenetrable darkness of the hole. I dropped a stone into it and there was a receding clatter which went on for a long time. Verne's hero who went to the centre of the earth might have had an easier time if he had picked this hole instead of Snaefellsjökull.

Before I popped Lindholm into his final resting-place I searched him. It was a messy business because the blood was still sticky and it was lucky I had not yet changed my suit. He had a Swedish passport made out in the name of Axel Lindholm, but that didn't mean a thing – passports are easy to come by. There were a few more bits and pieces but nothing of importance, and all I retained were the cosh and the pistol, a Smith & Wesson .38.

Then I carried him up to the vent and dropped him into it. There were a few soggy thumps and then silence – a silence I hoped would be eternal. I went back to the car and changed into a clean suit and pulled the stained clothing inside out so that the blood would not touch the inside of my suitcase. The cosh, the pistol and Slade's damned package I also tossed into the suitcase before I closed it, and then I set off on the wearisome way to Reykjavik.

I was very tired.

II

It was late evening when I pulled up in front of the Hotel Saga, although it was still light with the brightness of the northern summer. My eyes were sore because I had been driving right into the western sun and I stayed in the car for a moment to rest them. If I had stayed in the car two minutes more the next fateful thing would not have happened, but I didn't; I got out and was just extracting the suitcase when a tall man came out of the hotel, paused, and hailed me. 'Alan Stewart!'

I looked up and cursed under my breath because the man in the uniform of an Icelandair pilot was the last man I wanted to see – Bjarni Ragnarsson. 'Hello, Bjarni,' I said.

We shook hands. 'Elin didn't tell me you were coming.'

'She didn't know,' I said. 'It was a last-minute decision; I didn't even have time to telephone.'

He looked at my suitcase resting on the pavement. 'You're not staying at the Saga!' he said in surprise.

It was a snap judgment and I had to make it fast. 'No,' I said. 'I'll be going to the apartment.' I didn't want to bring Elin into this but now her brother knew I was in Reykjavik he would be sure to tell her and I didn't want her to be hurt in that way. Elin was very special.

I saw Bjarni looking at the car. 'I'll leave it here,' I said lightly. 'It's just a delivery job for a friend. I'll take a taxi to the apartment.'

He accepted that, and said, 'Staying long?'

'For the rest of the summer, as usual,' I said easily.

'We must go fishing,' he said.

I agreed. 'Have you become a father yet?'

'Another month,' he said glumly. 'I'm dreading it.'

I laughed. 'I should think that's Kristin's worry; you aren't even in the country half the time. No nappy-changing for you.'

We spent another few minutes in the usual idle-small-talk of old friends just met and then he glanced at his watch. 'I have a flight to Greenland,' he said. 'I must go. I'll ring you in a couple of days.'

'Do that.' I watched him go and then captured a taxi which had just dropped a fare at the hotel and told the driver where to go. Outside the building I paid him off and then stood uncertainly on the pavement wondering whether I was doing the right thing.

Elin Ragnarsdottir was someone very special.

She was a schoolteacher but, like many other Icelanders of her type, she held down two jobs. There are certain factors about Iceland – the smallness of population, the size of the country and its situation in high northern latitudes – which result in a social system which outsiders are apt to find weird. But since the system is designed to suit Icelanders they don't give a damn what outsiders think, which is just as it should be.

One result of this social system is that all the schools close down for four months in the summer and a lot of them are used as hotels. The teachers thus have a lot of spare time and many of them have quite a different summer occupation. When I first met her three years earlier, Elin had been a courier for *Ferdaskrifstofaa Nordri,* a travel agency in Reykjavik, and had shown visitors around the country.

A couple of seasons before, I had persuaded her to become my personal courier on a full-time summer basis. I had been afraid that her brother, Bjarni, might have thought that a touch irregular and put in an objection, but he didn't – presumably he thought his sister to be grown-up enough to handle her own affairs. She was an undemanding person and it was an easy relationship, but obviously it couldn't go on like that for ever and I intended to do something about it, but I doubted if this was the appropriate time – it takes someone with a stronger stomach than mine to propose marriage on the same day one has dropped a body down a hole.

I went up to the apartment and, although I had a key, I didn't use it; instead I knocked on the door. Elin opened it and looked at me with an expression of surprise changing to delight, and something in me jumped at the sight of her trim figure and corn-coloured hair. 'Alan!' she said. 'Why didn't you tell me you were coming?'

'A quick decision,' I said, and held up the cased fishing-rod. 'I've got a new one.'

Her lips curved down in mock glumness. 'That makes six,' she said severely, and held the door wide. 'Oh, come in, darling!'

I went in, dropped the suitcase and the rod, and took her in my arms. She held me closely and said, with her head against my chest, 'You didn't write, and I thought . . .'

'You thought I wasn't coming.' The reason I hadn't written was because of something Slade had said, but I couldn't tell her that. I said, 'I've been very busy, Elin.'

She drew back her head and looked at me intently. 'Yes, your face is drawn; you look tired.'

I smiled. 'But I feel hungry.'

She kissed me. 'I'll prepare something.' She broke away. 'Don't worry about unpacking your bag; I'll do it after supper.'

I thought of the bloody suit. 'Not to worry,' I said. 'I can do it.' I picked up the suitcase and the rod and took them into my room. I call it my room because it was the place where my gear was stored. Actually, the whole apartment was mine because, although it was in Elin's name, I paid the rent. Spending one-third of every year in Iceland, it was convenient to have a *pied-à-terre*.

I put the rod with the others and laid down the suitcase, wondering what to do with the suit. Until that moment I had never had any secrets I wanted to keep from Elin – with the one important exception – and there wasn't a lockable cupboard or drawer in the place. I opened the wardrobe and surveyed the line of suits and jackets, each on its hanger and neatly encased in its zippered plastic bag. It would be very risky to let the suit take its place in that line; Elin was meticulous in the care of my clothes and would be certain to find it.

In the end I emptied the suitcase of everything but the suit and the weapons, locked it, and heaved it on top of the wardrobe where it usually lived when not in use. It was unlikely that Elin would pull it down and even then it was locked, although that was not usual.

I took off my shirt and examined it closely and discovered a spot of blood on the front so I took it into the bathroom and cleaned it under the cold tap. Then I scrubbed my face in cold water and felt better for it. By the time Elin called that supper was ready I was cleaned up and already in the living-room looking through the window.

I was about to turn away when my attention was caught by a flicker of movement. On the other side of the street there was an alley between two buildings and it had seemed that someone had moved quickly out of sight when I twitched the curtains. I stared across the street but saw nothing more, but when Elin called again I was thoughtful as I turned to her.

Over supper I said, 'How's the Land-Rover?'

'I didn't know when you were coming but I had a complete overhaul done last week. It's ready for anything.'

Icelandic roads being what they are, Land-Rovers are as thick as fleas on a dog. The Icelanders prefer the short wheelbase Land-Rover, but ours was the long wheelbase job, fitted out as a camping van. When we travelled we were self-contained and could, and did, spend many weeks away from civilization, only being driven into a town by running out of food. There were worse ways of spending a summer than to be alone for weeks on end with Elin Ragnarsdottir.

In other summers we had left as soon as I arrived in Reykjavik, but this time it had to be different because of Slade's package, and I wondered how I was to get to Akureyri alone without arousing her suspicions. Slade had said the job was going to be easy but the late Mr Lindholm made all the difference and I didn't want Elin involved in any part of it. Still, all I had to do was to deliver the package and the job would be over and the summer would be like all the other summers. It didn't seem too difficult.

I was mulling this over when Elin said, 'You really do look tired. You must have been overworking.'

I managed a smile. 'An exhausting winter. There was too much snow on the hills – I lost a lot of stock.' Suddenly I remembered. 'You wanted to see what the glen was like; I brought you some photographs.'

I went and got the photographs and we pored over them. I pointed out Bheinn Fhada and Sgurr Dearg, but Elin was more interested in the river and the trees. 'All those trees,' she said luxuriously. 'Scotland must be beautiful.' That was an expected reaction from an Icelander; the island is virtually treeless. 'Are there salmon in your river?'

'Just trout,' I said. 'I come to Iceland for salmon.'

She picked up another photograph – a wide landscape. 'What on here is yours?'

I looked at it and grinned. 'All you can see.'

'Oh!' She was silent for a while, then said a little shyly, 'I've never really thought about it, Alan; but you must be rich.'

'I'm no Croesus,' I said. 'But I get by. Three thousand acres of heather isn't very productive, but sheep on the hills and forestry in the glen bring in the bread, and Americans who come to shoot the deer put butter on the bread.' I stroked her arm. 'You'll have to come to Scotland.'

'I'd like that,' she said simply.

I put it to her fast. 'I have to see a man in Akureyri tomorrow – it's a favour I'm doing for a friend. That means I'll have to fly. Why don't you take up the Land-Rover and meet me there? Or would it be too much for you to drive all that way?'

She laughed at me. 'I can drive the Land-Rover better than you.' She began to calculate. 'It's 450 kilometres; I wouldn't want to do that in one day so I'd stop somewhere near Hvammstangi. I could be in Akureyri at mid-morning the next day.'

'No need to break your neck,' I said casually. I was relieved; I could fly to Akureyri, get rid of the package before Elin got there and all would be well. There was no need to involve her at all. I said, 'I'll probably stay at the Hotel Vardborg. You can telephone me there.'

But when we went to bed I found I was strung up with unrelieved tensions and I could do nothing for her. While holding Elin in the darkness, Lindholm's face hovered ghost-like in my inner vision and again I tasted the nausea in my throat. I choked a little, and said, 'I'm sorry.'

'It doesn't matter, darling,' she said quietly. 'You're tired. Just go to sleep.'

But I couldn't. I lay on my back and reviewed the whole of an unpleasant day. I went over every word that had been said by my uncommunicative contact at Keflavik airport, the man whom Slade had said would pass me the package. *'Don't take the main road to Reykjavik,'* he had said. *'Go by Krysuvik.'*

So I had gone by Krysuvik and come within an ace of being killed. Chance or design? Would the same thing have happened had I gone by the main road? Had I been set up as a patsy deliberately?

The man at the airport had been Slade's man, or at least he had the password that Slade had arranged. But supposing he wasn't Slade's man and still had the password – it wasn't too hard to think up ways and means of that coming about. Then why had he set me up for Lindholm? Certainly not for the package – he already had the package! Scratch that one and start again.

Supposing he *had* been Slade's man and had still set me up for Lindholm – that made less sense. And, again, it couldn't have been for the package; he needn't have given it to me in the first place. It all boiled down to the fact that the man at the airport and Lindholm had nothing to do with each other.

But Lindholm had definitely been waiting for me. He had even made sure of my name before attacking. So how in hell did he know I'd be on the Krysuvik road? That was one I couldn't answer.

Presently, when I was sure Elin was sound asleep, I got out of bed quietly and went into the kitchen, not bothering to turn on a light. I opened the refrigerator and poured myself a glass of milk, then wandered into the living-room and sat by the window. The short northern night was almost over but it was still dark enough to see the sudden glow from the alley across the street as the watching man drew on a cigarette.

He worried me because I was no longer certain Elin was safe.

III

We were both up early, Elin because she wanted to make a quick start for Akureyri, and I because I wanted to get at the Land-Rover before Elin did. I had some things to stow in the Land-Rover that I didn't want Elin to know about; Lindholm's gun, for instance. I taped it securely to one of the main chassis girders and well out of sight. His cosh I put in my pocket. It had occurred to me that if things did not go well I might be in need of weaponry in Akureyri.

I didn't have to go out of the front door to get at the Land-Rover because the garage was at the back, and so the watcher in the alley got no sight of me. But I saw him because the next thing I did was to take a pair of field glasses one flight up to a landing where there was a window overlooking the street.

He was a tall, lean man with a neat moustache and he looked cold. If he had been there all night without a break he would be not only frozen to the marrow but starving. I made sure I would know him again if I saw him and lowered the glasses just as someone came downstairs from an upstairs flat. It was a middle-aged grey-haired woman who looked at me and then at the glasses and gave a meaningful sniff.

I grinned. It was the first time I had been suspected of voyeurism.

I enjoyed breakfast all the more because of my hungry friend across the street. 'You're looking more cheerful,' said Elin.

'It's your cooking,' I said.

She looked at the herring, the cheese, the bread and the eggs. 'What cooking? Anyone can boil an egg.'

'Not like you,' I assured her.

But I *was* more cheerful. The dark thoughts of the night had gone and in spite of all the unanswered questions the death of Lindholm no longer oppressed me. He had tried to kill me and failed, and had suffered the penalty for failure. The fact that I had killed him didn't weigh too heavily upon my conscience. My only lingering worry was for Elin.

I said, 'There's a flight for Akureyri from Reykjavik City Airport at eleven.'

'You'll have lunch there,' said Elin. 'Spare a thought for me bouncing about down in Kaldidalur.' She swallowed hot coffee hastily. 'I'd like to leave as soon as possible.'

I waved at the laden table. 'I'll clean up here.'

She got ready to leave, then picked up the binoculars. 'I thought these were in the Land-Rover.'

'I was just checking them,' I said. 'They seemed a bit out of focus last time I used them. They're all right, though.'

'Then I'll take them,' she said.

I went with her down to the garage and kissed her goodbye. She looked at me closely, and said, 'Everything *is* all right, isn't it, Alan?'

'Of course; why do you ask?'

'I don't really know. I'm just being feminine, I suppose. See you in Akureyri.'

I waved her off and watched as she drove away. Nobody seemed to bother; no heads popped around corners and no one followed in hot pursuit. I went back into the flat and checked on the watcher in the alley. He wasn't to be seen, so I made a mad dash for the upstairs landing from where I could get a better view and I breathed easier when I saw him leaning against the wall, beating his hands against his arms.

It would seem that he was not aware that Elin had left or, if he was, he didn't care. It lifted a considerable load off my mind.

I washed the breakfast crockery and then went to my room where I took a camera bag and emptied it of its contents. Then I took the hessian-covered steel box and found that it fitted neatly into the leather bag. From now on it was not going to leave my person until I handed it over in Akureyri.

At ten o'clock I rang for a taxi and left for the airport, a move which resulted in some action. I looked back along the street and saw a car draw up near the alley into which my watcher jumped. The car followed the taxi all the way to the airport, keeping a discreet distance.

On arrival I went to the reservation counter. 'I have a reservation on the flight to Akureyri. My name is Stewart.'

The receptionist checked a list. 'Oh, yes; Mr Stewart.' She looked at the clock. 'But you're early.'

'I'll have a coffee,' I said. 'It passes the time.'

She gave me the ticket and I paid for it, then she said, 'Your luggage is weighed over there.'

I touched the camera case. 'This is all I have. I travel light.'

She laughed. 'So I see, Mr Stewart. And may I compliment you on how you speak our language.'

'Thank you.' I turned and saw a recognized face lurking close by – my watcher was still watching. I ignored him and headed for the coffee-counter where I bought a newspaper and settled down to wait.

My man had a hurried conversation at the reservation counter, bought a ticket, and then came my way and both of us ignored each other completely. He ordered a late breakfast and ate ravenously, his eyes flicking in my direction infrequently. Presently I had a stroke of luck; the announcement loudspeaker cleared its throat and said in Icelandic, 'Mr Buchner is wanted on the telephone.' When it repeated this in fluent German my man looked up, got to his feet, and went to answer the call.

At least I could now put a name to him, and whether the name was accurate or not was really immaterial.

He could see me from the telephone-box and spoke facing outwards as though he expected me to make a break for it. I disappointed him by languidly ordering another coffee and becoming immersed in a newspaper account of how many salmon Bing Crosby had caught on his latest visit to Iceland.

In airport waiting lounges time seems to stretch interminably and it was a couple of eons before the flight to Akureyri was announced. Herr Buchner was close behind me in the queue and in the stroll across the apron towards the aircraft, and he chose a seat on the aisle just behind me.

We took off and flew across Iceland, over the cold glaciers of Langjökull and Hofsjökull, and soon enough we were circling over Eyjafjördur preparatory to landing at Akureyri, a city of fully ten thousand souls, the metropolis of Northern Iceland. The aircraft lurched to a halt and I undid my seat-belt, hearing the answering click as Buchner, behind me, did the same.

The attack, when it came, was made with smoothness and efficiency. I left the airport building and was walking towards the taxi rank when suddenly they were all about me – four of them. One stood in front of me and grabbed my right hand, pumping it up and down while babbling in a loud voice about how good it was to see me again and the enormous pleasure it would give him to show me the marvels of Akureyri.

The man on my left crowded hard and pinned my left arm. He put his mouth close to my ear, and said in Swedish, 'Don't make trouble, Herr Stewartsen; or you will be dead.' I could believe him because the man behind me had a gun in my back.

I heard a snip and turned my head just as the man on my right cut through the shoulder-strap of the camera case with a small pair of shears. I felt the strap snake loose and then he was gone and the camera case with him, while the man behind me took his place with one arm thrown carelessly over my shoulder and the other digging the gun into my ribs.

I could see Buchner standing by a taxi about ten yards away. He looked at me with a blank face and then turned and bent to get into the car. It drove away and I saw the white smudge of his face as he looked through the back window.

They kept up the act for two minutes more to give the man with the camera case time to get clear, and the man on my left said, again in Swedish, 'Herr Stewartsen: we're going to let you go now, but I wouldn't do anything foolish if I were you.'

They released me and each took a step away, their faces hard and their eyes watchful. There were no guns in sight but that didn't mean a damn thing. Not that I intended to start anything; the camera case was gone and the odds were too great anyway. As though someone had given a signal they all turned and walked away, each in a different direction, and left me standing there. There was quite a few people around but not one of the good people of Akureyri had any idea that anything untoward had just happened in their line of sight.

I felt ruffled so I straightened my jacket and then took a taxi to the Hotel Vardborg. There wasn't anything else to do.

IV

Elin had been right; I was in time to lunch at the Vardborg. I had just stuck my fork into the mutton when Herr Buchner walked in, looked around and spotted me, and headed in my direction. He stood on the other side of the table, twitched his moustache, and said, 'Mr Stewart?'

I leaned back. 'Well, if it isn't Herr Buchner! What can I do for you?'

'My name is Graham,' he said coldly. 'And I'd like to talk to you.'

'You were Buchner this morning,' I said. 'But if I had a name like that I'd want to change it, too.' I waved him towards a chair. 'Be my guest – I can recommend the soup.'

He sat down stiffly. 'I'm not in the mood for acting straight man to your comedian,' he said, extracting his wallet from his pocket. 'My credentials.' He pushed a scrap of paper across the table.

I unfolded it to find the left half of a 100-kronur banknote. When I matched it against the other half from my own wallet the two halves fitted perfectly. I looked up at him. 'Well, Mr Graham; that seems to be in order. What can I do for you?'

'You can give me the package,' he said. 'That's all I want.'

I shook my head regretfully. 'You know better than that.'

He frowned. 'What do you mean?'

'I mean that I can't give you the package because I haven't got it.'

His moustache twitched again and his eyes turned cold. 'Let's have no games, Stewart. The package.' He held out his hand.

'Damn it!' I said. 'You were there – you know what happened.'

'I don't know what you're talking about. I was where?'

'Outside Akureyri Airport. You were taking a taxi.'

His eyes flickered. 'Was I?' he said colourlessly. 'Go on!'

'They grabbed me before I knew what was happening, and they got clean away with the package. It was in my camera case.'

His voice cracked. 'You mean you haven't got it!'

I said sardonically, 'If you were supposed to be my bodyguard you did a bloody awful job. Slade isn't going to like it.'

'By God, he's not!' said Graham with feeling. A tic pulsed under his right eye. 'So it was in the camera case.'

'Where else would it be? It was the only luggage I carried. You ought to know that – you were standing right behind me with your big ears flapping when I checked in at Reykjavik airport.'

He gave me a look of dislike. 'You think you're clever, don't you?' He leaned forward. 'There's going to be a Godawful row about this. You'd better stay available, Stewart; you'd better be easy to find when I come back.'

I shrugged. 'Where would I go? Besides, I have the Scottish sense of thrift, and my room here is paid for.'

'You take this damned coolly.'

'What do you expect me to do? Burst into tears?' I laughed in his face. 'Grow up, Graham.'

His face tightened but he said nothing; instead he stood up and walked away. I put in fifteen minutes of deep thought while polishing off the mutton and at the end of that time I came to a decision, and the decision was that I could do with a drink, so I went to find one.

As I walked through the hotel foyer I saw Buchner-Graham hard at work in a telephone-box. Although it wasn't particularly warm he was sweating.

V

I came out of a dreamless sleep because someone was shaking me and hissing, 'Stewart, wake up!' I Opened my eyes and found Graham leaning over me.

I blinked at him. 'Funny! I was under the impression I locked my door.'

He grinned humourlessly. 'You did. Wake up – you're going to be interviewed. You'd better have your wits sharpened.'

'What time is it?'

'Five a.m.'

I smiled. 'Gestapo technique, eh! Oh, well: I suppose I'll feel better when I've shaved.'

Graham seemed nervous. 'You'd better hurry. He'll be here in five minutes.'

'Who will?'

'You'll see.'

I ran hot water into the basin and began to lather my face. 'What *was* your function on this particular exercise, Graham? As a bodyguard you're a dead loss, so it can't have been that.'

'You'd better stop thinking about me and start to think about yourself,' he said. 'You have a lot of explaining to do.'

'True,' I said, and put down the brush and picked up the razor. The act of scraping one's face with a sliver of sharp metal always seems futile and a little depressing; I would have been happier in one of the hairier ages – counter-espionage agent by appointment to Her Majesty Queen Victoria would have been the ideal ticket.

I must have been more nervous than I thought because I shaved myself down to the blood on the first pass. Then someone knocked perfunctorily on the door and Slade came into the room. He kicked the door shut with his foot and glowered at me with a scowl on his jowly face, his hands thrust deep into his overcoat pockets. Without an overture he said briefly, 'What's the story, Stewart?'

There's nothing more calculated to put a man off his stroke than having to embark on complicated explanations with a face full of drying lather. I turned back to the mirror and continued to shave – in silence.

Slade made one of those unspellable noises – an explosive outrush of air expelled through mouth and nose. He sat on the bed and the springs creaked in protest at the excessive weight. 'It had better be good,' he said. 'I dislike being hauled out of bed and flown to the frozen north.'

I continued to shave, thinking that whatever could bring Slade from London to Akureyri must be important. After the last tricky bit around the Adam's apple, I said, 'The package must have been more important than you told me.' I turned on the cold tap and rinsed the soap from my face.

'. . . that bloody package,' he said.

'I'm sorry,' I apologized. 'I didn't hear that. I had water in my ears.'

He contained himself with difficulty. 'Where's the package?' he asked with synthetic patience.

'As of this moment I couldn't tell you.' I dried my face vigorously. 'It was taken from me at midday yesterday by four unknown males – but you know that already from Graham.'

His voice rose. 'And you let them take it – just like that!'

'There wasn't much I could do about it at the time,' I said equably. 'I had a gun in my kidneys.' I nodded towards Graham. 'What was he supposed to be doing about it – if it isn't a rude answer?'

Slade folded his hands together across his stomach. 'We thought they'd tagged Graham – that's why we brought you in. We thought they'd tackle Graham and give you a free run to the goal line.'

I didn't think much of that one. If they – whoever they were – had tagged Graham, then it wasn't at all standard procedure for him to draw attention to me by lurking outside my flat. But I let it go because Slade always had been a slippery customer and I wanted to keep something in reserve.

Instead, I said, 'They didn't tackle Graham – they tackled me. But perhaps they don't know the rules of rugby football; it's not a game they go for in Sweden.' I gave myself a last dab behind the ears and dropped the towel. 'Or in Russia,' I added as an afterthought.

Slade looked up. 'And what makes you think of Russians?'

I grinned at him. 'I always think of Russians,' I said drily. 'Like the Frenchman who always thought of sex.' I leaned over him and picked up my cigarettes. 'Besides, they called me Stewartsen.'

'So?'

'So they knew who I was – not who I am now, but what I was once. There's a distinction.'

Slade shifted his eyes to Graham and said curtly, 'Wait outside.'

Graham looked hurt but obediently went to the door. When he'd closed it I said, 'Oh, goody; now the children are out of the room we can have a grown-up conversation. And where, for Christ's sake, did you get that one? I told you I wouldn't stand for trainees on the operation.'

'What makes you think he's a trainee?'

'Come, now; he's still wet behind the ears.'

'He's a good man,' said Slade, and shifted restlessly on the bed. He was silent for a while, then he said, 'Well, you've really cocked this one up, haven't you? Just a simple matter of carrying a small parcel from A to B and you fall down on it. I knew you were past it but, by God, I didn't think you were so bloody decrepit.' He wagged his finger. 'And they called you Stewartsen! You know what that means?'

'Kennikin,' I said, not relishing the thought. 'Is he here – in Iceland?'

Slade hunched his shoulders. 'Not that I know of.' He looked at me sideways. 'When you were contacted in Reykjavik what were you told?'

I shrugged. 'Not much. There was a car provided which I had to drive to Reykjavik by way of Krysuvik and leave parked outside the Saga. I did all that.'

Slade grunted in his throat. 'Run into any trouble?'

'Was I supposed to?' I asked blandly.

He shook his head irritably. 'We had word that something might happen. It seemed best to re-route you.' He stood up with a dissatisfied look on his face and went to the door. 'Graham!'

I said, 'I'm sorry about all this, Slade; I really am.'

'Being sorry butters no bloody parsnips. We'll just have to see what we can salvage from this mess. Hell, I brought you in because the Department is short-handed – and now we have a whole country to seal off because of your stupidity.' He turned to Graham. 'Put a call through to the Department in London; I'll take it downstairs. And talk to Captain Lee at the airport; I want that plane to be ready to take off at five minutes' notice. We may have to move fast.'

I coughed delicately. 'Me, too?'

Slade looked at me malevolently. 'You! You've caused enough of a shambles on this operation.'

'Well, what do I do?'

'You can go to hell for all I care,' he said. 'Go back to Reykjavik and shack up with your girl-friend for the rest of the summer.' He turned and bumped into Graham. 'What the hell are you waiting for?' he snarled, and Graham fled.

Slade paused at the door and said without turning, 'But you'd better watch out for Kennikin because I'll not lift a finger to stop him. By God, I hope he *does* nail you!'

The door slammed and I sat on the bed and brooded. I knew that if ever I met Kennikin again I would be meeting death.

TWO

Elin rang up as I was finishing breakfast. From the static and the slight fading I could tell she was using the radio-telephone in the Land-Rover. Most vehicles travelling long distances in Iceland are fitted with radio-telephones, a safety measure called for by the difficult nature of the terrain. That's the standard explanation, but not the whole truth. The fact is that Icelanders *like* telephoning and constitute one of the gabbiest nations on earth, coming just after the United States and Canada in the number of calls per head.

She asked if I had slept well and I assured her I had, then I said, 'When will you get here?'

'About eleven-thirty.'

'I'll meet you at the camp site,' I said.

That gave me two hours which I spent in walking around Akureyri like a tourist, ducking in and out of shops, unexpectedly retracing my steps and, in general acting the fool. But when I joined Elin at the camp site I was absolutely sure that I didn't have a tail. It seemed as though Slade had been telling the truth when he said he had no further use for me.

I opened the door of the Land-Rover, and said, 'Move over; I'll drive.'

Elin looked at me in surprise. 'Aren't we staying?'

'We'll drive a little way out of town and then have lunch. There's something I want to talk to you about.'

I drove along the north road by the coast, moving fast and keeping a close check behind. As it became clear that no one was following I began to relax, although not so much as to take the worry from Elin's eyes. She could see I was preoccupied and tactfully kept silent, but at last she said, 'There's something wrong, isn't there?'

'You're so damn right,' I said. 'That's what I want to discuss.'

Back in Scotland Slade had warned me about involving Elin in the operation; he had also invoked the Official Secrets Act with its penalties for blabbermouths. But if my future life with Elin was going to mean anything at all I had to tell her the truth and to hell with Slade and to hell with the Official Secrets Act.

I slowed down and left the road to bump over turf, and stopped overlooking the sea. The land fell away in a rumble of boulders to the grey water and in the distance the island of Grimsey loomed hazily through the mist. Apart from the scrap of land there wasn't a damned thing between us and the North Pole. This was the Arctic Ocean.

I said, 'What do you know about me, Elin?'

'That's a strange question. You're Alan Stewart – whom I like very much.'

'Is that all?'

She shrugged. 'What else do I need to know?'

I smiled. 'No curiosity. Elin?'

'Oh, I have my curiosity but I keep it under control. If you want me to know anything, you'll tell me,' she said tranquilly, then hesitated. 'I do know one thing about you.'

'What's that?'

She turned to face me. 'I know that you have been hurt, and it happened not long before we met. That is why I keep my questions to myself – I don't want to bring the hurt back.'

'You're very perceptive,' I said. 'I didn't think it showed. Would it surprise you to know I was once a British agent – a spy?'

She regarded me curiously. 'A spy,' she said slowly, as though rolling the word about her mouth to taste it. 'Yes, it surprises me very much. It is not a very honourable occupation – you are not the type.'

'So someone else told me recently,' I said sardonically. 'Nevertheless, it is true.'

She was silent for a while, then she said, 'You *were* a spy. Alan, what you were in the past doesn't matter. I know you as you are now.'

'Sometimes the past catches up with you,' I said. 'It did with me. There's a man called Slade . . .' I stopped, wondering if I was doing the right thing.

'Yes?' she prompted me.

'He came to see me in Scotland. I'll tell you about that – about Slade in Scotland.'

II

The shooting was bad that day. Something had disturbed the deer during the night because they had left the valley where my calculations had placed them and had drifted up the steep slopes of Bheinn Fhada. I could see them through the telescopic sight – pale grey-brown shapes grazing among the heather. The way the wind was blowing the only chance I had of getting near them was by sprouting wings and so, since it was the last day of the season, the deer were safe from Stewart for the rest of the summer.

At three in the afternoon I packed up and went home and was scrambling down Sgurr Mor when I saw the car parked outside the cottage and the minuscule figure of a man pacing up and down. The cottage is hard to get to – the rough track from the clachan discourages casual tourists – and so anyone who arrives usually wants to see me very much. The reverse doesn't always apply; I'm of a retiring nature and I don't encourage visitors.

So I was very careful as I approached and stopped under cover of the rocks by the burn. I unslung the rifle, checked it again to make sure it was unloaded, and set it to my shoulder. Through the telescopic sight the man sprang plainly to view. He had his back to me but when he turned I saw it was Slade.

I centred the cross-hairs on his large pallid face and gently squeezed the trigger, and the hammer snapped home with a harmless click. I wondered if I would have done the same had there been a bullet up the spout. The world would be a better place without men like Slade. But to load was too deliberate an act, so I put up the gun and walked towards the cottage. I should have loaded the gun.

As I approached he turned and waved. 'Good afternoon,' he called, as coolly as though he were a regular and welcome guest.

I stepped up to him. 'How did you find me?'

He shrugged. 'It wasn't too hard. You know my methods.'

I knew them and I didn't like them. I said, 'Quit playing Sherlock. What do you want?'

He waved towards the door of the cottage. 'Aren't you going to invite me inside?'

'Knowing you, I'll bet you've searched the place already.'

He held up his hands in mock horror. 'On my word of honour, I haven't.'

I nearly laughed in his face because the man had no honour. I turned from him and pushed open the door and he followed me inside, clicking his tongue deprecatingly. 'Not locked? You're very trusting.'

'There's nothing here worth stealing,' I said indifferently.

'Just your life,' he said, and looked at me sharply.

I let that statement lie and put up the rifle on its rack. Slade looked about him curiously. 'Primitive – but comfortable,' he remarked. 'But I don't see why you don't live in the big house.'

'It happens to be none of your business.'

'Perhaps,' he said, and sat down. 'So you hid yourself in Scotland and didn't expect to be found. Protective coloration, eh? A Stewart hiding among a lot of Stewarts. You've caused us some little difficulty.'

'Who said I was hiding? I am a Scot, you know.'

He smiled fatly. 'Of a sort. Just by your paternal grandfather. It's not long since you were a Swede – and before that you were Finnish. You were Stewartsen then, of course.'

'Have you travelled five hundred miles just to talk of old times?' I asked tiredly.

'You're looking very fit,' he said.

'I can't say the same for you; you're out of condition and running to fat,' I said cruelly.

He chuckled. 'The fleshpots, dear boy; the fleshpots – all those lunches at the expense of Her Majesty's Government.' He waved a pudgy hand. 'But let's get down to it, Alan.'

'To you I'm Mr Stewart,' I said deliberately.

'Oh, you don't like me,' he said in a hurt voice. 'But no matter – it makes no difference in the end. I . . . we . . . want you to do a job for us. Nothing too difficult, you understand.'

'You must be out of your mind,' I said.

'I know how you must feel, but . . .'

'You don't know a damn thing,' I said sharply. 'If you expect me to work for you after what happened then you're crazier than I thought.'

I was wrong, of course; Slade knew perfectly well how I felt – it was his business to know men and to use them like tools. I waited for him to put on the pressure and, sure enough, it came, but in his usual oblique manner.

'So let's talk of old times,' he said. 'You must remember Kennikin.'

I remembered – I'd have to have total amnesia to forget Kennikin. A vision of his face swam before me as I had last seen him; eyes like grey pebbles set above high Slavic cheekbones, and the scar ran from his right temple to the corner of his mouth standing out lividly against the suddenly pale skin. He had been angry enough to kill me at that moment.

'What about Kennikin?' I said slowly.

'Just that I hear he's been looking for you, too. You made a fool of him and he didn't like it. He wants to have you . . .' Slade paused as though groping for a thought. 'What's that delicate phrase our American colleagues of the CIA use? Oh, yes – Kennikin wants to have you "terminated with extreme prejudice." Although I daresay the KGB don't employ that exact wording.'

A damned nice term for a bullet in the back of the head one dark night. 'So?' I said.

'He's still looking for you,' Slade pointed out.

'Why?' I asked. 'I'm no longer with the Department.'

'Ah, but Kennikin doesn't know that.' Slade examined his fingernails. 'We've kept the information from him – quite successfully, I believe. It seemed useful to do so.'

I saw what was coming but I wanted to make Slade come right out with it, to commit himself in plain language – something he abhorred. 'But he doesn't know where I am.'

'Quite right, dear boy – but what if someone should tell him?'

I leaned forward and looked closely at Slade. 'And who would tell him?'

'I would,' he said blandly. 'If I thought it necessary. I'd have to do it tactfully and through a third party, of course; but it could be arranged.'

So there it was – the threat of betrayal. Nothing new for Slade; he made a life's work out of corruption and betrayal. Not that I was one to throw stones; it had been my work too, once. But the difference between us was that Slade liked his work.

I let him waffle on, driving home the point unnecessarily. 'Kennikin runs a very efficient *Mordgruppe*, as we know to our cost, don't we? Several members of the Department have been . . . er . . . terminated by Kennikin's men.'

'Why don't you just say murdered?'

He frowned and his piggy eyes sank deeper into the rolls of fat that larded his face. 'You always were blunt, Stewart; perhaps too blunt for your own good. I haven't forgotten the time you tried to get me in trouble with Taggart. I remember you mentioned that word then.'

'I'll mention it again,' I said. 'You murdered Jimmy Birkby.'

'Did I?' Slade asked softly. 'Who put the gelignite in his car? Who carefully connected the wire from the detonator to the ignition system? You did!' He cut me off with a chopping motion of his hand. 'And it was only that which got you next to Kennikin, only that induced Kennikin to trust you enough so that we could break him. You did very well, Stewart – all things considered.'

'Yes, you used me,' I said.

'And I'll use you again,' he said brutally. 'Or would you rather be thrown to Kennikin?' He laughed suddenly. 'You know, I don't think Kennikin gives a damn if you're with the Department or not. He wants you for your own sweet self.'

I stared at him. 'And what do you mean by that?'

'Didn't you know that Kennikin is impotent now?' Slade said in surprise. 'I know you intended to kill him with that last shot, but the light was bad and you thought you'd merely wounded him. Indeed you had, but not merely – you castrated the poor man.' His hands, which were folded across his belly, shook with his sniggers. 'To put it crudely – or bluntly, if you like, dear boy – you shot his balls off. Can you imagine what he'll do to you if – and when – he catches up with you?'

I felt cold and there was a yawning emptiness in the pit of my stomach. 'There's only one way of opting out of the world and that's by dying,' said Slade with phoney philosophy. 'You tried your way and it doesn't work.'

He was right; I shouldn't have expected otherwise. 'What it comes to is this,' I said. 'You want me to do a job. If I don't do it, you'll tip off the opposition and the opposition will knock me off – and your hands will be theoretically clean.'

'Very succinctly put,' said Slade. 'You always did write good, clear reports.' He sounded like a schoolmaster complimenting a boy on a good essay.

'What's the job?'

'Now you're being sensible,' he said approvingly. He produced a sheet of paper and consulted it. 'We know you are in the habit of taking an annual holiday in Iceland.' He looked up. 'Still sticking to your northern heritage, I see. You couldn't very well go back to Sweden – and Finland would be even more risky. Too close to the Russian border for comfort.' He spread his hands. 'But who goes to Iceland?'

'So the job is in Iceland?'

'Indeed it is.' He tapped the paper with his fingernail. 'You take long holidays – three and four months at a time. What it is to have a private income – the Department did very well by you.'

'The Department gave me nothing that wasn't mine,' I said shortly.

He ignored that. 'I note you've been doing very well for yourself in Iceland. All the home comforts down to a love-nest. A young lady, I believe, is . . .'

'We'll leave her out of it.'

'Just the point I'm making, dear boy. It would be most unwise if she became involved. It could be most dangerous for her, don't you think? I wouldn't tell her anything about it.' His voice was kindly.

Slade had certainly done his homework. If he knew about Elin then he must have tapped me a long time before. All the time I thought I was in cover I'd been under a microscope.

'Come to the job.'

'You will collect a package at Keflavik International Airport.' He sketched dimensions with his hands. 'About eight inches by four inches by two inches. You will deliver it to a man in Akureyri – you know where that is?'

'I know,' I said, and waited for him to continue, but he didn't. 'That's all?' I asked.

'That's all; I'm sure you will be able to accomplish it quite easily.'

I stared at him incredulously. 'Have you gone through all this rigmarole of blackmail just to give me a messenger boy's job?'

'I wish you wouldn't use such crude language,' he said peevishly. 'It's a job suitable for one who is out of practice, such as yourself. It's important enough and you were to hand, so we're using you.'

'This is something that's blown up quite quickly, isn't it?' I hazarded. 'You're forced to use me.'

Slade waggled his hand. 'We're a bit stretched for manpower, that's all. Don't get delusions of grandeur – in using you I'm scraping the bottom of the barrel.'

Slade could be blunt enough when it suited his purpose. I shrugged, and said, 'Who is the man in Akureyri?'

'He'll make himself known,' Slade took a slip of paper from his wallet and tore it jaggedly across. One piece he passed to me and it proved to be half of a 100-kronur banknote. 'He'll have the other half. Old ways are best, don't you think? Effective and uncomplicated.'

I looked at the ruined Icelandic currency in my hand and said ironically, 'I don't suppose I'll be paid for this enterprise?'

'Of course you will, dear boy. Her Majesty's Government is never niggardly when it comes to valuable services rendered. Shall we say two hundred pounds?'

'Send it to Oxfam, you bastard.'

He shook his head deprecatingly. 'Such language – but I shall do as you say. You may depend on it.'

I studied Slade and he looked back at me with eyes as candid as those of a baby. I didn't like the smell of this operation – it sounded too damned phoney. It occurred to me that perhaps he was setting up a training exercise with me as the guinea pig. The Department frequently ran games of that sort to train the new boys, but all the participants usually knew the score. If Slade was ringing me into a training scheme without telling me I'd strangle the sadistic bastard.

To test him, I said, 'Slade, if you're using me as the football in a training game it could be dangerous. You could lose some of your budding spies that way.'

He looked shocked. 'Oh, I wouldn't do that to you.'

'All right; what do I do if someone tries to take the package?'

'Stop him,' he said succinctly.

'At any cost?'

He smiled. 'You mean – should you kill? Do it any way you want. Just deliver the package to Akureyri.' His paunch shook with amusement. 'Killer Stewart!' he mocked gently. 'Well, well!'

I nodded. 'I just wanted to know. I'd hate to make your manpower problems more difficult. After Akureyri – what happens then?'

'Then you may go on your way rejoicing. Complete your holiday. Enjoy the company of your lady friend. Feel free as air.'

'Until the next time you drop by.'

'That is a highly unlikely eventuality,' said Slade decisively. 'The world has passed you by. Things are not the same in the Department as they were – techniques are different – many changes you would not understand. You would be quite useless, Stewart, in any real work; but this job is simple and you're just a messenger boy.' He looked around the room a little disdainfully. 'No, you may come back here and rusticate peacefully.'

'And Kennikin?'

'Ah, I make no promises there. He may find you – he may not; but if he does it will not be because of my doing, I assure you.'

'That's not good enough,' I said. 'You'll tell him I haven't been a member of the Department for four years?'

'I may,' he said carelessly. 'I may.' He stood and buttoned his coat. 'Of course, whether he would believe it is one thing, and whether it would make any difference is yet another. He has his own, strictly unprofessional, reasons for wanting to find you, and I'm inclined to think that he'll want to operate on you with a sharp knife rather than to ask you to share his bottle of Calvados.'

He picked up his hat and moved over to the door. 'You will receive further instructions about picking up the package before you leave. It's been nice to see you again, Mr Stewart.'

'I wish I could say the same,' I said, and he laughed jollily.

I walked with him to his car and pointed to the rocks from where I had watched him waiting outside the cottage. 'I had you in rifle sights from up there. I even squeezed the trigger. Unfortunately the rifle wasn't loaded.'

He looked at me, his face full of confidence. 'If it had been loaded you wouldn't have pulled the trigger. You're a civilized man, Stewart; too civilized. I sometimes wonder how you lasted so long in the Department – you were always a little too soft-centred for the big jobs. If it had been my decision you'd have been out long before you decided to . . . er . . . retire.'

I looked into his pale cold eyes and knew that if it *had* been his decision I would never have been allowed to retire. He said, 'I trust you remember the terms of the Official Secrets Act.' Then he smiled. 'But, of course, you remember.'

I said, 'Where are you in the hierarchy now, Slade?'

'Quite close to the top, as a matter of fact,' he said cheerfully. 'Right next to Taggart. I *do* make the decisions now. I get to have lunch with the Prime Minister from time to time.' He gave a self-satisfied laugh and got into the car. He rolled down the window, and said, 'There's just one thing. That package – don't open it, dear boy. Remember what curiosity did to the cat.'

He drove away, bumping down the track, and when he had disappeared the glen seemed cleaner. I looked up at Sgurr Mor and at Sgurr Dearg beyond and felt depressed. In less than twenty minutes my world had been smashed to pieces and I wondered how the hell I was going to pick up the bits.

And when I woke up next morning after a broken night I knew there was only one thing to do; to obey Slade, carry out his orders and deliver the damned package to Akureyri and hope to God I could get clear without further entanglement.

III

My mouth was dry with talking and smoking. I pitched the cigarette butt from the window and it lay on a stone sending a lonely smoke signal to the North Pole. 'That's it,' I said. 'I was blackmailed into it.'

Elin shifted in her seat. 'I'm glad you've told me. I was wondering why you had to fly to Akureyri so suddenly.'

She leaned forward and stretched. 'But now you've delivered this mysterious package you have nothing more to worry about.'

'That's it,' I said. 'I didn't deliver it.' I told her about the four men at Akureyri Airport and she went pale. 'Slade flew here from London. He was annoyed.'

'He was *here* – in Iceland?'

I nodded. 'He said that I'm out of it, anyway; but I'm not, you know. Elin, I want you to stay clear of me – you might get hurt.'

She regarded me intently. 'I don't think you've told me everything.'

'I haven't,' I said. 'And I'm not going to. You're better out of this mess.'

'I think you'd better complete your story,' she said.

I bit my lip. 'Have you anywhere to stay – out of sight, I mean?'

She shrugged. 'There's the apartment in Reykjavik.'

'That's compromised,' I said. 'Slade knows about it and one of his men has it tagged.'

'I could visit my father,' she said.

'Yes, you could.' I had met Ragnar Thorsson once only; he was a tough old farmer who lived in the wilds of Strandasysla. Elin would be safe enough there. I said, 'If I tell you the full story will you go and stay with him until I send for you?'

'I give no guarantees,' she said uncompromisingly.

'Christ!' I said. 'If I get out of this you're going to make me one hell of a wife. I don't know if I'll be able to stand it.'

She jerked her head. 'What did you say?'

'In a left-handed way I was asking you to marry me.'

Things immediately got confused and it was a few minutes before we got ourselves untangled. Elin, pink-faced and tousle-haired, grinned at me impishly. 'Now tell!'

I sighed and opened the door. 'I'll not only tell you, but I'll show you.'

I went to the back of the Land-Rover and took the flat metal box from the girder to which I had taped it. I held it out to Elin on the palm of my hand. 'That's what the trouble is all about,' I said. 'You brought it up from Reykjavik yourself.'

She poked at it tentatively with her forefinger. 'So those men didn't take it.'

I said, 'What they got was a metal box which originally contained genuine Scottish fudge from Oban – full of cotton wadding and sand and sewn up in the original hessian.'

IV

'What about some beer?' asked Elin.

I grimaced. The Icelandic brew is a prohibition beer, tasteless stuff bearing the same relationship to alcohol as candyfloss bears to sugar. Elin laughed. 'It's all right; Bjarni brought back a case of Carlsberg on his last flight from Greenland.'

That was better; the Danes really know about beer. I watched Elin open the cans and pour out the Carlsberg. 'I want you to go to stay with your father,' I said.

'I'll think about it.' She handed me a glass. 'I want to know why you still have the package.'

'It was a phoney deal,' I said. 'The whole operation stank to high heaven. Slade said Graham had been tagged by the opposition so he brought me in at the last minute. But Graham wasn't attacked – I was.' I didn't tell Elin about Lindholm; I didn't know how much strain I could put upon her. 'Doesn't that seem odd?'

She considered it. 'Yes, it is strange.'

'And Graham was watching our apartment which is funny behaviour for a man who knows he may be under observation by the enemy. I don't think Graham had been tagged at all; I think Slade has been telling a pack of lies.'

Elin seemed intent on the bubbles glistening on the side of her glass. 'Talking of the enemy – who is the enemy?'

'I think it's my old pals of the KGB,' I said. 'Russian Intelligence. I could be wrong, but I don't think so.'

I could see by her set face that she didn't like the sound of that, so I switched back to Slade and Graham. 'Another thing – Graham saw me being tackled at Akureyri Airport and he didn't do a bloody thing to help me. He could at least have followed the man who ran off with the camera case, but he didn't do a damned thing. What do you make of that?'

'I don't know.'

'Neither do I,' I admitted. 'That's why the whole thing smells rotten. Consider Slade – he is told by Graham that I've fallen down on the job so he flies from London. And what does he do? He gives me a slap on the wrist and tells me I've been a naughty boy. And that's too bloody uncharacteristic coming from Slade.'

Elin said, 'You don't trust Slade.' It was a statement.

I pointed over the sea towards Grimsey. 'I trust Slade as far as I can throw that island. He's cooked up a complicated deal and I'd like to find out where I fit in before the chopper falls because it might be designed to fall right on my neck.'

'And what about the package?'

'That's the ace.' I lifted the metal box. 'Slade thinks the opposition have it, but as long as they haven't there's no great harm done. The opposition think they have it, assuming they haven't opened it yet.'

'Is that a fair assumption?'

'I think so. Agents are not encouraged to pry too much. The quartet who took the package from me will have orders to take it to the boss unopened, I think.'

Elin looked at the box. 'I wonder what's in it?'

I looked at it myself, and it looked right back at me and said nothing. 'Maybe I'd better get out the can-opener,' I said. 'But not just yet. Perhaps it might be better not to know.'

Elin made a sound of exasperation. 'Why must you men make everything complicated? So what are you going to do?'

'I'm going to lie low,' I said mendaciously. 'While I do some heavy thinking. Maybe I'll post the damned thing to *post restante*, Akureyri, and telegraph Slade telling him where to pick it up.'

I hoped Elin would swallow that because I was going to do something quite different and infinitely more dangerous. Somebody was soon going to find out he'd been sold a pup; he was going to scream loudly and I wanted to be around to find out who was screaming. But I didn't want to have Elin around when that happened.

'Lie low,' repeated Elin thoughtfully. She turned to me. 'What about Asbyrgi for tonight?'

'Asbyrgi!' I laughed and drained my glass. 'Why not?'

V

In that dim and faraway time when the gods were young and Odin rode the arctic wastelands, he was out one day when his horse, Sleipnir, stumbled and planted a hoof in Northern Iceland. The place where the hoof hit the ground is now known as Asbyrgi. So runs the legend but my geologist friends tell it a little differently.

Asbyrgi is a hoof-shaped rock formation about two miles across. Within it the trees, sheltered from the killing wind, grow quite strongly for Iceland, some of them attaining a height of nearly twenty feet. It is a green and fertile place nestling between the towering rock walls which surround it. There is nothing to draw one there but the legend and the unaccustomed sight of growing trees, but although it is a tourist attraction they don't stay the night. More to the point, it is quite off the main road.

We pushed through the narrow entrance to Asbyrgi and along the track made by the wheels of visiting cars until we were well inside at a place where the rock walls drew together and the trees were thick, and there we made camp. It was our custom to sleep on the ground when the climate allowed so I erected the awning which fitted on to the side of the Land-Rover, and brought out the air mattresses and sleeping bags while Elin began to prepare supper.

Perhaps we were sybaritic about our camping because we certainly didn't rough it. I took out the folding chairs and the table and set them up and Elin put down a bottle of Scotch and two glasses and joined me in a drink before she broiled the steak. Beef is a luxury I insist upon in Iceland; one can get awfully tired of mutton.

It was quiet and peaceful and we sat and enjoyed the evening, savouring the peaty taste of the whisky and talking desultorily of the things farthest from our minds. I think we both needed a respite from the nagging problem of Slade and his damned package, and the act of setting out our camp was a return to happier days which we both eagerly grasped.

Elin got up to cook supper and I poured another drink and wondered how I was to get rid of her. If she wouldn't go voluntarily then perhaps the best way would be to decamp early in the morning leaving her a couple of cans of food and a water bottle. With those and the sleeping bag she would be all right for a day or two until someone came into Asbyrgi and gave her a lift into civilization. She would be mad as a hornet but she would still be alive.

Because lying low wasn't good enough. I had to become visible – set myself up like a tin duck at a shooting gallery so that someone would have a crack at me. I didn't want Elin around when the action started.

Elin brought the supper and we started to eat. She said, 'Alan, why did you leave the . . . the Department?'

I hesitated with my fork in the air. 'I had a difference of opinion,' I said shortly.

'With Slade?'

I laid down the fork gently. 'It was about Slade – yes. I don't want to talk about it, Elin.'

She brooded for a while, then said, 'It might be better if you talked about it. You don't want to keep things locked up.'

I laughed silently. 'That's funny,' I said. 'Telling that to an agent of the Department. Haven't you heard of the Official Secrets Act?'

'What's that?'

'If the Department found I'd talked out of turn I'd be slung into jail for the rest of my life.'

'Oh, that!' she said disparagingly. 'That doesn't count – not with me.'

'Try telling that to Sir David Taggart,' I said. 'I've told you more than enough already.'

'Then why not get it all out? You know I won't tell anyone.'

I looked down at my plate. 'Not of your own free will. I wouldn't want anyone to hurt you, Elin.'

'Who would hurt me?' she asked.

'Slade would, for one. Then there's a character called Kennikin who may be around, but I hope not.'

Elin said slowly, 'If I ever marry anyone it will be a man who has no secrets. This is not good, Alan.'

'So you think that a trouble shared is a trouble halved. I don't think the Department would go along with you on that. The powers that be don't think confession is good for the soul, and Catholic priests and psychiatrists are looked upon with deep suspicion. But since you're so persistent I'll tell you some of it – not enough to be dangerous.'

I cut into the steak again. 'It was on an operation in Sweden. I was in a counter-espionage group trying to penetrate the KGB *apparat* in Scandinavia. Slade was masterminding the operation. I'll tell you one thing about Slade; he's very clever – devious and tricky, and he likes a ploy that wins coming and going.'

I found I had lost my appetite and pushed the plate away. 'A man called V. V. Kennikin was bossing the opposition, and I got pretty close to him. As far as he was concerned I was a Swedish Finn called Stewartsen, a fellow traveller who was willing to be used. Did you know I was born in Finland?'

Elin shook her head. 'You didn't tell me.'

I shrugged. 1 suppose I've tried to close off that part of my life. Anyway, after a lot of work and a lot of fright I was inside and accepted by Kennikin; not that he trusted me, but he used me on minor jobs and I was able to gather a lot of information which was duly passed on to Slade. But it was all trivial stuff. I was close to Kennikin, but not close enough.'

Elin said, 'It sounds awful. I'm not surprised you were frightened.'

'I was scared to death most of the time; double agents usually are.' I paused, trying to think of the simplest way to explain a complicated situation. I said deliberately, 'The time came when I had to kill a man. Slade warned me that my cover was in danger of being blown. He said the man responsible had not reported to Kennikin and the best thing to do was to eliminate him. So I did it with a bomb.' I swallowed. 'I never even saw the man I killed – I just put a bomb in a car.'

There was horror in Elin's eyes. I said harshly, 'We weren't playing patty-cake out there.'

'But someone you didn't know – that you had never seen!'

'It's better that way,' I said. 'Ask any bomber pilot. But that's not the point. The point is that I had trusted Slade and it turned out that the man I killed was a British agent – one of my own side.'

Elin was looking at me as though I had just crawled out from under a stone. I said, 'I contacted Slade and asked what the hell was going on. He said the man was a freelance agent whom neither side trusted – the trade is lousy with them. He recommended that I tell Kennikin what I'd done, so I did and my stock went up with Kennikin. Apparently he had been aware of a leak in his organization and there was enough evidence around to point to the man I had killed. So I became one of his blue-eyed boys – we got really chummy – and that was his mistake because we managed to wreck his network completely.'

Elin let out her breath. 'Is that all?'

'By Christ, it's not all!' I said violently. I reached for the whisky bottle and found my hand was trembling. 'When it was all over I went back to England. I was congratulated on doing a good job. The Scandinavian branch of the Department was in a state of euphoria and I was a minor hero, for God's sake! Then I discovered that the man I had killed was no more a freelance agent than I was. His name – if it matters – was Birkby, and he had been a member of the Department, just as I was.'

I slopped whisky into the glass. 'Slade had been playing chess with us. Neither Birkby nor I were deep enough in Kennikin's outfit to suit him so he sacrificed a pawn to put another in a better position. But he had broken the rules as far as I was concerned – it was as though a chess player had knocked off one of his own pieces to checkmate the king, and that's not in the rules.'

Elin said in a shaking voice, 'Are there any rules in your dirty world?'

'Quite right,' I said. 'There aren't any rules. But I thought there were. I tried to raise a stink.' I knocked back the undiluted whisky and felt it burn my throat. 'Nobody would listen, of course – the job had been successful and was now being forgotten and the time had come to go on to bigger and better things. Slade had pulled it off and no one wanted to delve too deeply into how he'd done it.' I laughed humourlessly. 'In fact, he'd gone up a notch in the Department and any muck-raking would be tactless – a reflection on the superior who had promoted him. I was a nuisance and nuisances are unwanted and to be got rid of.'

'So they got rid of you,' she said flatly.

'If Slade had his way I'd have been got rid of the hard way – permanently. In fact, he told me so not long ago. But he wasn't too high in the organization in those days and he didn't carry enough weight.' I looked into the bottom of the glass. 'What happened was that I had a nervous breakdown.'

I raised my eyes to Elin. 'Some of it was genuine – I'd say about fifty-fifty. I'd been living on my nerves for a long time and this was the last straw. Anyway, the Department runs a hospital with tame psychiatrists for cases like mine. Right now there's a file stashed away somewhere full of stuff that would make Freud blush. If I step out of line there'll be a psychiatrist ready to give evidence that I suffer everything from enuresis to paranoic delusions of grandeur. Who would disbelieve evidence coming from an eminent medical man?'

Elin was outraged. 'But that's unethical! You're as sane as I am.'

'There are no rules – remember?' I poured out another drink, more gently this time. 'So I was allowed to retire. I was no use to the Department anyway; I had become that anomaly, the well-known secret service agent. I crept away to a Scottish glen to lick my wounds. I thought I was safe until Slade showed up.'

'And blackmailed you with Kennikin. Would he tell Kennikin where you are?'

'I wouldn't put it past him, on his past record. And it's quite true that Kennikin has a score to settle. The word is that he's no good to the girls any more, and he blames me for it. I'd just as soon he doesn't know where to find me.'

I thought of the last encounter in the dimness of the Swedish forest. I knew I hadn't killed him; I knew it as soon as I had squeezed the trigger. There is a curious prescience in the gunman which tells him if he has hit the mark at which he aims, and I knew the bullet had gone low and that I had only wounded him. The nature of the wound was something else, and I could expect no mercy from Kennikin if he caught up with me.

Elin looked away from me and across the little glade which was quiet and still in the fading light apart from the sleepy chirrup of birds bedding down for the night. She shivered and put her arms about her body, 'You come from another world – a world I don't know.'

'It's a world I'm trying to protect you from.'

'Was Birkby married?'

'I don't know,' I said. 'One thing did occur to me. If Slade had thought that Birkby had a better chance of getting next to Kennikin, then he'd have told him to kill me, and for the same reason. Sometimes I think it would have been better that way.'

'No, Alan!' Elin leaned forward and took my hand in hers. 'Never think that.'

'Don't worry; I'm not suicidally minded,' I said. 'Anyway, you now know why I don't like Slade and why I distrust him – and why I'm suspicious of this particular operation.'

Elin looked at me closely, still holding my hand. 'Alan, apart from Birkby, have you killed anyone else?'

'I have,' I said deliberately.

Her face seemed to close tight and her hand slipped from mine. She nodded slowly. 'I have a lot to think about, Alan. I'd like to take a walk.' She rose. 'Alone – if you don't mind.'

I watched her walk into the trees and then picked up the bottle hefting it in my hand and wondering if I wanted another drink. I looked at the level of liquid and discovered that four of my unmeasured slugs had nearly half-emptied the bottle. I put it down again – I have never believed in drowning my problems and this was no time to start.

I knew what was wrong with Elin. It's a shock for a woman to realize that the man accepted into her bed is a certified killer, no matter in how laudable a cause. And I had no illusions that the cause for which I had worked was particularly commendable – not to Elin. What would a peaceful Icelander know about the murkier depths of the unceasing undercover war between the nations?

I collected the dirty dishes and began to wash them, wondering what she would do. All I had going for me were the summers we had spent together and the hope that those days and nights of happiness would weigh in the balance of her mind. I hoped that what she knew of me as a man, a lover and a human being would count for more than my past.

I finished cleaning up and lit a cigarette. Light was slowly ebbing from the sky towards the long twilight of summer in northern lands. It would never really get dark – it was too close to Midsummer Day – and the sun would not be absent for long.

I saw Elin coming back, her white shirt glimmering among the trees. As she approached the Land-Rover she looked up at the sky. 'It's getting late.'

'Yes.'

She stooped, unzipped the sleeping bags, and then zipped them together to make one large bag. As she turned her head towards me her lips curved in a half-smile. 'Come to bed, Alan,' she said, and I knew that nothing was lost and everything was going to be all right.

Later that night I had an idea. I unzipped my side of the bag and rolled out, trying not to disturb Elin. She said sleepily, 'What are you doing?'

'I don't like Slade's mysterious box being in the open. I'm going to hide it.'

'Where?'

'Somewhere under the chassis.'

'Can't it wait until morning?'

I pulled on a sweater. 'I might as well do it now. I can't sleep – I've been thinking too much.'

Elin yawned. 'Can I help – hold a torch or something?'

'Go back to sleep.' I took the metal box, a roll of insulating tape and a torch, and went over to the Land-Rover. On the theory that I might want to get at the box quickly I taped it inside the rear bumper. I had just finished when a random sweep of my hand inside the bumper gave me pause, because my fingers encountered something that shifted stickily.

I nearly twisted my head off in an attempt to see what it was. Squinting in the light of the torch I saw another metal box, but much smaller and painted green, the same colour as the Land-Rover but definitely not standard equipment as provided by the Rover Company. Gently I grasped it and pulled it away. One side of the small cube was magnetized so it would hold on a metal surface and, as I held it in my hand, I knew that someone was being very clever.

It was a radio bug of the type known as a 'bumper-bleeper' and, at that moment, it would be sending out a steady scream, shouting, *'Here I am! Here I am!'* Anyone with a radio direction finder turned to the correct frequency would know exactly where to find the Land-Rover any time he cared to switch on.

I rolled away and got to my feet, still holding the bug, and for a moment was tempted to smash it. How long it had been on the Land-Rover I didn't know – probably ever since Reykjavik. And who else could have bugged it but Slade or his man, Graham. Not content with warning me to keep Elin out of it, he had coppered his bet by making it easy to check on her. Or was it me he wanted to find?

I was about to drop it and grind it under my heel when I paused. That wouldn't be too clever – there were other, and better, ways of using it. Slade knew I was bugged, I knew I was bugged, but Slade didn't know that I knew, and that fact might yet be turned to account. I bent down and leaned under the Land-Rover to replace the bug. It attached itself to the bumper with a slight click.

And at that moment something happened. I didn't know what it was because it was so imperceptible – just a fractional alteration of the quality of the night silence – and if the finding of the bug had not made me preternaturally alert I might have missed it. I held my breath and listened intently and heard it again – the faraway metallic grunt of a gear change. Then there was nothing more, but that was enough.

THREE

I leaned over Elin and shook her. 'Wake up!' I said quietly.

'What's the matter?' she asked, still half-asleep.

'Keep quiet! Get dressed quickly.'

'But what . . .?'

'Don't argue – just get dressed.' I turned and stared into the trees, dimly visible in the half light. Nothing moved, nor could I hear anything – the quiet of the night was unbroken. The narrow entrance to Asbyrgi lay just under a mile away and I thought it likely that the vehicle would stop there. That would be a natural precaution – the stopper in the neck of the bottle.

It was likely that further investigation of Asbyrgi would be made on foot in a known direction given by radio direction finder and a known distance as given by a signal strength meter. Having a radio bug on a vehicle is as good as illuminating it with a searchlight.

Elin said quietly, 'I'm ready.'

I turned to her. 'We're about to have visitors,' I said in a low voice. 'In fifteen minutes – maybe less. I want you to hide.' I pointed. 'Over there would be best; find the closest cover you can among the trees and lie down – and don't come out until you hear me calling you.'

'But . . .'

'Don't argue – just do it,' I said harshly. I had never spoken to her before in that tone of voice and she blinked at me in surprise, but she turned quickly and ran into the trees.

I dived under the Land-Rover and groped for Lindholm's pistol which I had taped there in Reykjavik, but it had gone and all that was left was a sticky strand of insulation tape to show where it had been. The roads in Iceland are rough enough to shake anything loose and I was bloody lucky not to have lost the most important thing – the metal box.

So all I had was the knife – the *sgian dubh.* I stooped and picked it up from where it was lying next to the sleeping bag and tucked it into the waistband of my trousers. Then I withdrew into the trees by the side of the glade and settled down to wait.

It was a long time, nearer to half an hour, before anything happened. He came like a ghost, a dark shape moving quietly up the track and not making a sound. It was too dark to see his face but there was just enough light to let me see what he carried. The shape and the way he held it was unmistakable – there are ways of holding tools, and a man carries a rifle in a different way from he carries a stick. This was no stick.

I froze as he paused on the edge of the glade. He was quite still and, if I hadn't known he was there, it would have been easy for the eye to pass over that dark patch by the trees without recognizing it for what it was – a man with a gun. I was worried about the gun; it was either a rifle or a shotgun, and that was the sign of a professional. Pistols are too inaccurate for the serious business of killing – ask any soldier – and are liable to jam at the wrong moment. The professional prefers something more deadly.

If I was going to jump him I'd have to get behind him. which meant letting him pass me, but that would mean laying myself wide open for his friend – if he had a friend behind him. So I waited to see if the friend would turn up or if he was alone. I wondered briefly if he knew what would happen if he fired that gun in Asbyrgi; if he didn't then he'd be a very surprised gunman when he pulled the trigger.

There was a flicker of movement and he was suddenly gone, and I cursed silently. Then a twig cracked and I knew he was in the trees on the other side of the glade. This was a professional all right – a really careful boy. Never come from the direction in which you are expected, even if you don't think you'll be expected. Play it safe. He was in the trees and circling the glade to come in from the other side.

I also began to circle, but in the opposite direction. This was tricky because sooner or later we'd come face to face. I plucked the *sgian dubh* from my waist and held it loosely – puny protection against a rifle but it was all I had. Every step I took I tested carefully to make sure there was no twig underfoot, and it was slow and sweaty work.

I paused beneath a scrawny birch tree and peered into the semi-darkness. Nothing moved but I heard the faint click as of one stone knocking against another. I remained motionless, holding my breath, and then I saw him coming towards me, a dark moving shadow not ten yards away. I tightened my hold on the knife and waited for him.

Suddenly the silence was broken by the rustle of bushes and something white arose at his feet. It could only be one thing – he had walked right on to Elin where she had crouched in hiding. He was startled, retreated a step, and raised the rifle, I yelled, 'Get down, Elin!' as he pulled the trigger and a flash of light split the darkness.

It sounded as though a war had broken out, as though an infantry company had let off a rather ragged volley of rifle fire. The noise of the shot bounced from the cliffs of Asbyrgi, repeating from rock face to rock face in a diminishing series of multiple echoes which died away slowly in the far distance. That unexpected result of pulling the trigger unnerved him momentarily and he checked in surprise.

I threw the knife and there was the soft thud as it hit him. He gave a bubbling cry and dropped the rifle to claw at his chest. Then his knees buckled and he fell to the ground, thrashing and writhing among the bushes.

I ignored him and ran to where I had seen Elin, pulling the flashlight from my pocket as I went. She was sitting on the ground, her hand to her shoulder and her eyes wide with shock. 'Are you all right?'

She withdrew her hand and her fingers were covered in blood. 'He shot me,' she said dully.

I knelt beside her and looked at her shoulder. The bullet had grazed her, tearing the pad of muscle on top of the shoulder. It would be painful later, but it was not serious. 'We'd better put a dressing on that,' I said.

'He shot me!' Her voice was stronger and there was something like wonder in her tone.

'I doubt if he'll shoot anyone again,' I said, and turned the light on him. He was lying quite still with his head turned away.

'Is he dead?' asked Elin, her eyes on the haft of the knife which protruded from his chest.

'I don't know. Hold the light.' I took his wrist and felt the quick beat of the pulse. 'He's alive,' I said. 'He might even survive.' I pulled his head around so that I could see his face. It was Graham – and that was something of a surprise. I mentally apologized for accusing him of having been wet behind the ears; the way he had approached our camp had been all professional.

Elin said, 'There's a first-aid box in the Land-Rover.'

'Carry on,' I said. 'I'll bring him over.' I stooped and picked up Graham in my arms and followed Elin. She spread out the sleeping bag and I laid him down. Then she brought out the first-aid box and sank to her knees.

'No,' I said. 'You first. Take off your shirt.' I cleaned the wound on her shoulder, dusted it with penicillin powder, and bound a pad over it. 'You'll have trouble in raising your arm above your shoulder for the next week,' I said. 'Otherwise it's not too bad.'

She seemed mesmerized by the amber light reflected from the jewelled pommel of the knife in Graham's chest. 'That knife – do you always carry it?'

'Always,' I said. 'We have to get it out of there.' It had hit Graham in the centre of the chest just below the sternum and it had an upwards inclination. The whole of the blade was buried in him and God knows what it had sliced through.

I cut away his shirt, and said, 'Get an absorbent pad ready,' and then I put my hand on the hilt and pulled. The serrated back edge admitted air into the wound and made extraction easy and the knife came away cleanly. I half expected a gush of arterial blood which would have been the end of Graham, but there was just a steady trickle which ran down his stomach and collected in his navel.

Elin put the pad on the wound and strapped it down with tape while I took his pulse again. It was a little weaker than it had been.

'Do you know who he is?' asked Elin, sitting back on her heels.

'Yes,' I said matter-of-factly. 'He said his name is Graham. He's a member of the Department working with Slade.' I picked up the *sgian dubh* and began to clean it. 'Right now I'd like to know if he came alone or if he has any pals around here. We're sitting ducks.'

I got up and walked back into the trees and hunted about for Graham's rifle. I found it and took it back to the Land-Rover; it was a Remington pump action carbine chambered for .30/06 ammunition – a good gun for a murderer. The barrel not too long to get in the way, the fire rapid – five aimed shots in five seconds – and a weight and velocity of slug enough to stop a man dead in his tracks. I operated the action and caught the round that jumped out. It was the ordinary soft-nosed hunting type, designed to spread on impact. Elin had been lucky.

She was bending over Graham wiping his brow. 'He's coming round.'

Graham's eyes flickered and opened and he saw me standing over him with the carbine in my hands. He tried to get up but a spasm of pain hit him and the sweat started out on his brow. 'You're not in a position to do much,' I said. 'You have a hole in your gut.'

He sagged back and moistened his lips. 'Slade said . . .' He fought for breath. '. . . said you weren't dangerous.'

'Did he, now? He was wrong, wasn't he?' I held up the carbine. 'If you'd come empty-handed without this you wouldn't be lying where you are now. What was supposed to be the idea?'

'Slade wanted the package,' he whispered.

'So? But the opposition have it. The Russians – I suppose they *are* Russians?'

Graham nodded weakly. 'But they didn't get it. That's why Slade sent me in here. He said you were playing a double game. He said you weren't straight.'

I frowned. 'Now, that's interesting,' I said, and sat on my heels next to him with the carbine across my knees. 'Tell me this, Graham – who told Slade the Russians hadn't got it? I didn't tell them, that's for sure. I suppose the Russkies obligingly told him they'd been fooled.'

A look of puzzlement came over his face. 'I don't know how he knew. He just told me to come and get it.'

I lifted the carbine. 'And he gave you this. I suppose I was to be liquidated.' I glanced at Elin, and then back at Graham. 'And what about Elin here? What was to happen to her?'

Graham closed his eyes. 'I didn't know she was here.'

'Maybe not,' I said. 'But Slade did. How the hell do you think that Land-Rover got here?' Graham's eyelids flickered. 'You know damned well you'd have to kill any witnesses.'

A trickle of blood crept from the corner of his mouth. 'You lousy bastard!' I said. 'If I thought you knew what you were doing I'd kill you now. So Slade told you I'd reneged and you took his word for it – you took the gun he gave you and followed his orders. Ever hear of a man called Birkby?'

Graham opened his eyes. 'No.'

'Before your time,' I said. 'It just happens that Slade has played that trick before. But never mind that now. Did you come alone?'

Graham closed his mouth tightly and a stubborn look came over his face. 'Don't be a hero,' I advised. 'I can get it out of you easily enough. How would you like me to stomp on your belly right now?' I heard Elin gasp, but ignored her. 'You have a bad gut wound, and you're liable to die unless we can get you to a hospital. And I can't do that if someone is going to take a crack at us as we leave Asbyrgi. I'm not going to put Elin into risk just for the sake of your hide.'

He looked beyond me to Elin, and then nodded. 'Slade,' he said. 'He's here . . . about a mile . . .'

'At the entrance to Asbyrgi?'

'Yes,' he said, and closed his eyes again. I took his pulse and found it very much fainter. I turned to Elin. 'Start to load; leave enough room for Graham to lie in the back on top of the sleeping bags.' I stood up and checked the load in the carbine.

'What are you going to do?'

'Maybe I can get close enough to Slade to talk to him,' I said. 'To tell him his boy is badly hurt. Maybe I won't – in that case I'll talk to him with this.' I held up the carbine.

She whitened. 'You'll kill him?'

'Christ, I don't know!' I said exasperatedly. 'All I know is that apparently he doesn't mind if I'm killed – and you, too. He's sitting at the entrance to Asbyrgi like a bloody cork in a bottle and this is the only corkscrew I've got.'

Graham moaned a little and opened his eyes. I bent down. 'How are you feeling?'

'Bad.' The trickle of blood at the corner of his mouth had increased to a rivulet which ran down his neck. 'It's funny,' he whispered. 'How *did* Slade know?'

I said, 'What's in the package?'

'Don't . . . know.'

'Who is bossing the Department these days?'

His breath wheezed. 'Ta . . . Taggart.'

If anyone could pull Slade off my back it would be Taggart. I said, 'All right; I'll go and see Slade. We'll have you out of here in no time.'

'Slade said . . .' Graham paused and began again. He seemed to have difficulty in swallowing and he coughed a little, bringing bright red bubbles foaming to his lips. 'Slade said . . .'

The coughing increased and there was sudden gush of red arterial blood from his mouth and his head fell sideways. I put my hand to his wrist and knew that Graham would never tell me what more Slade had said because he was dead. I closed his staring eyes, and stood up. 'I'd better talk to Slade.'

'He's dead!' said Elin in a shocked whisper.

Graham was dead – a pawn suddenly swept from the board. He had died because he followed orders blindly, just as I had done in Sweden; he had died because he didn't really understand what he was doing. Slade had told him to do something and he had tried and failed and come to his death. I didn't really understand what I was doing, either, so I'd better not fail in anything I attempted.

Elin was crying. The big tears welled from her eyes and trickled down her cheeks. She didn't sob but just stood there crying silently and looking down at the body of Graham. I said harshly, 'Don't cry for him – he was going to kill you. You heard him.'

When she spoke it was without a tremor, but still the tears came. 'I'm not crying for Graham,' she said desolately. 'I'm crying for you. Someone must.'

II

We struck camp quickly and loaded everything into the Land-Rover, and everything included the body of Graham. 'We can't leave him here,' I said. 'Someone will be sure to stumble across him soon – certainly within the week. To quote the Bard, we lug the guts into the neighbour room.'

A wan smile crossed Elin's face as she caught the allusion. 'Where?'

'Dettifoss,' I said. 'Or maybe Selfoss.' To go over a couple of waterfalls, one the most powerful in Europe, would batter the body beyond recognition and, with luck, disguise the fact that Graham had been stabbed. He would be a lone tourist who had had an accident.

So we put the body in the back of the Land-Rover. I picked up the Remington carbine, and said, 'Give me half an hour, then come along as fast as you can.'

'I can't move fast if I have to be quiet,' she objected.

'Quietness won't matter – just belt towards the entrance as fast as you can, and use the headlights. Then slow down a bit so I can hop aboard.'

'And then?'

'Then we head for Dettifoss – but not by the main road. We keep on the track to the west of the river.'

'What are you going to do about Slade? You're going to kill him, aren't you?'

'He might kill me first,' I said. 'Let's have no illusions about Slade.'

'No more killing, Alan,' she said. 'Please – no more killing.'

'It might not be up to me. If he shoots at me then I'll shoot back.'

'All right,' she said quietly.

So I left her and headed towards the entrance to Asbyrgi, padding softly along the track and hoping that Slade wouldn't come looking for Graham. I didn't think it likely. Although he must have heard the shot he would have been expecting it, and then it would have taken Graham a half-hour to return after searching for the package. My guess was that Slade wouldn't be expecting Graham for another hour.

I made good time but slowed as I approached the entrance. Slade had not bothered to hide his car; it was parked in full sight and was clearly visible because the short northern night was nearly over and the sky was light. He knew what he was doing because it was impossible to get close to the car without being seen, so I settled behind a rock and waited for Elin. I had no relish for walking across that open ground only to stop a bullet.

Presently I heard her coming. The noise was quite loud as she changed gear and I saw a hint of movement from inside the parked car. I nestled my cheek against the stock of the carbine and aimed. Graham had been professional enough to put a spot of luminous paint on the foresight but it was not necessary in the pre-dawn light.

I settled the sight on the driving side and, as the noise behind me built up to a crescendo, I slapped three bullets in as many seconds through the windscreen which must have been made of laminated glass because it went totally opaque. Slade took off in a wide sweep and I saw that the only thing that had saved him was that the car had right-hand drive, English style, and I had shot holes in the wrong side of the windscreen.

But he wasn't waiting for me to correct the error and bucked away down the track as fast as he could go. The Land-Rover came up behind me and I jumped for it. 'Get going!' I yelled. 'Make it fast.'

Ahead, Slade's car skidded around a corner in a four-wheel drift, kicking up a cloud of dust. He was heading for the main road, but when we arrived at the corner Elin turned the other way as I had instructed her. It would have been useless chasing Slade – a Land-Rover isn't built for that and he had the advantage.

We turned south on to the track which parallels the *Jökulsá á Fjöllum,* the big river that takes the melt water north from Vatnajökull, and the roughness of the ground dictated a reduction in speed. Elin said, 'Did you talk to Slade?'

'I couldn't get near him.'

'I'm glad you didn't kill him.'

'It wasn't for want of trying,' I said. 'If he had a left-hand drive car he'd be dead by now.'

'And would that make you feel any better?' she asked cuttingly.

I looked at her. 'Elin,' I said, 'The man's dangerous. Either he's gone off his nut – which I think is unlikely – or . . .'

'Or what?'

'I don't know,' I said despondently. 'It's too damned complicated and I don't know enough. But I do know that Slade wants me dead. There's something I know – or something he thinks I know – that's dangerous for him; dangerous enough for him to want to kill me. Under the circumstances I don't want you around – you could get in the line of fire. You *did* get in the line of fire this morning.'

She slowed because of a deep rut. 'You can't survive alone,' she said. 'You need help.'

I needed more than help; I needed a new set of brains to work out this convoluted problem. But this wasn't the time to do it because Elin's shoulder was giving her hell. 'Pull up,' I said. 'I'll do the driving.'

We travelled south for an hour and a half and Elin said, 'There's Dettifoss.'

I looked out over the rocky landscape towards the cloud of spray in the distance which hung over the deep gorge which the *Jökulsá á Fjöllum* has cut deep into the rock. 'We'll carry on to Selfoss,' I decided. 'Two waterfalls are better than one. Besides, there are usually campers at Dettifoss.'

We went past Dettifoss and, three kilometres farther on, I pulled off the road. 'This is as close to Selfoss as we can get.'

I got out. 'I'll go towards the river and see if anyone's around,' I said. 'It's bad form to be seen humping bodies about. Wait here and don't talk to any strange men.'

I checked to see if the body was still decently shrouded by the blanket with which we had covered it, and then headed towards the river. It was still very early in the morning and there was no one about so I went back and opened the rear door of the vehicle and climbed inside.

I stripped the blanket away from Graham's body and searched his clothing. His wallet contained some Icelandic currency and a sheaf of Deutschmarks, together with a German motoring club card identifying him as Dieter Buchner, as also did his German passport. There was a photograph of him with his arm around a pretty girl and a fascia board of a shop behind them was in German. The Department was always thorough about that kind of thing.

The only other item of interest was a packet of rifle ammunition which had been broken open. I put that on one side, pulled out the body and replaced the wallet in the pocket, and then carried him in a fireman's lift towards the river with Elin close on my heels.

I got to the lip of the gorge and put down the body while I studied the situation. The gorge at this point was curved and the river had undercut the rock face so that it was a straight drop right into the water. I pushed the body over the edge and watched it fall in a tumble of arms and legs until it splashed into the grey, swirling water. Buoyed by air trapped in the jacket it floated out until it was caught in the quick midstream current. We watched it go downstream until it disappeared over the edge of Selfoss to drop into the roaring cauldron below.

Elin looked at me sadly. 'And what now?'

'Now I go south,' I said, and walked away quickly towards the Land-Rover. When Elin caught up with me I was bashing hell out of the radio-bug with a big stone.

'Why south?' she asked breathlessly.

'I want to get to Keflavik and back to London. There's a man I want to talk to – Sir David Taggart.'

'We go by way of Myvatn?'

I shook my head, and gave the radio-bug one last clout, sure now that it would tell no more tales. 'I'm keeping off the main roads – they're too dangerous. I go by way of the *Odádahraun* and by Askja – into the desert. But you're not coming.'

'We'll see,' she said, and tossed the car key in her hand.

III

God has not yet finished making Iceland.

In the last 500 years one-third of all the lava extruded from the guts of the earth to the face of the planet has surfaced in Iceland and, of 200 known volcanoes, thirty are still very much active. Iceland suffers from a bad case of geological acne.

For the last thousand years a major eruption has been recorded, on average, every five years. Askja – the ash volcano – last blew its top in 1961. Measurable quantities of volcanic ash settled on the roofs of Leningrad, 1,500 miles away. That didn't trouble the Russians overmuch but the effect was more serious nearer home. The country to north and east of Askja was scorched and poisoned by deep deposits of ash and, nearer to Askja, the lava flows overran the land, overlaying desolation with desolation. Askja dominates north-east Iceland and has created the most awesome landscape in the world.

It was into this wilderness, the *Odádahraun*, as remote and blasted as the surface of the moon, that we went. The name, loosely translated, means 'Murderers' Country', and was the last foothold of the outlaws of olden times, the shunned of men against whom all hands were raised.

There are tracks in the *Odádahraun* – sometimes. The tracks are made by those who venture into the interior; most of them scientists – geologists and hydrographers – few travel for pleasure in that part of the *Óbyggdir.* Each vehicle defines the track a little more, but when the winter snows come the tracks are obliterated – by water, by snow avalanche, by rock slip. Those going into the interior in the early summer, as we were, are in a very real sense trail blazers, sometimes finding the track anew and deepening it a fraction, very often not finding it and making another.

It was not bad during the first morning. The track was reasonable and not too bone-jolting and paralleled the *Jökulsá á Fjöllum* which ran grey-green with melt water to the Arctic Ocean. By midday we were opposite Mödrudalur which lay on the other side of the river, and Elin broke into that mournfully plaintive song which describes the plight of the Icelander in winter: 'Short are the mornings in the mountains of Mödrudal. There it is mid-morning at daybreak.' I suppose it fitted her mood; I know mine wasn't very much better.

I had dropped all thoughts of giving Elin the slip. Slade knew that she had been in Asbyrgi – the bug planted on the Land-Rover would have told him that – and it would be very dangerous for her to appear unprotected in any of the coastal towns. Slade had been a party to attempted murder and she was a witness, and I knew he would take extreme measures to silence her. As dangerous as my position was she was as safe with me as anywhere, so I was stuck with her.

At three in the afternoon we stopped at the rescue hut under the rising bulk of the great shield volcano called Herdubreid or 'Broad Shoulders'. We were both tired and hungry, and Elin said, 'Can't we stop here for the day?'

I looked across at the hut. 'No,' I said. 'Someone might be expecting us to do just that. We'll push on a little farther towards Askja. But there's no reason why we can't eat here.'

Elin prepared a meal and we ate in the open, sitting outside the hut. Halfway through the meal I was in mid-bite of a herring sandwich when an idea struck me like a bolt of lightning. I looked up at the radio mast next to the hut and then at the whip antenna on the Land-Rover. 'Elin, we can raise Reykjavik from here, can't we? I mean we can talk to anyone in Reykjavik who has a telephone.'

Elin looked up. 'Of course. We contact Gufunes Radio and they connect us into the telephone system.'

I said dreamily, 'Isn't it fortunate that the transatlantic cables run through Iceland? If we can be plugged into the telephone system there's nothing to prevent a further patching so as to put a call through to London.' I stabbed my finger at the Land-Rover with its radio antenna waving gently in the breeze. 'Right from there.'

'I've never heard of it being done,' said Elin doubtfully.

I finished the sandwich. 'I see no reason why it can't be done. After all, President Nixon spoke to Neil Armstrong when he was on the moon. The ingredients are there – all we have to do is put them together. Do you know anyone in the telephone department?'

'I know Svein Haraldsson,' she said thoughtfully.

I would have taken a bet that she would know someone in the telephone department; everybody in Iceland knows somebody. I scribbled a number on a scrap of paper and gave it to her. 'That's the London number. I want Sir David Taggart in person.'

'What if this . . . Taggart . . . won't accept the call?'

I grinned. 'I have a feeling that Sir David will accept any call coming from Iceland right now.'

Elin looked up at the radio mast. 'The big set in the hut will give us more power.'

I shook my head. 'Don't use it – Slade might be monitoring the telephone bands. He can listen to what I have to say to Taggart but he mustn't know where it's coming from. A call from the Land-Rover could be coming from anywhere.'

Elin walked over to the Land-Rover, switched on that set and tried to raise Gufunes. The only result was a crackle of static through which a few lonely souls wailed like damned spirits, too drowned by noise to be understandable. 'There must be storms in the western mountains,' she said. 'Should I try Akureyri?' That was the nearest of the four radio-telephone stations.

'No,' I said. 'If Slade is monitoring at all he'll be concentrating on Akureyri. Try Seydisfjördur.'

Contacting Seydisfjördur in eastern Iceland was much easier and Elin was soon patched into the landline network to Reykjavik and spoke to her telephone friend, Svein. There was a fair amount of incredulous argument but she got her way. 'There's a delay of an hour,' she said.

'Good enough. Ask Seydisfjördur to contact us when the call comes through.' I looked at my watch. In an hour it would be 3:45 p.m. British Standard Time – a good hour to catch Taggart.

We packed up and on we pushed south towards the distant ice blink of Vatnajökull. I left the receiver switched on but turned it low and there was a subdued babble from the speaker.

Elin said, 'What good will it do to speak to this man, Taggart?'

'He's Slade's boss,' I said. 'He can get Slade off my back.'

'But will he?' she asked. 'You were supposed to hand over the package and you didn't. You disobeyed orders. Will Taggart like that?'

'I don't think Taggart knows what's going on here. I don't think he knows that Slade tried to kill me – and you. I think Slade is working on his own, and he's out on a limb. I could be wrong, of course, but that's one of the things I want to get from Taggart.'

'And if you *are* wrong? If Taggart instructs you to give the package to Slade? Will you do it?'

I hesitated. 'I don't know.'

Elin said. 'Perhaps Graham was right. Perhaps Slade really thought you'd defected – you must admit he would have every right to think so. Would he then . . .?'

'Send a man with a gun? He would.'

'Then I think you've been stupid, Alan; very, very stupid. I think you've allowed your hatred of Slade to cloud your judgment, and I think you're in very great trouble.'

I was beginning to think so myself. I said, 'I'll find that out when I talk to Taggart. If he backs Slade . . .' If Taggart backed Slade then I was Johnny-in-the-middle in danger of being squeezed between the Department and the opposition. The Department doesn't like its plans being messed around, and the wrath of Taggart would be mighty.

And yet there were things that didn't fit – the pointlessness of the whole exercise in the first place, Slade's lack of any real animosity when I apparently boobed, the ambivalence of Graham's role. And there was something else which prickled at the back of my mind but which I could not bring to the surface. Something which Slade had done or had not done, or had said or had not said – something which had rung a warning bell deep in my unconscious.

I braked and brought the Land-Rover to a halt, and Elin looked at me in surprise. I said, 'I'd better know what cards I hold before I talk to Taggart. Dig out the can-opener – I'm going to open the package.'

'Is that wise? You said yourself that it might be better not to know.'

'You may be right. But if you play stud poker without looking at your hole card you'll probably lose. I think I'd better know what it is that everyone wants so much.'

I got out and went to the rear bumper where I stripped the tape from the metal box and pulled it loose. When I got back behind the wheel Elin already had the can-opener – I think she was really as curious as I was.

The box was made of ordinary shiny metal of the type used for cans, but it was now flecked with a few rust spots due to its exposure. A soldered seam ran along four edges so I presumed that face to be the top. I tapped and pressed experimentally and found that the top flexed a little more under pressure than any of the other five sides, so it was probably safe to stab the blade of the can-opener into it.

I took a deep breath and jabbed the blade into one corner and heard the hiss of air as the metal was penetrated. That indicated that the contents had been vacuum-packed and I hoped I wasn't going to end up with a couple of pounds of pipe tobacco. The belated thought came to me that it could have been booby-trapped; there are detonators that operate on air pressure and that sudden equalization could have made the bloody thing blow up in my face.

But it hadn't, so I took another deep breath and began to lever the can-opener. Luckily it was one of the old-fashioned type that didn't need a rim to operate against; it made a jagged, sharp-edged cut – a really messy job – but it opened up the box inside two minutes.

I took off the top and looked inside and saw a piece of brown, shiny plastic with a somewhat electrical look about it – you can see bits of it in any radio repair shop. I tipped the contents of the box into the palm of my hand and looked at the gadget speculatively and somewhat hopelessly.

The piece of brown plastic was the base plate for an electronic circuit, a very complex one. I recognized resistors and transistors but most of it was incomprehensible. It had been a long time since I had studied radio and the technological avalanche of advances had long since passed me by. In my day a component was a component, but the micro-circuitry boys are now putting an entire and complicated circuit with dozens of components on to a chip of silicon you'd need a microscope to see.

'What is it?' asked Elin with sublime faith that I would know the answer.

'I'm damned if I know,' I admitted. I looked closer and tried to trace some of the circuits but it was impossible. Part of it was of modular construction with plates of printed circuits set on edge, each plate bristled with dozens of components; elsewhere it was of more conventional design, and set in the middle was a curious metal shape for which there was no accounting – not by me, anyway.

The only thing that made sense were the two ordinary screw terminals at the end of the base plate with a small engraved brass plate screwed over them. One terminal was marked ' + ' and the other ' – ', and above was engraved, '110 v. 60~.' I said, 'That's an American voltage and frequency. In England we use 240 volts and 50 cycles. Let's assume that's the input end.'

'So whatever it is, it's American.'

'Possibly American,' I said cautiously. There was no power pack and the two terminals were not connected so that the gadget was not working at the moment. Presumably it would do what it was supposed to do when a 110 volt, 60 cycle current was applied across those terminals. But what it would do I had no idea at all.

Whatever kind of a whatsit it was, it was an advanced whatsit. The electronic whiz-kids have gone so far and fast that this dohickey, small enough to fit in the palm of my hand, could very well be an advanced computer capable of proving that $e=mc^2$ or, alternatively, disproving it.

It could also have been something that a whiz-kid might have jack-legged together to cool his coffee, but I didn't think so. It didn't have the jack-leg look about it; it was coolly professional, highly sophisticated and had the air of coming off a very long production line – a production line in a building without windows and guarded by hard-faced men with guns.

I said thoughtfully, 'Is Lee Nordlinger still at the base at Keflavik?'

'Yes,' said Elin. 'I saw him two weeks ago.'

I poked at the gadget. 'He's the only man in Iceland who might have the faintest idea of what this is.'

'Are you going to show it to him?'

'I don't know,' I said slowly. 'He might recognize it as a piece of missing US government property and, since he's a commander in the US Navy, he might think he has to take action. After all, I'm not supposed to have it, and there'd be a lot of questions.'

I put the gadget back into its box, laid the lid on top and taped it into place. 'I don't think this had better go underneath again now that I've opened it.'

'Listen!' said Elin. 'That's our number.'

I reached up and twisted the volume control and the voice became louder. 'Seydisfjördur calling seven, zero, five; Seydisfjördur calling seven, zero, five.'

I unhooked the handset. 'Seven, zero, five answering Seydisfjördur.'

'Seydisfjördur calling seven, zero, five; your call to London has come through. I am connecting.'

'Thank you, Seydisfjördur.'

The characteristics of the noise coming through the speaker changed suddenly and a very faraway voice said, 'David Taggart here. Is that you, Slade?'

I said. 'I'm speaking on an open line – a very open line. Be careful.'

There was a pause, then Taggart said, 'I understand. Who is speaking? This is a very bad line.'

He was right, it was a bad line. His voice advanced and receded in volume and was mauled by an occasional burst of static. I said, 'This is Stewart here.'

An indescribable noise erupted from the speaker. It could have been static but more likely it was Taggart having an apoplexy. 'What the hell do you think you're doing?' he roared.

I looked at Elin and winced. From the sound of that it appeared that Taggart was not on my side, but it remained to be found if he backed Slade. He was going full blast. 'I talked to Slade this morning. He said you . . . er . . . tried to terminate his contract.' Another useful euphemism. 'And what's happened to Philips?'

'Who the hell is Philips?' I interjected.

'Oh! You might know him better as Buchner – or Graham.'

'His contract I did terminate,' I said.

'For Christ's sake!' yelled Taggart. 'Have you gone out of your mind?'

'I got in first just before he tried to terminate my contract,' I said. 'The competition is awful fierce here in Iceland. Slade sent him.'

'Slade tells it differently.'

'I'll bet he does,' I said. 'Either he's gone off his rocker or he's joined a competing firm. I came across some of their representatives over here, too.'

'Impossible!' said Taggart flatly.

'The competing representatives?'

'No – Slade. It's unthinkable.'

'How can it be unthinkable when I'm thinking it?' I said reasonably.

'He's been with us so long. You know the good work he's done.'

'Maclean,' I said. 'Burgess, Kim Philby. Blake, the Krogers, Lonsdale – all good men and true. What's wrong with adding Slade?'

Taggart's voice got an edge to it. 'This is an open line – watch your language. Stewart, you don't know the score. Slade says you still have the merchandise – is that true?'

'Yes,' I admitted.

Taggart breathed hard. 'Then you must go back to Akureyri. I'll fix it so that Slade finds you there. Let him have it.'

'The only thing I'll let Slade have is a final dismissal notice,' I said. 'The same thing I gave Graham – or whatever his name was.'

'You mean you're not going to obey orders,' said Taggart dangerously.

'Not so far as Slade is concerned,' I said. 'When Slade sent Graham my fiancée happened to be in the way.'

There was a long pause before Taggart said in a more conciliatory tone. 'Did anything . . .? Is she . . .?'

'She's got a hole in her,' I said baldly, and not giving a damn if it was an open line. 'Keep Slade away from me, Taggart.'

He had been called Sir David for so long that he didn't relish the unadorned sound of his own name, and it took some time for him to swallow it. At last he said, in a subdued voice, 'So you won't accept Slade.'

'I wouldn't accept Slade with a packet of Little Noddy's Rice Crispies. I don't trust him.'

'Who would you accept?'

That I had to think about. It had been a long time since I had been with the Department and I didn't know what the turnover had been. Taggart said, 'Would you accept Case?'

Case was a good man; I knew him and trusted him as far as I'd trust anyone in the Department. 'I'll accept Jack Case.'

'Where will you meet him? And when?'

I figured out the logic of time and distance. 'At Geysir – five p.m. the day after tomorrow.'

Taggart was silent and all I heard were the waves of static beating against my eardrum. Then he said, 'Can't be done – I still have to get him back here. Make it twenty-four hours later.' He slipped in a fast one. 'Where are you now?'

I grinned at Elin. 'Iceland.'

Even the distortion could not disguise the rasp in Taggart's voice; he sounded like a concrete-mixer. 'Stewart, I hope you know that you're well on your way to ruining a most important operation. When you meet Case you take your orders from him and you'll do precisely as he says. Understand?'

'He'd better not have Slade with him,' I said. 'Or all bets are off. Are you putting your dog on a leash, Taggart?'

'All right,' said Taggart reluctantly. 'I'll pull him back to London. But you're wrong about him, Stewart. Look what he did to Kennikin in Sweden.'

It happened so suddenly that I gasped. The irritant that had been festering at the back of my mind came to the surface and it was like a bomb going off. 'I want some information,' I said quickly. 'I might need it if I'm to do this job properly.'

'All right; what is it?' said Taggart impatiently.

'What have you got on file about Kennikin's drinking habits?'

'What the hell!' he roared. 'Are you trying to be funny?'

'I need the information,' I repeated patiently. I had Taggart by the short hairs and he knew it. I had the electronic gadget and he didn't know where I was. I was bargaining from strength and I didn't think he'd hold back apparently irrelevant information just to antagonize me. But he tried.

'It'll take time,' he said. 'Ring me back.'

'Now *you're* being funny,' I said. 'You have so many computers around you that electrons shoot out of your ears. All you have to do is to push a button and you'll have the answer in two minutes. Push it!'

'All right,' he said in an annoyed voice. 'Hold on.' He had every right to be annoyed – the boss isn't usually spoken to in that way.

I could imagine what was going on. The fast, computer-controlled retrieval of microfilm combined with the wonders of closed circuit television would put the answer on to the screen on his desk in much less than two minutes providing the right coding was dialled. Every known member of the opposition was listed in that microfilm file together with every known fact about him, so that his life was spread out like a butterfly pinned in a glass case. Apparent irrelevancies about a man could come in awfully useful if known at the right time or in the right place.

Presently Taggart said in a dim voice, 'I've got it.' The static was much worse and he was very far away. 'What do you want to know?'

'Speak up – I can hardly hear you. I want to know about his drinking habits.'

Taggart's voice came through stronger, but not much. 'Kennikin seems to be a bit of a puritan. He doesn't drink and, since his last encounter with you, he doesn't go out with women.' His voice was sardonic. 'Apparently you ruined him for the only pleasure in his life. You'd better watch . . .' The rest of the sentence was washed out in noise.

'What was that?' I shouted.

Taggart's voice came through the crashing static like a thin ghost. '. . . best of . . . knowledge . . . Kenni . . . Iceland . . . he's . . .'

And that was all I got, but it was enough. I tried unavailingly to restore the connection but nothing could be done. Elin pointed to the sky in the west which was black with cloud. 'The storm is moving east; you won't get anything more until it's over.'

I put the handset back into its clip. 'That bastard, Slade!' I said. 'I was right.'

'What do you mean?' asked Elin.

I looked at the clouds which were beginning to boil over Dyngjufjöll. 'I'd like to get off this track,' I said. 'We have twenty-four hours to waste and I'd rather not do it right here. Let's get up into Askja before that storm really breaks.'

FOUR

The great caldera of Askja is beautiful – but not in a storm. The wind lashed the waters of the crater lake far below and someone, possibly old Odin, pulled the plug out of the sky so that the rain fell in sheets and wind-driven curtains. It was impossible to get down to the lake until the water-slippery ash had dried out so I pulled off the track and we stayed right there, just inside the crater wall.

Some people I know get jumpy even at the thought of being inside the crater of what is, after all, a live volcano; but Askja had said his piece very loudly in 1961 and would probably be quiet for a while apart from a few minor exuberancies. Statistically speaking, we were fairly safe. I put up the top of the Land-Rover so as to get headroom, and presently there were lamb chops under the grill and eggs spluttering in the pan, and we were dry, warm and comfortable.

While Elin fried the eggs I checked the fuel situation. The tank held sixteen gallons and we carried another eighteen gallons in four jerrycans, enough for over 600 miles on good roads. But we weren't on good roads and, in the *Óbyggdir*, we'd be lucky to get even ten miles from a gallon. The gradients and the general roughness meant a lot of low gear work and that swallows fuel greedily, and the nearest filling station was a long way south. Still, I reckoned we'd have enough to get to Geysir.

Miraculously, Elin produced two bottles of Carlsberg from the refrigerator, and I filled a glass gratefully. I watched her as she spooned melted fat over the eggs and thought she looked pale and withdrawn. 'How's the shoulder?'

'Stiff and tender,' she said.

It would be. I said, 'I'll put another dressing on it after supper.' I drank from the glass and felt the sharp tingle of cold beer. 'I wish I could have kept you out of this, Elin.'

She turned her head and offered me a brief smile. 'But you haven't.' With a dextrous twist of a spatula she lifted an egg on to a plate. 'I can't say I'm enjoying it much, though.'

'Entertainment isn't the object,' I said.

She put the plate down before me. 'Why did you ask about Kennikin's drinking habits? It seems pointless.'

'That goes back a long way,' I said. 'As a very young man Kennikin fought in Spain on the Republican side, and when that war was lost he lived in France for a while, stirring things up for Leon Blum's Popular Front, but I think even then he was an undercover man. Anyway, it was there he picked up a taste for Calvados – the Normandy applejack. Got any salt?'

Elin passed the salt cellar. 'I think maybe he had a drinking problem at one time and decided to cut it out because, as far as the Department is aware, he's a non-drinker. You heard Taggart on that.'

Elin began to cut into a loaf of bread. 'I don't see the point of all this,' she complained.

'I'm coming to it. Like a lot of men with an alcohol problem he can keep off the stuff for months at a time, but when the going becomes tough and the pressures build up then he goes on a toot. And, by God, there are enough tensions in our line of work. But the point is that he's a secret drinker; I only found out when I got next to him in Sweden. I visited him unexpectedly and found him cut to the eyeballs on Calvados – it's the only stuff he inhales. He was drunk enough to talk about it, too. Anyway, I poured him into bed and tactfully made my exit, and he never referred to the incident again when I was with him.'

I accepted a piece of bread and dabbed at the yolk of an egg. 'When an agent goes back to the Department after a job he is debriefed thoroughly and by experts. That happened to me when I got back from Sweden, but because I was raising a stink about what had happened to Jimmy Birkby maybe the debriefing wasn't as thorough as it should have been, and the fact that Kennikin drinks never got put on record. It still isn't on record, as I've just found out.'

'I still don't see the point,' said Elin helplessly.

'I'm just about to make it,' I said. 'When Slade came to see me in Scotland he told me of the way I had wounded Kennikin, and made the crack that Kennikin would rather operate on me with a sharp knife than offer to split a bottle of Calvados. How in hell would Slade know about the Calvados? He's never been within a hundred miles of Kennikin and the fact isn't on file in the Department. It's been niggling at me for a long time, but the penny only dropped this afternoon.'

Elin sighed. 'It's a very small point.'

'Have you ever witnessed a murder trial? The point which can hang a man can be very small. But add this to it – the Russians took a package which they presumably discovered to be a fake. You'd expect them to come after the real thing, wouldn't you? But who did come after it, and with blood in his eye? None other than friend Slade.'

'You're trying to make out a case that Slade is a Russian agent,' said Elin. 'But it won't work. Who was really responsible for the destruction of Kennikin's network in Sweden?'

'Slade master-minded it,' I said. 'He pointed me in the right direction and pulled the trigger.'

Elin shrugged. 'Well, then? Would a Russian agent do that to his own side?'

'Slade's a big boy now,' I said. 'Right next to Taggart in a very important area of British Intelligence. He even lunches with the Prime Minister – he told me so. How important would it be to the Russians to get a man into that position?'

Elin looked at me as though I'd gone crazy. I said quietly, 'Whoever planned this has a mind like a pretzel, but it's all of a piece. Slade is in a top slot in British Intelligence – but how did he get there? Answer – by wrecking the Russian organization in Sweden. Which is more important to the Russians? To retain their Swedish network – which could be replaced if necessary? Or to put Slade where he is now?'

I tapped the table with the handle of my knife. 'You can see the same twisted thinking throughout. Slade put me next to Kennikin by sacrificing Birkby; the Russkies put Slade next to Taggart by sacrificing Kennikin and his outfit.'

'But this is silly!' burst out Elin. 'Why would Slade have to go to all that trouble with Birkby and you when the Russians would be co-operating with him, anyway?'

'Because it had to look good,' I said. 'The operation would be examined by men with very hard eyes and there had to be real blood, not tomato ketchup – no fakery at all. The blood was provided by poor Birkby – and Kennikin added some to it.' A sudden thought struck me. 'I wonder if Kennikin knew what was going on? I'll bet his organization was blasted from under him – the poor bastard wouldn't know his masters were selling him out just to bring Slade up a notch.' I rubbed my chin. 'I wonder if he's still ignorant of that?'

'This is all theory,' said Elin. 'Things don't happen that way.'

'Don't they? My God, you only have to read the *published* accounts of some of the spy trials to realize that bloody funny things happen. Do you know why Blake got a sentence of forty-two years in jail?'

She shook her head. 'I didn't read about it.'

'You won't find it in print, but the rumour around the Department was that forty-two was the number of our agents who came to a sticky end because he'd betrayed them. I wouldn't know the truth of it because he was in a different outfit – but think of what Slade could do!'

'So you can't trust anyone,' said Elin. 'What a life to lead!'

'It's not as bad as that. I trust Taggart to a point – and I trust Jack Case, the man I'm meeting at Geysir. But Slade is different; he's become careless and made two mistakes – one about the Calvados, and the other in coming after the package himself.'

Elin laughed derisively. 'And the only reason you trust Taggart and Case is because they've made no mistakes, as you call them?'

'Let me put it this way,' I said. 'I've killed Graham, a British intelligence agent, and so I'm in a hot spot. The only way I can get out of it is to prove that Slade is a Russian agent. If I can do that I'll be a bloody hero and the record will be wiped clean. And it helps a lot that I hate Slade's guts.'

'But what if you're wrong?'

I put as much finality into my voice as I could. 'I'm not wrong,' I said, and hoped it was true. 'We've had a long hard day, Elin; but we can rest tomorrow. Let me put a dressing on your shoulder.'

As I smoothed down the last piece of surgical tape, she said, 'What did you make of what Taggart said just before the storm came?'

I didn't like to think of that. 'I think,' I said carefully, 'that he was telling me that Kennikin is in Iceland.'

II

Tired though I was after a hard day's driving I slept badly. The wind howled from the west across the crater of Askja, buffeting the Land-Rover until it rocked on its springs, and the heavy rain drummed against the side. Once I heard a clatter as though something metallic had moved and I got up to investigate only to find nothing of consequence and got drenched to the skin for my pains. At last I fell into a heavy sleep, shot through with bad dreams.

Still, I felt better in the morning when I got up and looked out. The sun was shining and the lake was a deep blue reflecting the cloudless sky, and in the clear, rain-washed air the far side of the crater seemed a mere kilometre away instead of the ten kilometres it really was. I put water to boil for coffee and when it was ready I leaned over and dug Elin gently in the ribs.

'Umph!' she said indistinctly, and snuggled deeper into the sleeping bag. I prodded her again and one blue eye opened and looked at me malignantly through tumbled blonde hair. 'Stop it!'

'Coffee,' I said, and waved the cup under her nose.

She came to life and clutched the cup with both hands. I took my coffee and a jug of hot water and went outside where I laid my shaving kit on the bonnet and began to whisk up a lather. After shaving, I thought, it would be nice to go down to the lake and clean up. I was beginning to feel grubby – the *Odàdahraun* is a dusty place – and the thought of clean water was good.

I finished scraping my face and, as I rinsed the lather away, I ran through in my mind the things I had to do, the most important of which was to contact Taggart as soon as it was a reasonable hour to find him in his office. I wanted to give him the detailed case against Slade.

Elin came up with the coffee pot. 'More?'

'Thanks,' I said, holding out my cup. 'We'll have a lazy day.' I nodded towards the lake at the bottom of the crater. 'Fancy a swim?'

She pulled a face and moved her wounded shoulder. 'I can't do the crawl, but perhaps I can paddle with one arm.' She looked up at the sky, and said, 'It's a lovely day.'

I watched her face change. 'What's the matter?'

'The radio antenna,' she said. 'It's not there.'

I whirled around. 'Damn!' That was very bad. I climbed up and looked at the damage. It was easy to see what had happened. The rough ground in Central Iceland is enough to shake anything loose that isn't welded down; nuts you couldn't shift with a wrench somehow loosen themselves and wind off the bolts; split-pins jump out, even rivets pop. A whip antenna with its swaying motion is particularly vulnerable; I know one geologist who lost three in a month. The question here was when did we lose it?

It was certainly after I had spoken to Taggart, so it might have gone during the mad dash for Askja when we raced the storm. But I remembered the metallic clatter I had heard during the night; the antenna might have been loosened enough by the bumping to have been swept away by the strong wind. I said, 'It may be around here – quite close. Let's look.'

But we didn't get that far because I heard a familiar sound – the drone of a small aircraft. 'Get down!' I said quickly. 'Keep still and don't look up.'

We dropped flat next to the Land-Rover as the light plane came over the edge of the crater wall flying low. As it cleared the edge it dipped down into the crater to our left. I said, 'Whatever you do, don't lift your head. Nothing stands out so much as a white face.'

The plane flew low over the lake and then turned, spiralling out into a search pattern to survey the interior of the crater. It looked to me like a four-seater Cessna from the brief glimpse I got of it. The Land-Rover was parked in a jumble of big rocks, split into blocks by ice and water, and maybe it wouldn't show up too well from the air providing there was no movement around it.

Elin said quietly, 'Do you think it's someone looking for us?'

'We'll have to assume so,' I said. 'It could be a charter plane full of tourists looking at the *Óbyggdir* from the air, but it's a bit early in the day for that – tourists aren't awake much before nine o'clock.'

This was a development I hadn't thought of. Damn it, Slade was right; I *was* out of practice. Tracks in the *Óbyggdir* are few and it would be no great effort to keep them under surveillance from the air and to direct ground transport by radio. The fact that my Land-Rover was the long wheelbase type would make identification easier – there weren't many of those about.

The plane finished quartering the crater and climbed again, heading north-west. I watched it go but made no move. Elin said, 'Do you think we were seen?'

'I don't know that, either. Stop asking unanswerable questions – and don't move because it may come back for another sweep.'

I gave it five minutes and used the time to figure out what to do next. There would be no refreshing swim in the lake, that was certain. Askja was as secluded a place as anywhere in Iceland but it had one fatal flaw – the track into the crater was a spur from the main track – a dead end – and if anyone blocked the way out of the crater there'd be no getting past, not with the Land-Rover. And I didn't have any illusions about the practicability of going anywhere on foot – you can get very dead that way in the *Óbyggdir*.

'We're getting out of here fast,' I said. 'I want to be on the main track where we have some choice of action. Let's move!'

'Breakfast?'

'Breakfast can wait.'

'And the radio antenna?'

I paused, indecisive and exasperated. We *needed* that antenna – I had to talk to Taggart – but if we had been spotted from the air then a car full of guns could be speeding towards Askja, and I didn't know how much time we had in hand. The antenna could be close by but, on the other hand, it might have dropped off somewhere up the track and miles away.

I made the decision. 'The hell with it! Let's go.'

There was no packing to do beyond collecting the coffee cups and my shaving kit and within two minutes we were climbing the narrow track on the way out of Askja. It was ten kilometres to the main track and when we got there I was sweating for fear of what I might find, but nothing was stirring. I turned right and we headed south.

An hour later I pulled up where the track forked. On the left ran the *Jökulsá á Fjöllum*, now near its source and no longer the mighty force it displayed at Dettifoss. I said, 'We'll have breakfast here.'

'Why here particularly?'

I pointed to the fork ahead. 'We have a three-way choice – we can go back or take either of those tracks. If that plane is going to come back and spot us I'd just as soon he did it here. He can't stay up there forever so we wait him out before we move on and leave him to figure which way we went.'

While Elin was fixing breakfast I took the rifle I had liberated from Graham and examined it. I unloaded it and looked down the bore. This was no way to treat a good gun; not to clean it after shooting. Fortunately, modern powder is no longer so violently corrosive and a day's wait before cleaning no longer such a heinous offence. Besides, I had neither gun oil nor solvent and engine oil would have to do.

I checked the ammunition after cleaning the rifle. Graham had loaded from a packet of twenty-five; he had shot one and I had popped off three at Slade – twenty-one rounds left. I set the sights of the rifle at a hundred yards. I didn't think that if things came to the crunch I'd be shooting at much over that range. Only film heroes can take a strange gun and unknown ammunition and drop the baddy at 500 yards.

I put the rifle where I could get at it easily and caught a disapproving glance from Elin. 'Well, what do you expect me to do?' I said defensively. 'Start throwing rocks?'

'I didn't say anything,' she said.

'No, you didn't,' I agreed. 'I'm going down to the river to clean up. Give me a shout when you're ready.'

But first I climbed a small knoll from where I could get a good view of the surrounding country. Nothing moved for as far as I could see, and in Iceland you can usually see a hell of a long way. Satisfied, I went down to the river which was the milky grey-green colour of melt water and shockingly cold, but after the first painful gasp it wasn't too bad. Refreshed, I went back to tuck into breakfast.

Elin was looking at the map. 'Which way are you going?'

'I want to get between Hofsjökull and Vatnajökull,' I said. 'So we take the left fork.'

'It's a one-way track,' said Elin and passed me the map.

True enough. Printed in ominous red alongside the dashed line which denoted the track was the stern injunction: *Adeins faert til austurs* – eastward travel only. We wanted to go to the west.

I frowned. Most people think that because Greenland is covered with ice and is wrongly named then so is Iceland, and there's not much ice about the place. They're dead wrong. Thirty-six icefields glaciate one-eighth of the country and one of them alone – Vatnajökull – is as big as all the glaciated areas in Scandinavia and the Alps put together.

The cold wastes of Vatnajökull lay just to the south of us and the track to the west was squeezed right up against it by the rearing bulk of Trölladyngja – the Dome of Trolls – a vast shield volcano. I had never been that way before but I had a good idea why the track was one way only. It would cling to the sides of cliffs and be full of hair-pin blind bends – quite hairy enough to negotiate without the unnerving possibility of running into someone head on.

I sighed and examined other possibilities. The track to the right would take us north, the opposite direction to which I wanted to go. More damaging, to get back again would triple the mileage. The geography of Iceland has its own ruthless logic about what is and what is not permitted and the choice of routes is restricted.

I said, 'We'll take our chances going the short way and hope to God we don't meet anyone. It's still early in the season and the chances are good.' I grinned at Elin. 'I don't think there'll be any police around to issue a traffic ticket.'

'And there'll be no ambulance to pick us up from the bottom of a cliff,' she said.

'I'm a careful driver; it may never happen.'

Elin went down to the river and I walked to the top of the knoll again. Everything was quiet. The track stretched back towards Askja and there was no tell-tale cloud of dust to indicate a pursuing vehicle, nor any mysterious aircraft buzzing about the sky. I wondered if I was letting my imagination get the better of me. Perhaps I was running away from nothing.

The guilty flee where no man pursueth. I was as guilty as hell! I had withheld the package from Slade on nothing more than intuition – a hunch Taggart found difficult to believe. And I had killed Graham! As far as the Department was concerned I would already have been judged, found guilty and sentenced, and I wondered what would be the attitude of Jack Case when I saw him at Geysir.

I saw Elin returning to the Land-Rover so I took one last look around and went down to her. Her hair was damp and her cheeks glowed pink as she scrubbed her face with a towel. I waited until she emerged, then said, 'You're in this as much as I am now, so you've got a vote. What do you think I should do?'

She lowered the towel and looked at me thoughtfully. 'I should do exactly what you are doing. You've made the plan. Meet this man at Geysir and give him that . . . that whatever-it-is.'

I nodded. 'And what if someone should try to stop us?'

She hesitated. 'If it is Slade, then give him the gadget. If it is Kennikin . . .' She stopped and shook her head slowly.

I saw her reasoning. I might be able to hand over to Slade and get away unscathed; but Kennikin would not be satisfied with that – he'd want my blood. I said, 'Supposing it is Kennikin – what would you expect me to do?'

She drooped. 'I think you would want to fight him – to use that rifle. You would want to kill him.' Her voice was desolate.

I took her by the arm. 'Elin, I don't kill people indiscriminately. I'm not a psychopath. I promise there will be no killing unless it is in self defence; unless my life is in danger – or yours.'

'I'm sorry, Alan,' she said. 'But a situation like this is so alien to me. I've never had to face anything like it.'

I waved towards the knoll. 'I was doing a bit of thinking up there. It occurred to me that perhaps my assessment of everything has been wrong – that I've misjudged people and events.'

'No!' she said definitely. 'You've made a strong case against Slade.'

'And yet you would want me to give him the gadget?'

'What is it to me?' she cried. 'Or to you? Let him have it when the time comes – let us go back to living our own lives.'

'I'd like to do that very much,' I said. 'If people would let me.' I looked up at the sun which was already high. 'Come on; let's be on our way.'

As we drove towards the fork I glanced at Elin's set face and sighed. I could quite understand her attitude, which was that of any other Icelander. Long gone are the days when the Vikings were the scourge of Europe, and the Icelanders have lived in isolation for so many years that the affairs of the rest of the world must seem remote and alien.

Their only battle has been to regain their political independence from Denmark and that was achieved by peaceful negotiation. True, they are not so isolated that their economy is separated from world trade – far from it – but trade is trade and war, whether open or covert, is something for other crazy people and not for sober, sensible Icelanders.

They are so confident that no one can envy their country enough to seize it that they have no armed forces. After all, if the Icelanders with their thousand years of experience behind them still find it most difficult to scratch a living out of the country then who else in his right mind would want it?

A peaceful people with no first-hand knowledge of war. It was hardly surprising that Elin found the shenanigans in which I was involved distasteful and dirty. I didn't feel too clean myself.

III

The track was bad.

It was bad right from where we had stopped and it got steadily worse after we had left the river and began to climb under Vatnajökull. I crunched down into low gear and went into four-wheel drive as the track snaked its way up the cliffs, doubling back on itself so often that I had a zany idea I might drive into my own rear. It was wide enough only for one vehicle and I crept around each corner hoping to God that no one was coming the other way.

Once there was a slide of rubble sideways and I felt the Land-Rover slip with rear wheels spinning towards the edge of a sheer drop. I poured on the juice and hoped for the best. The front wheels held their grip and hauled us to safety. Soon after that I stopped on a reasonably straight bit, and when I took my hands from the wheel they were wet with sweat.

I wiped them dry. 'This is bloody tricky.'

'Shall I drive for a while?' asked Elin.

I shook my head. 'Not with your bad shoulder. Besides, it's not the driving – it's the expectation of meeting some-one around every corner.' I looked over the edge of the cliff. 'One of us would have to reverse out and that's a flat impos-sibility.' That was the best that could happen; the worst didn't bear thinking about. No wonder this track was one way only.

'I could walk ahead,' Elin said. 'I can check around the corners and guide you.'

'That would take all day,' I objected. 'And we've a long way to go.'

She jerked her thumb downwards. 'Better than going down there. Besides, we're not moving at much more than a walking pace as it is. I can stand on the front bumper while we go on the straight runs and jump off at the corners.'

It was an idea that had its points but I didn't like it much. 'It won't do your shoulder much good.'

'I can use the other arm,' she said impatiently, and opened the door to get out.

At one time in England there was a law to the effect that every mechanically propelled vehicle on the public highway must be preceded by a man on foot bearing a red flag to warn the unwary citizenry of the juggernaut bearing down upon them. I had never expected to be put in the same position, but that's progress.

Elin would ride the bumper until we approached a corner and jump off as I slowed down. Slowing down was no trick at all, even going down hill; all I had to do was to take my foot off the accelerator. I had dropped into the lowest gear possible which, on a Land-Rover is something wondrous. That final drive ratio of about 40:1 gives a lot of traction and a lot of engine braking. Driven flat out when cranked as low as that the old girl would make all of nine miles an hour when delivering ninety-five horsepower – and a hell of a lot of traction was just what I needed on that Icelandic roller-coaster. But it was hell on fuel consumption.

So Elin would guide me around a corner and then ride the bumper to the next one. It sounds as though it might have been a slow job but curiously enough we seemed to make better time. We went on in this dot-and-carry-one manner for quite a long way and then Elin held up her hand and pointed, not down the track but away in the air to the right. As she started to hurry back I twisted my neck to see what she had seen.

A helicopter was coming over Trölladyngja like a grasshopper, the sun making a spinning disc of its rotor and striking reflections from the greenhouse which designers put on choppers for their own weird reasons. I've flown by helicopter on many occasions and on a sunny day you feel like a ripening tomato under glass.

But I wasn't thinking about that right then because Elin had come up on the wrong side of the Land-Rover. 'Get to the other side,' I shouted. 'Get under cover.' I dived out of the door on the other side where the cliff face was.

She joined me. 'Trouble?'

'Could be.' I held open the door and grabbed the carbine. 'We've seen no vehicles so far, but two aircraft have been interested in us. That seems unnatural.'

I peered around the rear end of the Land-Rover, keeping the gun out of sight. The helicopter was still heading towards us and losing height. When it was quite close the nose came up and it bobbed and curtsied in the air as it came to a hovering stop about a hundred yards away. Then it came down like a lift until it was level with us.

I sweated and gripped the carbine. Sitting on the ledge we were like ducks in a shooting gallery, and all that was between us and any bullets was the Land-Rover. It's a stoutly built vehicle but at that moment I wished it was an armoured car. The chopper ducked and swayed and regarded us interestedly, but I could see no human movement beyond the reflections echoed from the glass of the cockpit.

Then the fuselage began to rotate slowly until it was turned broadside on, and I let out my breath in a long sigh. Painted in large letters along the side was the single word – NAVY – and I relaxed, put down the carbine and went into the open. If there was one place where Kennikin would not be it was inside a US Navy Sikorsky LH-34 chopper.

I waved, and said to Elin, 'It's all right; you can come out.'

She joined me and we looked at the helicopter. A door in the side slid open and a crewman appeared wearing a white bone-dome helmet. He leaned out, holding on with one hand, and made a whirling motion with the other and then put his fist to the side of his face. He did this two or three times before I tumbled to what he was doing.

'He wants us to use the telephone,' I said. 'A pity we can't.' I climbed on top of the Land-Rover and pointed as eloquently as I could to where the whip antenna had been. The crewman caught on fast; he waved and drew himself back inside and the door closed. Within a few seconds the helicopter reared up and gained height, the fuselage turning until it was pointing south-west, and then away it went until it disappeared into the distance with a fading roar.

I looked at Elin. 'What do you suppose that was about?'

'It seemed they want to talk to you. Perhaps the helicopter will land farther down the track.'

'It certainly couldn't land here,' I said. 'Maybe you're right. I could do with a trip back to Keflavik in comfort.' I looked into the thin air into which the chopper had vanished. 'But nobody told me the Americans were in on this.'

Elin gave me a sidelong look. 'In on what?'

'I don't know, damn it! I wish to hell I did.' I retrieved the carbine. 'Let's get on with it.'

So on we went along that bastard of a track, round and round, up and down, but mostly up, until we had climbed right to the edge of Vatnajökull, next to the ice. The track could only go one way from there and that was away, so it turned at right-angles to the ice field and from then on the direction was mostly down. There was one more particularly nasty bit where we had to climb an outlying ridge of Trölladyngja but from then on the track improved and I called Elin aboard again.

I looked back the way we had come and was thankful for one thing; it had been a bright, sunny day. If there had been mist or much rain it would have been impossible. I checked the map and found we were through the one-way section for which I was heartily thankful.

Elin looked tired. She had done a lot of walking over rough ground and a lot of jumping up and down, and her face was drawn. I checked the time, and said, 'We'll feel better after we've eaten, and hot coffee would go down well. We'll stop here a while.'

And that was a mistake.

I discovered it was a mistake two and a half hours later. We had rested for an hour and eaten, and then continued for an hour and a half until we came to a river which was brimming full. I pulled up at the water's edge where the track disappeared into the river, and got out to look at the problem.

I estimated the depth and looked at the dry stones in the banks. 'It's still rising, damn it! If we hadn't stopped we could have crossed an hour ago. Now, I'm not so sure.'

Vatnajökull is well named the 'Water Glacier'. It dominates the river system of Eastern and Southern Iceland – a great reservoir of frozen water which, in slowly melting, covers the land with a network of rivers. I had been thankful it had been a sunny day, but now I was not so sure because sunny days mean full rivers. The best time to cross a glacier is at dawn when it is low. During the day, especially on a clear, sunny day, the melt water increases and the flow grows to a peak in the late afternoon. This particular river had not yet reached its peak but it was still too damned deep to cross.

Elin consulted the map. 'Where are you making for? Today, I mean.'

'I wanted to get to the main Sprengisandur route. That's more or less a permanent track; once we're on it getting to Geysir should be easy.'

She measured the distance. 'Sixty kilometres,' she said, and paused.

I saw her lips moving. 'What's the matter?'

She looked up, 'I was counting,' she said. 'Sixteen rivers to cross in that sixty kilometres before we hit the Sprengisandur track.'

'For Christ's sake!' I said. Normally in my travels in Iceland I had never been in a particular hurry to get anywhere. I had never counted the rivers and if an unfordable one had barred my path it was no great hardship to camp for a few hours until the level dropped. But the times were a-changing.

Elin said, 'We'll have to camp here.'

I looked at the river and knew I had to make up my mind quickly. 'I think we'll try to get over,' I said.

Elin looked at me blankly. 'But why? You won't be able to cross the others until tomorrow.'

I tossed a pebble into the water. If it made any ripples I didn't see them because they were obliterated by the swift flowing current. I said, ' "By the pricking of my thumbs, something evil this way comes." ' I swung around and pointed back along the track. 'And I think it will come from that direction. If we have to stop I'd rather it was on the other side of this river.'

Elin looked doubtfully at the fast rip in the middle. 'It will be dangerous.'

'It might be more dangerous to stay here.' I had an uneasy feeling which, maybe, was no more than the automatic revulsion against being caught in a position from which it was impossible to run. It was the reason I had left Askja, and it was the reason I wanted to cross this river. Perhaps it was just my tactical sense sharpening up after lying dormant for so long. I said, 'And it'll be more dangerous to cross in fifteen minutes, so let's move it.'

I checked whether, in fact, the place where the track crossed the river was the most practicable. This turned out to be a waste of time but it had to be done. Anywhere upstream or downstream was impossible for various reasons, either deep water or high banks – so I concentrated on the ford and hoped the footing was sound.

Dropping again into the lowest gear possible I drove slowly into the river. The quick water swirled against the wheels and built up into waves which slapped against the side of the cab. Right in midstream the water was deep and any moment I expected to find it flowing under the door. More ominously the force of the water was so great that for one hair-raising second I felt the vehicle shift sideways and there was a curiously lifting lurch preparatory to being swept downstream.

I rammed my foot down and headed for shallower water and the opposite bank. The front wheels bit into the bed of the river but the back of the Land-Rover actually lifted and floated so that we got to the other side broadside on and climbed out awkwardly over a moss-crusted hummock of lava, streaming water like a shaggy dog just come from a swim.

I headed for the track and we bucked and lurched over the lava, and when we were finally on reasonably level ground I switched off the engine and looked at Elin. 'I don't think we'll cross any more rivers today. That one was enough. Thank God for four-wheel drive.'

She was pale. 'That was an unjustifiable risk,' she said. 'We could have been swept downstream.'

'But we weren't,' I said, and switched on the engine again. 'How far to the next river? We'll camp there and cross at dawn.'

She consulted the map. 'About two kilometres.'

So we pushed on and presently came to river number two which was also swollen with sun-melted water from Vatnajökull. I turned the vehicle and headed towards a jumble of rocks behind which I parked, out of sight of both the river and the track – again on good tactical principles.

I was annoyed. It was still not very late and there were several hours of daylight left which we could have used for mileage if it hadn't been for those damned rivers. But there was nothing for it but to wait until the next day when the flow would drop. I said, 'You look tired; you've had a hard day.'

Elin nodded dispiritedly and got out of the cab. I noticed her favouring her right arm, and said, 'How is the shoulder?'

She grimaced. 'Stiff.'

'I'd better take a look at it.'

I put up the collapsible top of the Land-Rover and set water to boil, and Elin sat on a bunk and tried to take off her sweater. She couldn't do it because she couldn't raise her right arm. I helped her take it off but, gentle though I was, she gasped in pain. Reasonably enough, she wasn't wearing a brassière under the sweater because the shoulder strap would have cut right into the wound.

I took off the pad and looked at her shoulder. The wound was angry and inflamed but there was no sign of any pus which would indicate infection. I said, 'I told you that you'd begin to feel it. A graze like this can hurt like the devil, so don't be too stiff-upper-lipped about it – I know how it feels.'

She crossed her arms across her breasts. 'Has it ever happened to you?'

'I was grazed across the ribs once,' I said, as I poured warm water into a cup.

'So that's how you got that scar.'

'Yours is worse because it's across the trapezius muscle and you keep pulling it. You really should have your arm in a sling – I'll see what I can find.' I washed the wound and put on a new medicated dressing from the first-aid box, then helped her put on the sweater. 'Where's your scarf – the new woollen one?'

She pointed. 'In that drawer.'

'Then that's your sling.' I took out the scarf and fitted it to her arm so as to immobilize the shoulder as much as possible. 'Now, you just sit there and watch me cook supper.'

I thought this was an appropriate time to open the goody box – the small collection of luxuries we kept for special occasions. We both needed cheering up and there's nothing like a first-class meal under the belt to lift the spirits. I don't know if Mr Fortnum and Mr Mason are aware of the joy they bring to sojourners in far-flung lands, but after the oyster soup, the whole roast quails and the pears pickled in cognac I felt almost impelled to write them a letter of appreciation.

The colour came back into Elin's cheeks as she ate. I insisted that she didn't use her right hand and she didn't have to – the dark, tender flesh fell away from the quail at the touch of a fork and she managed all right. I made coffee and we accompanied it with brandy which I carried for medicinal purposes.

As she sipped her coffee she sighed. 'Just like old times, Alan.'

'Yes,' I said lazily. I was feeling much better myself. 'But you'd better sleep. We make an early start tomorrow.' I calculated it would be light enough to move at three a.m. when the rivers would also be at their lowest. I leaned over and took the binoculars.

'Where are you going?' she asked.

'Just to have a look around. You go to bed.'

Her eyes flickered sleepily. 'I *am* tired,' she admitted.

That wasn't surprising. We'd been on the run for a long time, and bouncing about in the *Óbyggdir* wasn't helping – we'd managed to fall into every damned pothole on the track. I said, 'Get your head down – I won't be long.'

I hung the lanyard of the binoculars around my neck, opened the back door and dropped to the ground. I was about to walk away when I turned back on impulse, reached into the cab and picked up the carbine. I don't think Elin saw me do that.

First I inspected the river we had to cross. It was flowing well but exposed wet stones showed that the level was already dropping. By dawn the crossing would be easy, and we should be able to get across all the other rivers that lay between us and Sprengisandur before the increased flow made it impossible.

I slung the carbine over my shoulder and walked back along the track towards the river we had crossed which lay a little over a mile away. I approached cautiously but everything was peaceful. The river flowed and chuckled and there was nothing in sight to cause alarm. I checked the distant view with the binoculars, then sat down with my back against a mossy boulder, lit a cigarette and started to think.

I was worried about Elin's shoulder; not that there was anything particularly alarming about its condition, but a doctor would do a better job than I could, and this bouncing about the wilderness wasn't helping. It might be difficult explaining to a doctor how Elin had come by an unmistakable gunshot wound, but accidents do happen and I thought I could get away with it by talking fast.

I stayed there for a couple of hours, smoking and thinking and looking at the river, and at the end of that time I had come up with nothing new despite my brain beating. The added factor of the American helicopter was a piece of the jigsaw that wouldn't fit anywhere. I looked at my watch and found it was after nine o'clock, so I buried all the cigarette stubs, picked up the carbine and prepared to go back.

As I stood up I saw something that made me tense – a plume of dust in the far distance across the river. I laid down the carbine and lifted the glasses and saw the little dot of a vehicle at the head of that feather of dust like a high-flying jet at the head of a contrail. I looked around – there was no cover near the river but about two hundred yards back a spasm of long gone energy had heaved up the lava into a ridge which I could hide behind. I ran for it.

The vehicle proved to be a Willys jeep – as good for this country in its way as my Land-Rover. It slowed as it came to the river, nosed forward and came to a stop at the water's edge. The night was quiet and I heard the click of the door handle as a man got out and walked forward to look at the water. He turned and said something to the driver and, although I could not hear the words, I knew he was speaking neither Icelandic nor English.

He spoke Russian.

The driver got out, looked at the water and shook his head. Presently there were four of them standing there, and they seemed to be having an argument. Another jeep came up behind and more men got out to study the problem until there were eight in all – two jeeps full. One of them, the one who made the decisive gestures and who seemed to be the boss, I thought I recognized.

I lifted the glasses and his face sprang into full view in the dimming light. Elin had been wrong; crossing the river had *not* been an unjustifiable risk, and the justification lay in the face I now saw. The scar was still there, running from the end of the right eyebrow to the corner of the mouth, and the eyes were still grey and hard as stones. The only change in him was that his close-cropped hair was no longer black but a grizzled grey and his face was puffier with incipient wattles forming on his neck.

Kennikin and I were both four years older but I think I may have worn better than he had.

FIVE

I put my hand out to the carbine and then paused. The light was bad and getting worse, the gun was strange and it hadn't the barrel to reach out and knock a man down at a distance. I estimated the range at a shade under three hundred yards and I knew that if I hit anyone at that range and in that light it would be by chance and not by intention.

If I had my own gun I could have dropped Kennikin as easily as dropping a deer. I have put a soft-nosed bullet into a deer and it has run for half a mile before dropping dead, and that with an exit wound big enough to put your fist in. A man can't do that – his nervous system is too delicate and can't stand the shock.

But I hadn't my own rifle, and there was no percentage in opening fire at random. That would only tell Kennikin I was close, and it might be better if he didn't know. So I let my fingers relax from the carbine and concentrated on watching what was going to happen next.

The arguing had stopped with Kennikin's arrival, and I knew why, having worked with him. He had no time for futile blathering; he would accept your facts – and God help you if they were wrong – and then he would make the decisions. He was busily engaged in making one now.

I smiled as I saw someone point out the tracks of the Land-Rover entering the water and then indicate the other bank of the river. There were no tracks where we had left the water because we had been swept sideways a little, and that must have been puzzling to anyone who hadn't seen it happen.

The man waved downstream eloquently but Kennikin shook his head. He wasn't buying that one. Instead he said something, snapping his fingers impatiently, and someone else rushed up with a map. He studied it and then pointed off to the right and four of the men got into a jeep, reversed up the track, and then took off across country in a bumpy ride.

That made me wrinkle my brows until I remembered there was a small group of lakes over in that direction called Gaesavötn. If Kennikin expected me to be camping at Gaesavötn he'd draw a blank, but it showed how thorough and careful he was.

The crew from the other jeep got busy erecting a camp just off the track, putting up tents rather inexpertly. One of them went to Kennikin with a vacuum flask and poured out a cup of steaming hot coffee which he offered obsequiously. Kennikin took it and sipped it while still standing at the water's edge looking across the impassable river. He seemed to be staring right into my eyes.

I lowered the glasses and withdrew slowly and cautiously, being careful to make no sound. I climbed down from the lava ridge and then slung the carbine and headed back to the Land-Rover at a fast clip, and checked to make sure there were no tyre marks to show where we had left the track. I didn't think Kennikin would have a man swim the river – he could lose a lot of men that way – but it was best to make sure we weren't stumbled over too easily.

Elin was asleep. She lay on her left side, buried in her sleeping bag, and I was thankful that she always slept quietly and with no blowing or snoring. I let her sleep; there was no reason to disturb her and ruin her night. We weren't going anywhere, and neither was Kennikin. I switched on my pocket torch shading it with my hand to avoid waking her, and rummaged in a drawer until I found the housewife, from which I took a reel of black thread.

I went back to the track and stretched a line of thread right across it about a foot from the ground, anchoring each end by lumps of loose lava. If Kennikin came through during the night I wanted to know it, no matter how stealthily he went about it. I didn't want to cross the river in the morning only to run into him on the other side.

Then I went down to the river and looked at it. The water level was still dropping and it might have been barely feasible to cross there and then had the light been better. But I wouldn't risk it without using the headlights and I couldn't do that because they'd certainly show in the sky. Kennikin's mob wasn't all that far away.

I dropped into my berth fully clothed. I didn't expect to sleep under the circumstances but nevertheless I set the alarm on my wrist watch for two a.m. And that was the last thing I remember until it buzzed like a demented mosquito and woke me up.

II

We were ready to move at two-fifteen. As soon as the alarm buzzed I woke Elin, ruthlessly disregarding her sleepy protests. As soon as she knew how close Kennikin was she moved fast. I said, 'Get dressed quickly. I'm going to have a look around.'

The black thread was still in place which meant that no vehicle had gone through. Any jeep moving at night would *have* to stick to the track; it was flatly impossible to cross the lava beds in the darkness. True, someone on foot might have gone through, but I discounted that.

The water in the river was nice and low and it would be easy to cross. As I went back I looked in the sky towards the east; already the short northern night was nearly over and I was determined to cross the river at the earliest opportunity and get as far ahead of Kennikin as I could.

Elin had different ideas. 'Why not stay here and let him get ahead? Just let him go past. He'd have to go a long way before he discovered he's chasing nothing.'

'No,' I said. 'We know he has two jeeps, but we don't know if he has more. It could happen that, if we let him get ahead, we could be the meat in a sandwich and that might be uncomfortable. We cross now.'

Starting an engine quietly is not easy. I stuffed blankets around the generator in an attempt to muffle that unmistakable rasp, the engine caught and purred sweetly, and I took the blankets away. And I was very light-footed on the accelerator as we drove towards the river. We got across easily, although making more noise than I cared for, and away we went towards the next river.

I told Elin to keep a sharp eye to the rear while I concentrated on moving as fast as possible compatible with quietness. In the next four kilometres we crossed two more rivers and then there was a long stretch where the track swung north temporarily, and I opened up. We were now far enough away from Kennikin to make speed more important than silence.

Sixteen rivers in sixty kilometres, Elin had said. Not counting the time spent in crossing rivers we were now averaging a bone-jarring twenty-five kilometres an hour – too fast for comfort in this country – and I estimated we would get to the main Sprengisandur track in about four hours. It actually took six hours because some of the rivers were bastards.

In reaching the Sprengisandur track we had crossed the watershed and all the rivers from now on would be flowing south and west instead of north and east. We hit the track at eight-thirty, and I said, 'Breakfast. Climb in the back and get something ready.'

'You're not stopping?'

'Christ, no! Kennikin will have been on the move for hours. There's no way of knowing how close he is and I've no urgent inclination to find out the hard way. Bread and cheese and beer will do fine.'

So we ate on the move and stopped only once, at ten o'clock, to fill up the tank from the last full jerrycan. While we were doing that up popped our friend of the previous day, the US Navy helicopter. It came from the north this time, not very low, and floated over us without appearing to pay us much attention.

I watched it fly south, and Elin said, 'I'm puzzled about that.'

'So am I,' I said.

'Not in the same way that I am,' she said. 'American military aircraft don't usually overfly the country.' She was frowning.

'Now you come to mention it, that *is* odd.' There's a certain amount of tension in Iceland about the continuing American military presence at Keflavik. A lot of Icelanders take the view that it's an imposition and who can blame them? The American authorities are quite aware of this tension and try to minimize it, and the American Navy in Iceland tries to remain as inconspicuous as possible. Flaunting military aircraft in Icelandic skies was certainly out of character.

I shrugged and dismissed the problem, concentrating on getting the last drop out of the jerrycan, and then we carried on with not a sign of anything on our tail. We were now on the last lap, running down the straight, if rough, track between the River Thjórsá and the ridge of Búdarháls with the main roads only seventy kilometres ahead, inasmuch as any roads in Iceland can be so described.

But even a lousy Icelandic road would be perfection when compared with the tracks of the *Óbyggdir*, especially when we ran into trouble with mud. This is one of the problems of June when the frozen earth of winter melts into a gelatinous car trap. Because we were in a Land-Rover it didn't stop us but it slowed us down considerably, and the only consolation I had was that Kennikin would be equally hampered when he hit the stuff.

At eleven o'clock the worst happened – a tyre blew. It was a front tyre and I fought the wheel as we jolted to a stop. 'Let's make this fast,' I said, and grabbed the wheel brace.

If we had to have a puncture it wasn't a bad place to have it. The footing was level enough to take the jack without slipping and there was no mud at that point. I jacked up the front of the Land-Rover and got busy on the wheel with the brace. Because of Elin's shoulder she wasn't of much use in this kind of job. so I said. 'What about making coffee – we could do with something hot.'

I took the wheel off, rolled it away and replaced it with the spare. The whole operation took a little under ten minutes, time we couldn't afford – not there and then. Once we were farther south we could lose ourselves on a more-or-less complex road network, but these wilderness tracks were too restricted for my liking.

I tightened the last wheel nut and then looked to see what had caused a blowout and to put the wheel back into its rack. What I saw made my blood run cold. I fingered the jagged hole in the thick tyre and looked up at the Búdarháls ridge which dominated the track.

There was only one thing that could make a hole like that – a bullet. And somewhere up on the ridge, hidden in some crevice, was a sniper – and even then I was probably in his sights.

III

How in hell did Kennikin get ahead of me? That was my first bitter thought. But idle thoughts were no use and action was necessary.

I heaved up the wheel with its ruined tyre on to the bonnet and screwed it down securely. While I rotated the wheel brace I glanced covertly at the ridge. There was a lot of open ground before the ridge heaved itself into the air – at least two hundred yards – and the closest a sniper could have been was possibly four hundred yards and probably more.

Any man who could put a bullet into a tyre at over four hundred yards – a quarter mile – was a hell of a good shot. So good that he could put a bullet into me any time he liked – so why the devil hadn't he? I was in plain view, a perfect target, and yet no bullets had come my way. I tightened down the last nut and turned my back to the ridge, and felt a prickling feeling between my shoulder blades – that was where the bullet would hit me if it came.

I jumped to the ground and put away the brace and jack, concentrating on doing the natural thing. The palms of my hands were slippery with sweat. I went to the back of the Land-Rover and looked in at the open door. 'How's the coffee coming?'

'Just ready,' said Elin.

I climbed in and sat down. Sitting in that confined space gave a comforting illusion of protection, but that's all it was – an illusion. For the second time I wished the Land-Rover had been an armoured car. From where I was sitting I could inspect the slopes of the ridge without being too obvious about it and I made the most of the opportunity.

Nothing moved among those red and grey rocks. Nobody stood up and waved or cheered. If anyone was still up there he was keeping as quiet as a mouse which, of course, was the correct thing to do. If you pump a bullet at someone you'd better scrunch yourself up small in case he starts shooting back.

But was anybody still up there? I rather thought there was. Who in his right mind would shoot a hole in the tyre of a car and then just walk away? So he was still up there, waiting and watching. But if he was still there why hadn't he nailed me? It didn't make much sense – unless he was just supposed to immobilize me.

I stared unseeingly at Elin who was topping up a jar with sugar. If that was so, then Kennikin had men coming in from both sides. It wouldn't be too hard to arrange if he knew where I was – radio communication is a wonderful thing. That character up on the ridge would have been instructed to stop me so that Kennikin could catch up; and that meant he wanted me alive.

I wondered what would happen if I got into the driving seat and took off again. The odds were that another bullet would rip open another tyre. It would be easier this time on a sitting target. I didn't take the trouble to find out – there was a limit to the number of spare tyres I carried, and the limit had already been reached.

Hoping that my chain of reasoning was not too shaky I began to make arrangements to get out from under that gun. I took Lindholm's cosh from under the mattress where I had concealed it and put it into my pocket, then I said, 'Let's go and . . .' My voice came out as a hoarse croak and I cleared my throat. 'Let's have coffee outside.'

Elin looked up in surprise. 'I thought we were in a hurry.'

'We've been making good time,' I said. 'I reckon we're far enough ahead to earn a break. I'll take the coffee pot and the sugar; you bring the cups.' I would have dearly loved to have taken the carbine but that would have been too obvious; an unsuspecting man doesn't drink his coffee fully armed.

I jumped out of the rear door and Elin handed out the coffee pot and the sugar jar which I set on the rear bumper before helping her down. Her right arm was still in the sling but she could carry the cups and spoons in her left hand. I picked up the coffee pot and waved it in the general direction of the ridge. 'Let's go over there at the foot of the rocks.' I made off in that direction without giving her time to argue.

We trudged over the open ground towards the ridge. I had the coffee pot in one hand and the sugar jar in the other, the picture of innocence. I also had the *sgian dubh* tucked into my left stocking and a cosh in my pocket, but those didn't show. As we got nearer the ridge a miniature cliff reared up and I thought our friend up on top might be getting worried. Any moment from now he would be losing sight of us, and he might just lean forward a little to keep us in view.

I turned as though to speak to Elin and then turned back quickly, glancing upwards as I did so. There was no one to be seen but I was rewarded by the glint of something – a reflection that flickered into nothing. It might have been the sun reflecting off a surface of glassy lava, but I didn't think so. Lava doesn't jump around when left to its own devices – not after it has cooled off, that is.

I marked the spot and went on, not looking up again, and we came to the base of the cliff which was about twenty feet high. There was a straggly growth of birch; gnarled trees all of a foot high. In Iceland bonsai grow naturally and I'm surprised the Icelanders don't work up an export trade to Japan. I found a clear space, set down the coffee pot and the sugar jar, then sat down and pulled up my trouser leg to extract the knife.

Elin came up. 'What are you doing?'

I said, 'Now don't jump out of your pants, but there's a character on the ridge behind us who just shot a hole in that tyre.'

Elin stared at me wordlessly. I said, 'He can't see us here, but I don't think he's worried very much about that. All he wants to do is to stop us until Kennikin arrives – and he's doing it very well. As long as he can see the Land-Rover he knows we aren't far away.' I tucked the knife into the waistband of my trousers – it's designed for a fast draw only when wearing a kilt.

Elin sank to her knees. 'You're sure?'

'I'm positive. You don't get a natural puncture like that in the side wall of a new tyre.' I stood up and looked along the ridge. 'I'm going to winkle out that bastard; I think I know where he is.' I pointed to a crevice at the end of the cliff, a four-foot high crack in the rock. 'I want you to get in there and wait. Don't move until you hear me call – and make bloody sure it is me.'

'And what if you don't come back?' she said bleakly.

She was a realist. I looked at her set face and said deliberately, 'In that case, if nothing else happens, you stay where you are until dark, then make a break for the Land-Rover and get the hell out of here. On the other hand, if Kennikin pitches up, try to keep out of his way – and do that by keeping out of sight.' I shrugged. 'But I'll try to get back.'

'Do you have to go at all?'

I sighed. 'We're stuck here, Elin. As long as that joker can keep the Land-Rover covered we're stuck. What do you want me to do? Wait here until Kennikin arrives and then just give myself up?'

'But you're not armed?'

I patted the hilt of the knife. 'I'll make out. Now, just do as I say.' I escorted her to the cleft and saw her inside. It can't have been very comfortable; it was a foot and a half wide by four feet high and so she had to crouch. But there are worse things than being uncomfortable.

Then I contemplated what I had to do. The ridge was seamed by gullies cut by water into the soft rock and they offered a feasible way of climbing without being seen. What I wanted to do was to get above the place where I had seen the sudden glint. In warfare – and this was war – he who holds the high ground has the advantage.

I set out, moving to the left and sticking close in to the rocks. There was a gully twenty yards along which I rejected because I knew it petered out not far up the ridge. The next one was better because it went nearly to the top, so I went into it and began to climb.

Back in the days when I was being trained I went to mountain school and my instructor said something very wise. 'Never follow a watercourse or a stream, either uphill or downhill,' he said. The reasoning was good. Water will take the quickest way down any hill and the quickest way is usually the steepest. Normally one sticks to the bare hillside and steers clear of ravines. Abnormally, on the other hand, one scrambles up a damned steep, slippery, waterworn crack in the rock or one gets one's head blown off.

The sides of the ravine at the bottom of the ridge were about ten feet high, so there was no danger of being seen. But higher up the ravine was shallower and towards the end it was only about two feet deep and I was snaking upwards on my belly. When I had gone as far as I could I reckoned I was higher than the sniper, so I cautiously pushed my head around a pitted chunk of lava and assessed the situation.

Far below me on the track, and looking conspicuously isolated, was the Land-Rover. About two hundred feet to the right and a hundred feet below was the place where I thought the sniper was hiding. I couldn't see him because of the boulders which jutted through the sandy skin of the ridge. That suited me; if I couldn't see him then he couldn't see me, and that screen of boulders was just what I needed to get up close.

But I didn't rush at it. It was in my mind that there might be more than one man. Hell, there could be a dozen scattered along the top of the ridge for all I knew! I just stayed very still and got back my breath, and did a careful survey of every damned rock within sight.

Nothing moved, so I wormed my way out of cover of the ravine and headed towards the boulders, still on my belly. I got there and rested again, listening carefully. All I heard was the faraway murmur of the river in the distance. I moved again, going upwards and around the clump of boulders, and now I was holding the cosh.

I pushed my head around a rock and saw them, fifty feet below in a hollow in the hillside. One was lying down with a rifle pushed before him, the barrel resting on a folded jacket; the other sat farther back tinkering with a walkie-talkie. He had an unlighted cigarette in his mouth.

I withdrew my head and considered. One man I might have tackled – two together were going to be tricky, especially without a gun. I moved carefully and found a better place from which to observe and where I would be less conspicuous – two rocks came almost together but not quite, and I had a peephole an inch across.

The man with the rifle was very still and very patient. I could imagine that he was an experienced hunter and had spent many hours on hillsides like this waiting for his quarry to move within range. The other man was more fidgety; he eased his buttocks on the rock on which he was sitting, he scratched, he slapped at an insect which settled on his leg, and he fiddled with the walkie-talkie.

At the bottom of the ridge I saw something moving and held my breath. The man with the rifle saw it, too, and I could see the slight tautening of his muscles as he tensed. It was Elin. She came out of cover from under the cliff and walked towards the Land-Rover.

I cursed to myself and wondered what the hell she thought she was doing. The man with the rifle settled the butt firmly into his shoulder and took aim, following her all the way with his eye glued to the telescopic sight. If he pulled that trigger I would take my chances and jump the bastard there and then.

Elin got to the Land-Rover and climbed inside. Within a minute she came out again and began to walk back towards the cliff. Half-way there she called out and tossed something into the air. I was too far away to see what it was but I thought it was a packet of cigarettes. The joker with the rifle would be sure of what it was because he was equipped with one of the biggest telescopic sights I had ever seen.

Elin vanished from sight below and I let out my breath. She had deliberately play-acted to convince these gunmen that I was still there below, even if out of sight. And it worked, too. The rifleman visibly relaxed and turned over and said something to the other man. I couldn't hear what was said because he spoke in low tones, but the fidget laughed loudly.

He was having trouble with the walkie-talkie. He extended the antenna, clicked switches and turned knobs, and then tossed it aside on to the moss. He spoke to the rifleman and pointed upwards, and the rifleman nodded. Then he stood up and turned to climb towards me.

I noted the direction he was taking, then turned my head to find a place to ambush him. There was a boulder just behind me about three feet high, so I pulled away from my peephole and dropped behind it in a crouch and took a firm hold of the cosh. I could hear him coming because he wasn't making much attempt to move quietly. His boots crunched on the ground and once there was a flow of gravel as he slipped and I heard a muttered curse. Then there was a change in the light as his shadow fell across me, and I rose up behind him and hit him.

There's quite a bit of nonsense talked about hitting men on the head. From some accounts – film and TV script writers – it's practically as safe as an anaesthetic used in an operating theatre; all that happens is a brief spell of unconsciousness followed by a headache not worse than a good hangover. A pity it isn't so because if it were the hospital anaesthetists would be able to dispense with the elaborate equipment with which they are now lumbered in favour of the time-honoured blunt instrument.

Unconsciousness is achieved by imparting a sharp acceleration to the skull bone so that it collides with the contents – the brain. This results in varying degrees of brain damage ranging from slight concussion to death, and there is always lasting damage, however slight. The blow must be quite heavy and, since men vary, a blow that will make one man merely dizzy will kill another. The trouble is that until you've administered the blow you don't know what you've done.

I wasn't in any mood for messing about so I hit this character hard. His knees buckled under him and he collapsed, and I caught him before he hit the ground. I eased him down and turned him so that he lay on his back. A mangled cigar sagged sideways from his mouth, half bitten through, and blood trickled from the cigar butt to show he had bitten his tongue. He was still breathing.

I patted his pockets and came upon the familiar hard shape, and drew forth an automatic pistol – a Smith & Wesson .38, the twin to the one I had taken from Lindholm. I checked the magazine to see if it was full and then worked the action to put a bullet into the breech.

The collapsed figure at my feet wasn't going to be much use to anybody even if he did wake up, so I didn't have to worry about him. All I had to do now was to take care of Daniel Boone – the man with the rifle. I returned to my peephole to see what he was doing.

He was doing precisely what he had been doing ever since I had seen him – contemplating the Land-Rover with inexhaustible patience. I stood up and walked into the hollow, gun first. I didn't worry overmuch about keeping quiet; speed was more important than quietness and I reckoned he might be more alarmed if I pussyfooted around than if I crunched up behind him.

He didn't even turn his head. All he did was to say in a flat Western drawl, 'You forgotten something, Joe?'

I caught my jaw before it sagged too far. A Russian I expected; an American I didn't. But this was no time to worry about nationalities – a man who throws bullets at you is automatically a bastard, and whether he's a Russian bastard or an American bastard makes little difference. I just said curtly, 'Turn around, but leave the rifle where it is or you'll have a hole in you.'

He went very still, but the only part of him that he turned was his head. He had china-blue eyes in a tanned, narrow face and he looked ideal for type-casting as Pop's eldest son in a TV horse opera. He also looked dangerous. 'I'll be goddamned!' he said softly.

'You certainly will be if you don't take your hands off that rifle,' I said. 'Spread your arms out as though you were being crucified.'

He looked at the pistol in my hand and reluctantly extended his arms. A man prone in that position finds it difficult to get up quickly. 'Where's Joe?' he asked.

'He's gone beddy-byes.' I walked over to him and put the muzzle of the pistol to the nape of his neck and I felt him shudder. That didn't mean much; it didn't mean he was afraid – I shudder involuntarily when Elin kisses me on the nape of the neck. 'Just keep quiet,' I advised, and picked up the rifle.

I didn't have time to examine it closely then, but I did afterwards, and it was certainly some weapon. It had a mixed ancestry and probably had started life as a Browning, but a good gunsmith had put in a lot of time in reworking it, giving it such refinements as a sculptured stock with a hole in it to put your thumb, and other fancy items. It was a bit like the man said, 'I have my grandfather's axe – my father replaced the blade and I gave it a new haft.'

What it had ended up as was the complete long-range assassin's kit. It was bolt action because it was a gun for a man who picks his target and who can shoot well enough not to want to send a second bullet after the first in too much of a hurry. It was chambered for a .375 magnum load, a heavy 300 grain bullet with a big charge behind it – high velocity, low trajectory. This rifle in good hands could reach out half a mile and snuff out a man's life if the light was good and the air still.

To help the aforesaid good hands was a fantastic telescopic sight – a variable-powered monster with a top magnification of 30. To use it when fully racked out would need a man with no nerves – and thus no tremble – or a solid bench rest. The scope was equipped with its own range-finding system, a multiple mounting of graduated dots on the vertical cross hair for various ranges, and was sighted in at five hundred yards.

It was a hell of a lot of gun.

I straightened and rested the muzzle of the rifle lightly against my friend's spine. 'That's your gun you can feel,' I said. 'You don't need me to tell you what would happen if I pulled the trigger.'

His head was turned sideways and I saw a light film of sweat coating the tan. He didn't need to let his imagination work because he was a good craftsman and knew his tools enough to *know* what would happen – over 5,000 foot-pounds of energy would blast him clean in two.

I said, 'Where's Kennikin?'

'Who?'

'Don't be childish,' I said. 'I'll ask you again – where's Kennikin?'

'I don't know any Kennikin,' he said in a muffled voice. He found difficulty in speaking because the side of his face was pressed against the ground.

'Think again.'

'I tell you I don't know him. All I was doing was following orders.'

'Yes,' I said. 'You took a shot at me.'

'No,' he said quickly. 'At your tyre. You're still alive, aren't you? I could have knocked you off any time.'

I looked down the slope at the Land-Rover. That was true; it would be like a Bisley champion shooting tin ducks at a fairground. 'So you were instructed to stop me. Then what?'

'Then nothing.'

I increased the pressure on his spine slightly. 'You can do better than that.'

'I was to wait until someone showed up and then quit and go home.'

'And who was the someone?'

'I don't know – I wasn't told.'

That sounded crazy; it was even improbable enough to be true. I said, 'What's your name?'

'John Smith.'

I smiled and said, 'All right, Johnny; start crawling – backwards and slowly. And if I see more than half an inch of daylight between your belly and the ground I'll let you have it.'

He wriggled back slowly and painfully away from the edge and down into the hollow, and then I stopped him. Much as I would have liked to carry on the interrogation I had to put an end to it because time was wasting. I said, 'Now, Johnny; I don't want you to make any sudden moves because I'm a very nervous man, so just keep quite still.'

I came up on his blind side, lifted the butt of the rifle and brought it down on the back of his head. It was no way to treat such a good gun but it was the only thing I had handy. The gun butt was considerably harder than the cosh and I regretfully decided I had fractured his skull. Anyway, he wouldn't be causing me any more trouble.

I walked over to pick up the jacket he had been using as a gun rest. It was heavy and I expected to find a pistol in the pocket, but the weight was caused by an unbroken box of rounds for the rifle. Next to the jacket was an open box. Both were unlabelled.

I checked the rifle. The magazine was designed to hold five rounds and contained four, there was one in the breech ready to pop off, and there were nineteen rounds in the opened box. Mr Smith was a professional; he had filled the magazine, jacked one into the breech, and then taken out the magazine and stuffed another round into it so he would have six rounds in hand instead of five. Not that he needed them – he had bust the tyre on a moving vehicle at over four hundred yards with just one shot.

He was a professional all right, but his name wasn't Smith because he carried an American passport in the name of Wendell George Fleet. He also carried a pass that would get him into the more remote corners of Keflavik Naval Base, the parts which the public are discouraged from visiting. He didn't carry a pistol; a rifleman as good as he usually despises handguns.

I put the boxes of ammunition into my pocket where they weighed heavy, and I stuck Joe's automatic pistol into the waistband of my trousers, unloading it first so I didn't do a Kennikin on myself. Safety catches are not all that reliable and a lot of men have ruined themselves for their wives by acting like a character in a TV drama.

I went to see how Joe was doing and found that he was still asleep and that his name wasn't even Joe according to his passport. It turned out he was Patrick Aloysius McCarthy. I regarded him speculatively; he looked more Italian than Irish to me. Probably all the names were phoney, just as Buchner who wasn't Graham turned out to be Philips.

McCarthy carried two spare magazines for the Smith & Wesson, both of them full, which I confiscated. I seemed to be building up quite an armoury on this expedition – from a little knife to a high-powered rifle in one week wasn't doing too bad. Next up the scale ought to be a burp gun or possibly a fully-fledged machine-gun. I wondered how long it would take me to graduate to something really lethal, such as an Atlas ICBM.

McCarthy had been going somewhere when I thumped him. He had been trying to contact someone by radio, but the walkie-talkie had been on the blink so he'd decided to walk, and that put whoever it was not very far away. I stared up towards the top of the ridge and decided to take a look over the next rise. It was a climb of perhaps two hundred yards and when I poked my head carefully over the top I caught my breath in surprise.

The yellow US Navy helicopter was parked about four hundred yards away and two crewmen and a civilian sat in front of it, talking casually. I lifted Fleet's rifle and looked at them through the big scope at maximum magnification. The crewmen were unimportant but I thought I might know the civilian. I didn't, but I memorized his face for future reference.

For a moment I was tempted to tickle them up with the rifle but I shelved the idea. It would be better to depart quietly and without fuss. I didn't want that chopper with me the rest of the way, so I withdrew and went back down the hill. I had been away quite a while and Elin would be becoming even more worried, if that were possible.

From where I was I had a good view along the track so I looked to see if Kennikin was yet in sight. He was! Through the scope I saw a minute black dot in the far distance crawling along the track, and I estimated that the jeep was about three miles away. There was a lot of mud along there and I didn't think he'd be making much more than ten miles an hour, so that put him about fifteen minutes behind.

I went down the hillside fast.

Elin was squashed into the crack in the rock but she came out when I called. She ran over and grabbed me as though she wanted to check whether I was all in one piece and she was laughing and crying at the same time. I disentangled myself from her arms. 'Kennikin's not far behind; let's move.'

I set out towards the Land-Rover at a dead run, holding Elin's arm, but she dragged free. 'The coffee pot!'

'The hell with it!' Women are funny creatures; this was not a time to be thinking of domestic economy. I grabbed her arm again and dragged her along.

Thirty seconds later I had the engine going and we were bouncing along the track too fast for either safety or comfort while I decided which potholes it would be safe to put the front wheels into. Decisions, decisions, nothing but bloody decisions – and if I decided wrongly we'd have a broken half-axle or be stuck in the mud and the jig would be up.

We bounced like hell all the way to the Tungnaá River and the traffic got thicker – one car passed us going the other way, the first we had seen since being in the *Óbyggdir.* That was bad because Kennikin was likely to stop it and ask the driver if he had seen a long wheelbase Land-Rover lately. It was one thing to chase me through the wilderness without knowing where I was, and quite another to know that I was actually within spitting distance. The psychological spur would stimulate his adrenal gland just that much more.

On the other hand, seeing the car cheered me because it meant that the car transporter over the Tungnaá would be on our side of the river and there would be no waiting. I have travelled a lot in places where water crossings are done by ferry – there are quite a few in Scotland – and it's a law of nature that the ferry is always on the other side when you arrive at the water's edge. But that wouldn't be so this time.

Not that this was a ferry. You cross the Tungnaá by means of a contraption – a platform slung on an overhead cable. You drive your car on to the platform and winch yourself across, averting your eyes from the white water streaming below. According to the *Ferdahandbokin,* which every traveller in the *Óbyggdir* ought to consult, extreme care is necessary for people not acquainted with the system. Personally, I don't recommend it for those with queasy stomachs who have to cross in a high wind.

We arrived at the Tungnaá and the contraption was, indeed, on our side. I checked that it was secured and safe, and then drove on carefully. 'Stay in the cab,' I said to Elin. 'You can't winch with that broken wing.'

I got out and began to operate the winch, keeping an eye open for Kennikin's imminent arrival. I felt very exposed and naked and I hoped I had kept my fifteen-minute lead because crossing the Tungnaá is a slow job. But we made it without incident and I drove off the platform with a great sense of relief.

'Now we can stop the bastard,' I said as we drove away.

Elin sat up straight. 'You're not going to break the cable!' There was a note of indignation in her voice. Being shot at was all right but the wanton destruction of public property was unethical.

I grinned at her. 'I'd do it if I could, but it would take a stronger man than me.' I pulled the car off the road and looked back; the river was out of sight. 'No, I'm going to chain up the platform so Kennikin can't pull it across. He'll be stuck on the other side until someone going the other way can release it, and God knows when that will be – there's not much traffic. Stay here.'

I got out, rummaged in the tool kit, and found the snow chains. It wasn't at all likely we'd need them in the summer and they could do a better job keeping Kennikin off my neck than lying where they were. I lifted them out and ran back down the track.

You can't really tie a chain into a knot but I tethered that platform with such a tangle of iron that would take anyone at least half an hour to free unless he happened to have an oxy-acetylene cutting torch handy. I had nearly completed the job when Kennikin arrived on the other side and the fun started.

The jeep came to a halt and four men got out, Kennikin in the lead. I was hidden behind the platform and no one saw me at first. Kennikin studied the cable and then read the instructions that are posted in Icelandic and English. He got the hang of it and ordered his men to haul the platform back across the river.

They duly hauled and nothing happened.

I was working like hell to finish the job and just got it done in time. The platform lurched away and then stopped, tethered by the chain. There was a shout from the other side and someone went running along the bank so as to get into a position to see what was stopping the platform. He saw it all right – he saw me. The next moment he had whipped out a gun and started to shoot.

The pistol is a much over-rated weapon. It has its place, which is about ten yards from its target or, better still, ten feet. The popgun that was shooting at me was a short-barrelled .38 revolver – a belly gun – with which I wouldn't trust to hit anything I couldn't reach out and touch. I was pretty safe as long as he aimed at me; if he started to shoot anywhere else I might get hit by accident, but that was a slim chance.

The others opened up as I snagged the last bit of chain into place. A bullet raised the dust two yards away and that was as close as they came. Yet it's no fun being shot at so I turned and belted away up the track at a dead run.

Elin was standing by the Land-Rover, her face full of concern, having heard the barrage of shots. 'It's all right,' I said. 'The war hasn't broken out.' I reached inside and took out Fleet's rifle. 'Let's see if we can discourage them.'

She looked at the rifle with abhorrence. 'Oh, God! Must you kill them? Haven't you done enough?'

I stared at her and then the penny dropped. She thought I'd got hold of that rifle by killing Fleet; she seemed to think that you couldn't take that much gun away from a man without killing him. I said, 'Elin; those men across the river were trying to kill me. The fact they didn't succeed doesn't alter their intention. Now, I'm not going to kill anyone – I said I'll discourage them.' I held up the rifle. 'And I didn't kill the man I took this from, either.'

I walked away down the track but veered away from it before I reached the river. I hunted around until I found suitable cover and then lay and watched Kennikin and his crew unsuccessfully trying to get at the platform. A 30-power scope was a bit too much optical glass for a range of a hundred yards but it had variable power so I dropped it to a magnification of six which was as low as it would go. A rock in front of me formed a convenient rest and I settled the butt against my shoulder and looked into the eyepiece.

I wasn't going to kill anyone. Not that I didn't want to, but bodies you can't get rid of are inconvenient and lead to the asking of awkward questions by the appropriate authorities. A wounded Russian, on the other hand, would be eliminated just as much as a dead one. He would be smuggled by his friends on to the trawler which was undoubtedly to hand, probably already in Reykjavik harbour. The Russians have more non-fishing trawlers than any other nation on earth.

No, I wasn't going to kill anyone, but someone would soon wish to God he were dead.

Kennikin had disappeared and the three other men were engaged in a heated discussion about how to solve their little problem. I broke it up by firing five spaced shots in thirty seconds. The first hit the man standing next to the jeep in the kneecap, and suddenly there wasn't anyone else around to shoot at. He lay on the ground, writhing and shouting, and he'd have one leg shorter than the other for the rest of his life – if he was got into a hospital quickly. If not, he'd be lucky to have a leg at all.

I re-sighted and squeezed the trigger again, this time shooting at the off-side front tyre of the jeep. The rifle was one of the best I've ever handled and, at a hundred yards, the trajectory was so flat that I could put a bullet exactly where I wanted it. The tyre wasn't just punctured; under the close-range hammer blow of that big .375 bullet it exploded into bits, as did the other front tyre when I let fly again.

Someone popped off with a pistol. I ignored that and fed another round into the breech. I centred the cross hairs on to the front of the radiator and fired again, and the jeep rocked on its springs under the impact. This rifle was chambered to shoot big game and anything that can crack open the frontal skull bone of a buffalo wouldn't do an engine block much good. I put the last bullet in the same place in the hope of putting the jeep permanently out of action and then withdrew, keeping my head down.

I walked up to the Land-Rover, and said to Elin, 'It's a good rifle.'

She looked at me nervously. 'I thought I heard someone scream.'

'I didn't kill anyone,' I said. 'But they won't be driving that jeep very far. Let's go on. You can drive for a bit.' I was suddenly very tired.

SIX

We drove out of the *Óbyggdir* and hit the main road system. Even if Kennikin was able to follow us we would have a good chance of losing him because this was one of the main areas of population and there was a network of roads harder to police than the simple choices of the *Óbyggdir.* Elin drove while I relaxed in the passenger seat, and once we were on the good roads were able to pick up speed.

'Where to?' she asked.

'I'd like to get this vehicle out of sight,' I said. 'It's too damned conspicuous. Any suggestions?'

'You have to be at Geysir tomorrow night,' she said. 'I have friends at Laugarvatn – you must remember Gunnar.'

'Weren't you running around with him before you met me?'

She smiled. 'It wasn't serious – and we're still friends. Besides, he's married now.'

Marriage, to a lot of men, doesn't mean an automatic cancellation of their hunting licence, but I let it lie; a more-or-less civilized butting match with Elin's old boyfriend was preferable to a more deadly encounter with Kennikin. 'All right,' I said. 'Head for Laugarvatn.'

We were silent for a while, then I said, 'Thank you for what you did back there when I was on Búdarháls. It was a damned silly thing to do, but it helped.'

'I thought it might distract their attention,' she said.

'It sure as hell distracted mine for a minute. Did you know you were in the sights of a rifle all the way – and there was a finger on the trigger?'

'I did feel uneasy,' she admitted, and shivered involuntarily. 'What happened up there?'

'I gave headaches to a couple of men. One of them will probably wind up in hospital at Keflavik.'

She looked at me sharply. 'Keflavik!'

'Yes,' I said. 'They were Americans.' I told her about Fleet, McCarthy and the waiting helicopter. 'I've been trying to make sense out of it ever since – without much success.'

She thought about it too, and said. 'But it *doesn't* make sense. Why would the Americans co-operate with the Russians? Are you sure they were Americans?'

'They were as American as Mom's apple-pie – at least Fleet was. I didn't get to talk to McCarthy.'

'They could be sympathizers,' said Elin. 'Fellow-travellers.'

'Then they're travelling closer than a flea to a dog.' I took out Fleet's pass to the remoter recesses of Keflavik Air Base. 'If they're fellow-travellers then the Yanks had better watch it – their furniture is riddled with woodworm.' I examined the pass and thought about the helicopter. 'It's just about the most ridiculous thing I've heard of.'

'Then what other explanation is there?'

The idea of a nest of communist sympathizers being convenient to hand at Keflavik and able to lay their hands on a navy helicopter at a moment's notice was untenable. I said, 'I doubt if Kennikin rang up Keflavik and said, "Look, boys; I'm chasing a British spy and I need your help. Can you lay on a chopper and a sharpshooter and stop him for me?" But there's someone else who could do it.'

'Who?'

'There's a man called Helms in Washington who could pick up a telephone and say, "Admiral, there'll be a couple of guys dropping in at Keflavik pretty soon. Let them have a helicopter and a crew – and don't ask too many questions about what they want it for." And the Admiral would say, "Yes, sir; yes, sir; three bags full, sir," because Helms is the boss of the CIA.'

'But why?'

'I'm damned if I know,' I said. 'But it's a bloody sight more likely than Keflavik being white-anted by Russian agents.' I thought of my brief and unsatisfactory conversation with Fleet. 'Fleet said that his orders were to pin us down until someone – presumably Kennikin – arrived. He said he'd never heard of Kennikin. He also said that when Kennikin arrived his job was over and he could go home. There's one more question I should have asked him.'

'What's that?'

'Whether his instructions called for him to show himself to Kennikin or whether they specifically forbade it. I'd give a lot to know the answer to that one.'

'You're sure we were chased by Russians? I mean, you're sure it *was* Kennikin?'

'That's a face I'll never forget,' I said. 'And there was a lot of swearing in Russian back at the Tungnaá River.'

I could almost see the wheels whizzing round as Elin thought about it. 'Try this,' she said. 'Supposing Slade is also chasing us, and suppose he asked the Americans to co-operate – but what he didn't know was that Kennikin was closer to us. The Americans were supposed to hold us up until Slade arrived – not Kennikin.'

'It's barely possible,' I conceded. 'But it shows lousy liaison. And why go to all the trouble of a sniper hidden on a hill? Why not have the Americans just make a simple pinch?' I shook my head. 'Besides, the Department isn't all that chummy with the CIA – the special relationship has its limits.'

'My explanation is the more reasonable,' said Elin.

'I'm not sure there *is* any reason involved – it's turning into a thoroughly unreasonable situation. It reminds me of what a physicist once said about his job: "The universe is not only queerer than we imagine but, perhaps, queerer than we can imagine." I can see his point now.'

Elin laughed, and I said, 'What the hell's so funny? Slade has already taken a crack at us, and may do again if Taggart hasn't pulled him off. Kennikin is sweating blood trying to get at me – and now the Americans have put in their oar. Any minute from now I'm expecting the West Germans to pitch up, or maybe the Chilean Secret Service. I wouldn't be surprised at anything. But there's one thing that really worries me.'

'What?'

I said, 'Suppose I give this gadget to Case tomorrow night. Kennikin won't know that, will he? I can't see Jack Case writing him a letter – "Dear Vaslav, Stewart doesn't have the football any more; I've got it – come and chase *me*." I'll be just as much up the creek as before. Farther, in fact, because if Kennikin catches me and I *haven't* got the damned thing then he'll be even madder than he is now, if that's possible.'

I wasn't so sure I was going to give the gadget to Case, after all. If I was going to be up the creek, I'd better retain the paddle.

II

Laugarvatn is a district educational centre which takes in children from a wide rural area. The country is so big relative to the population, and the population so scattered, that the educational system is rather peculiar. Most of the rural schools are boarding schools and in some of them the pupils spend a fortnight at school and a fortnight at home, turn and turn about, during the winter teaching terms. The children from farther away spend all winter at school. In the summer the schools are turned into hotels for four months.

Because Laugarvatn is conveniently close to Thingvellir, Geysir, Gullfoss and other tourist attractions its two large schools come in very useful as summer hotels, and Laugarvatn had become a pony-trekking centre very popular with visitors. Personally, I've never cared much for horses, not even the multi-coloured Icelandic variety which is better-looking than most. I think the horse is a stupid animal – any animal which allows another to ride it must be stupid – and I prefer to be bounced by a Land-Rover rather than by a stubborn pony who would rather go home.

Gunnar Arnarsson was a schoolteacher in the winter and in summer ran a pony-trekking operation. Very versatile people, these Icelanders. He was away when we arrived, but his wife, Sigurlin Asgeirsdottir, made us welcome with much clucking at the sight of Elin's arm in an improvised sling.

One of the problems in Iceland is sorting out the single from the married people, because the woman does not change her name when she gets married. In fact, the whole problem of names is a trap into which foreigners usually fall with a loud thump. The surname just tells everyone who your father was; Sigurlin was the daughter of Asgeir, just as Gunnar was the son of Arnar. If Gunnar had a son and decided to name the boy after his grandfather he'd be called Arnar Gunnarsson. All very difficult and the reason why the Icelandic telephone directory is listed alphabetically under given names. Elin Ragnarsdottir was listed under 'E'.

Gunnar appeared to have done well for himself because Sigurlin was one of those tall, leggy, svelte, Scandinavian types who go over big when they get to Hollywood, and what the hell has acting got to do with it, anyway? The widespread belief that the Nordic nations are populated exclusively on the distaff side by these tow-headed goddesses is, however, a regrettable illusion.

From the way she welcomed us Sigurlin knew about me, but not all, I hoped. At any rate she knew a lot – enough to hear the distant chime of wedding bells. It's funny, but as soon as a girl gets married she wants to get all her old girl-friends caught in the same trap. Because of Kennikin there weren't going to be any immediate wedding bells – the tolling of a single funeral note was more likely – but, disregarding Kennikin, I wasn't going to be pressured by any busty blonde with a match-making glint in her eye.

I put the Land-Rover into Gunnar's empty garage with some relief. Now it was safely off the road and under cover I felt much better. I saw that the collection of small arms was decently concealed and then went into the house to find Sigurlin just coming downstairs. She gave me a peculiar look and said abruptly, 'What did Elin do to her shoulder?'

I said cautiously, 'Didn't she tell you?'

'She said she was climbing and fell against a sharp rock.'

I made an indeterminate noise expressive of agreement, but I could see that Sigurlin was suspicious. A gunshot wound tends to look like nothing else but, even to someone who has never seen one before. I said hastily, 'It's very good of you to offer us a bed for the night.'

'It's nothing,' she said. 'Would you like some coffee?'

'Thank you, I would.' I followed her into the kitchen. 'Have you known Elin long?'

'Since we were children.' Sigurlin dumped a handful of beans into a coffee grinder. 'And you?'

'Three years.'

She filled an electric kettle and plugged it in, then swung around to face me. 'Elin looks very tired.'

'We pushed it a bit in the *Óbyggdir.*'

That can't have sounded convincing because Sigurlin said, 'I wouldn't want her to come to any harm. That wound . . .'

'Well?'

'She didn't fall against a rock, did she?'

There was a brain behind those beautiful eyes. 'No,' I said. 'She didn't.'

'I thought not,' she said. 'I've seen wounds like that. Before I married I was a nurse at Keflavik. An American sailor was brought into hospital once – he'd been cleaning his gun and shot himself accidentally. Whose gun was Elin cleaning?'

I sat down at the kitchen table. 'There's a certain amount of trouble,' I said carefully. 'And it's best you're not involved, so I'm not going to tell you anything about it – for your own good. I tried to keep Elin out of it from the beginning, but she's headstrong.'

Sigurlin nodded. 'Her family always was stubborn.'

I said, 'I'm going to Geysir tomorrow evening and I'd like Elin to stay here. I'll want your co-operation on that.'

Sigurlin regarded me seriously. 'I don't like trouble with guns.'

'Neither do I. I'm not exactly shouting for joy. That's why I want Elin out of it. Can she stay here for a while?'

'A gunshot wound should be reported to the police.'

'I know,' I said wearily. 'But I don't think your police are equipped to cope with this particular situation. It has international ramifications and there is more than one gun involved. Innocent people could get killed if it's not carefully handled, and with no disrespect to your police, I think they'd be likely to blunder.'

'This trouble, as you call it – is it criminal?'

'Not in the normal sense. You might call it an extreme form of political action.'

Sigurlin turned down the corners of her mouth. 'The only good thing I've heard about this is that you want to keep Elin out of it,' she said waspishly. 'Tell me, Alan Stewart; are you in love with her?'

'Yes.'

'Are you going to marry her?'

'If she'll have me after all this.'

She offered me a superior smile. 'Oh, she'll have you. You're hooked like a salmon and you won't get away now.'

'I'm not so sure of that,' I said. 'There are certain things that have come up lately that don't add to my charms in Elin's eyes.'

'Such as guns?' Sigurlin poured coffee. 'You don't need to answer that. I won't probe.' She put the cup before me. 'All right; I'll keep Elin here.'

'I don't know how you're going to do it,' I said. 'I've never been able to make her do anything she didn't want to do.'

'I'll put her to bed,' said Sigurlin. 'Strict medical supervision. She'll argue, but she'll do it. You do what you have to do and Elin will stay here. But I won't be able to keep her long. What happens if you don't come back from Geysir?'

'I don't know,' I said. 'But don't let her go back to Reykjavik. To go to the apartment would be extremely unwise.'

Sigurlin took a deep breath. 'I'll see what I can do.' She poured herself a cup of coffee and sat down. 'If it weren't for the concern you show for Elin I'd be inclined to . . .' She shook her head irritably. 'I don't like any of this, Alan. For God's sake get it cleared up as quickly as you can.'

'I'll do my best.'

III

The next day seemed very long.

At breakfast Sigurlin read the paper and suddenly said, 'Well, well! Someone tied up the cable transport on the

Tungnaá just the other side of Hald. A party of tourists was stranded on the farther side for several hours. I wonder who could have done that?'

'It was all right when we came across,' I said blandly. 'What does it say about the tourists? Anyone hurt?'

She looked at me speculatively across the breakfast table. 'Why should anyone be hurt? No, it says nothing about that.'

I changed the subject quickly. 'I'm surprised that Elin is still asleep.'

Sigurlin smiled. 'I'm not. She didn't know it, but she had a sleeping draught last night. She'll be drowsy when she wakes and she won't want to jump out of bed.'

That was one way of making sure of Elin. I said, 'I noticed your garage was empty – don't you have a car?'

'Yes. Gunnar left it at the stables.'

'When will he be back?'

'In two days – providing the party doesn't get saddle-sore.'

'When I go to Geysir I'd just as soon not use the Land-Rover,' I said.

'You want the car? All right – but I want it back in one piece.' She told me where to find it. 'You'll find the key in the glove locker.'

After breakfast I regarded the telephone seriously and wondered whether to ring Taggart. I had a lot to tell him but I thought it would be better to let it go until I heard what Jack Case had to say. Instead I went out to the Land-Rover and cleaned Fleet's rifle.

It really was a good tool. With its fancy hand-grip and free-style stock it had obviously been tailor-made to suit Fleet, whom I suspected of being an enthusiast. In every field of human endeavour there are those who push perfection to its ultimate and absurd end. In hi-fi, for example, there is the maniac who has seventeen loud-speakers and one test record. In shooting there is the gun nut.

The gun nut believes that there is no standard, off-the-shelf weapon that could be possibly good enough for him and so he adapts and chisels until he finally achieves something that looks like one of the more far-out works of modern sculpture. He also believes that the ammunition manufacturers know damn-all about their job and so he loads his own cases, carefully weighing each bullet and matching it with an amount of powder calculated to one-tenth of a grain. Sometimes he shoots very well.

I checked the ammunition from the opened box and, sure enough, found the telltale scratches from a crimping tool. Fleet was in the habit of rolling his own, something I have never found necessary, but then my own shooting has not been of the type necessary to get a perfect grouping at x-hundred yards. It also explained why the box was unlabelled.

I wondered why Fleet should have carried as many as fifty rounds; after all, he was a good shot and had brought us to a standstill with one squeeze of the trigger. He had loaded the rifle with ordinary hunting ammunition, soft-nosed and designed to spread on impact. The closed box contained twenty-five rounds of jacketed ammunition – the military load.

It's always seemed odd to me that the bullet one shoots at an animal is designed to kill as quickly and as mercilessly as possible, whereas the same bullet shot at a man is illegal under the Geneva Convention. Shoot a hunting load at a man and you're accused of using dum-dum bullets and that's against the rules. You can roast him to death with napalm, disembowel him with a jump mine, but you can't shoot him with the same bullet you would use to kill a deer cleanly.

I looked at the cartridge in the palm of my hand and wished I had known about it earlier. One of those going into the engine of Kennikin's jeep was likely to do a hell of a lot more damage than the soft-nosed bullet I had used. While a .375 jacketed bullet with a magnum charge behind it probably wouldn't drill through a jeep from end to end at a range of a hundred yards, I wouldn't like to bet on it by standing behind the jeep.

I filled the magazine of the rifle with a mixed load, three soft-nosed and two jacketed, laid alternately. Then I examined McCarthy's Smith & Wesson automatic pistol, a more prosaic piece of iron than Fleet's jazzed-up rifle. After checking that it was in order I put it into my pocket, together with the spare clips. The electronic gadget I left where it was under the front seat. I wasn't taking it with me when I went to see Jack Case, but I wasn't going empty-handed either.

When I got back to the house Elin was awake. She looked at me drowsily, and said, 'I don't know why I'm so tired.'

'Well,' I said judiciously. 'You've been shot and you've been racketing around the *Óbyggdir* for two days with not much sleep. I'm not surprised you're tired. I haven't been too wide awake myself.'

Elin opened her eyes wide in alarm and glanced at Sigurlin who was arranging flowers in a vase. I said, 'Sigurlin knows you didn't fall on any rock. She knows you were shot, but not how or why – and I don't want you to tell her. I don't want you to discuss it with Sigurlin or anyone else.' I turned to Sigurlin. 'You'll get the full story at the right time, but at the moment the knowledge would be dangerous.'

Sigurlin nodded in acceptance. Elin said, 'I think I'll sleep all day. I'm tired now, but I'll be ready by the time we have to leave for Geysir.'

Sigurlin crossed the room and began to plump up the pillows behind Elin's head. The heartless professionalism spoke of the trained nurse. 'You're not leaving for anywhere,' she said sharply. 'Not for the next two days at least.'

'But I must,' protested Elin.

'But you must not. Your shoulder is bad enough.' Her lips compressed tightly as she looked down at Elin. 'You should really see a doctor.'

'Oh, no!' said Elin.

'Well, then, you'll do as I say.'

Elin looked at me appealingly. I said, 'I'm only going to see a man. As a matter of fact, Jack Case wouldn't say a word in your presence, anyway – you're not a member of the club. I'm just going to Geysir, have a chat with the man, and then come back here – and you might as well keep your turned-up nose out of it for once.'

Elin looked flinty, and Sigurlin said, 'I'll leave you to whisper sweet nothings into each other's ear.' She smiled. 'You two are going to lead interesting lives.'

She left the room, and I said gloomily, 'That sounds like the Chinese curse – "May you live in interesting times."'

'All right,' said Elin in a tired voice. 'I won't give you any trouble. You can go to Geysir alone.'

I sat on the edge of the bed. 'It's not a matter of you giving trouble; I just want you out of this. You disturb my concentration, and if I run into difficulties I don't want to have to watch out for you as well as myself.'

'Have I been a drag?'

I shook my head. 'No, Elin; you haven't. But the nature of the game may change. I've been chased across Iceland and I'm pretty damn tired of it. If the opportunity offers I'll turn around and do a bit of chasing myself.'

'And I'd get in the way,' she said flatly.

'You're a civilized person,' I said. 'Very law-abiding and full of scruples. I doubt if you've had as much as a parking ticket in your life. I might manage to retain a few scruples while I'm being hunted; not many, but some. But when I'm the hunter I can't afford them. I think you might be horrified at what I'd do.'

'You'd kill,' she said. It was a statement.

'I might do worse,' I said grimly, and she shivered. 'It's not that I want to – I'm no casual murderer; I didn't want to have any part of this but I've been conscripted against my will.'

'You dress it in fine words,' she said. 'You don't have to kill.'

'No fine words,' I said. 'Just one – survival. A drafted American college boy may be a pacifist, but when the Viet Cong shoot at him with those Russian 7.62 millimetre rifles he'll shoot right back, you may depend on it. And when Kennikin comes after me he'll deserve all he runs into. I didn't ask him to shoot at me on the Tungnaá River – he didn't need my permission – but he can't have been very surprised when I shot back. Hell, he would expect it!'

'I can see the logic,' said Elin. 'But don't expect me to like it.'

'Christ!' I said. 'Do you think I like it?'

'I'm sorry, Alan,' she said, and smiled wanly.

'So am I.' I stood up. 'After that bit of deep philosophy you'd better have breakfast. I'll see what Sigurlin can offer.'

IV

I left Laugarvatn at eight that night. Punctuality may be a virtue but it has been my experience that the virtuous often die young while the ungodly live to a ripe age. I had arranged to meet Jack Case at five o'clock but it would do him no great harm to stew for a few hours, and I had it in mind that the arrangement to meet him had been made on an open radio circuit.

I arrived at Geysir in Gunnar's Volkswagen beetle and parked inconspicuously quite a long way from the summer hotel. A few people, not many, were picking their way among the pools of boiling water, cameras at the ready.

Geysir itself – the Gusher – which has given its name to all the other spouters in the world, was quiescent. It has been a long time since Geysir spouted. The habit of prodding it into action by tossing rocks into the pool finally proved too much as the pressure chamber was blocked. However, Strokkur – the Churn – was blasting off with commendable efficiency and sending up its feathery plume of boiling water at seven-minute intervals.

I stayed in the car for a long time and used the field-glasses assiduously. There were no familiar faces to be seen in the next hour, a fact that didn't impress me much, however. Finally I got out of the car and walked towards the Hotel Geysir, one hand in my pocket resting on the butt of the pistol.

Case was in the lounge, sitting in a corner and reading a paperback. I walked up to him and said, 'Hello, Jack; that's a nice tan – you must have been in the sun.'

He looked up. 'I was in Spain. What kept you?'

'This and that.'

I prepared to sit down, but he said, 'This is too public – let's go up to my room. Besides, I have a bottle.'

'That's nice.'

I followed him to his room. He locked the door and turned to survey me. 'That gun in your pocket spoils the set of your coat. Why don't you use a shoulder holster?'

I grinned at him. 'The man I took the gun from didn't have one. How are you, Jack? It's good to see you.'

He grunted sourly. 'You might change your mind about that.' With a flip of his hand he opened a suitcase lying on a chair and took out a bottle. He poured a heavy slug into a tooth glass and handed it to me. 'What the devil have you been doing? You've got Taggart really worked up.'

'He sounded pretty steamy when I spoke to him,' I said, and sipped the whisky. 'Most of the time I've been chased from hell-and-gone to here.'

'You weren't followed here?' he asked quickly.

'No.'

'Taggart tells me you killed Philips. Is that true?'

'If Philips was a man who called himself Buchner and Graham it's true.'

He stared at me. 'You admit it!'

I relaxed in the chair. 'Why not, since I did it? I didn't know it was Philips, though. He came at me in the dark with a gun.'

'That's not how Slade described it. He says you took a crack at him too.'

'I did – but that was after I'd disposed of Philips. He and Slade came together.'

'Slade says differently. He says that he was in a car with Philips when you ambushed it.'

I laughed. 'With what?' I drew the *sgian dubh* from my stocking and flipped it across the room, where it stuck in the top of the dressing-table, quivering. 'With that?'

'He says you had a rifle.'

'Where would I get a rifle?' I demanded. 'He's right, though; I took the rifle from Philips after I disposed of him with that little pig-sticker. I put three shots into Slade's car and missed the bastard.'

'Christ!' said Case. 'No wonder Taggart is doing his nut. Have you gone off your little rocker?'

I sighed. 'Jack, did Taggart say anything about a girl?'

'He said you'd referred to a girl. He didn't know whether to believe you.'

'He'd better believe me,' I said. 'That girl isn't far from here, and she has a bullet wound in her shoulder that was given to her by Philips. He was within an ace of killing her. Now, there's no two ways about that, and I can take you to her and show you the wound. Slade says I ambushed him. Is it likely I'd do it with my fiancée watching? And why in hell would I want to ambush him?' I slid in a trick question. 'What did he say he'd done with Philips's body?'

Case frowned. 'I don't think the question came up.'

'It wouldn't,' I said. 'The last I saw of Slade he was driving away like a maniac – and there was no body in his car. I disposed of it later.'

'This is all very well,' said Case. 'But it happened after Akureyri, and in Akureyri you were supposed to deliver a package to Philips. You didn't, and you didn't give it to Slade either. Why not?'

'The operation stank,' I said, and went into it in detail.

I talked for twenty minutes and by the time I had finished Case was pop-eyed. He swallowed and his Adam's apple jumped convulsively. 'Do you really believe that Slade is a Russian agent? How do you expect Taggart to swallow that? I've never heard such a cock-and-bull story in my life.'

I said patiently, 'I followed Slade's instructions at Keflavik and nearly got knocked off by Lindholm; Slade sent Philips after me into Asbyrgi – how *did* he know the Russians were holding a fake? There's the Calvados; there's . . .'

Case held up his hands. 'There's no need to go through it all again. Lindholm might have been lucky in catching you – there's nothing to say all the roads around Keflavik weren't staked out. Slade says he didn't go after you in Asbyrgi. As for the Calvados . . .' He threw up his hands. 'There's only your word for that.'

'What the hell are you, Jack? Prosecutor, judge and jury, too? Or have I already been judged and you're the executioner?'

'Don't fly off the handle,' he said wearily. 'I'm just trying to find out how complicated a cock-up you've made, that's all. What did you do after you left Asbyrgi?'

'We went south in the wilderness,' I said. 'And then Kennikin pitched up.'

'The one who drinks Calvados? The one you had the hassle with in Sweden?'

'The same. My old pal, Vaslav. Don't you think that was bloody coincidental, Jack? How would Kennikin know which track to chase along? But Slade knew, of course; he knew which way we went after we left Asbyrgi.'

Case regarded me thoughtfully. 'You know you're very convincing sometimes. I'm getting so I might believe this silly story if I'm not careful. But Kennikin didn't catch you.'

'It was nip and tuck,' I said. 'And the bloody Yanks didn't help.'

Case sat up. 'How do they come into this?'

I pulled out Fleet's pass and skimmed it across the room into Case's lap. 'That chap shot a hole in my tyre at very long range. I got out of there with Kennikin ten minutes behind.' I told Case all about it.

His mouth was grim. 'Now you really have gone overboard. I suppose you'll now claim Slade is a member of the CIA,' he said sarcastically. 'Why should the Americans hold you up just so Kennikin could grab you?'

'I don't know,' I said feelingly. 'I wish I did.'

Case examined the card. 'Fleet – I know that name; it came up when I was in Turkey last year. He's a CIA hatchetman and he's dangerous.'

'Not for the next month,' I said. 'I cracked his skull.'

'So what happened next?'

I shrugged. 'I went hell-for-leather with Kennikin and his boys trying to climb up my exhaust pipe – there was a bit of an affray at a river, and then I lost him. I suppose he's around here somewhere.'

'And you've still got the package?'

'Not on me, Jack,' I said softly. 'Not on me – but quite close.'

'I don't want it,' he said, and crossed the room to take my empty glass. 'The plan's changed. You're to take the package to Reykjavik.'

'Just like that,' I said. 'What if I don't want to?'

'Don't be a fool. Taggart wants it that way, and you'd better not annoy him any more. Not only have you loused up his operation but you've killed Philips, and for that he can have your hide. I have a message from him – take the package to Reykjavik and all is forgiven.'

'It must be really important,' I said, and checked my fingers. 'Let's see – I've killed two men, damn near shot the leg off another, and maybe fractured a couple of skulls – and Taggart says he can sweep all that under the carpet?'

'The Russkies and the Americans can take care of their own – they bury their own dead, if any,' said Case brutally. 'But Taggart – and only Taggart – can clear you on our side. By killing Philips you set yourself up as a legitimate target. Do as he says or he'll set the dogs on you.'

I remembered I had used a phrase like that when speaking to Taggart. I said, 'Where is Slade now?'

Case turned away from me and I heard the clink of glass against bottle. 'I don't know. When I left London Taggart was trying to contact him.'

'So he could still be in Iceland,' I said slowly. 'I don't know that I like that.'

Case whirled around. 'What you like has ceased to matter. For God's sake, what's got into you, Alan? Look, it's only a hundred kilometres to Reykjavik; you can be there in two hours. Take the bloody package and go.'

'I have a better idea,' I said. 'You take it.'

He shook his head. 'That's not on. Taggart wants me back in Spain.'

I laughed. 'Jack, the easiest way to get to the International Airport at Keflavik is through Reykjavik. You could drop off the package on the way. What's so important about me and the package together?'

He shrugged. 'My instructions are that you take it. Don't ask me why because I don't know.'

'What's in the package?'

'I don't know that either; and the way this operation is shaping I don't want to know.'

I said, 'Jack, at one time I'd have called you a friend. But you've just tried to con me with this nonsense about being pulled back to Spain, and I don't believe a bloody word of it. But I do believe you when you say you don't know what's going on. I don't think anyone in this operation knows what's going on except, maybe, one man.'

Case nodded. 'Taggart has his hands on the strings,' he said. 'Neither you nor I need to know much in order to do the job.'

'I wasn't thinking of Taggart,' I said. 'I don't think he knows what's going on either. He might think he does, but he doesn't.' I looked up. 'I was thinking of Slade. This whole weird operation is warped to the pattern of his mind. I've worked with him before and I know how he thinks.'

'So we get back to Slade,' said Case grimly. 'You're obsessed, Alan.'

'Maybe,' I said. 'But you can make Taggart happy by telling him I'll take his damned package to Reykjavik. Where do I deliver it?'

'That's better.' Case looked down at my glass which had been held, forgotten, in his hand. He gave it to me. 'You know the Nordri Travel Agency?'

'I know it.' It was the firm for which Elin had once worked.

'I don't, but I'm told that as well as running the agency they have a big souvenir shop.'

'You were told correctly.'

'I have here a piece of wrapping paper from the souvenir shop; it's the standard stuff they gift-wrap with. You have the package neatly wrapped up. You walk in and go to the back of the shop where they sell the woollen goods. A man will be standing there carrying a copy of the *New York Times,* and under his arm will be an identical package. You make light conversation by saying, "It's colder here than in the States," to which he will reply . . .'

' "It's even colder than Birmingham." I've been through the routine before.'

'All right; once there's a mutual identification you put your package on the counter, and so will he. From then on it's a simple exchange job.'

'And when is this simple exchange job to take place?'

'At midday tomorrow.'

'Supposing I'm not there at midday tomorrow? For all I know there may be a hundred Russians spaced out along that road at one kilometre intervals.'

'There'll be a man in the shop every midday until you turn up,' said Case.

'Taggart has a touching faith in me,' I said. 'According to Slade the Department is afflicted with a manpower shortage, and here is Taggart being spendthrift. What happens if I don't turn up for a year?'

Case didn't smile. 'Taggart brought up that problem. If you're not there within a week then someone will come looking for you, and I'd regret that because, in spite of that snide crack you made about friendship, I still love you, you silly bastard.'

'Smile when you say that, stranger.'

He grinned and sat down again. 'Now let's go through all this again, right from the beginning – right from the time Slade came to see you in Scotland.'

So I repeated my tale of woe again in great detail, with all the pros and cons, and we talked for a long time. At the end of it Case said seriously, 'If you're right and Slade has been got at then this is big trouble.'

'I don't think he's been got at,' I said. 'I think he's been a Russian agent all along. But there's something else worrying me just as much as Slade – where do the Americans fit in? It's not like them to be cosy with people like Kennikin.'

Case dismissed the Americans. 'They're just a problem of this particular operation. Slade is different. He's a big boy now and has a hand in planning and policy. If he's gone sour the whole department will have to be organized.'

He made a sudden sweeping motion with his hand. 'Jesus, you've got me going now! I'm actually beginning to believe you. This is nonsense, Alan.'

I held out my empty glass. 'I could do with a refill – this is thirsty work.' As Case picked up the depleted bottle, I said, 'Let me put it this way. The question has been asked and, once asked, it can't be unasked. If you put my case against Slade to Taggart, just as I've put it to you, then he'll be forced to take action. He can't afford not to. He'll have Slade under a microscope and I don't think Slade can stand close inspection.'

Case nodded. 'There's just one thing, Alan. Be sure – be very, very sure – that your prejudices aren't shouting too loud. I know why you left the Department and I know why you hate Slade's guts. You're biased. This is a serious accusation you're making, and if Slade comes out of it cleaner than the driven snow then you're in big trouble. He'll demand your head on a platter – and he'll get it.'

'He'll deserve it,' I said. 'But the problem won't arise. He's as guilty as hell.' I may have sounded confident but there was the nagging fear that perhaps I was wrong. Case's warning about bias and prejudice was sound, and I hastily re-examined the indictment against Slade. I found no flaw.

Case looked at his watch. 'Eleven-thirty.'

I put down the whisky untasted. 'It's late – I'd better be going.'

'I'll tell Taggart all about it,' said Case. 'And I'll also tell him about Fleet and McCarthy. Maybe he can get a line on that angle through Washington.'

I retrieved the *sgian dubh* from the dressing-table and slipped it into my stocking-top. 'Jack, you really haven't any idea of what this operation is all about?'

'Not the faintest clue,' he said. 'I didn't know anything about it until I was pulled out of Spain. Taggart was angry, and justifiably so, in my opinion. He said you refused to have anything to do with Slade, and you wouldn't even tell him where you were. He said you'd agree to meet me here. All I am is a messenger boy, Alan.'

'That's what Slade told me I was,' I said morosely. 'I'm getting tired of running blind; I'm getting tired of *running*. Maybe if I stood my ground for once in a while I'd be better off.'

'I wouldn't advise it,' said Case. 'Just follow orders and get the package to Reykjavik.' He put on his jacket. 'I'll walk with you to your car. Where is it?'

'Up the road.'

He was about to unlock the door when I said, 'Jack, I don't think you've been entirely frank with me. You've dodged a couple of issues in this conversation. Now there have been some bloody funny things going on lately, such as a member of the Department coming after me with a gun – so I just want to tell you one thing. It's likely that I'll be stopped on the way to Reykjavik, and if you have any part in that I'll go right through you, friendship or no friendship. I hope you understand that.'

He smiled and said, 'For God's sake, you're imagining things.'

But the smile was strained and there was something about his expression I couldn't place, and it worried me. It was only a long time afterwards that I identified the emotion. It was pity but by then the identification had come too late.

SEVEN

We went outside to find it was as dark as it ever gets in the Icelandic summer. There was no moon but there was visibility of sorts in a kind of ghostly twilight. There was a soft explosion among the hot pools and the eerie spectre of Strokkur rose into the air, a fading apparition which dissipated into wind-blown shreds. There was a stink of sulphur in the air.

I shivered suddenly. It's no wonder that the map of Iceland is littered with place names which tell of the giant trolls who dwell in the roots of the mountains, or that the old men still hand down the legends of man in conflict with spirits. The young Icelanders, geared to the twentieth century with their transistor radios and casual use of aircraft, laugh and call it superstition. Maybe they're right, but I've noticed that they tend to force their laughter sometimes and it has a quality of unease about it. All I know is that if I had been one of the old Vikings and had come upon Strokkur unexpectedly one dark night I'd have been scared witless.

I think Case caught something of the atmosphere because he looked across at the thinning curtain of mist as Strokkur disappeared, and said softly, 'It's really something, isn't it?'

'Yes,' I said shortly. 'The car's over there. It's quite a way.'

We crunched on the crushed lava of the road and walked past the long row of white-painted pillars which separate the road from the pools. I could hear the bubbling of hot water and the stench of sulphur was stronger. If you looked at the pools in daylight you would find them all colours, some as white and clear as gin, others a limpid blue or green, and all close to boiling point. Even in the darkness I could see the white vapour rising in the air.

Case said, 'About Slade. What was the . . .?'

I never heard the end of that question because three heavier patches of darkness rose up about us suddenly. Someone grabbed me and said, *'Stewartsen, stanna! Förstar Ni?'* Something hard jabbed into my side.

I stopped all right, but not in the way that was expected. I let myself go limp, just as McCarthy had done when I hit him with the cosh. My knees buckled and I went down to the ground. There was a muffled exclamation of surprise and momentarily the grip on my arm relaxed and the movement in a totally unexpected direction dislodged the gun from my ribs.

As soon as I was down I spun around fast with one leg bent and the other extended rigidly. The outstretched leg caught my Swedish-speaking friend behind the knees with a great deal of force and he fell to the ground. His pistol was ready for use because there was a bang as he fell and I heard the whine of a ricocheting bullet.

I rolled over until I was prone against one of the pillars. I would be too conspicuous against that painted whiteness so I wormed off the road and into the darkness, pulling the pistol from my pocket as I went. Behind me there was a shout of *'Spheshíte!'* and another voice in a lower tone said, *'Net! Slúshayte!'* I kept very still and heard the thudding of boots as someone ran towards the hotel.

Only Kennikin's mob would have addressed me as Stewartsen and in Swedish, and now they were bellowing in Russian. I kept my head close to the ground and looked back towards the road so I could see anyone there silhouetted against the paler sky. There was a flicker of movement quite close and a crunch of footsteps, so I put a bullet in that direction, picked myself up, and ran for it.

And that was damned dangerous because, in the darkness, I could very well run headlong into a bottomless pool of boiling water. I counted my paces and tried to visualize the hot pools area as I had often seen it in daylight under less unnerving conditions. The pools vary in size from a piddling little six inches in diameter to the fifty-foot giant economy size. Heated by the subterranean volcanic activity, the water continually wells out of the pools to form a network of hot streams which covers the whole area.

After I had covered a hundred yards I stopped and dropped on one knee. Ahead of me steam rose and lay in a level blanket and I thought that was Geysir itself. That means that Strokkur was somewhere to my left and a little behind. I wanted to keep clear of Strokkur – getting too close would be dicey in the extreme.

I looked back and saw nothing, but I heard footsteps following in the line I had come, and others away to the right and getting closer. I didn't know if my pursuers knew the lie of the ground or not but, intentionally or accidentally, I was being herded right into the pools. The man on the right switched on a flash lamp, a big thing like a miniature searchlight. He directed it at the ground which was lucky for me, but he was more troubled about turning himself into goulash.

I lifted my pistol and banged off three shots in that direction and the light went out suddenly. I don't think I hit him but he had come to the acute realization that his light made a good target. I wasn't worried about making a noise; the more noise the better as far as I was concerned. Five shots had been fired, five too many in the quiet Icelandic night, and already lights were popping on in the hotel and I heard someone call from that direction.

The man behind me let fly with two shots and I saw the muzzle flare of his pistol very close, not more than ten yards away. The bullets went wide; one I don't know where, but the other raised a fountain in the pool of Geysir. I didn't return the fire but ran to the left, skirting the pool. I stumbled through a stream of hot water, but it was barely two inches deep and I went through fast enough not to do any damage to myself and being more concerned that the splashing noise would give away my position.

There were more cries from the hotel and the slam of windows opening. Someone started up a car with a rasping noise and headlights were switched on. I paid little attention to that, but carried on, angling back towards the road. Whoever started that car had a bright idea – and no pun intended. He swung around and drove towards the pools, his headlamps illuminating the whole area.

It was fortunate for me that he did because it prevented me from running headlong into one of the pools. I saw the reflections strike from the water just in time to skid to a halt, and I teetered for a moment right on the edge. My balancing act wasn't improved much when someone took a shot at me from an unexpected direction – the other side of the pool – and something tugged briefly at the sleeve of my jacket.

Although I was illuminated by the lights of that damned car my attacker was in an even worse position because he was between me and the light and marvellously silhouetted. I slung a shot at him and he flinched with his whole body and retreated. Briefly the headlights of the car swung away and I hastily ran around the pool while he put a bullet in roughly the place I had been.

Then the lights came back and steadied and I saw him retreating backwards, his head moving from side to side nervously. He didn't see me because by this time I was flat on my belly. Slowly he went backwards until he put a foot into six inches of boiling water and jerked apprehensively. He moved fast but not fast enough, because the big gas bubble which heralds the blasting of Strokkur was already rising in the pool behind him like a monster coming to the surface.

Strokkur exploded violently. Steam, superheated by the molten magma far below, drove a column of boiling water up the shaft so that it fountained sixty feet above the pool and descended in a downpour of deadly rain. The man screamed horribly, but his shrill piping was lost in the roar of Strokkur. He flung his arms wide and toppled into the pool.

I moved fast, casting a wide circle away from the revealing lights and heading eventually towards the road. There was a confused babble of shouting and more cars were started up to add their lights to the scene, and I saw a crowd of people running towards Strokkur. I came to a pool and tossed the pistol into it, together with the spare clips of ammunition. Anyone found carrying a gun that night would be likely to spend the rest of his life in jail.

At last I got to the road and joined the crowd. Someone said, 'What happened?'

'I don't know,' I flung my hand towards the pool. 'I heard shooting.'

He dashed past me, avid for vicarious excitement – he would have run just as fast to see a bloody motor smash – and I discreetly melted into the darkness behind the line of parked cars drawn up with headlamps blazing.

After I had gone a hundred yards up the road in the direction of the Volkswagen I turned and looked back. There was a lot of excitement and waving of arms, and long shadows were cast on to the shifting vapour above the hot pools, and there was a small crowd about Strokkur, edging closer but not too close because Strokkur has a short, seven-minute cycle. I realized, with some astonishment, that from the time Case and I had seen Strokkur blow when we left the hotel until the man had fallen into the pool had been only seven minutes.

Then I saw Slade.

He was standing clearly visible in the lights of a car and looking out towards Strokkur. I regretted throwing away the pistol because I would have shot him there and then had I been able, regardless of the consequences. His companion raised his arm and pointed and Slade laughed. Then his friend turned around and I saw it was Jack Case.

I found myself trembling all over, and it was with an effort that I dragged myself away up the road and looked for the Volkswagen. It was where I had left it and I got behind the driving wheel, switched on the engine, and then sat there for a moment, letting the tension drain away. No one I know has ever been shot at from close range and retained his equanimity – his autonomic nervous system sees to that. The glands work overtime and the chemicals stir in the blood, the muscles tune up and the belly goes loose, and it's even worse when the danger has gone.

I found that my hands were trembling violently and rested them on the wheel, and presently they grew still and I felt better. I had just put the car into gear when I felt a ring of cold metal applied to the back of my neck, and a harsh, well-remembered voice said, *'God dag, Herr Stewartsen. Var forsiktig.'*

I sighed, and switched off the engine. 'Hello, Vaslav,' I said.

II

'I am surrounded by a pack of idiots of an incomparable stupidity,' said Kennikin. 'Their brains are in their trigger fingers. It was different in our day; eh, Stewartsen?'

'My name is Stewart now,' I said.

'So? Well. Herr Stewart; you may switch on your engine and proceed. I will direct you. We will let my incompetent assistants find their own way.'

The muzzle of the gun nudged me. I switched on, and said, 'Which way?'

'Head towards Laugarvatn.'

I drove out of Geysir slowly and carefully. The gun no longer pressed into the back of my neck but I knew it wasn't far away, and I knew Kennikin well enough not to go in for any damn-fool heroics. He was disposed to make light conversation. 'You've caused a lot of trouble, Alan – and you can solve a problem that's been puzzling me. Whatever happened to Tadeusz?'

'Who the hell is Tadeusz?'

'The day you landed at Keflavik he was supposed to stop you.'

'So that was Tadeusz – he called himself Lindholm. Tadeusz – that sounds Polish.'

'He's Russian; his mother is Polish, I believe.'

'She'll miss him,' I said.

'So!' He was silent for a while, then he said, 'Poor Yuri had his leg amputated this morning.'

'Poor Yuri ought to have known better than to wave a belly gun at a man armed with a rifle,' I said.

'But Yuri didn't know you had a rifle,' said Kennikin. 'Not that rifle, anyway. It came as quite a surprise.' He clicked his tongue. 'You really shouldn't have wrecked my jeep like that. It wasn't nice.'

Not *that* rifle! He expected a rifle, but not the blockbuster I'd taken from Fleet. That was interesting because the only other rifle was the one I'd taken from Philips and how could he know about that? Only from Slade – another piece of evidence.

I said, 'Was the engine wrecked?'

'There was a hole shot through the battery,' he said. 'And the cooling system was wrecked. We lost all the water. That must be quite a gun.'

'It is,' I said. 'I hope to use it again.'

He chuckled. 'I doubt if you will. That little episode was most embarrassing; I had to talk fast to get out of it. A couple of inquisitive Icelanders asked a lot of questions which I didn't really feel like answering. Such as why the cable car was tied up, and what had happened to the jeep. And there was the problem of keeping Yuri quiet.'

'It must have been most uncomfortable,' I said.

'And now you've done it again,' said Kennikin. 'And in public this time. What really happened back there?'

'One of your boys got himself parboiled,' I said. 'He got too close to a spouter.'

'You see what I mean,' said Kennikin. 'Incompetents, the lot of them. You'd think three to one would be good odds, wouldn't you? But no; they bungled it.'

The odds had been three to two, but what had happened to Jack Case? He hadn't lifted a finger to help. The image of him standing and talking to Slade still burned brightly in my mind and I felt the rage boil up within me. Every time I had turned to those I thought I could trust I had been betrayed, and the knowledge burned like acid.

Buchner/Graham/Philips I could understand; he was a member of the Department fooled by Slade. But Case knew the score – he knew my suspicions of Slade – and he had not done one damned thing to help when I had been jumped by Kennikin's men. And ten minutes later he was hobnobbing with Slade. It seemed as though the whole Department was infiltrated although, Taggart excepted, Case was the last man I would have thought to have gone over. I thought sourly that even Taggart might be on the Moscow pay-roll – that would wrap the whole bundle into one neat package.

Kennikin said, 'I'm glad I didn't underestimate you. I rather thought you'd get away from the morons I've had wished on me, so I staked out this car. A little forethought always pays, don't you think?'

I said, 'Where are we going?'

'You don't need to know in detail,' he said. 'Just concentrate on the driving. And you will go through Laugarvatn very carefully, observing all the speed limits and refraining from drawing attention. No sudden blasts on the horn, for example.' The cold steel momentarily touched my neck. 'Understand?'

'I understand.' I felt a sudden relief. I had thought that perhaps he knew where I had spent the last twenty-four hours and that we were driving to Gunnar's house. It wouldn't have surprised me overmuch; Kennikin seemed to know everything else. He had been lying in wait at Geysir, and that had been a neat trick. The thought of Elin being taken and what might have happened to Sigurlin had made my blood freeze.

We went through Laugarvatn and on to Thingvellir, and took the Reykjavik road, but eight kilometres out of Thingvellir Kennikin directed me to turn left on a secondary road. It was a road I knew well, and it led around the lake of Thingvallavatn. I wondered where the hell we were going.

I didn't have to wonder long because at a word from Kennikin I turned off the road again and we went down a bumpy track towards the lake and the lights of a small house. One of the status symbols in Reykjavik is to have a summer chalet on the shores of Thingvallavatn, even more prized because the building restrictions have forbidden new construction and so the price has shot up. Owning a chalet on Thingvallavatn is the Icelandic equivalent of having a Rembrandt on the wall.

I pulled up outside the house, and Kennikin said, 'Blow the horn.'

I tooted and someone came out. Kennikin put the pistol to my head. 'Careful, Alan,' he said. 'Be very careful.'

He also was very careful. I was taken inside without the faintest possibility of making a break. The room was decorated in that generalized style known as Swedish Modern; when done in England it looks bleak and a little phoney, but when done by the Scandinavians it looks natural and good. There was an open fire burning which was something of a surprise. Iceland has no coal and no trees to make log fires, and an open blaze is something of a rarity; a lot of the houses are heated by natural hot water, and those that aren't have oil-fired central heating. This fire was of peat which glowed redly with small flickering blue flames.

Kennikin jerked his gun. 'Sit by the fire, Alan; make yourself warm. But first Ilyich will search you.'

Ilyich was a squarely-built man with a broad, flat face. There was something Asiatic about his eyes which made me think that at least one of his parents hailed from the farther side of the Urals. He patted me thoroughly, then turned to Kennikin and shook his head.

'No gun?' said Kennikin. 'That was wise of you.' He smiled pleasantly at Ilyich, then turned to me and said, 'You see what I mean, Alan? I am surrounded by idiots. Draw up the left leg of your trousers and show Ilyich your pretty little knife.'

I obeyed, and Ilyich blinked at it in astonishment while Kennikin reamed him out. Russian is even richer than English in cutting invective. The *sgian dubh* was confiscated and Kennikin waved me to the seat while Ilyich, red-faced, moved behind me.

Kennikin put away his gun. 'Now, what will you have to drink, Alan Stewart?'

'Scotch – if you have it.'

'We have it.' He opened a cupboard near the fireplace and poured a drink. 'Will you have it neat or with water? I regret we have no soda.'

'Water will do,' I said. 'Make it a weak one.'

He smiled. 'Oh, yes; you have to keep a clear head,' he said sardonically. 'Section four. Rule thirty-five; when offered a drink by the opposition request a weak one.' He splashed water into the glass then brought it to me. 'I hope that is to your satisfaction.'

I sipped it cautiously, then nodded. If it had been any weaker it wouldn't have been able to crawl out of the glass and past my lips. He returned to the cupboard and poured himself a tumbler-full of Icelandic *brennivin* and knocked back half the contents with one gulp. I watched with some astonishment as he swallowed the raw spirit without twitching a hair. Kennikin was going downhill fast if he now did his drinking openly. I was surprised the Department hadn't caught on to it.

I said, 'Can't you get Calvados here in Iceland, Vaslav?'

He grinned and held up the glass. 'This is my first drink in four years, Alan. I'm celebrating.' He sat in the chair opposite me. 'I have reason to celebrate – it's not often that old friends meet in our profession. Is the Department treating you well?'

I sipped the watery scotch and set the glass on the low table next to my chair. 'I haven't been with the Department for four years.'

He raised his eyebrows. 'My information is different.'

'Maybe,' I said. 'But it's wrong. I quit when I left Sweden.'

'I also quit,' said Kennikin. 'This is my first assignment in four years. I have you to thank for that. I have you to thank for many things.' His voice was slow and even. 'I didn't quit of my own volition. Alan; I was sent to sort papers in Ashkhabad. Do you know where that is?'

'Turkmenistan.'

'Yes.' He thumped his chest. 'Me – Vaslav Viktorovich Kennikin – sent to comb the border for narcotics smugglers and to shuffle papers at a desk.'

'Thus are the mighty fallen,' I said. 'So they dug you up for this operation. That must have pleased you.'

He stretched out his legs. 'Oh, it did. I was very pleased when I discovered you were here. You see, at one time I thought you were my friend.' His voice rose slightly. 'You were as close to me as my own brother.'

'Don't be silly,' I said. 'Don't you know intelligence agents have no friends?' I remembered Jack Case and thought bitterly that I was learning the lesson the hard way, just as Kennikin had.

He went on as though I had not spoken. 'Closer to me than my brother. I would have put my life in your hands – I *did* put my life in your hands.' He stared into the colourless liquid in his glass. 'And you sold me out.' Abruptly he lifted the glass and drained it.

I said derisively, 'Come off it, Vaslav; you'd have done the same in my position.'

He stared at me. 'But I trusted you,' he said almost plaintively. 'That is what hurt most.' He stood up and walked to the cupboard. Over his shoulder he said, 'You know what my people are like. Mistakes aren't condoned. And so . . .' He shrugged '. . . the desk in Ashkhabad. They wasted me.' His voice was harsh.

'It could have been worse,' I said. 'It could have been Siberia. Khatanga, for instance.'

When he returned to his chair the tumbler was full again. 'It very nearly was,' he said in a low voice. 'But my friends helped – my true Russian friends.' With an effort he pulled himself back to the present. 'But we waste time. You have a certain piece of electronic equipment which is wrongfully in your possession. Where is it?'

'I don't know what you're talking about.'

He nodded. 'Of course, you would have to say that; I expected nothing else. But you must realize that you will give it to me eventually.' He took a cigarette case from his pocket. 'Well?'

'All right,' I said. 'I know I've got it, and you know I've got it; there's no point in beating around the bush. We know each other too well for that, Vaslav. But you're not going to get it.'

He took a long Russian cigarette from the case. 'I think I will. Alan; I *know* I will.' He put the case away and searched his pockets for a lighter. 'You see, this is not just an ordinary operation for me. I have many reasons for wanting to hurt you that are quite unconnected with this electronic gear. I am quite certain I shall get it. Quite certain.'

His voice was cold as ice and I felt an answering shudder run down my spine. *Kennikin will want to operate on you with a sharp knife*. Slade had said that, and Slade had delivered me into his hands.

He made a sound of annoyance as he discovered he had no means of lighting his cigarette, and Ilyich stepped from behind me, a cigarette lighter in his hand. Kennikin inclined his head to accept a light as the flint sparked. It sparked again but no flame appeared, and he said irritably, 'Oh, never mind!'

He leaned forward and picked up a spill of paper from the hearth, ignited it at the fire, and lit his cigarette. I was interested in what Ilyich was doing. He had not returned to his post behind my chair but had gone to the cupboard where the liquor was kept – behind Kennikin.

Kennikin drew on the cigarette and blew a plume of smoke, and then looked up. As soon as he saw that Ilyich was not in sight the pistol appeared in his hand. 'Ilyich, what are you doing?' The gun pointed steadily at me.

Ilyich turned with a refill cylinder of butane gas in his hand. 'Filling the lighter.'

Kennikin blew out his cheeks and rolled his eyes upwards. 'Never mind that,' he said curtly. 'Go outside and search the Volkswagen. You know what to look for.'

'It's not there, Vaslav,' I said.

'Ilyich will make sure of it,' said Kennikin.

Ilyich put the butane cylinder back into the liquor cupboard and left the room. Kennikin did not put away the pistol again but held it casually. 'Didn't I tell you? The team they have given me has been scraped from the bottom of the barrel. I'm surprised you didn't try to take advantage.'

I said, 'I might have done if you hadn't been around.'

'Ah, yes,' he said. 'We know each other very well. Perhaps too well.' He balanced the cigarette in an ashtray and picked up his glass. 'I don't really know if I will get any pleasure from working on you. Don't you English have a proverb – "It hurts me as much as it hurts you."' He waved his hand. 'But perhaps I've got it wrong.'

'I'm not English,' I said. 'I'm a Scot.'

'A difference that makes no difference is no difference. But I'll tell you something – you made a great difference to me and to my life.' He took a gulp of *brennivin*. 'Tell me – that girl you've been running around with – Elin Ragnarsdottir; are you in love with her?'

I felt myself tighten. 'She's got nothing to do with this.'

He laughed. 'Do not trouble yourself. I have no intention of harming her. Not a hair of her head shall be touched. I don't believe in the Bible, but I'm willing to swear on it.' His voice turned sardonic. 'I'll even swear it on the Works of Lenin, if that's an acceptable substitute. Do you believe me?'

'I believe you,' I said. I did, too. There was no comparison between Kennikin and Slade. I wouldn't have taken Slade's word had he sworn on a thousand bibles, but in this I would accept Kennikin's lightest word and trust him as he had once trusted me. I knew and understood Kennikin and I liked his style; he was a gentleman – savage, but still a gentleman.

'Well, then; answer my question. Are you in love with her?'

'We're going to be married.'

He laughed. 'That's not exactly a straight answer, but it will do.' He leaned forward. 'Do you sleep with her, Alan? When you come to Iceland do you lie under the stars together and clasp each other's bodies, and work at each other until your sweat mingles? Do you call each other by names that are sweet and soft and handle each other until that last gust of passion, that flare of ecstasy in each of you, mutually quenches the other and ebbs away into languor? Is that how it is, Alan?'

His voice was purring and cruel. 'Do you remember our last encounter in the pine woods when you tried to kill me? I wish you had been a better shot. I was in hospital in Moscow for a long time while they patched me up, but there was one patch they couldn't put back, Alan. And that is why, if you come out of this alive – and that is something I haven't yet decided – you will be no good to Elin Ragnarsdottir or to any other woman.'

I said, 'I'd like another drink.'

'I'll make it stronger this time,' he said. 'You look as though you need it.' He came across and took my glass, and backed towards the liquor cupboard. Still holding the pistol he poured whisky into the glass and added a little water. He brought it back. 'You need some colour in your cheeks,' he said.

I took the whisky from him. 'I understand your bitterness – but any soldier can expect to be wounded; it's an occupational hazard. What really hurts is that you were sold out. That's it, Vaslav; isn't it?'

'That among other things,' he agreed.

I sampled the whisky; it was strong this time. 'Where you go wrong is in your identification of who did it. Who was your boss at that time?'

'Bakayev – in Moscow.'

'And who was my boss?'

He smiled. 'That eminent British nobleman, Sir David Taggart.'

I shook my head. 'No. Taggart wasn't interested; there were bigger fish to occupy his attention at the time. You were sold out by Bakayev, your own boss, in collaboration with my boss, and I was just the instrument.'

Kennikin roared with laughter. 'My dear Alan; you've been reading too much Fleming.'

I said, 'You haven't asked who my boss was.'

He was still shaking with chuckles as he said, 'All right; who was he?'

'Slade,' I said.

The laughter suddenly stopped. I said, 'It was very carefully planned. You were sacrificed to give Slade a good reputation. It had to look good – it had to look very authentic. That's why you weren't told. All things considered, you put up a good fight, but all the time your foundations were being nibbled away by Bakayev who was passing information to Slade.'

'This is nonsense, Stewartsen,' he said; but his face had gone pale and the livid cicatrice stood out on his cheek.

'So you failed,' I said. 'And, naturally, you had to be punished, or it still wouldn't look right. Yes, we know how your people do things, and if you hadn't been sent to Ashkhabad or somewhere like it we'd have been suspicious. So you spent four years in exile to make it look right; four years of paper shuffling for doing your duty. You've been had, Vaslav.'

His eyes were stony. 'This Slade I don't know,' he said shortly.

'You ought to. He's the man you take orders from in Iceland. You thought it natural, perhaps, that you shouldn't be in command on this operation. Your people wouldn't want to give sole responsibility to a man like yourself who failed once. A reasonable attitude, you would think; and maybe you could retrieve your reputation and your honour and aspire to your former dizzy heights by a successful completion of this mission.' I laughed. 'And who do they give you for a boss? None other than the man who torpedoed you in Sweden.'

Kennikin stood up. The pistol pointed unwaveringly at my chest. 'I know who ruined the Swedish operation,' he said. 'And I can touch him from here.'

'I just took orders,' I said. 'Slade did the brainwork. Do you remember Jimmy Birkby?'

'I've never heard of the man,' said Kennikin stonily.

'Of course not. You'd know him better as Sven Hornlund – the man I killed.'

'The British agent,' said Kennikin. 'I remember. It was that one act of yours that made me sure of you.'

'Slade's idea,' I said. 'I didn't know who I killed. That's why I left the Department – I had a flaming row.' I leaned forward. 'Vaslav, it fits the pattern, don't you see that? Slade sacrificed one good man to make you trust me. It meant nothing to him how many of our agents were killed. But he and Bakayev sacrificed you to make Taggart trust Slade the more.'

Kennikin's grey eyes were like stones. His face was quite still except for one corner of his mouth where the scar ran down which twitched with a slight tic.

I leaned back in the chair and picked up the glass. 'Slade's sitting pretty now. He's here in Iceland running both sides of an operation. My God, what a position to be in! But it went wrong when one of the puppets refused to jump when he pulled the strings. That must have worried the hell out of him.'

'I don't know this man Slade,' repeated Kennikin woodenly.

'No? Then why are you all worked up?' I grinned at him. 'I'll tell you what to do. Next time you speak to him why don't you ask him for the truth. Not that he'll tell you; Slade never told anyone the truth in his life. But he might give himself away to such a perceptive person as yourself.'

Lights flickered through the drawn curtains and there was the sound of a car pulling up outside. I said, 'Think of the past, Vaslav; think of the wasted years in Ashkhabad. Put yourself in the position of Bakayev and ask yourself which is the more important – an operation in Sweden which can be reconstituted at any time, or the chance to put a man high in the hierarchy of British Intelligence – so high that he lunches with the British Prime Minister?'

Kennikin moved uneasily and I knew I had got to him. He was deep in thought and the pistol no longer pointed directly at me. I said, 'As a matter of interest, how long did it take to build up another Swedish outfit? Not long, I'll bet. I daresay Bakayev had an organization already working in parallel ready to go into action when you dropped out.'

It was a shot at random but it went home. It was like watching a one-armed bandit come up with the jackpot; the wheels went round and whirred and clicked and a mental bell rang loud and clear. Kennikin snorted and turned away. He looked down into the fire and the hand holding the pistol was down at his side.

I tensed myself, ready to jump him, and said softly, 'They didn't trust you, Vaslav. Bakayev didn't trust you to wreck your own organization and make it look good. I wasn't trusted either; but I was sold out by Slade who is one of your mob. You're different; you've been kicked in the teeth by your own people. How does it feel?'

Vaslav Kennikin was a good man – a good agent – and he gave nothing away. He turned his head and looked at me.

'I've listened to this fairy-story with great interest,' he said colourlessly. 'The man, Slade, I don't know. You tell a fine tale, Alan, but it won't get you out of trouble. You're not . . .'

The door opened and two men came in. Kennikin turned impatiently, and said, 'Well?'

The bigger of the men said in Russian, 'We've just got back.'

'So I see,' said Kennikin emotionlessly. He waved at me. 'Let me introduce Alan Stewartsen, the man you were supposed to bring here. What went wrong? Where's Igor?'

They looked at each other, and the big man said, 'He was taken to hospital. He was badly scalded when . . .'

'That's fine!' said Kennikin caustically. 'That's marvellous!' He turned and appealed to me. 'What do you think of this, Alan? We get Yuri safely and secretly to the trawler but Igor must go to a hospital where questions are asked. What would you do with an idiot like this?'

I grinned, and said hopefully, 'Shoot him.'

'It's doubtful if a bullet would penetrate his thick skull,' said Kennikin acidly. He looked balefully at the big Russian. 'And why, in God's name, did you start shooting? It sounded like the outbreak of revolution.'

The man gestured towards me helplessly. 'He started it.'

'He should never have been given the opportunity. If three men can't take another one quietly, then . . .'

'There were two of them.'

'Oh!' Kennikin glanced at me. 'What happened to him?'

'I don't know – he ran away,' said the big man.

I said casually, 'It's hardly surprising. He was just a guest from the hotel.' I seethed internally. So Case had just run away and left me to it. I wouldn't sell him to Kennikin but there'd be an account to settle if I got out of this mess.

'He probably raised the alarm at the hotel,' said Kennikin. 'Can't you do anything right?'

The big man started to expostulate, but Kennikin cut him short. 'What's Ilyich doing?'

'Taking a car to pieces,' His voice was sullen.

'Go and help him.' They both turned, but Kennikin said sharply, 'Not you, Gregor. Stay here and watch Stewartsen.' He handed his pistol to the smaller man.

I said, 'Can I have another drink, Vaslav?'

'Why not?' said Kennikin. 'There's no danger of you turning into an alcoholic. You won't live that long. Watch him, Gregor.'

He left the room, closing the door behind him, and Gregor planted himself in front of it and looked at me expressionlessly. I drew up my legs very slowly and got to my feet. Gregor lifted the pistol and I grinned at him, holding up my empty glass. 'You heard what the boss said; I'm allowed a last drink.'

The muzzle of the pistol dropped. 'I'll be right behind you,' he said.

I walked across to the liquor cupboard, talking all the time. 'I'll bet you're from the Crimea, Gregor. That accent is unmistakable. Am I right?'

He was silent, but I persevered with my patter. 'There doesn't seem to be any vodka here, Gregor. The nearest to it is *brennivin*, but that comes a bad second – I don't go for it myself. Come to that, I don't like vodka very much either. Scotch is my tipple, and why not, since I'm a Scot?'

I clattered bottles and heard Gregor breathing down my neck. The scotch went into the glass to be followed by water, and I turned with it raised in my hand to find Gregor a yard away with the pistol trained on my navel. As I have said, there *is* a place for the pistol, and this was it. It's a dandy indoor weapon. If I had done anything so foolish as to throw the drink into his face he would have drilled me clear through the spine.

I held up the glass at mouth level. '*Skal* – as we say in Iceland.' I had to keep my hand up otherwise the cylinder of butane gas would have dropped out of my sleeve, so I walked across the room in a pansyfied manner and sat in my chair again. Gregor looked at me with something like contempt in his eyes.

I sipped from the glass and then transferred it from one hand to the other. When I had finished wriggling about the butane cylinder was tucked in between the cushion and the arm of the chair. I toasted Gregor again and then looked at the hot-burning peat fire with interest.

On each refill cylinder of butane there is a solemn warning: EXTREMELY INFLAMMABLE MIXTURE, DO NOT USE NEAR FIRE OR FLAME. KEEP OUT OF THE REACH OF CHILDREN. DO NOT PUNCTURE OR INCINERATE. Commercial firms do not like to put such horrendous notices on their products and usually do so only under pressure of legislation, so that in all cases the warnings are thoroughly justified.

The peat fire was glowing hot with a nice thick bed of red embers. I thought that if I put the cylinder into the fire one of two things were likely to happen – it would either explode like a bomb or take off like a rocket – and either of these would suit me. My only difficulty was that I didn't know how long it would take to blow up. Putting it into the fire might be easy, but anyone quick enough could pull it out – Gregor, for instance. Kennikin's boys couldn't possibly be as incompetent as he made them out to be.

Kennikin came back. 'You were telling the truth,' he said.

'I always do; the trouble is most people don't recognize it when they hear it. So you agree with me about Slade.'

He frowned. 'I don't mean that stupid story. What I am looking for is not in your car. Where is it?'

'I'm not telling you, Vaslav.'

'You will.'

A telephone bell rang somewhere. I said, 'Let's have a bet on it.'

'I don't want to get blood on the carpet in here,' he said. 'Stand up.' Someone took the telephone receiver off the hook.

'Can't I finish my drink first?'

Ilyich opened the door and beckoned to Kennikin, who said, 'You'd better have finished that drink by the time I get back.'

He left the room and Gregor moved over to stand in front of me. That wasn't very good because as long as he stood there I wouldn't have a chance of jamming the butane cylinder into the fire. I touched my forehead and found a thin film of sweat.

Presently Kennikin came back and regarded me thoughtfully. 'The man you were with at Geysir – a guest at the hotel, I think you said.'

'That's right.'

'Does the name – John Case – mean anything to you?'

I looked at him blankly. 'Not a thing.'

He smiled sadly. 'And you are the man who said he always told the truth.' He sat down. 'It seems that what I am looking for has ceased to have any importance. More accurately, its importance has diminished relative to yourself. Do you know what that means?'

'You've lost me,' I said, and I really meant it. This was a new twist.

Kennikin said, 'I would have gone to any length necessary to get the information from you. However, my instructions have changed. You will not be tortured, Stewartsen, so put your mind at ease.'

I let out my breath. 'Thanks!' I said wholeheartedly.

He shook his head pityingly. 'I don't want your thanks. My instructions are to kill you immediately.'

The telephone bell rang again.

My voice came out in a croak. 'Why?'

He shrugged. 'You are getting in the way.'

I swallowed. 'Hadn't you better answer that telephone? It might be a change of instruction.'

He smiled crookedly. 'A last-minute reprieve, Alan? I don't think so. Do you know why I told you of these instructions? It's not normally done, as you know.'

I knew all right, but I wouldn't give him the satisfaction of telling him. The telephone stopped ringing.

'There are some good things in the Bible,' he said. 'For instance – "An eye for an eye, and a tooth for a tooth." I had everything planned for you, and I regret my plans cannot now be implemented. But at least I can watch you sweat as you're sweating now.'

Ilyich stuck his head around the door. 'Reykjavik,' he said.

Kennikin made a gesture of annoyance. 'I'm coming.' He rose. 'Think about it – and sweat some more.'

I put out my hand. 'Have you a cigarette?'

He stopped in mid-stride and laughed aloud. 'Oh, very good, Alan. You British are strong on tradition. Certainly you may have the traditional last cigarette.' He tossed me his cigarette case. 'Is there anything else you would like?'

'Yes,' I said. 'I would like to be in Trafalgar Square on New Year's Eve in the year 2000.'

'My regrets,' he said, and left the room.

I opened the case, stuck a cigarette in my mouth, and patted my pockets helplessly; then I stooped very slowly to pick up one of the paper spills from the hearth. I said to Gregor, 'I'm just going to light my cigarette,' and bent forward to the fire, hoping to God he wouldn't move from the door.

I held the spill in my left hand and leaned forward so that my right hand was screened by my body, and thrust the cylinder into the embers at the same time as I lifted the flaming spill and returned to my seat. Waving it in a circle to attract Gregor's eyes from the fire, I applied it to the tip of the cigarette, drew in smoke and blew a plume in his direction. I deliberately allowed the flame to burn down so that it touched my fingers.

'Ouch!' I exclaimed, and shook my hand vigorously. Anything to keep him from looking directly at the fire. It took all the willpower I had to refrain from glancing at it myself.

The telephone was slammed down and Kennikin came stalking back. 'Diplomats!' he said in a scathing voice. 'As though I don't have enough troubles.' He jerked his thumb at me. 'All right; on your feet.'

I held up the cigarette. 'What about this?'

'You can finish it outside. There'll be just enough . . .'

The blast of the exploding cylinder was deafening in that enclosed area, and it blew the peat fire all over the room. Because I was expecting it I was quicker off the mark than anyone else. I ignored the red-hot ember which stung my neck, but Gregor found he couldn't do the same with the ember which alighted on the back of his hand. He gave a yell and dropped the gun.

I dived across the room, seized the pistol and shot him twice through the chest. Then I turned to nail Kennikin before he could recover. He had been beating red-hot bits of peat from his jacket but now he was turning at the sound of the shots. I lifted the pistol and he grabbed a table-lamp and threw it at me. I ducked, my shot went wild, and the table-lamp sailed over my head to hit Ilyich straight in the face as he opened the door to find out what the hell was going on.

That saved me the trouble of opening it. I shouldered him aside and stumbled into the hall to find that the front door was open. Kennikin had given me a bad time, and much as I would have liked to have fought it out with him this was not the time for it. I ran out of the house and past the Volkswagen which was minus all four wheels, and on the way took a snap shot at the big Russian to encourage him to keep his head down. Then I ran into the darkness which, by now, was not as dark as I would have liked, and took to the countryside fast.

The countryside thereabouts consisted of humpy lava covered by a thick layer of moss and occasional patches of dwarf birch. At full speed and in broad daylight a man might make one mile an hour without breaking an ankle. I sweated over it, knowing that if I broke my ankle, or as much as sprained it, I would be picked up easily and probably shot on the spot.

I went about four hundred yards, angling away from the lake shore and up towards the road, before I stopped. Looking back I saw the windows of the room in which I had been held; there was a curious flickering and I saw that the curtains were going up in flames. There were distant shouts and someone ran in front of the window, but it seemed that no one was coming after me. I don't think any of them knew which direction I'd taken.

The view ahead was blocked by the bulk of an old lava flow and I reckoned the road was on the other side of that. I moved forward again and began to climb over it. It would be dawn soon and I wanted to get out of sight of the house.

I went over the top of the lava flow on my belly and once safely screened on the other side I got to my feet. Dimly, in the distance, I could see a straight dark line which could only be the road, and I was just about to make for it when someone put a stranglehold on my neck and a hand clamped on my wrist with bone-crushing pressure. 'Drop the gun!' came a hoarse whisper in Russian.

I dropped the pistol and was immediately flung away so that I stumbled and fell. I looked up into the glare of a flashlight which illumined a pistol held on me. 'Christ, it's you!' said Jack Case.

'Put that bloody light out,' I said, and massaged my neck. 'Where the hell were you when the whistle blew at Geysir?'

'I'm sorry about that,' said Case. 'He was at the hotel when I arrived.'

'But you said . . .'

There was a note of exasperation in Case's voice. 'Jesus, I couldn't tell you he was there. In the mood you were in you'd have slaughtered him.'

'A fine friend you turned out to be,' I said bitterly. 'But this is no time to go into it. Where's your car – we can talk later.'

'Just off the road down there.' He put away his gun.

I came to a snap decision; this was no time to trust Case or anyone else. I said, 'Jack, you can tell Taggart I'll deliver his package to Reykjavik.'

'All right, but let's get out of here.'

I moved close to him. 'I don't trust you. Jack,' I said, and sank three rigid fingers into his midriff. The air exploded violently from his lungs and he doubled up. I chopped at the back of his neck and he collapsed at my feet. Jack and I had always been level on the unarmed combat mat and I don't think I could have taken him so easily had he known what was coming.

In the distance a car started and its engine throbbed. I saw the glow of headlights to my right and dropped flat. I could hear the car coming up the spur track towards the road, but it turned away and moved in the opposite direction – the way I had driven in from Thingvellir.

When it was out of earshot I reached out and began to search Case's pockets. I took his keys and stripped him of his shoulder holster and pistol. Gregor's pistol I wiped clean and threw away. Then I went to look for Case's car.

It was a Volvo and I found it parked just off the road. The engine turned over easily at the touch of a button and I moved away without lights. I would be going all the way around Thingvallavatn and it would be a long way to Laugarvatn, but I certainly didn't feel like going back.

EIGHT

I got into Laugarvatn just before five in the morning and parked the car in the drive. As I got out I saw the curtains twitch and Elin ran out and into my arms before I got to the front door. 'Alan!' she said. 'There's blood on your face.'

I touched my cheek and felt the caked blood which had oozed from a cut. It must have happened when the butane cylinder went up. I said, 'Let's get inside.'

In the hall we met Sigurlin. She looked me up and down, then said, 'Your jacket's burnt.'

I glanced at the holes in the fabric. 'Yes,' I said. 'I was careless, wasn't I?'

'What happened?' asked Elin urgently.

'I had . . . I had a talk with Kennikin,' I said shortly. The reaction was hitting me and I felt very weary. I had to do something about it because there was no time to rest. 'Do you have any coffee?' I asked Sigurlin.

Elin gripped my arm. 'What happened? What did Kenni . . .?'

'I'll tell you later.'

Sigurlin said, 'You look as though you haven't slept for a week. There's a bed upstairs.'

I shook my head. 'No. I . . . we . . . are moving out.'

She and Elin exchanged glances, and then Sigurlin said practically, 'You can have your coffee, anyway. It's all ready – we've been drinking the stuff all night. Come into the kitchen.'

I sat down at the kitchen table and spooned a lot of sugar into a steaming cup of black coffee. It was the most wonderful thing I've ever tasted. Sigurlin went to the window and looked at the Volvo in the drive. 'Where's the Volkswagen?'

I grimaced. 'It's a write-off.' The big Russian had said that Ilyich was taking it to pieces, and from the fleeting glimpse I had of it he had been right. I said, 'What's it worth, Sigurlin?' and put my hand in my pocket for my cheque-book.

She made an impatient gesture. 'That can wait.' There was an edge to her voice. 'Elin told me everything. About Slade – about Kennikin – everything.'

'You shouldn't have done that, Elin,' I said quietly.

'I had to talk about it to someone,' she burst out.

'You must go to the police,' said Sigurlin.

I shook my head. 'So far this has been a private fight. The only casualties have been among the professionals – the men who know the risks and accept them. No innocent bystanders have been hurt. I want to keep it that way. Anyone who monkeys around with this without knowing the score is in for trouble – whether he's wearing a police uniform or not.'

'But it needn't be handled at that level,' she said. 'Let the politicians handle it – the diplomats.'

I sighed and leaned back in my chair. 'When I first came to this country someone told me that there are three things which an Icelander can't explain – not even to another Icelander: the Icelandic political system, the Icelandic economic system, and the Icelandic drinking laws. We're not worried about alcohol right now, but politics and economics are right at the top of my list of worries.'

Elin said, 'I don't really know what you're talking about.'

'I'm talking about that refrigerator,' I said. 'And that electric coffee-grinder.' My finger stabbed out again. 'And the electric kettle and the transistor radio. They're all imported and to afford imports you have to export – fish, mutton, wool. The herring shoals have moved a thousand miles away, leaving your inshore herring fleet high and dry. Aren't things bad enough without making them worse?'

Sigurlin wrinkled her brow. 'What do you mean?'

'There are three nations involved – Britain, America and Russia. Supposing a thing like this is handled at diplomatic level with an exchange of Notes saying: "Stop fighting your battles on Icelandic territory." Do you really think a thing like that could be kept secret? Every country has political wild men – and I'm sure Iceland is no exception – and they'd all jump on the bandwagon.'

I stood up. 'The anti-Americans would shout about the Base at Keflavik; the anti-communists would have a good handle to grab hold of; and you'd probably restart the Fishing War with Britain because I know a lot of Icelanders who aren't satisfied with the settlement of 1961.'

I swung around to face Sigurlin. 'During the Fishing War your trawlers were denied entry to British ports, so you built up a fair trade with Russia, which you still have. What do you think of Russia as a trading partner?'

'I think they're very good,' she said instantly. 'They've done a lot for us.'

I said deliberately, 'If your government is placed in the position of having to take official notice of what's going on then that good relationship might be endangered. Do you want that to happen?'

Her face was a study in consternation. I said grimly, 'If this lark ever comes into the open it'll be the biggest *cause célèbre* to bite Iceland since Sam Phelps tried to set up Jorgen Jorgensen as king back in 1809.'

Elin and Sigurlin looked at each other helplessly. 'He's right,' said Sigurlin.

I knew I was right. Under the placid level of Icelandic society were forces not safe to tamper with. Old animosities still linger among the longer-memoried and it wouldn't take much to stir them up. I said, 'The less the politicians know, the better it will be for everybody. I like this country, damn it; and I don't want the mud stirred up.' I took Elin's hand. 'I'll try to get this thing cleaned up soon. I think I know a way.'

'Let them have the package,' she said urgently. 'Please, Alan; let them have it.'

'I'm going to,' I said. 'But in my own way.'

There was a lot to think about. The Volkswagen, for instance. It wouldn't take Kennikin long to check the registration and find out where it came from. That meant he'd probably be dropping in before the day was over. 'Sigurlin,' I said. 'Can you take a pony and join Gunnar?'

She was startled. 'But why . . .?' She took the point. 'The Volkswagen?'

'Yes; you might have unwelcome visitors. You'd be better out of the way.'

'I had a message from Gunnar last night, just after you left. He's staying out another three days.'

'That's good,' I said. 'In three days everything should be over.'

'Where are you going?'

'Don't ask,' I warned. 'You know too much already. Just get yourself in a place where there's no one to ask questions.' I snapped my fingers. 'I'll shift the Land-Rover too. I'm abandoning it, but it had better not be found here.'

'You can park it in the stables.'

'That's a thought. I'm going to move some things from the Land-Rover into the Volvo. I'll be back in a few minutes.'

I went into the garage and took out the electronic gadget, the two rifles and all the ammunition. The guns I wrapped in a big piece of sacking which I found and they went into the boot. Elin came out, and said, 'Where *are* we going?'

'Not we,' I said. 'Me.'

'I'm coming with you.'

'You're going with Sigurlin.'

That familiar stubborn, mulish look came on to her face. 'I liked what you said in there,' she said. 'About not wanting to cause trouble for my country. But it is my country and I can fight for it as well as anyone else.'

I nearly laughed aloud. 'Elin,' I said. 'What do you know about fighting?'

'As much as any other Icelander,' she said evenly.

She had something there. 'You don't know what's going on,' I said.

'Do you?'

'I'm beginning to catch on. I've just about proved that Slade is a Russian agent – and I loaded Kennikin just like a gun and pointed him at Slade. When they meet he's likely to go off, and I wouldn't like to be in Slade's position when it happens. Kennikin believes in direct action.'

'What happened last night? Was it bad?'

I slammed the boot closed. 'It wasn't the happiest night of my life,' I said shortly. 'You'd better get some things together. I want this house unoccupied within the hour.' I took out a map and spread it out.

'Where are you going?' Elin was very persistent.

'Reykjavik,' I said. 'But I want to go to Keflavik first.'

'That's the wrong way round,' she pointed out. 'You'll get to Reykjavik first – unless you go south through Hveragerdi.'

'That's the problem,' I said slowly, and frowned as I looked at the map. The web of roads I had visualized existed all right but not as extensively as I had imagined. I didn't know about the Department's supposed manpower shortage, but Kennikin certainly wasn't suffering that way; I had counted ten different men with Kennikin at one time or another.

And the map showed that the whole of the Reykjanes Peninsula could be sealed off from the east by placing men at two points – Thingvellir and Hveragerdi. If I went through either of those towns at a normal slow speed I'd be spotted; if I went through hell-for-leather I'd attract an equivalent amount of attention. And the radio-telephone which had worked for me once would now work against me, and I'd have the whole lot of them down on me.

'Christ!' I said. 'This is bloody impossible.'

Elin grinned at me cheerfully. 'I know an easy way,' she said too casually. 'One that Kennikin won't think of.'

I looked at her suspiciously. 'How?'

'By sea.' She laid her finger on the map. 'If we go to Vik I know an old friend who will take us to Keflavik in his boat.'

I regarded the map dubiously. 'It's a long way to Vik, and it's in the wrong direction.'

'All the better,' she said. 'Kennikin won't expect you to go there.'

The more I studied the map, the better it looked. 'Not bad,' I said.

Elin said innocently, 'Of course, I'll have to come with you to introduce you to my friend.'

She'd done it again.

II

It was an odd way to get to Reykjavik because I pointed the Volvo in the opposite direction and put my foot down.

It was with relief that I crossed the bridge over the Thjòrsà River because that was a bottleneck I was sure Kennikin would cover, but we got across without incident and I breathed again.

Even so, after we passed Hella I had a belated attack of nerves and left the main road to join the network of bumpy tracks in Landeyjasandur, feeling that anyone who could find me in that maze would have to have extrasensory perception.

At midday Elin said decisively, 'Coffee.'

'What have you got? A magic wand?'

'I've got a vacuum flask – and bread – and pickled herring. I raided Sigurlin's kitchen.'

'Now I'm glad you came,' I said. 'I never thought of that.' I pulled the car to a halt.

'Men aren't as practical as women,' said Elin.

As we ate I examined the map to check where we were. We had just crossed a small river and the farmstead we had passed was called Bergthórshvoll. It was with wonder that I realized we were in the land of Njal's Saga. Not far away was Hlidarendi, where Gunnar Hamundarsson was betrayed by Hallgerd, his wife, and had gone down fighting to the end. Skarp-Hedin had stalked over this land with death on his face and his war-axe raised high, tormented by the devils of revenge. And here, at Bergthórshvoll, Njal and his wife, Bergthóra, had been burned to death with their entire family.

All that had happened a thousand years ago and I reflected, with some gloom, that the essential nature of man had not changed much since. Like Gunnar and Skarp-Hedin I travelled the land in imminent danger of ambush by my enemies and, like them, I was equally prepared to lay an ambush if the opportunity arose. There was another similarity; I am a Celt and Njal had a Celtic name, nordicized from Neil. I hoped the Saga of

Burnt Njal would not be echoed by the Saga of Burnt Stewart.

I aroused myself from these depressing thoughts, and said, 'Who is your friend in Vik?'

'Valtýr Baldvinsson, one of Bjarni's old school friends. He's a marine biologist studying the coastal ecology. He wants to find out the extent of the changes when Katla erupts.'

I knew about Katla. 'Hence the boat,' I said. 'And what makes you think he'll run us to Keflavik?'

Elin tossed her head. 'He will if I ask him to.'

I grinned. 'Who is this fascinating woman with a fatal power over men? Can it be none other than Mata Hari, girl spy?'

She turned pink but her voice was equable as she said, 'You'll like Valtýr.'

And I did. He was a square man who, but for his colouring, looked as though he had been rough-hewn from a pillar of Icelandic basalt. His torso was square and so was his head, and his hands had stubby, spatulate fingers which appeared to be too clumsy for the delicate work he was doing when we found him in his laboratory. He looked up from the slide he was mounting and gave a great shout. 'Elin! What are you doing here?'

'Just passing by. This is Alan Stewart from Scotland.'

My hand was enveloped in a big paw. 'Good to meet you,' he said, and I had the instant feeling he meant it.

He turned to Elin. 'You're lucky to have caught me here. I'm leaving tomorrow.'

Elin raised her eyebrows. 'Oh! Where for?'

'At last they've decided to put a new engine into that relic of a longship they've given me instead of a boat. I'm taking her round to Reykjavik.'

Elin glanced at me and I nodded. In the course of events you have to be lucky sometimes. I had been wondering how

Elin was going to cajole him into taking us to Keflavik without arousing too many suspicions, but now the chance had fallen right into our laps.

She smiled brilliantly. 'Would you like a couple of passengers? I told Alan I hoped you could take us to have a look at Surtsey, but we wouldn't mind going on to Keflavik. Alan has to meet someone there in a couple of days.'

'I'd be glad to have company,' Valtýr said jovially. 'It's a fair distance and I'd like someone to spell me at the wheel. How's your father?'

'He's well,' said Elin.

'And Bjarni? Has Kristin given him that son yet?'

Elin laughed. 'Not yet – but soon. And how do you know it won't be a daughter?'

'It will be a boy!' he said with certainty. 'Are you on holiday, Alan?' he asked in English.

I replied in Icelandic, 'In a manner of speaking. I come here every year.'

He looked startled, and then grinned. 'We don't have many enthusiasts like you,' he said.

I looked around the laboratory; it appeared to be a conventional biological set-up with the usual rows of bottles containing chemicals, the balance, the two microscopes and the array of specimens behind glass. An odour of formalin was prevalent. 'What are you doing here?' I asked.

He took me by the arm and led me to the window. With a large gesture he said, 'Out there is the sea with a lot of fish in it. It's hazy now but in good weather you can see Vestmannaeyjar where there is a big fishing fleet. Now come over here.'

He led me to a window on the other side of the room and pointed up toward Mýrdalsjökull. 'Up there is the ice and, under the ice, a big bastard called Katla. You know Katla?'

'Everybody in Iceland knows of Katla,' I said.

He nodded. 'Good! I've been studying the sea off this coast and all the animals in it, big and small – and the plants too. When Katla erupts sixty cubic kilometres of ice will be melted into fresh water and it will come into the sea here; as much fresh water as comes out of all the rivers of Iceland in a year will come into the sea in one week and in this one place. It will be bad for the fish and the animals and the plants because they aren't accustomed to so much fresh water all at once. I want to find out how badly they will be hit and how long they take to recover.'

I said, 'But you have to wait until Katla erupts. You might wait a long time.'

He laughed hugely. 'I've been here five years – I might be here another ten. but I don't think so. The big bastard is overdue already.' He thumped me on the arm. 'Could blow up tomorrow – then we don't go to Keflavik.'

'I won't lose any sleep over it,' I said drily.

He called across the laboratory, 'Elin, in your honour I'll take the day off.' He took three big strides, picked her up and hugged her until she squealed for mercy.

I didn't pay much attention to that because my eyes were attracted to the headline of a newspaper which lay on the bench. It was the morning newspaper from Reykjavik and the headline on the front page blared: GUN BATTLE AT GEYSIR.

I read the story rapidly. Apparently a war had broken out at Geysir to judge from this account, and everything short of light artillery had been brought into play by persons unknown. There were a few eye-witness reports, all highly inaccurate, and it seemed that a Russian tourist, one Igor Volkov, was now in hospital after having come too close to Strokkur. Mr Volkov had no bullet wounds. The Soviet Ambassador had complained to the Icelandic Minister of Foreign Affairs about this unprovoked assault on a Soviet citizen.

I opened the paper to see if there was a leading article on the subject and, of course, there was. In frigid and austere tones the leader writer inquired of the Soviet Ambassador the reason why the aforesaid Soviet citizen, Igor Volkov, was armed to the teeth at the time, since there was no record of his having declared any weapons to the Customs authorities when he entered the country.

I grimaced. Between us, Kennikin and I were in a fair way to putting a crimp into Icelandic-Soviet relations.

III

We left Vik rather late the next morning and I wasn't in a good mood because I had a thick head. Valtýr had proved to be a giant among drinkers and, since I was suffering from lack of sleep, my efforts to keep up with him had been disastrous. He put me to bed, laughing boisterously, and woke up himself as fresh as a daisy while I had a taste in my mouth as though I had been drinking the formalin from his specimen jars.

My mood wasn't improved when I telephoned London to speak to Taggart only to find he was absent from his office. The bland official voice declined to tell me where he was but offered to pass on a message, an invitation which I, in my turn, declined to accept. The curious actions of Case had led me to wonder who in the Department was trustworthy, and I wouldn't speak to anyone but Taggart.

Valtýr's boat was anchored in a creek, a short distance from the open beach, and we went out to it in a dinghy. He looked curiously at the two long, sackcloth-covered parcels I took aboard but made no comment, while I hoped they did not look too much like what they actually were. I wasn't going to leave the rifles behind because I had an idea I might need them.

The boat was about twenty-five feet overall, with a tiny cabin which had sitting headroom and a skimpy wooden canopy to protect the man at the wheel from the elements. I had checked the map to find the sea distance from Vik to Keflavik and the boat seemed none too large. I said, 'How long will it take?'

'About twenty hours,' said Valtýr, and added cheerfully, 'If the bastard engine keeps going. If not, it takes forever. You get seasick?'

'I don't know,' I said. 'I've never had the chance to find out.'

'You have the chance now.' He bellowed with laughter.

We left the creek and the boat lifted alarmingly to the ocean swells and a fresh breeze streamed Elin's hair. 'It's clearer today,' said Valtýr. He pointed over the bows. 'You can see Vestmannaeyjar.'

I looked towards the group of islands and played the part which Elin had assigned me. 'Where is Surtsey from here?'

'About twenty kilometres to the south-west of Heimaey – the big island. You won't see much of it yet.'

We plunged on, the little boat dipping into the deep swells and occasionally burying her bows in the water and shaking free a shower of spray when she came up. I'm not any kind of a seaman and it didn't look too safe to me, but Valtýr took it calmly enough, and so did Elin. The engine, which appeared to be a toy diesel about big enough to go with a Meccano set, chugged away, aided by a crack from Valtýr's boot when it faltered, which it did too often for my liking. I could see why he was pleased at the prospect of having a new one.

It took six hours to get to Surcey, and Valtýr circled the island, staying close to shore, while I asked the appropriate questions. He said, 'I can't land you, you know.'

Surtsey, which came up thunderously and in flames from the bottom of the sea, is strictly for scientists interested in finding out how life gains hold in a sterile environment. Naturally they don't want tourists clumping about and bringing in seeds on their boots. 'That's all right,' I said. 'I didn't expect to go ashore.'

Suddenly he chuckled. 'Remember the Fishing War?'

I nodded. The so-called Fishing War was a dispute between Iceland and Britain about off-shore fishing limits, and there was a lot of bad blood between the two fishing fleets. Eventually it had been settled, with the Icelanders making their main point of a twelve-mile limit.

Valtýr laughed, and said, 'Surtsey came up and pushed our fishing limit thirty kilometres farther south. An English skipper I met told me it was a dirty trick – as though we'd done it deliberately. So I told him what a geologist told me; in a million years our fishing limit will be pushed as far south as Scotland.' He laughed uproariously.

When we left Surtsey I abandoned my pretended interest and went below to lie down. I was in need of sleep and my stomach had started to do flip-flops so that I was thankful to stretch out, and I fell asleep as though someone had hit me on the head.

IV

My sleep was long and deep because when I was awakened by Elin she said, 'We're nearly there.'

I yawned. 'Where?'

'Valtýr is putting us ashore at Keflavik.'

I sat up and nearly cracked my head on a beam. Overhead a jet plane whined and when I went aft into the open I saw that the shore was quite close and a plane was just dipping in to land. I stretched, and said, 'What time is it?'

'Eight o'clock,' said Valtýr. 'You slept well.'

'I needed it after a session with you,' I said, and he grinned.

We tied up at eight-thirty, Elin jumped ashore and I handed her the wrapped rifles. 'Thanks for the ride, Valtýr.'

He waved away my thanks. 'Any time. Maybe I can arrange to take you ashore on Surtsey – it's interesting. How long are you staying?'

'For the rest of the summer,' I said. 'But I don't know where I'll be.'

'Keep in touch,' he said.

We stood on the dockside and watched him leave, and then Elin said, 'What are we doing here?'

'I want to see Lee Nordlnger. It's a bit chancy, but I want to know what this gadget is. Will Bjarni be here, do you think?'

'I doubt it,' said Elin. 'He usually flies out of Reyjkavik Airport.'

'After breakfast I want you to go to the Icelandair office at the airport here,' I said. 'Find out where Bjarni is, and stay there until I come.' I rubbed my cheek and felt unshaven bristles. 'And stay off the public concourse. Kennikin is sure to have Keflavik Airport staked out and I don't want you seen.'

'Breakfast first,' she said. 'I know a good café here.'

When I walked into Nordlinger's office and dumped the rifles in a corner he looked at me with some astonishment, noting the sagging of my pockets under the weight of the rifle ammunition, my bristly chin and general uncouthness. His eyes flicked towards the corner. 'Pretty heavy for fishing tackle,' he commented. 'You look beat, Alan.'

'I've been travelling in rough country,' I said, and sat down. 'I'd like to borrow a razor, and I'd like you to look at something.'

He slid open a drawer of his desk and drew out a battery-powered shaver which he pushed across to me. 'The washroom's two doors along the corridor,' he said. 'What do you want me to look at?'

I hesitated. I couldn't very well ask Nordlinger to keep his mouth shut no matter what he found. That would be asking him to betray the basic tenets of his profession, which he certainly wouldn't do. I decided to plunge and take a chance, so I dug the metal box from my pocket, took off the tape which held the lid on, and shook out the gadget. I laid it before him. 'What's that, Lee?'

He looked at it for a long time without touching it, then he said, 'What do you want to know about it?'

'Practically everything,' I said. 'But to begin with – what nationality is it?'

He picked it up and turned it around. If anyone could tell me anything about it, it was Commander Lee Nordlinger. He was an electronics officer at Keflavik Base and ran the radar and radio systems, both ground-based and airborne. From what I'd heard he was damned good at his job.

'It's almost certainly American,' he said. He poked his finger at it. 'I recognize some of the components – these resistors, for instance, are standard and are of American manufacture.' He turned it around again. 'And the input is standard American voltage and at fifty cycles.'

'All right,' I said. 'Now – what is it?'

'That I can't tell you right now. For God's sake, you bring in a lump of miscellaneous circuitry and expect me to identify it at first crack of the whip. I may be good but I'm not that good.'

'Then can you tell me what it's not?' I asked patiently.

'It's no teenager's transistor radio, that's for sure,' he said, and frowned. 'Come to that, it's like nothing I've ever seen before.' He tapped the odd-shaped piece of metal in the middle of the assembly. 'I've never seen one of these, for example.'

'Can you run a test on it?'

'Sure.' He uncoiled his lean length from behind the desk. 'Let's run a current through it and see if it plays "The Star-Spangled Banner."'

'Can I come along?'

'Why not?' said Nordlinger lightly. 'Let's go to the shop.' As we walked along the corridor he said, 'Where did you get it?'

'It was given to me,' I said uncommunicatively.

He gave me a speculative glance but said no more. We went through swing doors at the end of the corridor and into a large room which had long benches loaded with electronic gear. Lee signalled to a petty officer who came over. 'Hi, Chief; I have something here I want to run a few tests on. Have you a test bench free?'

'Sure, Commander.' The petty officer looked about the room. 'Take number five; I guess we won't be using that for a while.'

I looked at the test bench; it was full of knobs and dials and screens which meant less than nothing. Nordlinger sat down. 'Pull up a chair and we'll see what happens.' He attached clips to the terminals on the gadget, then paused. 'We already know certain things about it. It isn't part of an airplane; they don't use such a heavy voltage. And it probably isn't from a ship for roughly the same reason. So that leaves ground-based equipment. It's designed to plug into the normal electricity system on the North American continent – it could have been built in Canada. A lot of Canadian firms use American manufactured components.'

I jogged him along. 'Could it come from a TV set?'

'Not from any TV I've seen.' He snapped switches. 'A hundred ten volts – fifty cycles. Now, there's no amperage given so we have to be careful. We'll start real low.' He twisted a knob delicately and a fine needle on a dial barely quivered against the pin.

He looked down at the gadget. 'There's a current going through now but not enough to give a fly a heart attack.' He paused, and looked up. 'To begin with, this thing is crazy; an alternating current with these components isn't standard. Now, let's see – first we have what seems to be three amplification stages, and that makes very little sense.'

He took a probe attached to a lead. 'If we touch the probe here we should get a sine wave on the oscilloscope . . .' He looked up. '. . . which we do. Now we see what happens at this lead going into this funny-shaped metal ginkus.'

He gently jabbed the probe and the green trace on the oscilloscope jumped and settled into a new configuration. 'A square wave,' said Nordlinger. 'This circuit up to here is functioning as a chopper – which is pretty damn funny in itself for reasons I won't go into right now. Now let's see what happens at the lead going *out* of the ginkus and into this mess of boards.'

He touched down the probe and the oscilloscope trace jumped again before it settled down. Nordlinger whistled. 'Just look at that spaghetti, will you?' The green line was twisted into a fantastic waveform which jumped rhythmically and changed form with each jump. 'You'd need a hell of a lot of Fourier analysis to sort that out,' said Nordlinger. 'But whatever else it is, it's pulsed by this metal dohickey.'

'What do you make of it?'

'Not a damn thing,' he said. 'Now I'm going to try the output stage; on past form this should fairly tie knots into that oscilloscope – maybe it'll blow up.' He lowered the probe and we looked expectantly at the screen.

I said, 'What are you waiting for?'

'I'm waiting for nothing.' Nordlinger looked at the screen blankly. 'There's no output.'

'Is that bad?'

He looked at me oddly. In a gentle voice he said, 'It's impossible.'

I said, 'Maybe there's something broken in there.'

'You don't get it,' said Nordlinger. 'A circuit is just what it says – a circle. You break the circle anywhere you get no current flow anywhere.' He applied the probe again. 'Here there's a current of a pulsed and extremely complex form.' Again the screen jumped into life. 'And here, in the same circuit, what do we get?'

I looked at the blank screen. 'Nothing?'

'Nothing,' he said firmly. He hesitated. 'Or, to put it more precisely, nothing that can show on this test rig.' He tapped the gadget. 'Mind if I take this thing away for a while?'

'Why?'

'I'd like to put it through some rather more rigorous tests. We have another shop.' He cleared his throat and appeared to be a little embarrassed. 'Uh . . . you won't be allowed in there.'

'Oh – secret stuff.' That would be in one of the areas to which Fleet's pass would give access. 'All right, Lee; you put the gadget through its paces and I'll go and shave. I'll wait for you in your office.'

'Wait a minute,' he said. 'Where did you get it, Alan?'

I said, 'You tell me what it does and I'll tell you where it came from.'

He grinned. 'It's a deal.'

I left him disconnecting the gadget from the test rig and went back to his office where I picked up the electric shaver. Fifteen minutes later I felt a lot better after having got rid of the hair. I waited in Nordlinger's office for a long time – over an hour and a half – before he came back.

He came in carrying the gadget as though it was a stick of dynamite and laid it gently on his desk. 'I'll have to ask you where you got this,' he said briefly.

'Not until you tell me what it does,' I said.

He sat behind his desk and looked at the complex of metal and plastic with something like loathing in his eyes. 'It does nothing,' he said flatly. 'Absolutely nothing.'

'Come off it,' I said. 'It must do *something*.'

'Nothing!' he repeated. 'There is no measurable output.' He leaned forward and said softly, 'Alan, out there I have instruments that can measure any damn part of the electromagnetic spectrum from radio waves of such low frequency you wouldn't believe possible right up to cosmic radiation – and there's nothing coming out of this contraption.'

'As I said before – maybe something has broken.'

'That cat won't jump; I tested everything.' He pushed at it and it moved sideways on the desk. 'There are three things I don't like about this. Firstly, there are components in here that are not remotely like anything I've seen before, components of which I don't even understand the function. I'm supposed to be pretty good at my job, and that, in itself, is enough to disturb me. Secondly, it's obviously incomplete – it's just part of a bigger complex – and yet I doubt if I would understand it even if I had everything. Thirdly – and this is the serious one – it shouldn't work.'

'But it isn't working,' I said.

He waved his hand distractedly. 'Perhaps I put it wrong. There should be an output of some kind. Good Christ, you can't keep pushing electricity into a machine – juice that gets used up – without getting something out. That's impossible.'

I said, 'Maybe it's coming out in the form of heat.'

He shook his head sadly. 'I got mad and went to extreme measures. I pushed a thousand watts of current through it in the end. If the energy output was in heat then the goddamn thing would have glowed like an electric heater. But no – it stayed as cool as ever.'

'A bloody sight cooler than you're behaving,' I said.

He threw up his hands in exasperation. 'Alan, if you were a mathematician and one day you came across an equation in which two and two made five without giving a nonsensical result then you'd feel exactly as I do. It's as though a physicist were confronted by a perpetual motion machine which works.'

'Hold on,' I said. 'A perpetual motion machine gets something for nothing – energy usually. This is the other way round.'

'It makes no difference,' he said. 'Energy can neither be created nor destroyed.' As I opened my mouth he said quickly, 'And don't start talking about atomic energy. Matter can be regarded as frozen, concentrated energy.' He looked at the gadget with grim eyes. 'This thing is destroying energy.'

Destroying energy! I rolled the concept around my cerebrum to see what I could make of it. The answer came up fast – nothing much. I said, 'Let's not go overboard. Let's see what we have. You put an input into it and you get out . . .'

'Nothing,' said Nordlinger.

'Nothing you can measure,' I corrected. 'You may have some good instrumentation here, Lee, but I don't think you've got the whole works. I'll bet that there's some genius somewhere who not only knows what's coming out of there but has an equally involved gadget that can measure it.'

'Then I'd like to know what it is,' he said. 'Because it's right outside my experience.'

I said, 'Lee, you're a technician, not a scientist. You'll admit that?'

'Sure; I'm an engineer from way back.'

'That's why you have a crew-cut – but this was designed by a long-hair.' I grinned. 'Or an egghead.'

'I'd still like to know where you got it.'

'You'd better be more interested in where it's going. Have you got a safe – a really secure one?'

'Sure.' He did a double-take. 'You want *me* to keep *this?*'

'For forty-eight hours,' I said. 'If I don't claim it in that time you'd better give it to your superior officer together with all your forebodings, and let him take care of it.'

Nordlinger looked at me with a cold eye.' I don't know but what I shouldn't give it to him right now. Forty-eight hours might mean my neck.'

'You part with it now and it will be my neck,' I said grimly.

He picked up the gadget. 'This is American and it doesn't belong here at Keflavik. I'd like to know where it does belong.'

'You're right about it not belonging here,' I said. 'But I'm betting it's Russian – and they want it back.'

'For God's sake!' he said. 'It's full of American components.'

'Maybe the Russians learned a lesson from Macnamara on cost-effectiveness. Maybe they're shopping in the best market. I don't give two bloody hoots if the components were made in the Congo – I still want you to hold on to it.'

He laid the gadget on his desk again very carefully. 'Okay – but I'll split the difference; I'll give you twenty-four hours. And even then you don't get it back without a full explanation.'

'Then I'll have to be satisfied with that,' I said. 'Providing you lend me your car. I left the Land-Rover in Laugarvatn.'

'You've got a goddamn nerve.' Nordlinger put his hand in his pocket and tossed the car key on the desk.

'You'll find it in the car park near the gate – the blue Chevrolet.'

'I know it.' I put on my jacket and went to the corner to pick up the rifles. 'Lee, do you know a man called Fleet?'

He thought for a moment. 'No.'

'Or McCarthy?'

'The CPO you met in the shop is McCarthy.'

'Not the same one,' I said. 'I'll be seeing you, Lee. We'll go fishing sometime.'

'Stay out of jail.'

I paused at the door. 'What makes you say a thing like that?'

His hand closed over the gadget. 'Anyone who walks around with a thing like this ought to be in jail,' he said feelingly.

I laughed, and left him staring at it. Nordlinger's sense of what was right had been offended. He was an engineer, not a scientist, and an engineer usually works to the rule book – that long list of verities tested through the centuries. He tends to forget that the rule book was originally compiled by scientists, men who see nothing strange in broken rules other than an opportunity to probe a little deeper into the inexplicable universe. Any man who can make the successful transition from Newtonian to quantum physics without breaking his stride can believe anything any day of the week and twice as much on Sundays. Lee Nordlinger was not one of these men, but I'd bet the man who designed the gadget was.

I found the car and put the rifles and the ammunition into the boot. I was still wearing Jack Case's pistol in the shoulder holster and so now there was nothing to spoil the set of my coat. Not that I was any more presentable; there were scorch marks on the front from the burning peat of Kennikin's fire, and a torn sleeve from where a bullet had come a shade too close at Geysir. It was stained with mud and so were my trousers, I was looking more and more like a tramp – but a clean-shaven tramp.

I climbed into the car and trickled in the direction of the International Airport, thinking of what Nordlinger hadn't been able to tell me about the gadget. According to Lee it was an impossible object and that made it scientifically important – so important that men had died and had their legs blown off and had been cooked in boiling water because of it.

And one thing made me shiver. By Kennikin's last words just before I escaped from the house at Thingvallavatn he had made it quite clear that I was now more important than the gadget. He had been prepared to kill me without first laying his hands on it and, for all he knew, once I was dead the gadget would have been gone forever with me.

I had Nordlinger's evidence that the gadget was of outstanding scientific importance, so what was it about me that made me even more important than that? It's not often in this drear, technological world that a single man becomes of more importance than a scientific breakthrough. Maybe we were returning to sanity at last, but I didn't think so.

There was a side entrance to the Icelandair office which one could use without going through the public concourse, so I parked the car and went in. I bumped pleasantly into a hostess, and asked, 'Is Elin Ragnarsdottir around?'

'Elin? She's in the waiting-room.'

I walked into the waiting-room and found her alone. She jumped up quickly. 'Alan, you've been so long!'

'It took longer than I expected.' Her face was strained and there seemed to be a sense of urgency about her. 'You didn't have trouble?'

'No trouble – not for me. Here's the newspaper.'

I took it from her. 'Then what's the matter?'

'I think you'd better . . . you'd better read the paper.' She turned away.

I shook it open and saw a photograph on the front page, a life-size reproduction of my *sgian dubh*. Underneath, the black headline screamed: HAVE YOU SEEN THIS KNIFE?

The knife had been found embedded in the heart of a man sitting in a car parked in the driveway of a house in Laugarvatn. The man had been identified as a British tourist called John Case. The house and the Volkswagen in which Case had been found belonged to Gunnar Arnarsson who was absent, being in charge of a pony-trekking expedition. The house had been broken into and apparently searched. In the absence of Gunnar Arnarsson and his wife, Sigurlin Asgeirsdottir, it was impossible to tell if anything had been stolen. Both were expected to be contacted by the police.

The knife was so unusual in form that the police had requested the newspaper to publish a photograph of it. Anyone who had seen this knife or a similar knife was requested to call at his nearest police station. There was a boxed paragraph in which the knife was correctly identified as a Scottish *sgian dubh,* and after that the paragraph degenerated into pseudo-historical blather.

The police were also trying to find a grey Volvo registered in Reykjavik; anyone having seen it was requested to communicate with the police at once. The registration number was given.

I looked at Elin. 'It's a mess, isn't it?' I said quietly.

'It *is* the man you went to see at Geysir?'

'Yes.' I thought of how I had mistrusted Jack Case and left him unconscious near Kennikin's house. Perhaps he had not been untrustworthy at all because I had no illusions about who had killed him. Kennikin had the *sgian dubh* and Kennikin had the Volkswagen – and probably Kennikin had stumbled across Case in his search for me.

But why had Case been killed?

'This is dreadful,' said Elin. 'Another man killed.' Her voice was filled with despair.

'I didn't kill him,' I said baldly.

She picked up the paper. 'How did the police know about the Volvo?'

'Standard procedure,' I said. 'As soon as Case was identified the police would dig into whatever he'd been doing since he entered the country. They'd soon find he hired a car – and it wasn't the Volkswagen he was found in.'

I was glad the Volvo was tucked away out of sight in Valtýr's garage in Vik. 'When is Valtýr going back to Vik?' I asked.

'Tomorrow,' said Elin.

It seemed as though everything was closing in on me. Lee Nordlinger had given me a twenty-four hour ultimatum; it was too much to hope that Valtýr wouldn't check on the Volvo as soon as he got back to Vik – he might even go to the Reykjavik police if he felt certain it was the car they were searching for. And when the police laid hands on Sigurlin then the balloon would certainly go up – I couldn't see her keeping silent in the face of a corpse parked in her home.

Elin touched my arm. 'What are you going to do?'

'I don't know,' I said. 'Right now I just want to sit and think.'

I began to piece the fragments together and gradually they made some kind of sense which hinged around Kennikin's sudden switch of attitude after he had captured me. At first he had been all for extracting the gadget from me and he was looking forward with unwholesome delight to the operation. But then he lost interest in the gadget and announced that my death was the more important, and that was just after he had received a telephone call.

I ticked off the sequence of events. At Geysir I had told Case of my suspicions of Slade, and Case had agreed to pass them on to Taggart. No matter what happened Slade would then be thoroughly investigated. But I had seen Slade talking to Case just before Kennikin took me. Suppose that Case had aroused Slade's suspicions in some way? Slade was a clever man – a handler of men – and maybe Case had shown his hand.

What would Slade do? He would contact Kennikin to find if I had been captured. He would insist that his cover next to Taggart should remain unbroken at all costs and that this was more important than the gadget. He would say, 'Kill the bastard!' That was why Kennikin had switched.

And it would be just as important to kill Jack Case before he talked to Taggart.

I had played right into Slade's hands and left Case for Kennikin to find, and Kennikin had stabbed him with my knife. Kennikin had traced where the Volkswagen had come from and gone looking for me, and he had left the body of Case. Terrorist tactics.

It all tied together except for one loose end which worried me. Why, when I had been jumped at Geysir by Kennikin's mob, had Jack Case run out on me? He hadn't lifted a finger to help; he hadn't fired a shot in my defence even though he was armed. I knew Jack Case and that was very unlike him, and that, together with his apparent chumminess with Slade, had been the basis of my mistrust of him. It worried me very much.

But it was all past history and I had the future to face and decisions to make. I said, 'Did you check on Bjarni?'

Elin nodded listlessly. 'He's on the Reykjavik-Höfn run. He'll be in Reykjavik this afternoon.'

'I want him over here,' I said. 'And you're to stick in this office until he comes. You're not to move out of it even for meals. You can have those sent up. And most emphatically you're not to go out into the concourse of the airport; there are too many eyes down there looking for you and me.'

'But I can't stay here forever,' she protested.

'Only until Bjarni comes. Then you can tell him anything you think fit – you can even tell him the truth. Then you're to tell him what he must do.'

She frowned. 'And that is?'

'He's got to get you on a plane and out of here, and he has to do it discreetly without going through normal channels. I don't care if he has to dress you up as a hostess and smuggle you aboard as one of the crew, but you mustn't go down into the concourse as an ordinary passenger.'

'But I don't think he could do that.'

'Christ!' I said. 'If he can smuggle in crates of Carlsberg from Greenland he can smuggle you out. Come to think of it, going to Greenland might not be such a bad idea; you could stay in Narsassuaq until all this blows over. Not even Slade, clever though he is, would think of looking there.'

'I don't want to go.'

'You're going,' I said. 'I want you from underfoot. If you think things have been rough for the last few days then compared to the next twenty-four hours they'll seem like an idyllic holiday. I want you out of it, Elin, and, by God, you'll obey me.'

'So you think I'm useless,' she said bitterly.

'No, I don't; and you've proved it during the last few days. Everything you've done in that time has been against your better judgment, but you've stuck by me. You've been shot and you've been shot at, but you still helped out.'

'Because I love you,' she said.

'I know – and I love you. That's why I want you out of here. I don't want you killed.'

'And what about you?' she demanded.

'I'm different,' I said. 'I'm a professional. I know what to do and how to do it; you don't.'

'Case was a professional too – and he's dead. So was Graham, or whatever his name really was. And that man, Volkov, was hurt at Geysir – and he was a professional. You said yourself that the only people hurt so far have been the professionals. I don't want you hurt, Alan.'

'I also said that no innocent bystanders have been hurt,' I said. 'You're an innocent bystander – and I want to keep it that way.'

I had to do something to impress the gravity of the situation upon her. I looked around the room to check its emptiness, then quickly took off my jacket and unslung Case's shoulder holster complete with gun. I held it in my hand and said, 'Do you know how to use this?'

Her eyes dilated. 'No!'

I pointed out the slide. 'If you pull this back a bullet is injected into the breech. You push over this lever, the safety catch, then you point it and pull the trigger. Every time you pull a bullet comes out, up to a maximum of eight. Got that?'

'I think so.'

'Repeat it.'

'I pull back the top of the gun, push over the safety catch and pull the trigger.'

'That's it. It would be better if you squeezed the trigger but this is no time for finesse.' I put the pistol back into the holster and pressed it into her reluctant hands. 'If anyone tries to make you do anything you don't want to do just point the gun and start shooting. You might not hit anyone but you'll cause some grey hairs.'

The one thing that scares a professional is a gun in the hands of an amateur. If another professional is shooting at you at least you know he's accurate and you have a chance of out-manoeuvring him. An amateur can kill you by accident.

I said, 'Go into the loo and put on the holster under your jacket. When you come back I'll be gone.'

She accepted the finality of the situation along with the pistol. 'Where are you going?'

'The worm is turning,' I said. 'I'm tired of running, so I'm going hunting. Wish me luck.'

She came close to me and kissed me gently and there were unshed tears in her eyes and the gun in its holster was iron-hard between us. I patted her bottom and said, 'Get along with you,' and watched as she turned and walked away. When the door closed behind her I also left.

NINE

Nordlinger's Chevrolet was too long, too wide and too soft-sprung and I wouldn't have given a thank you for it in the *Óbyggdir,* but it was just what I needed to get into Reykjavik fast along the International Highway which is the only good bit of paved road in Iceland. I did the twenty-five miles to Hafnarfjördur at 80 mph and cursed when I was slowed down by the heavy traffic building up around Kopavogur. I had an appointment at midday in the souvenir shop of the Nordri Travel Agency and I didn't want to miss it.

The Nordri Travel Agency was in Hafnarstraeti. I parked the car in a side street near Naust and walked down the hill towards the centre of town. I had no intention at all of going into Nordri; why would I when Nordlinger had the gadget tucked away in his safe? I came into Hafnarstraeti and ducked into a bookshop opposite Nordri. There was a café above the shop with a flight of stairs leading directly to it so that one could read over a cup of coffee. I bought a newspaper as cover and went upstairs.

It was still before the midday rush so I got a seat at the window and ordered pancakes and coffee. I spread open the paper and then glanced through the window at the crowded street below and found that, as I had planned, I had a good view of the travel agency which was on the other side of the street. The thin gauze curtains didn't obstruct my view but made it impossible for anyone to recognize me from the street.

The street was fairly busy. The tourist season had begun and the first hardy travellers had already started to ransack the souvenir shops and carry home their loot. Camera-hung and map in hand they were easy to spot, yet I inspected every one of them because the man I was looking for would probably find it convenient to be mistaken for a tourist.

This was a long shot based on the fact that everywhere I had gone in Iceland the opposition had shown up. I had followed instructions on arrival and gone the long way around to Reykjavik and Lindholm had been there. I had gone to earth in Asbyrgi and Graham had pitched up out of the blue. True, that was because of the radio bug planted on the Land-Rover, but it had happened. Fleet had lain in wait and had shot up the Land-Rover in a deliberate ambush, the purpose of which was still a mystery. Yet he, like Lindholm, had known *where* to wait. Kennikin had jumped me at Geysir and I'd got away from that awkward situation by the thickness of a gnat's whisker.

And now I was expected to call at the Nordri Travel Agency. It was a thin chance but it seemed logical to suppose that if past form was anything to go on then the place would be staked out. So I took a more than ordinary interest in those below who window-shopped assiduously, and I hoped that if Kennikin was laying for me I'd be able to recognize his man. He couldn't have brought a whole army to Iceland and, one way or another, I'd already laid eyes on a lot of his men.

Even so, it was a full half-hour before I spotted him, and that was because I was looking at him from an unfamiliar angle – from above. It is very hard to forget a face first seen past the cross hairs of a telescopic sight, yet it was only when he lifted his head that I recognized one of the men who had been with Kennikin on the other side of the Tungnaá River.

He was pottering about and looking into the window of the shop next to Nordri and appeared to be the perfect tourist complete with camera, street map and sheaf of picture postcards. I whistled up the waitress and paid my bill so that I could make a quick getaway, but reserved the table for a little longer by ordering another coffee.

He wouldn't be alone on a job like this and so I was interested in his relationship with the passers-by. As the minutes ticked on he appeared to become increasingly restless and consulted his watch frequently and, at one o'clock exactly, he made a decisive move. He lifted his hand and beckoned, and another man came into my line of sight and crossed the street towards him.

I gulped my coffee and went downstairs to lurk at the newspaper counter while observing my friends through the glass doors of the bookshop. They had been joined by a third man whom I recognized immediately – none other than Ilyich who had unwittingly provided me with the butane bomb. They nattered for a while and then Ilyich stuck out his arm and tapped his wrist-watch, shrugging expressively. They all set off up the street towards Posthusstraeti and I followed.

From the bit of action with the watch it seemed that they not only knew the rendezvous I was supposed to keep but the time I was to keep it. They had pulled off duty at one o'clock like workmen clocking off the job. It wouldn't have surprised me overmuch if they knew the passwords as well.

At the corner of Posthusstraeti two of them got into a parked car and drove away, but Ilyich turned smartly to the right across the street and headed at a quick clip towards the Hotel Borg, into which he disappeared like a rabbit diving into its hole. I hesitated for a moment and then drifted in after him.

He didn't stop to collect a key at the desk but went immediately upstairs to the second floor, with me on his heels. He walked along a corridor and knocked at a door, so I did a smart about-turn and went downstairs again where I sat at a table in the lounge from where I had a good view of the foyer. This meant another obligatory cup of coffee with which I was already awash, but that's the penalty of a trailing job. I spread my newspaper at arm's length and waited for Ilyich to appear again.

He wasn't away long – a matter of ten minutes – and when he came back I knew triumphantly that all my suspicions had been correct and that everything I had done in Iceland was justified. He came downstairs talking to someone – and that someone was Slade!

They came through the lounge on their way to the dining-room and Slade passed my table no farther away than six feet. It was to be expected that he would wait in his room for a report, positive or negative, and then head for the fleshpots. I shifted in my chair and watched where they would sit and, during the brouhaha of the seating ceremony. I left quickly and walked into the foyer and out of sight.

Two minutes later I was on the second floor and tapping at the same door Ilyich had knocked on, hoping that no one would answer. No one did and so, by a bit of trickery involving a plastic sheet from my wallet, I went inside. That was something I had learned at school – the Department had trained me well.

I wasn't stupid enough to search Slade's luggage. If he was as smart as I thought he would have gimmicked it so that he could tell at a glance whether a suitcase had been opened. Standard operating procedure when on a job, and Slade had a double advantage – he'd been trained by both sides. But I did inspect the door of his wardrobe, checking to see if there were any fine hairs stuck down with dabs of saliva which would come free if the door was opened. There was nothing, so I opened the door, stepped inside, and settled down to wait in the darkness.

I waited a long time. That I expected, having seen the way Slade gourmandized, yet I wondered how he would take to the Icelandic cuisine which is idiosyncratic, to say the least. It takes an Icelander to appreciate *hakarl* – raw shark meat buried in sand for several months – or pickled whale blubber.

It was quarter to three when he came back and by that time my own stomach was protesting at the lack of attention; it had had plenty of coffee but very little solid food. Ilyich was with him and it came as no surprise that Slade spoke Russian like a native. Hell, he probably *was* a Russian, as had been Gordon Lonsdale, another of his stripe.

Ilyich said, 'Then there's nothing until tomorrow?'

'Not unless Vaslav comes up with something,' said Slade.

'I think it's a mistake,' said Ilyich. 'I don't think Stewartsen will go near the travel agency. Anyway, are we sure of that information?'

'We're sure,' said Slade shortly. 'And he'll be there within the next four days. We've all underestimated Stewart.'

I smiled in the darkness. It was nice to have an unsolicited testimonial. I missed what he said next, but Ilyich said, 'Of course, we don't do anything about the package he will carry. We let him get rid of it in the agency and then we follow him until we get him alone.'

'And then?'

'We kill him,' said Ilyich unemotionally.

'Yes,' said Slade. 'But there must be no body found. There has been too much publicity already; Kennikin was mad to have left the body of Case where he did.' There was a short silence and then he said musingly, 'I wonder what Stewart did with Philips?'

To this rhetorical question Ilyich made no answer, and Slade said, 'All right; you and the others are to be at the

Nordri Agency at eleven tomorrow. As soon as you spot Stewart I must be notified by telephone immediately. Is that understood?'

'You will be informed,' said Ilyich. I heard the door open. 'Where is Kennikin?' he asked.

'What Kennikin does is no concern of yours,' said Slade sharply. 'You may go.'

The door slammed.

I waited and heard a rustle as of paper and a creak followed by a metallic click. I eased open the wardrobe door a crack and looked into the room with one eye. Slade was seated in an armchair with a newspaper on his knee and was applying a light to a fat cigar. He got the end glowing to his satisfaction and looked about for an ashtray. There was one on the dressing-table so he got up and moved his chair so that the ashtray would be conveniently to hand.

It was convenient for me too, because the action of moving the chair had turned his back to me. I took my pen from my pocket and opened the wardrobe door very slowly. The room was small and it only needed two steps to get behind him. I made no sound and it must have been the fractional change of the quality of the light in the room that made him begin to turn his head. I rammed the end of the pen in the roll of fat at the back of his neck and said, 'Stop right there or you'll be minus a head.'

Slade froze, and I snaked my other hand over his shoulder to the inside of his jacket where I found a pistol in a shoulder holster. Everyone seemed to be wearing guns these days and I was becoming exceptionally competent at disarming people.

'I don't want a move from you,' I said, and stepped back. I worked the action of the pistol to make sure it was loaded, and threw off the safety catch. 'Stand up.'

Obediently he stood, still clutching the newspaper. I said, 'Walk straight forward to the wall in front of you lean against it with your hands high and your arms held wide.'

I stepped back and watched him critically as he went through the evolution. He knew what I was going to do; this was the safest way of searching a man. Being Slade, he tried to pull a fast one, so I said, 'Pull your feet out from the wall and lean harder.' That meant he would be off-balance to begin with if he tried anything – just enough to give me that extra fraction of a second that is all-important.

He shuffled his feet backwards and I saw the telltale quiver of his wrists as they took up the weight of his body. Then I searched him swiftly, tossing the contents of his pockets on to the bed. He carried no other weapon, unless you consider a hypodermic syringe a weapon, which I was inclined to do when I saw the wallet of ampoules that went with it. Green on the left for a six-hour certain knock-out; red on the right for death in thirty seconds equally certainly.

'Now bend your knees and come down that wall very slowly.' His knees sagged and I brought him into the position in which I had had Fleet – belly down and arms wide stretched. It would take a better man than Slade to jump me from that position; Fleet might have done it had I not rammed his rifle in the small of his back, but Slade was not as young and he had a bigger paunch.

He lay with his head on one side, his right cheek pressed to the carpet and his left eye glaring at me malevolently. He spoke for the first time. 'How do you know I won't have visitors this afternoon?'

'You're right to worry about that,' I said. 'If anyone comes through that door you're dead.' I smiled at him. 'It would be a pity if it was a chambermaid, then you'd be dead for nothing.'

He said, 'What the devil do you think you're doing, Stewart? Have you gone out of your mind? I think you must have – I told Taggart so and he agrees with me. Now, put away that gun and let me stand up.'

'I must say you try,' I said admiringly. 'Nevertheless, if you move a muscle towards getting up I'll shoot you dead.' His only reaction to that was a rapid blinking of the one eye I could see.

Presently he said, 'You'll hang for this, Stewart. Treason is still a capital crime.'

'A pity,' I said. 'At least *you* won't hang, because what you are doing isn't treason – merely espionage. I don't think spies are hanged – not in peacetime, anyway. It would be treason if you were English, but you're not; you're a Russian.'

'You're out of your mind,' he said disgustedly. 'Me – a Russian!'

'You're as English as Gordon Lonsdale was Canadian.'

'Oh, wait until Taggart gets hold of you,' he said. 'He'll put you through the wringer.'

I said, 'What are you doing consorting with the opposition, Slade?'

He actually managed to summon up enough synthetic indignation to splutter. 'Dammit!' he said. 'It's my job. You did the same; you were Kennikin's right-hand man at one time. I'm just following orders – which is more than you are doing.'

'That's interesting,' I said. 'Your orders are very curious. Tell me more.'

'I'll tell nothing to a traitor,' he said virtuously.

I must say that at that moment I admired Slade for the first time. Lying in a most undignified position and with a gun at his head he wasn't giving an inch and was prepared to fight to the end. I had been in his position myself when I had got next to Kennikin in Sweden and I knew how nerve-abrading a life it was – never knowing from one day to another whether one's cover had been blown. Here he was, still trying to convince me that he was as pure as the latest brand of detergent, and I knew that if I let up on him for a fraction of a second so that he could get the upper hand I would be a dead man in that very second.

I said, 'Come off it, Slade. I heard you tell Ilyich to kill me. Don't tell me that was an order passed on from Taggart.'

'Yes,' he said, without the flicker of an eyelash. 'He thinks you've gone over. I can't say I blame him, either, considering the way you've been behaving.'

I almost burst out laughing at his effrontery. 'By God, but you're good!' I said. 'You lie there with your face hanging out and tell me that. I suppose Taggart also told you to ask the Russkies to do the job for him.'

Slade's exposed cheek wrinkled up into the rictus of a half smile. 'It's been done before,' he said. 'You killed Jimmy Birkby.'

Involuntarily my finger tightened on the trigger, and I had to take a deep breath before I relaxed. I tried to keep my voice even as I said, 'You've never been nearer death than now, Slade. You shouldn't have mentioned Birkby – that's a sore point. Let's not have any more comedy. You're finished and you know it quite well. You're going to tell me a lot of things I'm interested in, and you're going to tell it fast, so speak up.'

'You can go to hell,' he said sullenly.

'You're a great deal nearer hell right now,' I said. 'Let me put it this way. Personally, I don't give a damn if you're English or Russian, a spy or a traitor. I don't give a damn for patriotism either; I've got past that. With me this is purely personal – on a man-to-man basis, if you like. The foundation for most murders. Elin was nearly killed in Asbyrgi on your instruction, and I've just heard you tell a man to kill me. If I kill you right now it will be self-defence.'

Slade lifted his head a little and turned it so that he could look at me straight. 'But you won't do it,' he said.

'No?'

'No,' he said with certainty. 'I told you before – you're too soft-centred. You might kill me under different circumstances; if I were running away, for instance, or if we were shooting at each other. But you won't kill me while I'm lying here. You're an English gentleman.' He made it sound like a swearword.

'I wouldn't bet on it,' I said. 'Maybe Scots are different.'

'Not enough to matter,' he said indifferently.

I watched him look into the muzzle of the pistol without a quiver and I had to give the devil his due. Slade knew men and he had my measure as far as killing was concerned. He also knew that if he came for me I would shoot to kill. He was safe enough while lying defenceless, but action was another thing.

He smiled. 'You've already proved it. You shot Yuri in the leg – why not in the heart? By Kennikin's account you were shooting accurately enough across that river to have given every man a free shave without benefit of barber. You could have killed Yuri – but you didn't!'

'Maybe I wasn't feeling in the mood at the time. I killed Gregor.'

'In the heat of action. Your death or his. Any man can make that kind of decision.'

I had the uneasy feeling that the initiative was passing from me and I had to get it back. I said, 'You can't talk if you're dead – and you're going to talk. Let's begin by you telling me about the electronic gadget – what is it?'

He looked at me contemptuously and tightened his lips.

I glanced at the pistol I held. God knows why Slade carried it because it was a .32 – a popgun just as heavy to lug about as a modern .38 but without the stopping power. But maybe he was a crack shot and could hit his target every time so that wouldn't matter much. What would matter when shooting in a populous place was that the muzzle blast was much less and so were the decibels. You could probably fire it in a busy street and no one would take much notice.

I looked him in the eye and then put a bullet into the back of his right hand. He jerked his hand convulsively and a strangled cry broke from his lips as the muzzle of the pistol centred on his head again. The noise of the shot hadn't even rattled the windows.

I said, 'I may not shoot to kill you but I'll cut you to pieces bit by bit if you don't behave yourself. I hear from Kennikin that I'm a fair hand at surgical operations too. There are worse things than getting yourself shot dead. Ask Kennikin some time.'

Blood oozed from the back of his hand and stained the carpet, but he lay still, staring at the gun in my hand. His tongue came out and licked dry lips. 'You bloody bastard!' he whispered.

The telephone rang.

We stared at each other for the time it took to ring four times. I walked around him, keeping clear of his legs, and I picked up the telephone whole and entire complete with base. I dumped it next to him, and said, 'You'll answer that, and you'll remember two things – I want to hear *both* ends of the conversation and that there are plenty of other parts of your fat anatomy. I can work on.' I jerked the gun. 'Pick it up.'

Awkwardly he picked up the handset with his left hand. 'Yes?'

I jerked the gun again and he held up the telephone so that I could hear the scratchy voice. 'This is Kennikin.'

'Be natural,' I whispered.

Slade licked his lips. 'What is it?' he asked hoarsely.

'What's the matter with your voice?' said Kennikin.

Slade grunted, his eye on the gun I held. 'I have a cold. What do you want?'

'I've got the girl.'

There was a silence and I could feel my heart thumping in my chest. Slade went pale as he watched my finger curl around the trigger and slowly take up the pressure. I breathed, 'Where from?'

Slade coughed nervously. 'Where did you find her?'

'At Keflavik Airport – hiding in the Icelandair office. We know her brother is a pilot, and I had the idea of looking for her there. We took her out without any trouble.'

That made it true. 'Where now?' I whispered into Slade's ear and put the gun to the nape of his neck.

He asked the question, and Kennikin said, 'In the usual place. When can I expect you?'

'You'll be right out.' I pressed the muzzle harder into his fat and felt him shiver.

'I'll leave straight away,' said Slade, and I quickly cut the contact by depressing the telephone bar.

I jumped back fast in case he tried to start something, but he just lay there gazing at the telephone. I felt like screaming, but there was no time for that. I said, 'Slade, you were wrong – I *can* kill you. You know that now, don't you?'

For the first time I detected fear in him. His fat jowl developed a tremor and his lower lip shook so that he looked like a fat boy about to burst into tears. I said, 'Where's the usual place?'

He looked at me with hatred and said nothing. I was in a quandary; if I killed him I would have got nothing out of him, yet I didn't want to damage him too much because I wanted him fit to walk the streets of Reykjavik without occasioning undue attention. Still, he didn't know my problem, so I said, 'You'll still be alive when I've finished with you, but you'll wish you weren't.'

I put a bullet just by his left ear and he jerked violently. Again the noise of the shot was very small and I think he must have doctored the cartridges by taking out some of the powder to reduce the bang. It's an old trick when you want to shoot without drawing notice to yourself and, if done carefully and the gun is fired at not too great a range, the bullet is still lethal. It's much better than using a silencer which is a much overrated contraption and dangerous to the user. A silencer is good for one quiet shot – after that the steel wool packing becomes compressed and the back pressure builds up so high that the user is in danger of blowing off his own hand.

I said, 'I'm a good shot, but not all that good. I intended to put that bullet exactly where I did, but only you know the accuracy of this popgun. I'm inclined to think it throws to the left a bit, so if I try to clip your right ear you stand a fair chance of stopping one in the skull.'

I shifted the gun a little and took aim. He broke – his nerve gone completely. 'For God's sake, stop!' This sort of Russian roulette wasn't to his taste.

I sighted on his right ear. 'Where's the usual place?'

There was a sheen of sweat on his face. 'At Thingvallavatn.'

'The house to which I was taken after Geysir?'

'That's it.'

'You'd better be right,' I said. 'Because I have no time to waste in chasing about Southern Iceland.' I lowered the gun and Slade's expression changed to one of relief. 'Don't start cheering yet,' I advised. 'I hope you don't think I'm going to leave you here.'

I went to the stand at the bottom of the bed and flipped open the lid of his suitcase. I took out a clean shirt and tossed it to him. 'Rip some strips off that and bind up your hand. Stay on the floor and don't get any smart ideas such as throwing it at me.'

While he tore up the shirt awkwardly I rummaged about in the suitcase and came up with two clips of .32 ammunition. I dropped them into my pocket then went to the wardrobe and took out Slade's topcoat, the pockets of which I had already searched. 'Stand up facing the wall and put that on.'

I watched him carefully, alert for any trickery. I knew that if I made one false step he would take full advantage of it. A man who could worm his way into the heart of British Intelligence hadn't done it by being stupid. The mistakes he had made weren't such as would normally have discommoded him and he had done his damnedest to rectify them by eliminating me. If I weren't careful he could still pull it off.

I picked up his passport and his wallet from the bed and pocketed them, then threw his hat across the room so that it landed at his feet. 'We're going for a walk. You'll keep that bandaged hand in your coat pocket and you'll behave like the English gentleman you're not. One wrong move from you and I'll shoot you dead and take my chances, and I don't care if it has to be in the middle of Hafnarstraeti. I hope you realize that Kennikin did exactly the wrong thing in taking Elin.'

He spoke to the wall. 'Back in Scotland I warned you about that. I told you not to let her get involved.'

'Very thoughtful of you,' I said. 'But if anything happens to her you're a dead man. You may have been right about my inability to kill before, but I hope you're not counting on it now because one of Elin's nail parings is of more importance to me than the whole of your lousy body. You'd better believe that, Slade. I protect my own.'

I saw him shudder. 'I believe you,' he said quietly.

I really think he did. He knew he had encountered something more primitive than patriotism or the loyalty of a man to his group. This was much more fundamental, and while I might not have killed him because he was a spy I would kill without mercy any man who got between me and Elin.

'All right,' I said. 'Pick up your hat and let's go.'

I escorted him into the corridor, made him lock the door, and then took the key. I had one of his jackets draped over my arm to hide the gun, and I walked one pace behind him and to the right. We left the hotel and walked the streets of Reykjavik to where I had left Nordlinger's car. 'You'll get behind the wheel,' I said.

We performed an intricate ballet in getting into the car. While unlocking it and getting him settled I had to make sure that never for one moment could he take advantage and, at the same time, our antics had to look reasonably normal to the passers-by. At last I managed to get him seated and myself behind him in the rear.

'Now you'll drive,' I said.

'But my hand,' he protested. 'I don't think I can.'

'You'll do it. I don't care how much it hurts – but you'll do it. And never for one moment will you exceed thirty miles an hour. You won't even think of putting the car into a ditch or crashing it in any other way. And the reason you won't think of such things is because of this.' I touched his neck with the cold metal of the pistol.

'This will be behind you all the way. Just imagine that you're a prisoner and I'm one of Stalin's boys back in the bad old days. The approved method of execution was an unexpected bullet in the back of the head, wasn't it? But if you do anything naughty this is one bullet you can expect for sure. Now, take off, and do it carefully – my trigger finger is allergic to sudden jerks.'

I didn't have to tell him where to drive. He drove along the Tjarnargata with the duck-strewn waters of the Tjörnin lake on our left, past the University of Iceland, and so into Miklabraut and out of town. He drove in silence and once on the open road he obeyed orders and never let the speed drift above thirty miles an hour. I think this was less out of sheer obedience and more because changing gears hurt his hand.

After a while he said, 'What do you think you're going to gain by this, Stewart?'

I didn't answer him: I was busy turning out the contents of his wallet. There wasn't anything in it of interest – no plans for the latest guided missile or laser death ray that a master spy and double agent might have been expected to carry. I transferred the thick sheaf of currency and the credit cards to my own wallet; I could use the money – I was out of pocket on this operation – and should he escape he would find the shortage of funds a serious disability.

He tried again. 'Kennikin won't believe anything you say, you know. He won't be bluffed.'

'He'd better be,' I said. 'For your sake. But there'll be no bluff.'

'Your work will be cut out convincing Kennikin of that,' said Slade.

'You'd better not push that one too hard,' I said coldly. 'I might convince him by taking him your right hand – the one with the ring on the middle finger.'

That shut him up for a while and he concentrated on his driving. The Chevrolet bounced and rolled on its soft springing as the wheels went over the corrugated dips and rises of the road. We would have got a smoother ride had we travelled faster but, as it was, we climbed up and down every minuscule hill and valley. I dared not order him to speed up, much as I wanted to get to Elin; 30 mph gave me the leeway both to shoot Slade and get out safely should he deliberately run the car off the road.

Presently I said, 'I notice you've given up your protestations of innocence.'

'You wouldn't believe me no matter what I told you – so why should I try?'

He had a point there. 'I'd just like to clear up a few things, though. How did you know I was going to meet Jack Case at Geysir?'

'When you make a call on open radio to London you can expect people to listen,' he said.

'You listened and you told Kennikin.'

He half-turned his head. 'How do you know it wasn't Kennikin who listened?'

'Keep your eyes on the road,' I said sharply.

'All right, Stewart,' he said. 'There's no point in fencing. I admit it all. You've been right all along the line. Not that it will do you much good; you'll never get out of Iceland.' He coughed. 'What gave me away?'

'Calvados,' I said.

'Calvados!' he repeated. He was at a loss. 'What the hell is that supposed to mean?'

'You knew that Kennikin drinks Calvados. No one else did, except me.'

'I see! That's why you asked Taggart about Kennikin's drinking habits. I was wondering about that.' His shoulders seemed to sag and he said musingly, 'It's the little things. You cover every possibility; you train for years, you get yourself a new identity – a new personality – and you think you're safe.' He shook his head slowly. 'And then it's a little thing like a bottle of Calvados that you saw a man drink years before. But surely that wasn't enough?'

'It started me thinking. There was something else, of course. Lindholm – who was conveniently in the right place at the right time – but that could have been coincidence. I didn't get around to suspecting you until you sent in Philips at Asbyrgi – that was a bad mistake. You ought to have sent Kennikin.'

'He wasn't immediately available.' Slade clicked his tongue. 'I ought to have gone in myself.'

I laughed gently. 'Then you'd be where Philips is now. Count your blessings, Slade.' I looked ahead through the windscreen and then leaned forward to check the position of his hands and feet to make sure he wasn't conning me – lulling me with conversation. 'I suppose there was a man called Slade once.'

'A boy,' said Slade. 'We found him in Finland during the war. He was fifteen then. His parents were British and had been killed in a bombing raid by our Stormoviks. We took him into our care, and later there was a substitution – me.'

'Something like Gordon Lonsdale,' I said. 'I'm surprised you survived inspection in the turmoil after the Lonsdale case.'

'So am I,' he said bleakly.

'What happened to young Slade?'

'Siberia perhaps. But I don't think so.'

I didn't think so either. Young Master Slade would have been interrogated to a fare-thee-well and then dispatched to some anonymous hole in the ground.

I said, 'What's your name – the real Russian one, I mean?'

He laughed. 'You know, I've quite forgotten. I've been Slade for the better part of my life, for so long that my early life in Russia seems like something I once dreamed.'

'Come off it! No one forgets his name.'

'I think of myself as Slade,' he said. 'I think we'll stick to it.'

I watched his hand hovering over the button of the glove compartment. 'You'd better stick to driving,' I said drily. 'There's only one thing you'll find in the glove compartment and that's a quick, sweet death.'

Without hurrying too much he withdrew his hand and put it back where it belonged – on the wheel. I could see that his first fright was over and he was regaining confidence. More than ever I would have to watch him.

An hour after leaving Reykjavik we arrived at the turn-off to Lake Thingvallavatn and Kennikin's house. Watching Slade, I saw that he was about to ignore it, so I said, 'No funny business – you know the way.'

He hastily applied the brakes and swung off to the right and we bumped over a road that was even worse. As near as I could remember from the night drive I had taken with Kennikin along this same road the house was about five miles from the turn-off. I leaned forward and kept one eye on the odometer, one eye on the countryside to see if I could recognize anything, and the other on Slade. Having three eyes would be useful to a man in my position, but I had to make do with two.

I spotted the house in the distance or, at least, what I thought was the house, although I could not be entirely sure since I had previously only seen it in darkness. I laid the gun against Slade's neck. 'You drive past it,' I said. 'You don't speed up and you don't slow down – you just keep the same pace until I tell you to stop.'

As we went past the drive that led to the house I glanced sideways at it. It was about four hundred yards off the road and I was certain this was the place. I was absolutely sure when I spotted the lava flow ahead and to the left where I had encountered Jack Case. I tapped Slade's shoulder. 'In a little while you'll see a level place to the left where they've been scooping out lava for road-making. Pull in there.'

I kicked the side of the door and swore loudly as though I had hurt myself. All I wanted to do was to make noise enough to cover the sound of my taking the clip out of the pistol and working the slide to eject the round in the breech. That would leave me unarmed and it wouldn't do for Slade to know it. I was going to hit him very hard with the butt of the pistol and to do that with a loaded gun was to ask for a self-inflicted gut shot.

He pulled off the road and even before the car rolled to a halt I let him have it, striking sideways in a chopping motion at the base of his neck. He moaned and fell forward and his feet slipped on the foot pedals. For one alarming moment the car bucked and lurched but then the engine stalled and it came to a standstill.

I dipped into my pocket and put a full clip into the pistol and jacked a round into the breech before I examined Slade at close quarters. What I had done to him was in a fair way towards breaking his neck, but I found that his head lolled forward because I had merely knocked him cold. I made sure of that by taking the hand which had a bullet hole through the palm and squeezing it hard. He didn't move a muscle.

I suppose I should have killed him. The knowledge in his head culled from his years in the Department was a deadly danger, and my duty as a member of the Department was to see that the knowledge was permanently erased. I didn't even think of it. I needed Slade as one hostage to set against another and I had no intention of exchanging dead hostages.

E. M. Forster once said that if he had to choose between betraying his country and betraying his friend then he hoped he would have the guts to betray his country. Elin was more than my friend – she was my life – and if the only way I could get her was to give up Slade then I would do so.

I got out of the car and opened the boot. The sacking which was wrapped around the rifles came in handy for tearing into strips and binding Slade hand and foot. I then put him in the boot and slammed the lid on him.

The Remington carbine I had taken from Philips I hid in a crevice of the lava close to the car, together with its ammunition, but Fleet's piece of light artillery I slung over my shoulder as I walked towards the house. It was very likely that I would need it.

II

The last time I had been anywhere near this house it had been dark and I had plunged away not knowing the lie of the land. Now, in the daylight, I found I could get to within a hundred yards of the front door without breaking cover. The ground was broken and three big lava flows had bled across the landscape during some long-gone eruption and had hardened and solidified while in full spate to form jagged ridges full of crevices and holes. The ever-present moss grew thickly, covering the spiky lava with soft vegetable cushions. The going was slow and it took me half an hour to get as close to the house as I dared.

I lay on the moss and studied it. It was Kennikin's hide-away, all right, because a window was broken in the room where I had been kept captive and there were no curtains at that window. The last time I had seen them they had been going up in flames.

A car stood outside the front door and I noticed that the air over the bonnet shimmered a little. That meant that the engine was still hot and someone had just arrived. Although my own journey had been slow, Kennikin had farther to travel from Keflavik – there was a good chance that whatever he intended to do to Elin to get her to tell him where I was had not yet begun. And, possibly, he would wait for Slade before starting. For Elin's sake I hoped so.

I loosened a big slab of moss and pushed Fleet's rifle out of sight beneath it, together with the ammunition for it. I had brought it along as insurance – it was useless in the boot of the car, anyway. It would also be useless in the house too, but now it was tucked away within a fast sprint of the front door.

I withdrew and began a painful retreat across the lava beds until I reached the driveway, and the walk towards the house was the longest distance I have ever walked, psychologically if not physically. I felt as a condemned man probably feels on his way to the scaffold. I was walking quite openly to the front door of the house and if anyone was keeping a watch I hoped his curiosity would get the better of him enough to ask *why* I was coming instead of shooting me down ten paces from the threshold.

I crunched my way to the car and casually put out my hand. I had been right; the engine was still warm. There was a flicker of movement at one of the windows so I carried on and walked to the door. I pressed the bell-push and heard the genteel peal of chimes inside the house.

Nothing happened for a while but soon I heard boots crushing loose lava chips and I looked sideways to see a man coming around the corner of the house to my left. I looked to the right and saw another, and both were strolling towards me with intent expressions on their faces.

I smiled at them and jabbed the bell-push again and the chimes jingled softly just as in any house in the stockbroker belt. The door opened and Kennikin stood there. He had a gun in his hand.

'I'm the man from the Prudential,' I said pleasantly. 'How's your insurance, Vaslav?'

TEN

Kennikin looked at me expressionlessly and his pistol was pointing at my heart. 'Why shouldn't I kill you now?'

'That's what I've come to talk to you about,' I said. 'It really would be a bad thing if you did.' I heard footsteps behind me as the outflankers moved in for the kill. 'Aren't you interested to know why I'm here? Why I walked up and rang the bell?'

'It did cross my mind that it was strange,' said Kennikin. 'You won't object to a slight search?'

'Not at all,' I said, and felt heavy hands on me. They took Slade's gun and the clips of ammunition. 'This is most inhospitable,' I said. 'Keeping me at the door like this. Besides, what will the neighbours think?'

'We have no neighbours for some considerable distance,' said Kennikin, and looked at me with a puzzled expression. 'You're very cool, Stewartsen. I think you must have gone mad. But come in.'

'Thanks,' I said, and followed him into the familiar room where we had talked before. I glanced at the burnt patches on the carpet and said, 'Heard any good explosions lately?'

'That was very clever,' said Kennikin. He waved his pistol. 'Sit down in the same chair. You will observe there is no fire.' He sat down opposite me. 'Before you say anything I must tell you that we have the girl, Elin Ragnarsdottir.'

I stretched out my legs. 'What on earth do you want her for?'

'We were going to use her to get you,' he said. 'But it seems that is no longer necessary.'

'Then there's no need to keep her. You can let her go.'

Kennikin smiled. 'You're really funny, Stewartsen. It's a pity the English music hall has gone into eclipse; you could make quite a good living as a comedian.'

'You ought to hear me wow them in the working men's clubs,' I said. 'That should appeal to a good Marxist such as yourself. But I wasn't being funny, Vaslav. She is going to walk out of this house unharmed, and you are going to let her go.'

He narrowed his eyes. 'You'd better elaborate on that.'

'I walked in here on my own feet,' I said. 'You don't think I'd do that unless I could trump your ace. You see, I've got Slade. Tit for tat.' His eyes opened wide, and I said, 'But I forget – you don't know a man called Slade. You told me so yourself, and we all know that Vaslav Viktorovich Kennikin is an honourable man who doesn't stoop to fibs.'

'Even supposing I did know this Slade, what proof have you of this? Your word?'

I put my hand to my breast pocket and stopped sharply as his gun came up. 'Not to worry,' I said. 'But do you mind if I dig for a bit of evidence?' I took the jerk of the gun as assent and extracted Slade's passport from my pocket and tossed it to him.

He stooped to where it had fallen and picked it up, flicking open the pages with one hand. He studied the photograph intently and then snapped the passport closed. 'This is a passport made out in the name of Slade. It is no proof of possession of the man. To hold a passport is meaningless; I, myself, possess many passports in many names. In any case, I know of no Slade. The name means nothing to me.'

I laughed. 'It's so unlike you to talk to yourself. I know for a fact that not two hours ago you spoke to a non-existent man at the Hotel Borg in Reykjavik. This is what you said, and this is what he said.' I recited the telephone conversation verbatim. 'Of course, I could have been wrong about what Slade said, since he doesn't exist.'

Kennikin's face tightened. 'You have dangerous knowledge.'

'I have more than that – I have Slade. I had him even as he spoke to you. My gun was in his fat neck.'

'And where is he now?'

'For Christ's sake, Vaslav!' I said. 'You're talking to me, not some muscle-bound, half-witted ape like Ilyich.'

He shrugged. 'I had to try.'

I grinned. 'You'll have to do a bloody sight better than that. I can tell you this, though – if you go looking for him, by the time you find him he'll be cold meat. Those are my orders.'

Kennikin pulled at his lower lip, thinking deeply. 'Orders you have received – or orders you have given?'

I leaned forward, preparing to lie heroically. 'Let's make no mistake about this, Vaslav. Those are orders I've given. If you, or anyone who even smells like you, gets close to Slade, then Slade dies. Those are the orders I have given and they'll be followed, you may depend upon it.'

At all costs I had to drive out of his mind any suggestion that I had been given orders. The only man who could give me orders was Taggart, and if he had issued such orders then the game was blown as far as Slade was concerned. If Kennikin believed for one minute that Taggart had penetrated Slade's cover then he'd cut his losses by killing me and Elin, and get the hell back to Russia as fast as he could move.

I buttressed the argument by saying, 'I may be rapped over the knuckles when the Department catches up with me, but until then those orders stand – Slade will catch a bullet if you go near him.'

Kennikin smiled grimly. 'And who will pull the trigger? You've said you're working independently of Taggart, and I know you're alone.'

I said, 'Don't sell the Icelanders short, Vaslav. I know them very well and I have a lot of friends here – and so does Elin Ragnarsdottir. They don't like what you've been doing in their country and they don't like one of their own being put in danger.'

I leaned back in the chair. 'Look at it this way. This is a biggish country with a small population. Everyone knows everyone else. Damn it, everyone is related to everyone else if you push it back far enough – and the Icelanders do. I've never known a people, other than the Scots, who are so genealogically minded. So everyone cares what happens to Elin Ragnarsdottir. This isn't a mass society where people don't even know their next-door neighbour. By taking Elin Ragnarsdottir you've laid yourself wide open.'

Kennikin looked thoughtful. I hoped I had given him something to chew over for a long time, but I didn't have the time so I pushed him. 'I want the girl down here in this room – intact and in one piece. If any harm has come to her then you've made a big mistake.'

He regarded me keenly, and said, 'It's obvious you haven't informed the Icelandic authorities. If you had, the police would be here.'

'You're so right,' I said. 'I haven't, and for good reasons. Firstly, it would cause an international brouhaha, which would be lamentable. Secondly, and more important, all the authorities could do would be to deport Slade. My friends are tougher-minded – they'll kill him if necessary.' I leaned over and jabbed Kennikin in the knee with a hard forefinger. 'And *then* they'll blow you off to the police, and you'll be up to your neck in uniforms and diplomats.'

I straightened up. 'I want to see the girl, and I want to see her now.'

'You talk straight,' he said. 'But, then, you always did . . .' His voice tailed away, and he whispered, '. . . until you betrayed me.'

'I don't see you have any options,' I said. 'And just to screw it tighter I'll tell you something else. There's a time limit. If my friends don't get the word from Elin's own lips within three hours then Slade gets what's coming to him.'

I could see Kennikin visibly debating it with himself. He had to make a choice and a damned thin one it was. He said, 'Your Icelandic friends – do they know who Slade is?'

'You mean that he's in Russian Intelligence?' I said. 'Or in British Intelligence, for that matter?' I shook my head. 'All they know is that he's a hostage for Elin. I didn't tell them anything else about him. They think you're a crowd of gangsters and, by God, they're not far wrong!'

That clinched it. He thought he had me isolated, that only Elin and I knew the truth that Slade was a double agent. Given that premise which, God knows, was true enough since my Icelandic friends were pure invention, then he could do a deal. He was faced with the choice of sacrificing Slade, who had been laboriously built up over many years into a superlative Trojan Horse, for a no-account Icelandic girl. The choice was obvious. He would be no worse off than before he had taken her, and his weasel mind would already be working out ways of double-crossing me.

He sighed. 'At least you can see the girl.' He signalled to the man standing behind him who left the room.

I said, 'You've really queered this one, Vaslav. I don't think Bakayev is going to be too cheerful about it. It'll be Siberia for sure this time, if not worse – and all because of Slade. It's funny, isn't it? You spent four years in Ashkhabad because of Slade, and now what do you have to look forward to?'

There was a look almost of pain in his eyes. 'Is it true – what you said about Slade and Sweden?'

'Yes, Vaslav,' I said. 'It was Slade who cut the ground from under you there.'

He shook his head irritably. 'There's one thing I don't understand,' he said. 'You say you are willing to trade Slade for the girl. Why should a member of your Department do that?'

'I swear to God you don't listen to me. I'm not a member of the Department – I quit four years ago.'

He pondered. 'Even so – where are your loyalties?'

'My loyalties are my business,' I said curtly.

'The world well lost for a woman?' he asked mockingly. 'I've been cured of that way of thinking – and you were the doctor.'

'Now, you're not still harping on that,' I said. 'If you hadn't jumped when you should have fallen flat you'd have been killed decently.'

The door opened and Elin came in under escort. I was about to get up but subsided again as Kennikin lifted his pistol warningly. 'Hello, Elin; you'll forgive me if I don't get up.'

Her face was pale and when she saw me it acquired a bleak look. 'You, too!'

'I'm here by choice,' I said. 'Are you all right? They didn't hurt you?'

'Not more than was necessary,' she said. 'Just some arm twisting.' She put her hand to her wounded shoulder.

I smiled at her. 'I've come to collect you. We'll be leaving soon.'

'That's a matter of opinion,' said Kennikin. 'How do you expect to do it?'

'In the normal way – through the front door,' I said.

'Just like that!' Kennikin smiled. 'And what about Slade?'

'He'll be returned unharmed.'

'My dear Alan! Not long ago you accused *me* of being unrealistic. You'll have to work out a better exchange mechanism than that.'

I grinned at him. 'I didn't think you'd fall for it but, as you said, one has to try. I daresay we can work out something equitable.'

'Such as?'

I rubbed my chin. 'Such as sending Elin away. She'll contact our friends and then you exchange Slade for me. The arrangements can be made by telephone.'

'That sounds logical,' said Kennikin. 'But I'm not sure it's reasonable. Two for one, Alan?'

'It's a pity you can't ask Slade if it's reasonable or not.'

'You make a point.' Kennikin moved restlessly. He was trying to find the flaws in it. 'We get Slade back unharmed?'

I smiled apologetically. 'Er . . . well – not entirely. He's been leaking blood through a hole, but it's minor and not fatal. And he might have a headache – but why should you care about that?'

'Why, indeed?' Kennikin stood up. 'I think I can go along with you on this, but I'd like to think about it a little more.'

'Not for too long,' I said warningly. 'Remember the time limit.'

Elin said, 'Have you really captured Slade?'

I stared at her, trying to pass an unspoken message and hoping to God she didn't let me down. 'Yes. Our friends are taking care of him – Valtýr is in charge.'

'Valtýr!' She nodded. 'He's big enough to handle anyone.'

I switched my eyes back to Kennikin and tried not to show too much relief at the way Elin had played that one. 'Buck it up, Vaslav,' I said. 'Time's a-wasting.'

He came to the decision quickly. 'Very well, it shall be as you say.' He looked at his watch. 'I also shall lay down a time limit. If there is no telephone call within two hours then you will die regardless of what may happen to Slade.' He swung on his heel and faced Elin. 'Remember that, Elin Ragnarsdottir.'

'There's just one thing,' I said. 'I'll have to talk to Elin before she leaves to tell her where to find Valtýr. She doesn't know, you see.'

'Then you'll do it in my hearing.'

I gave him a pained look. 'Don't be an idiot. You'd know as much as I do, and that might be unwise. You'd know where Slade is and you might be tempted to get him out. And where would that leave me?' I stood cautiously. 'I talk to Elin privately or not at all. It's another stalemate, Vaslav, but I'm sure you understand that I have to look out for my own skin.'

'Yes, I'm sure you do,' he said contemptuously. He gestured with the gun. 'You may talk in the corner, but I remain in the room.'

'Fair enough.' I jerked my head at Elin and we walked over to the corner. I stood with my back to Kennikin because, for all I knew, lip-reading in six languages might have been one of his minor talents.

Elin whispered, 'Have you really got Slade?'

'Yes, but Valtýr doesn't know about it, nor anyone else. I've sold Kennikin a credible story but not the true one. But I *have* got Slade.'

She put her hand to my chest. 'They took me so quickly,' she said. 'I couldn't do anything. I was afraid, Alan.'

'That doesn't matter now,' I said. 'You're going to walk out of here, and this is how you do it. You . . .'

'But you are staying.' There was pain in her eyes.

'I won't be staying long if you do as I say. Listen carefully. You'll leave here, walk up to the road and turn left. About half a mile along you'll come to a big dream-boat of an American car. Whatever you do, don't open the boot. Just climb into it and go like a bat out of hell to Keflavik. Got that?'

She nodded. 'What do I do there?'

'See Lee Nordlinger. Raise a storm and demand to see a CIA agent. Lee and everyone else will deny having such an article on the premises, but if you persist long enough they'll dig one up. You can tell Lee it's about the gadget he tested; that might help. Tell the CIA man the whole story and then tell him to open the boot of the car.' I grinned wryly. 'But don't call it the boot or he won't know what the hell you're talking about. Call it the trunk.'

'So what is in there?'

'Slade,' I said.

She stared at me. 'He's *here*! Just outside this house!'

'It was all I could do at short notice,' I said. 'I had to act quickly.'

'But what about you?'

'Get the CIA man to make the telephone call. You'll have just on two hours from the time you leave here, so you'll have to be bloody persuasive. If you can't do it in time or if the CIA man won't be persuaded, then make the call yourself and spin Kennikin some kind of yarn. Set up a meeting to exchange me for Slade. It might be phoney but it will buy me time.'

'What if the Americans won't believe me?'

'Tell them you know about Fleet and McCarthy. Tell them you'll give it to the Icelandic newspapers. That should produce some kind of reaction. Oh, yes; and tell them that all your friends know exactly where you are – just as insurance.' I was trying to cover all the possibilities.

She closed her eyes briefly as she memorized her instructions. When she opened them, she asked, 'Is Slade alive?'

'Of course he is. I told Kennikin the truth about that. He's damaged but alive.'

She said, 'I was thinking the CIA might believe Slade rather than me. He might even know the CIA people at Keflavik.'

'I know,' I said. 'But we have to take that risk. That's why you must tell the whole story before producing Slade. Get your oar in first. If you pitch it really hot they won't just let him walk out.'

She didn't seem too happy about that, and neither was I, but it was the best we could do. I said, 'Make it fast, but not so fast that you have an accident in that car.' I put my hand under her chin and tipped her head up. 'Everything will be all right. You'll see.'

She blinked rapidly. 'There's something you must know. That gun you gave me – I've still got it.'

It was my turn to blink. *'What!'*

'They didn't search me. I have it on me – in the holster under this anorak.'

I looked at her. Her anorak was admittedly very loose and no sign of the gun was visible. Someone had slipped. It was unlikely that an Icelandic girl would be armed, but even so it was bad workmanship. No wonder Kennikin went off pop periodically about the quality of his team. Elin said, 'Can I pass it to you safely?'

'Not a chance,' I said regretfully, aware of Kennikin at my back. He would be watching like a hawk, and a Smith & Wesson .38 pistol isn't something you can palm in your hand like a playing-card. 'You'd better keep it. Who knows, you might need it.'

I put my hand on her good shoulder and drew her towards me. Her lips were cold and hard under mine, and she trembled slightly. I drew back my head, and said, 'You'd better go,' and turned to face Kennikin.

'Very touching,' he said.

'There's one thing,' I said. 'Your time limit is too short. Two hours isn't enough.'

'It will have to do,' he said uncompromisingly.

'Be reasonable, Vaslav. She has to drive through Reykjavik. The day is getting on and by the time she reaches town it will be just after five o'clock – right in the middle of the rush hour when people are going home. You wouldn't want to lose Slade because of a traffic jam, would you?'

'You're not thinking of Slade,' he said. 'You're thinking of yourself. You're thinking of the bullet in your head.'

'Maybe I am, but you'd better think of Slade because if I'm dead then so is he.'

He nodded shortly. 'Three hours,' he said. 'Not a minute more.'

Kennikin was a logical man and susceptible to a reasoned argument. I had won Elin another hour in which to convince the top brass at Keflavik. 'She goes alone,' I said. 'No one follows her.'

'That is understood.'

'Then give her the telephone number she is to call. It would be a pity if she walked out without it.'

Kennikin took out a notebook and scribbled down a number, then ripped out the sheet and gave it to her. 'No tricks,' he said. 'Especially no police. If there is an undue number of strangers around here, then he dies. You'd better know that I mean it.'

In a colourless voice she said, 'I understand. There will be no tricks.'

She looked at me and there was something in her eyes that made my heart turn over, and then Kennikin took her by the elbow and led her to the door. A minute later I saw her through the window, walking away from the house up towards the road.

Kennikin returned. 'We'll put you somewhere safe,' he said, and jerked his head at the man who held a gun on me.

I was led upstairs and into an empty room. Kennikin surveyed the bare walls and shook his head sadly. 'They did these things so much better in medieval times,' he said.

I was in no mood for light conversation but I played along with him. I had the idea that, perhaps, he wouldn't mind at all if Slade didn't show up. Then he would be able to get down to the delightful business of killing me – slowly. And I had put the idea into his mind; I had tried to antagonize him towards Slade. Maybe it hadn't been such a good idea.

I said, 'What do you mean?'

'In those days they built with stone.' He strode to the window and thumped on the exterior wall. It responded with a wooden hollowness. 'This place is built like an eggshell.'

That was true enough. The chalets around Thingvallavatn are holiday cottages, not designed for permanent occupancy. A timber frame, skinned on each side with thin planking and with a filling of foamed polystyrene for insulation, finished off with a skim of plaster maybe half an inch thick on the interior to make the place look nice. The nearest thing to a permanent tent.

Kennikin went to the opposite wall and rapped on it with his knuckles. It echoed even more hollowly. 'You could get through this partition wall in fifteen minutes, using nothing more than your hands. Therefore this man will stay in here with you.'

'You needn't worry,' I said sourly. 'I'm not Superman.'

'You don't need to be Superman to tangle the feet of the incompetents I've been given for this operation,' said Kennikin, equally sourly. 'You've proved that already. But I think the orders I give now will penetrate the thickest head.' He turned to the man with the gun. 'Stewartsen will sit in that corner. You will stand in front of the door. Do you understand?'

'Yes.'

'If he moves, shoot him. Understand?'

'Yes.'

'If he speaks, shoot him. Understand?'

'Yes.'

'If he does anything else at all, shoot him. Understand?'

'Yes,' said the man with the gun stolidly.

Kennikin's orders weren't leaving much room for manoeuvre. He said musingly, 'Now, have I forgotten anything? Oh, yes! You said that Slade had a hole in him – right?'

'Not much of one,' I said. 'Just in the hand.'

He nodded, and said to the guard, 'When you shoot him, don't kill him. Shoot him in the stomach.' He turned on his heel and left the room. The door slammed behind him.

II

I looked at the guard and the guard looked right back at me. His gun was trained on my belly and didn't deviate a hair's-breadth. With his other hand he gestured wordlessly towards the corner, so I backed into it until my shoulder-blades touched and then bent my knees until I was squatting on my heels.

He looked at me expressionlessly. 'Sit!' he said economically.

I sat. He wasn't going to be bluffed. He stood in front of the door about fifteen feet away and he was impregnable. He had the look of a man who would obey orders to the letter; if I rushed him I'd catch a bullet and I couldn't even con him into doing anything stupid. It was going to be a long three hours.

Kennikin had been right. Left alone in the room and I'd have gone through the partition wall, and it wouldn't have taken me any fifteen minutes either. True, once through the wall I would still be in the house, but I'd be in an unexpected place, and surprise, as all generals know, wins battles. Now that Elin was gone I was prepared to do anything to get away, and Kennikin knew it.

I looked at the window. All I could see was a small patch of blue sky and a fleecy cloud drifting by. The time oozed on, maybe half an hour, and I heard the crunch of tyres as a car drew up outside. I didn't know how many men had been in the house when I arrived, although I knew of three, but now there were more and the odds had lengthened.

I turned my wrist slowly and drew back the cuff of my jacket to look at my watch, hoping to God that the guard would not interpret that as an unnatural action. I kept my eye on him and he looked back at me blankly, so I lowered my gaze to see what time it was. It had not been half an hour – only fifteen minutes had passed. It was going to be a longer three hours than I had thought.

Five minutes after that there was a tap at the door and I heard the raised voice of Kennikin. 'I'm coming in.'

The guard stepped to one side as the door opened. Kennikin came in and said, 'I see you've been a good boy.' There was something in the way he said it that made me uneasy. He was too damned cheerful.

'I'd like to go over what you told me again,' he said. 'According to you, Slade is being kept with friends of yours – Icelandic friends – I think you said. These friends will kill him unless they get you in exchange. I think that was the argument. Am I right?'

'Yes,' I said.

He smiled. 'Your girl-friend is waiting downstairs. Shall we join her?' He waved largely. 'You can get up – you will not be shot.'

I stood up stiffly, and wondered what the hell had gone wrong. I was escorted downstairs and found Elin standing in front of the empty fireplace flanked by Ilyich. Her face was pale as she whispered, 'I'm sorry, Alan.'

'You must think I'm stupid,' said Kennikin. 'You don't suppose I thought you had walked here? You tramped up to the front door and immediately I wondered where you had left your car. You had to have a car because this is no country for walking, so I sent a man to look for it even before you rang the bell.'

'You always were logical,' I said.

He was enjoying himself. 'And what do you suppose my man found? A large American car complete with key. He had not been there long when this young lady came up in a very great hurry, so he brought her – and the car – back here. You see, he was unaware of the agreement we had reached. We can't blame him for that, can we?'

'Of course not,' I said flatly. *But had he opened the boot?* 'I don't see that this makes any difference.'

'No, you wouldn't. But my man had standing orders. He knew we were looking for a small package containing electronic equipment, and so he searched the car. He didn't find the package.'

Kennikin stopped and looked at me expectantly. He was really relishing this. I said, 'Do you mind if I sit down? And for God's sake, give me a cigarette – I've run out.'

'My dear Alan – but of course,' he said solicitously. 'Take your usual chair.' He produced his cigarette case and carefully lit my cigarette. 'Mr Slade is very angry with you. He doesn't like you at all.'

'Where is he?'

'In the kitchen having his hand bound up. You're a very good diagnostician, Alan; he *does* have a headache.'

My stomach felt as though it had a ball of lead in it. I drew on the cigarette, and said, 'All right; where do we go from here?'

'We carry on from where we left off the night we came here from Geysir. Nothing has changed.'

He was wrong – Elin was here. I said, 'So now you shoot me.'

'Perhaps. Slade wants to talk to you first.' He looked up. 'Ah, here he is.'

Slade looked bad. His face was grey and he staggered slightly as he walked in. When he came closer I saw that his eyes had a curiously unfocused appearance and I guessed he was still suffering from concussion. Someone had bound up his hand neatly with clean gauze bandages, but his clothes were rumpled and stained and his hair stood on end. As he was a man who usually cared very much for outward appearances, I guessed he was probably very disturbed.

I was right, and I found out how much he was disturbed pretty damned quick.

He walked up and looked down at me, and gestured with his left hand. 'Pick him up and take him over there – to the wall.'

I was grabbed before I could move. Someone put a hammer lock on me from behind and I was dragged from the chair and hustled across the room. As I was slammed against the wall, Slade said, 'Where's my gun?'

Kennikin shrugged. 'How should I know?'

'You must have taken it from Stewart.'

'Oh, that one.' Kennikin pulled it from his pocket. 'Is this it?'

Slade took the pistol and walked over to me. 'Hold his right hand against the wall,' he said, and held up his bandaged hand before my eyes. 'You did that, Stewart, so you know what's going to happen now.'

A hard hand pinned my wrist to the wall and Slade raised his gun. I had just sense enough and time enough to stop making a fist and to spread my fingers so he wouldn't shoot through them before he pulled the trigger and I took the bullet in the palm of my hand. Curiously enough, after the first stabbing shock it didn't hurt. All I felt was a dead numbness from shoulder to finger-tip. It would hurt soon enough as the shock wore off, but it didn't hurt then.

My head swam and I heard Elin scream, but the cry seemed to come from a long way away. When I opened my eyes I saw Slade looking at me unsmilingly. He said curtly, 'Take him back to his chair.' It had been a purely vindictive act of revenge and now it was over and he was back to business as usual.

I was dumped back into the chair and I raised my head to see Elin leaning against the chimney piece with tears streaming down her face. Then Slade moved between us and I lost sight of her.

'You know too much, Stewart,' he said. 'So you must die – you know that.'

'I know you'll do your best,' I said dully. I now knew why Slade had cracked in the hotel room because the same thing was happening to me. I found I couldn't string two consecutive thoughts together to make sense and I had a blinding headache. The penetration of a bullet into flesh has that effect.

Slade said, 'Who knows about me – apart from the girl?'

'No one,' I said. 'What about the girl?'

He shrugged. 'You'll be buried in the same grave.' He turned to Kennikin. 'He might be telling the truth. He's been on the run and he hasn't had a chance to let anyone know.'

'He might have written a letter,' said Kennikin doubtfully.

'That's a risk I'll have to take. I don't think Taggart has any suspicions. He might be annoyed because I've dropped out of sight but that will be all. I'll be a good boy and take the next plane back to London.' He lifted his wounded hand and grinned tightly at Kennikin. 'And I'll blame this on you.

I've been wounded trying to save this fool.' He reached out and kicked my leg.

'What about the electronic equipment?'

'What about it?'

Kennikin took out his cigarette case and selected a cigarette. 'It seems a pity not to complete the operation as planned. Stewartsen knows where it is, and I can get the information from him.'

'So you could,' said Slade thoughtfully. He looked down at me. 'Where is it, Stewart?'

'It's where you won't find it.'

'That car wasn't searched,' said Kennikin. 'When you were found in the boot everything else was forgotten.' He snapped out orders and his two men left the room. 'If it's in the car they'll find it.'

'I don't think it's in the car,' said Slade.

'I didn't think *you* were in the car,' said Kennikin waspishly. 'I wouldn't be at all surprised to find it there.'

'You may be right,' said Slade. His voice indicated that he didn't think so. He bent over me. 'You're going to die, Stewart – you may depend upon it. But there are many ways of dying. Tell us where the package is and you'll die cleanly and quickly. If not, I'll let Kennikin work on you.'

I kept my mouth firmly shut because I knew that if I opened it he would see the tremulous lower lip that is a sign of fear.

He stood aside. 'Very well. You can have him, Kennikin.' A vindictive note entered his voice. 'The best way to do it is to shoot him to pieces slowly. He threatened to do it to me.'

Kennikin stepped in front of me, gun in hand. 'Well, Alan; we come to the end of the road, you and I. Where is the radar equipment?'

Even then when facing his gun I noted that new piece of information. *Radar equipment.* I screwed up my face and managed a smile. 'Got another cigarette. Vaslav?'

No answering smile crossed his face. His eyes were bleak and his mouth was set in grim lines. He had the face of an executioner. 'There is no time for tradition – we are done with that foolery.'

I looked past him. Elin was still standing there, forgotten, and there was an expression of desperation on her face. But her hand was inside her anorak and coming out slowly, grasping something. The jolting realization came that she still had the gun!

That was enough to bring me to my senses fast. When all hope is gone and there is nothing more to look forward to than death one sinks into a morass of fatalism as I had done. But given the faintest hint that all is not lost and then a man can act – and my action now was to talk and talk fast.

I turned my head and spoke to Slade. I had to attract his attention to me so he would not even think of looking at Elin. 'Can't you stop him?' I pleaded.

'You can stop him. All you have to do is to tell him what we want to know.'

'I don't know about that,' I said. 'I'll still die, anyway.'

'But easier,' said Slade. 'Quickly and without pain.'

I looked back to Kennikin and, over his shoulder, saw that Elin had now withdrawn the pistol and it was in plain sight. She was fiddling with it and I hoped to God she remembered the sequence of actions she would have to go through before it would fire.

'Vaslav,' I said. 'You wouldn't do this to an old mate. Not you.'

His pistol centred on my belly and then dropped lower. 'You don't have to guess to know where I'm going to put the first bullet,' he said. His voice was deadly quiet. 'I'm just following Slade's orders – and my own inclination.'

'Tell us,' urged Slade, leaning forward.

I heard the snap of metal as Elin pulled back the slide of the pistol. So did Kennikin and he began to turn. Elin held the pistol in both hands and at arm's length and as Kennikin began his turn she fired and kept on firing.

I distinctly heard the impact of the first bullet in Kennikin's back. His hand tightened convulsively around his gun and it exploded in my face, the bullet burying itself in the arm of the chair next to my elbow. By then I was moving. I dived for Slade head first and rammed him in the paunch. My skull was harder than his belly and the breath came out of him in a great whoosh and he folded up and lay gasping on the floor.

I rolled over, aware that Elin was still shooting and that bullets were still whanging across the room. 'Stop!' I yelled.

I scooped up Slade's popgun and came up under Elin's elbow, grabbing her by the wrist. 'For Christ's sake, stop!'

I think she had shot off the whole magazine. The opposite wall was pock-marked and Kennikin lay in front of the chair in which I had been sitting. He lay face upwards gazing sightlessly at the ceiling. Elin had hit him twice more which was hardly surprising, considering she had been shooting at a range of less than six feet. Come to think of it, I was fortunate she hadn't put a bullet into me. There was a ragged red spot dead centre in Kennikin's forehead to prove he'd had the vitality to turn around and try to shoot back. Another bullet had caught him in the angle of the jaw and had blown off the bottom half of his face.

He was very dead.

I didn't stop to ruminate about how in the midst of life we are in death. I dragged Elin behind me and headed for the door. The boys outside might be prepared for the odd shot, especially after Slade's little demonstration, but the barrage Elin had laid down would be a matter for urgent investigation and that had to be discouraged.

At the door I let go of Elin's wrist with my left hand and swapped it for the gun I held in my wounded right hand. With a hole through the palm I couldn't possibly use a gun in that hand, even one with as little recoil as Slade's gimmicked weapon. I'm a lousy pistol shot at the best of times and even worse when shooting left-handed; but one of the nice things about gun battles is that the man you're shooting at doesn't ask you for a proficiency certificate before he decides to duck.

I glanced at Elin. She was obviously in a state of shock. No one can shoot a man to death without undergoing an emotional upheaval – especially for the first time, especially when a civilian, especially when a woman. I put a snap in my voice. 'You'll do exactly as I say without question. You'll follow me and you'll run like hell without any hesitation.'

She choked back a rasping sob and nodded breathlessly, so I went out of the front door, and I went out shooting. Even as we went someone took a crack at us from the *inside* of the house and a bullet clipped the architrave by my ear. But I had no time to worry about that because the pair who had been sent to search the Chevrolet were heading right at me.

I shot at them and kept on squeezing the trigger and they vanished from view, diving right and left, and we belted between them. There was a tinkle of glass as somebody decided it was quicker to smash a window than to open it, and then the bullets came after us. I dropped Slade's gun and again grasped Elin by the wrist and forced her to follow me in a zigzag. Behind I could hear the heavy thud of boots as someone chased us.

Then Elin was hit. The bullet pushed her forward into a stumble but, as her knees gave in, I managed to put my arm around her to hold her up. We were then ten yards from the edge of the lava flow where I had hidden the rifle, and how we managed to travel that short distance I still don't know. Elin could still use her legs and that helped, and we scrambled up towards the top of the flow, over the mossy humps, until I stooped and laid my hands on the butt of Fleet's rifle.

I was jacking a round into the breech even before I got it clear of the moss. Elin fell to the ground as I swung around holding the rifle in my left hand. Even with a hole in the palm of my right hand I could still pull the trigger, and I did so to some effect.

The magazine contained the mixed load I had carefully put into it – steel-jacketed and soft-nosed bullets. The first one that came out was jacketed; it hit the leading pursuer in the chest and went through him as though he wasn't there. He came on for four more paces before his heart realized it had a hole in it and it was time to quit beating, then he dropped on the spot, nearly at my feet, with a surprised look on his face.

By that time I had shot the man just behind him, and that was spectacular. A man hit by a big, soft-nosed bullet driven by a magnum charge at a range of twenty yards isn't as much killed as disintegrated, and this character came apart at the seams. The bullet hit him in the sternum and then started to expand, lifted him clear off the ground and throwing him back four feet before lifting his spine out and splattering it over the landscape.

Everything was suddenly quiet. The deep-throated bellow of Fleet's gun had told everyone concerned that something new had been added to the game and they held their fire while they figured what was going on. I saw Slade by the door of the house, his hand clutched to his belly. I lifted the rifle again and took a shot at him, too quickly and with shaking hands. I missed him but gave him a hell of a fright because he ducked back in haste and there was no one to be seen.

Then a bullet nearly parted my hair and from the sound of the report I knew someone in the house also had a rifle. I got down off the skyline and reached for Elin. She was lying on the moss, her face screwed up with pain and trying to control her laboured breathing. Her hand was at her side and, when she withdrew it, it was red with blood.

I said. 'Does it hurt much?'

'When I breathe,' she said with a gasp. 'Only then.'

That was a bad sign, yet from the apparent position of the wound she had not been hit in the lung. There wasn't anything I could do there and then. For the next few minutes I'd be busy making sure we stayed alive for the next few minutes. There's not much point in worrying about dying of septicaemia in the next week when you might have your head blown off in the next thirty seconds.

I scrabbled for the box of ammunition, took the magazine from the rifle and reloaded it. The numbness had left my hand and it was now beginning to really hurt. Even the experimental flexing of my trigger finger sent a shock up my arm as though I'd grabbed a live wire, and I didn't know if I could do much more shooting. But it's surprising what you can do when you're pushed to it.

I poked my head carefully around a slab of lava and took a look at the house. Nobody and nothing moved. Just to my front lay the bodies of the men I had shot, one lying as though peacefully asleep and the other dreadfully shattered. In front of the house were the two cars; Kennikin's car appearing to be quite normal, but Nordlinger's Chevrolet was a bit of a wreck – they had ripped the seats out in the search for the package and the two nearer doors gaped open. I'd be running up quite a bill for damage to people's cars.

Those cars were less than a hundred yards away and, dearly as I wanted one of them, I knew it was hopeless to try. I also knew we couldn't leave on foot. Apart from the fact that walking on the lava beds is a sport which even the Icelanders aren't keen on, there was Elin to consider. I couldn't leave her, and if we made a break for it we'd be picked up within fifteen minutes.

Which left only one thing – since neither the Mounties nor the US Cavalry were going to show up on the horizon in the time-honoured manner, I had to fight a pitched battle against an unknown number of men securely ensconced in that house – and win.

I studied the house. Kennikin hadn't thought much of it as a prison. *'Built like an eggshell,'* he had said. A couple of planks thick, a half-inch of plaster and a few inches of foamed polystyrene. Most people would regard a house as bullet-proof, but I laugh every time I see a Western film when the hero takes refuge in a clapboard hut and the baddies carefully shoot at the windows.

Even a 9 mm bullet from a Luger will penetrate nine inches of pine board from very close range, and that's a pee-wee bullet compared to the .44 fired by the Western Colt. A few well placed shots would whittle away the shack from around our hero.

I looked at the house and wondered how those flimsy walls would stand up against the awesome power of Fleet's rifle. The soft-nosed bullets mightn't do much – they would tend to splash on impact; but the jacketed bullets should have a hell of a lot of penetrative power. It was time to find out, but first I had to locate that rifleman.

I withdrew my head and looked at Elin. She seemed better now that she had her breathing under control. 'How are you feeling now?'

'My God!' she said. 'How do you think I feel?'

I grinned at her with some relief. That spurt of temper showed she had improved. 'Everything will get better from now on.'

'They can hardly get worse.'

'Thanks for what you did in there,' I said. 'It was very brave.' Considering the attitude she had previously shown towards killing it was much more than that.

She shivered. 'It was horrible!' she said in a low voice. 'I shall see it as long as I live.'

'You won't,' I said with certainty. 'The mind has a knack of forgetting things like that. That's why wars are so long and frequent. But just so you don't have to do it again, you can do something for me.'

'If I can.'

I pointed to a lump of lava above her head. 'Can you push that over the edge when I tell you to? But don't expose yourself or you'll get a bullet.'

She looked up at the lava fragment. 'I'll try.'

'Don't do it until I say.' I pushed the rifle ahead of me and looked at the house. Still nothing moved and I wondered what Slade was up to. 'Right,' I said. 'Shove it over.'

There was a clatter as the rock moved and rolled down the slope of the lava flow. A rifle spoke and a bullet sang overhead and then another, better aimed, struck rock splinters a little to the left. Whoever was shooting knew his work, but I had him spotted. He was in an upstairs room and, by the shadowy movement I had seen, he was kneeling at the window with his head barely showing.

I took aim, not at the window but at the wall below it and a little to the left. I squeezed the trigger and, through the scope, saw the wood of the wall planking splinter under the impact. There was a faint cry and a shift of light at the window, and then I saw the man in full sight standing with his hands to his chest. He staggered backwards and vanished.

I had been right – Fleet's rifle would shoot through walls.

I shifted sights to the downstairs rooms and methodically put a bullet into the wall alongside every window on the ground floor, just where it would be natural for a man to wait in cover. Every time I squeezed the trigger the torn sinews in my hand shrieked in protest and I relieved my feelings by bellowing at the top of my voice.

I felt Elin tug at my trouser leg. 'What's the matter?' she said worriedly.

'Don't hinder the man on the job,' I said, and dropped back. I took out the empty magazine. 'Fill that up – it's difficult for me.' These periods with an empty gun worried me and I wished Fleet had had a spare clip. To be jumped on by somebody now would be slightly disastrous.

I saw that Elin was coping with reloading the clip with the right bullets and took a look at the house again. Someone was wailing over there and there were confused shouts. I had no doubt that the house was now filled with a considerable amount of consternation; the idea that a bullet can rip through a wall and hit the man behind it is highly unsettling for the man behind the wall.

'Here,' said Elin, and passed me the full clip of five rounds. I slotted it into the gun and poked it forward again just in time to see a man break from the front door and take cover behind the Chevrolet. I could see his feet through the telescopic sight. The door nearer to me was swung wide open and, with a mental apology to Lee Nordlinger, I put a bullet through the car and through the metal of the opposite door. The feet moved and the man came into view and I saw it was Ilyich. His hand was at his neck and blood spurted from between his fingers. He tottered a few more steps then dropped, rolled over and lay still.

It was becoming very difficult for me to work the bolt action with my ruined hand. I said to Elin, 'Can you crawl over here beside me?' She came up on my right side, and I said, 'Lift up that lever, pull it back, and ram it forward again. But keep your head down while you're doing it.'

She operated the bolt while I held the rifle firm with my left hand, and she cried out as the empty brass case jumped out into her face unexpectedly. In this dot-and-carry-one manner I put another three rounds into selected points of the house where I thought they would do most damage.

When Elin put the last round into the breech I took out the magazine and told her to fill it again.

I felt happier with that one round in the breech as an insurance against emergency, and I settled down to observe the house and to compile an interim report. I had killed three men for certain, wounded another – the rifleman upstairs – and possibly yet another, judging from the moaning still coming from the house. That was five – six if Kennikin was included. I doubted if there were many more, but that didn't mean that more weren't on their way – someone could have used a telephone.

I wondered if it was Slade who was doing the wailing. I knew his voice but it was difficult to tell from that inarticulate and unstructured sound. I glanced down at Elin. 'Hurry up!' I said.

She was fiddling desperately. 'One of them is stuck.'

'Do your best.' Again I peered around the rock in front of me and my eye was caught by a movement beyond the house. Someone was doing what they all ought to have done at the start of this action – getting away from the back of the house. It was only because of the sheer unexpectedness of the gun power I wielded that they hadn't done it before – and it was dangerous because I could be outflanked.

I racked up the telescopic sight to a greater magnification and looked at the distant figure. It was Slade and he was apparently unhurt except for his bandaged hand. He was leaping like a bloody chamois from hummock to hummock at a breakneck speed, his coat tails flying in the breeze and his arms outstretched to preserve his balance. By the convenient range-finder system built into the sight I estimated that he was a little under three hundred yards away and moving farther every second.

I took a deep breath and let it out slowly to steady myself and then took aim carefully. I was in considerable pain and had difficulty in controlling the wavering sight. Three times

I almost squeezed off the shot and three times I relaxed the pressure on the trigger because the sight had drifted off target.

My father bought me my first rifle when I was twelve and, wisely, he chose a .22 single-shot. When a boy hunts rabbits and hares and knows that he has only one shot at his disposal then he also knows that the first and only shot must count, and no finer training in good shooting habits is possible. Now, again, I had only one shot available and I was back to my boyhood again, but it was no rabbit I was shooting – more like a tiger.

It was difficult to concentrate and I felt dizzy and a wash of greyness passed momentarily in front of my eyes. I blinked and it cleared away and Slade stood out preternaturally clearly in the glass. He had begun to move away at an angle and I led him in the sight and let him run into the aiming point. There was a roaring of blood in my ears and the dizziness came again.

My finger painfully took up the final pressure and the butt of the rifle jolted my shoulder and Slade's nemesis streaked towards him at 2,000 miles an hour. The distant figure jerked like a marionette with suddenly cut strings, toppled over, and disappeared from sight.

I rolled over as the roaring in my ears increased. The dizziness built up again and the recurring waves of greyness turned to black. I saw the sun glowing redly through the darkness and then I passed out, the last thing I heard being Elin's voice crying my name.

III

'It was a deception operation,' said Taggart.

I was lying in a hospital bed in Keflavik and there was a guard on the door, not so much to keep me imprisoned as to shield me from prying eyes. I was a potential *cause célèbre,* a *casus belli* and all those other foreign phrases which the leader writers of *The Times* trot out so readily in moments of crisis, and all attempts were being made to keep the situation potential and to prevent it from becoming actual. All parties concerned wanted the whole thing hushed up, and if the Icelandic government knew what had been going on they were damned careful not to say so.

Taggart was with another man, an American, whom he introduced as Arthur Ryan. I recognized Ryan; the last time I had seen him was through the sights of Fleet's rifle – he had been standing beside a helicopter on the other side of Búdarháls ridge.

It was the second time they had come to see me. The first time I was drowsy with dope and not very coherent, but still coherent enough to ask two questions.

'How's Elin?'

'She's all right,' said Taggart soothingly. 'In better shape than you are, as a matter of fact.' He told me that the bullet had been a ricochet and had the force taken out of it; it had just penetrated the flesh and lodged between two ribs. 'She's as right as rain,' said Taggart heartily.

I looked at him with dislike but I was too wobbly to push it then. I said, 'How did I get here?'

Taggart glanced at Ryan who took a pipe from his pocket, looked at it uncertainly, and then put it away again. He said in a slow voice, 'That's quite a girl you have, Mr Stewart.'

'What happened?'

'Well, when you passed out she didn't know what to do. She thought about it a bit, then she loaded the rifle and started to put even more holes into that house.'

I thought of Elin's attitude towards killing. 'Did she hit anyone?'

'I guess not,' said Ryan. 'I think you did most of the damage. She shot off all the ammunition – and there was a hell of a lot of it – and then she waited a while to see what would happen. Nothing did, so she stood up and walked into the house. I think that was a very brave thing to do, Mr Stewart.'

I thought so too.

Ryan said, 'She found the telephone and rang the Base, here, and contacted Commander Nordlinger. She was very forceful and got him really stirred up. He got even more stirred up when the phone went dead.' He grimaced. 'It's not surprising she fainted – that place was like a slaughterhouse. Five dead and two badly wounded.'

'Three wounded,' said Taggart. 'We found Slade afterwards.'

Soon after that they went away because I was in no shape for serious conversation, but twenty-four hours later they were back and Taggart was talking about deception.

'When can I see Elin?' I said abruptly.

This afternoon,' said Taggart. 'She's quite all right, you know.'

I looked at him stonily. 'She'd better be.'

He gave an embarrassed cough. 'Don't you want to know what it was all about?'

'Yes,' I said. 'I would. I'd certainly like to know why the Department did its damnedest to get me killed.' I switched my eyes to Ryan. 'Even to the extent of getting the co-operation of the CIA.'

'As I say, it was a deception operation, a scheme cooked up by a couple of American scientists.' Taggart rubbed his chin. 'Have you ever considered *The Times* crossword puzzle?'

'For God's sake!' I said. 'No, I haven't.'

Taggart smiled. 'Let us assume it takes some maniacal genius eight hours to compile it; then it has to be set up in type, a block made, and printed in the paper. This involves quite a few people for a short time. Let us say that a total of forty man-hours is used up in this way – one working man-week.'

'So?'

'So consider the consumer end of the operation. Let's assume that ten thousand readers of *The Times* apply their brain power to working out the damned thing – and that each one takes an hour. That's ten thousand hours – five man-years. You see the implication? One man-week of labour has tied up five man-years of brain power in totally unproductive activity.' He looked at Ryan. 'I think you can take it from there.'

Ryan had a low, even voice. 'There are a lot of discoveries made in the physical sciences which have no immediate application, or any conceivable application, for that matter. One example is silly putty. Have you ever seen the stuff?'

'I've heard of it,' I said, wondering what they were getting at. 'I've never seen it.'

'It's funny stuff,' said Ryan. 'You can mould it like putty, but if you leave it alone it flows like water. Furthermore, if you hit it with a hammer it shatters like glass. You'd think that a substance with such diverse properties would be useful, but so far no one has thought of a single goddamn thing to do with it.'

'I believe they're now putting it into the middle of golf balls,' offered Taggart.

'Yeah, a real technological breakthrough,' said Ryan ironically. 'In electronics there are quite a few effects like that. The electret, for example, carries a permanent electric charge like a magnet carries a magnetic field. That idea has been around for forty years and only now has a use been found for it. When the scientists began to kick the quantum theory around they came up with any number of odd effects – the tunnel diode, the Josephson effects, and a lot more – some of them usable and some not. A fair number of these discoveries have been made in laboratories working on defence contracts and they're not generally known.'

He shifted uneasily in his chair. 'Mind if I smoke?'

'Go ahead.'

Thankfully he took out his pipe and began to fill it. 'One scientist, a guy called Davies, surveyed the field and came up with an idea. As a scientist he's not very bright – certainly not of the first rank – but his idea was bright enough even if he merely intended it as a practical joke. He figured it was possible to put together an electronic package, utilizing a number of these mysterious but unusable effects, which would baffle a really big brain. In fact, he did put together such a package, and it took five top research men at Caltech six weeks to discover they'd been fooled.'

I began to get the drift. 'The deception operation.'

Ryan nodded. 'One of the men who was fooled was a Dr Atholl, and he saw possibilities in it. He wrote a letter to someone important and in due course the letter was passed on to us. One of the sentences in that letter is outstanding – Dr Atholl said this was a concrete example of the aphorism: "Any fool can ask a question which the wisest of men cannot answer." Davies's original package was relatively unsophisticated, but what we finally came up with was really complex – and it was designed to do precisely nothing.'

I thought of how Lee Nordlinger had been baffled and began to smile. 'What are you laughing at?' asked Taggart.

'Nothing much. Carry on.'

Taggart said, 'You see the principle, Stewart; it's just like *The Times* crossword. The design of the package didn't take much brain power – three scientists worked on it for a year. But if we could get it into the hands of the Russians it could tie up some of their finest minds for a hell of a long time. And the joke is that the problem was fundamentally unsolvable – there was no answer.'

'But we had a problem,' said Ryan. 'How to get it into the hands of the Russians. We started by feeding them a line by a series of carefully controlled leaks. The word was that American scientists had invented a new form of radar with fascinating properties. It had over the horizon capability, it showed a detailed picture and not just a green blob on a screen, and it wasn't affected by ground-level clutter and so could detect a low-level air attack. Any nation would sell its Premier's daughter into white slavery for a gadget like that, and the Russians began to bite.'

He pointed out of the window. 'You see that funny antenna out there – that's supposed to be it. The radar is supposed to be having a field test here at Keflavik, and we've had jet fighters skimming the waves for five hundred miles around here for the last six weeks just to add to the plausibility. And that's when we brought you British in.'

Taggart said, 'We sold another story to the Russians. Our American friends were keeping this radar to themselves and we were annoyed about it, so annoyed that we decided to have a look at it ourselves. In fact, one of our agents was sent to pinch a bit of it – an important bit.' He flicked a finger at me. 'You, of course.'

I swallowed. 'You mean I was intended to let the Russians have it!'

'That's right,' said Taggart blandly. 'And you were handpicked. Slade pointed out – and I agreed – that you were probably not a good agent any more, but you had the advantage, for our purposes, of being known to the Russians as a good agent. Everything was set up and then you fooled everybody – us and the Russians. In fact, you were a devil of a lot better than anyone supposed.'

I felt the outrage beginning to build up, and said deliberately, 'You lousy, amoral son of a bitch! Why didn't you let me in on it? It would have saved a hell of a lot of trouble.'

He shook his head. 'It had to look authentic.'

'By God!' I said. 'You sold me – just as Bakayev sold Kennikin in Sweden.' I grinned tightly. 'It must have complicated things when Slade turned out to be a *Russian* agent.'

Taggart glanced sideways at Ryan and appeared to be embarrassed. 'Our American friends are a bit acid about that. It wrecked the operation.' He sighed, and said plaintively, 'Counter-espionage work is the very devil. If we don't catch any spies then everybody is happy; but when we do our job and catch a spy then there's a scream to high heaven that we *haven't* been doing our job.'

'You break my heart,' I said. '*You* didn't catch Slade.'

He changed the subject quickly. 'Well, there Slade was – in charge of the operation.'

'Yeah,' said Ryan. 'In charge on *both* sides. What a sweet position to be in. He must have thought he couldn't lose.' He leaned forward. 'You see, once the Russians knew about the operation they decided they had no objection to grabbing the package if they thought it would fool us into believing they'd been fooled. A sort of double blind thing.'

I looked at Taggart with distaste. 'What a bastard you are,' I said. 'You must have known that Kennikin would do his best to kill me.'

'Oh, no!' he said earnestly. 'I didn't know about Kennikin. I think Bakayev must have realized they were wasting a good man so they decided to rehabilitate him by sending him on this operation. Perhaps Slade had something to do with it too.'

'He would!' I said bitterly. 'And because I was supposed to be a pushover they gave Kennikin a scratch team. He was complaining about that.' I looked up. 'And what about Jack Case?' I demanded.

Taggart didn't bat an eyelid. 'He had my orders to steer you to the Russians – that's why he didn't help you at Geysir. But when he talked to Slade you had already filled him up with your suspicions. He must have tried to pump Slade, but Slade is a clever man and realized it. That was the end of Case. Slade was doing everything to make sure his cover wasn't blown and in the end you were more important to him than that damned package.'

'Write off Jack Case,' I said sourly. 'He was a good man. When did you catch on to Slade?'

'I was slow there,' said Taggart. 'When you telephoned me I thought you'd done your nut, but after I sent Case here I found I couldn't get hold of Slade. He'd made himself unobtainable. That's against all procedure so I began to look into his record. When I found he'd been in Finland as a boy and that his parents were killed during the war I remembered that you'd mentioned Lonsdale and I wondered if the same trick hadn't been played.' He grimaced. 'But when Case's body was discovered with your pet knife in it, I didn't know what the hell to think.' He nudged Ryan. 'The knife.'

'What! Oh, yes – the knife.' Ryan put his hand into his breast pocket and produced the *sgian dubh*. 'We managed to get it from the police. I guess you'd like to have it back.' He held it out. 'It's a real cute knife; I like that jewel in the hilt.'

I took it. A Polynesian would have said it had *mana;* my own distant ancestors would have named it and called it *Weazand Slitter* or *Blood Drinker,* but to me it was just my grandfather's knife and his grandfather's before him. I laid it gently on the bedside table.

I said to Ryan, 'Your people shot at me. What was the idea of that?'

'Hell!' he said. 'You'd gone crazy and the whole operation was in danger. We were floating about in a chopper above that goddamn wilderness and we saw you, and we saw the Russians chasing you, and we reckoned you had a good chance of getting clear away. So we dropped a guy to stop you in your tracks. And we couldn't be too obvious about it because it had to look good to the Russians. We didn't know then that the whole operation was a bust, anyway.'

Neither Taggart nor Ryan had a grain of morality, but I didn't expect it. I said, 'You're lucky to be alive. The last time I saw you was through the sights of Fleet's rifle.'

'Jesus!' he said. 'I'm glad I didn't know it at the time. Talking about Fleet; you busted him up but good – but he'll survive.' He rubbed his nose. 'Fleet is sort of married to that rifle of his. He'd like to have it back.'

I shook my head. 'I've got to get something out of this deal. If Fleet is man enough let him come and get it.'

Ryan scowled. 'I'll doubt if he will. We've all had a bellyful of you.'

There was just one more thing. I said, 'So Slade is still alive.'

'Yes,' said Ryan. 'You shot him through the pelvis. If he ever walks again he'll need steel pins through his hips.'

'The only walking Slade will do for the next forty years is in the exercise yard of a prison,' said Taggart. He stood up. 'All this comes under the Official Secrets Act, Stewart. Everything has to be hushed. Slade is in England already; he was flown across yesterday in an American aircraft. He'll stand trial as soon as he comes out of hospital but the proceedings will be in camera. You'll keep quiet, and so will that girl-friend of yours. The sooner you turn her into a British subject the better I'll be pleased. I'd like to have some control over her.'

'Christ Almighty!' I said wearily. 'You can't even act as Cupid without an ulterior motive.'

Ryan joined Taggart at the door. He turned, and said, 'I think Sir David owes you a lot, Mr Stewart; a lot more than thanks, anyway – which I notice he hasn't proffered.' He looked at Taggart from the corner of his eye, and I thought there was no love lost between them.

Taggart was impervious; he didn't turn a hair. 'Oh, yes,' he said casually. 'I dare say something can be arranged. A medal, perhaps – if you like such trinkets.'

I found that my voice was shaking. 'All I want is your permanent absence,' I said. 'I'll keep quiet for just as long as you stay away from us, but if you, or any of the boys from the Department, come within shouting distance, I'll blow the gaff.'

'You won't be disturbed again,' he said, and they went out. A moment later he popped his head around the door. 'I'll send in some grapes.'

IV

Elin and I were flown to Scotland by courtesy of the CIA and the US Navy in a plane laid on by Ryan, and we were married in Glasgow by a special licence provided by Taggart. Both of us were still in bandages.

I took Elin back to the glen under Sgurr Dearg. She liked the scenery, especially the trees – the marvellous un-Icelandic trees – but she didn't think much of the cottage. It was small and it depressed her and I wasn't at all surprised; what suits a bachelor is not good for a married man.

'I'm not going to live in the big house,' I said. 'We'd rattle around in there and, anyway, I usually rent it to Americans who come for the shooting. We'll let a gillie have the cottage and we'll build our own house a little farther up the glen, by the river.'

So we did.

I still have Fleet's rifle. I don't keep it over the fireplace as a trophy but decently in the gun cabinet along with all the other working tools. I use it sometimes when the deer herd needs culling, but not often. It doesn't give the deer much of a chance.

THE FREEDOM TRAP

To Ron and Peggy Hulland

ONE

Mackintosh's office was, unexpectedly, in the City. I had difficulty in finding it because it was in that warren of streets between Holborn and Fleet Street which is a maze to one accustomed to the grid-iron pattern of Johannesburg. I found it at last in a dingy building; a well-worn brass plate announcing innocuously that this Dickensian structure held the registered office of Anglo-Scottish Holdings, Ltd.

I smiled as I touched the polished plate, leaving a smudged fingerprint. It seemed that Mackintosh knew his business; this plate, apparently polished by generations of office boys, was a sign of careful planning that augured well for the future – the professional touch. I'm a professional and I don't like working with amateurs – they're unpredictable, careless and too dangerous for my taste. I had wondered about Mackintosh because England is the spiritual home of amateurism, but Mackintosh was a Scot and I suppose that makes a difference.

There was no lift, of course, so I trudged up four flights of stairs – poor lighting and marmalade-coloured walls badly in need of a repaint – and found the Anglo-Scottish office at the end of a dark corridor. It was all so normal that I wondered if I had the right address but I stepped forward to the desk and said, 'Rearden – to see Mr Mackintosh.'

The red-headed girl behind the desk favoured me with a warm smile and put down the tea-cup she was holding. 'He's expecting you,' she said. 'I'll see if he's free.' She went into the inner office, closing the door carefully behind her. She had good legs.

I looked at the scratched and battered filing cabinets and wondered what was in them and found I could not possibly guess. Perhaps they were stuffed full of Angles and Scots. There were two eighteenth-century prints on the wall – Windsor Castle and the Thames at Richmond. There was a Victorian steel engraving of Princes Street, Edinburgh. All very Anglic and Scottish. I admired Mackintosh more and more – this was going to be a good careful job; but I did wonder how he'd done it – did he call in an interior decorator or did he have a pal who was a set dresser in a film studio?

The girl came back. 'Mr Mackintosh will see you now – you can go right through.'

I liked her smile so I returned it and walked past her into Mackintosh's sanctum. He hadn't changed. I hadn't expected him to change – not in two months – but sometimes a man looks different on his home ground where he has a sense of security, a sense of knowing what's what. I was pleased Mackintosh hadn't changed in that way because it meant he would be sure of himself anywhere and at any time. I like people I can depend on.

He was a sand-coloured man with light gingery hair and invisible eyebrows and eyelashes which gave his face a naked look. If he didn't shave for a week probably no one would notice. He was slight in build and I wondered how he would use himself in a rough-house; flyweights usually invent nasty tricks to make up for lack of brawn. But then Mackintosh would never get into a brawl in the first place; there are all sorts of different ways of using your brains.

He put his hands flat on the desk. 'So you are,' he paused, holding his breath, and then spoke my name in a gasp, 'Rearden. And how was the flight, Mr Rearden?'

'Not bad.'

'That's fine. Sit down, Mr Rearden. Would you like some tea?' He smiled slightly. 'People who work in offices like this drink tea all the time.'

'All right,' I said, and sat down.

He went to the door. 'Could you rustle up another pot of tea, Mrs Smith?'

The door clicked gently as he closed it and I cocked my head in that direction. 'Does she know?'

'Of course,' he said calmly. 'I couldn't do without Mrs Smith. She's a very capable secretary, too.'

'Smith?' I asked ironically.

'Oh, it's her real name. Not too incredible – there are plenty of Smiths. She'll be joining us in a moment so I suggest we delay any serious discussion.' He peered at me. 'That's a rather lightweight suit for our English weather. You mustn't catch pneumonia.'

I grinned at him. 'Perhaps you'll recommend a tailor.'

'Indeed I will; you must go to my man. He's a bit expensive but I think we can manage that.' He opened a drawer and took out a fat bundle of currency. 'You'll need something for expenses.'

I watched unbelievingly as he began to count out the fivers. He parted with thirty of them, then paused. 'We'd better make it two hundred,' he decided, added another ten notes, then pushed the wad across to me. 'You don't mind cash, I trust? In my business cheques are rather looked down upon.'

I stuffed the money into my wallet before he changed his mind. 'Isn't this a little unusual? I didn't expect you to be so free and easy.'

'I daresay the expense account will stand it,' he said tolerantly. 'You are going to earn it, you know.' He offered a cigarette. 'And how was Johannesburg when you left?'

'Still the same in a changing sort of way,' I said. 'Since you were there they've built another hundred-and-sixty-foot office block in the city.'

'In two months? Not bad!'

'They put it up in twelve days,' I said drily.

'Go-ahead chaps, you South Africans. Ah, here's the tea.'

Mrs Smith put the tea tray on to the desk and drew up a chair. I looked at her with interest because anyone Mackintosh trusted was sure to be out of the ordinary. Not that she looked it, but perhaps that was because she was disguised as a secretary in a regulation twin-set – just another office girl with a nice smile. Yet in other circumstances I thought I could get on very well with Mrs Smith – in the absence of Mr Smith, of course.

Mackintosh waved his hand. 'Will you be Mother, Mrs Smith?' She busied herself with the cups, and Mackintosh said, 'There's no real need for further introductions, is there? You won't be around long enough for anything but the job, Rearden. I think we can get down to cases now.'

I winked at Mrs Smith. 'A pity.'

She looked at me unsmilingly. 'Sugar?' was all she asked.

He tented his fingers. 'Did you know that London is the world centre of the diamond business?'

'No, I didn't. I thought it was Amsterdam.'

'That's where the cutting is done. London is where diamonds are bought and sold in all stages of manufacture from uncut stones to finished pieces of jewellery.' He smiled. 'Last week I was in a place where packets of diamonds are sold like packets of butter in a grocer's shop.'

I accepted a cup of tea from Mrs Smith. 'I bet they have bags of security.'

'Indeed they have,' said Mackintosh. He held his arms wide like a fisherman describing the one that got away. 'The safe doors are that thick and the place is wired up with so many electronic gimmicks that if you blink an eyelash in the wrong place at the wrong time half the metropolitan police begin to move in.'

I sipped the tea, then put down the cup. 'I'm not a safe cracker,' I said. 'And I wouldn't know where to begin – you need a peterman for that. Besides, it would have to be a team job.'

'Rest easy,' said Mackintosh. 'It was the South African angle that set me thinking about diamonds. Diamonds have all the virtues; they're relatively anonymous, portable and easily sold. Just the thing a South African would go for, don't you think? Do you know anything about the IDB racket?'

I shook my head. 'Not my line of country – so far.'

'It doesn't matter, perhaps it's for the better. You're a clever thief, Rearden; that's why you've stayed out of trouble. How many times have you been inside?'

I grinned at him. 'Once – for eighteen months. That was a long time ago.'

'Indeed it was. You change your methods and your aims, don't you? You don't leave any recurring statistics for a computer to sort out – no definite *modus operandi* to trip over. As I say – you're a clever thief. I think that what I have in mind will be just up your street. Mrs Smith thinks so, too.'

'Let's hear about it,' I said cautiously.

'The British GPO is a marvellous institution,' said Mackintosh inconsequentially. 'Some say ours is the best postal system in the world; some think otherwise if you judge by the readers' letters in the *Daily Telegraph*, but grousing is an Englishman's privilege. Insurance companies, however, regard the GPO very highly. Tell me, what is the most outstanding property of the diamond?'

'It sparkles.'

'An uncut diamond doesn't,' he pointed out. 'An uncut stone looks like a bit of sea-washed bottle glass. Think again.'

'It's hard,' I said. 'Just about the hardest thing there is.'

Mackintosh clicked his tongue in annoyance. 'He's not thinking, is he, Mrs Smith? Tell him.'

'The size – or the lack of it,' she said quietly.

Mackintosh pushed his hand under my nose and curled his fingers into a fist. 'You can hold a fortune in your hand and no one would know it was there. You could put diamonds worth a hundred thousand pounds into this matchbox – then what would you have?'

'You tell me.'

'You'd have a parcel, Rearden; a package. Something that can be wrapped up in brown paper with enough room to write an address and accept a postage stamp. Something that can be popped into a letter-box.'

I stared at him. 'They send diamonds through the *post*!'

'Why not? The postal system is highly efficient and very rarely is anything lost. Insurance companies are willing to bet large sums of money on the efficiency of the GPO and those boys know what they're doing. It's a matter of statistics, you know.'

He toyed with the matchbox. 'At one time there was a courier system and that had a lot of disadvantages. A courier would personally carry a parcel of diamonds and deliver it to its destination by hand. That fell through for a number of reasons; the couriers got to be known by the wide boys, which was very sad because a number of them were severely assaulted. Another thing was that human beings are but human, after all, and a courier could be corrupted. The supply of trustworthy men isn't bottomless and the whole courier system was not secure. Far from it.

'But consider the present system,' he said enthusiastically. 'Once a parcel is swallowed into the maw of the Post Office not even God can extract it until it reaches its destination. And why? Because nobody knows precisely where the hell it is. It's just one of millions of parcels circulating through the system and to find it would *not* be like finding a needle in a haystack – it would be like searching a haystack for a particular wisp of hay. Do you follow me?'

I nodded. 'It sounds logical.'

'Oh, it is,' said Mackintosh. 'Mrs Smith did all the necessary research. She's a very clever girl.' He flapped his hand languidly. 'Carry on, Mrs Smith.'

She said coolly, 'Once the insurance company actuaries analysed the GPO statistics regarding losses, they saw they were on to a good thing providing certain precautions were taken. To begin with, the stones are sent in all sizes and shapes of parcel from matchbox size to crates as big as a tea chest. The parcels are labelled in a multitude of different ways, very often with the trade label of a well-known firm – anything to confuse the issue, you see. The most important thing is the anonymity of the destination. There are a number of accommodation addresses having nothing to do with the diamond industry to which the stones are sent, and the same address is never used twice running.'

'Very interesting,' I said. 'Now how do we crack it?'

Mackintosh leaned back in his chair and put his fingertips together. 'Take a postman walking up a street – a familiar sight. He carries a hundred thousand pounds' worth of diamonds but – and this is the interesting point – he doesn't know it and neither does anyone else. Even the recipient who is eagerly awaiting the diamonds doesn't know when they'll arrive because the Post Office doesn't guarantee delivery at any specific time, regardless of what they say about first-class post in their specious advertising. The parcels are sent by ordinary post; no special delivery nonsense which would be too easy to crack open.'

I said slowly, 'It seems to me that you're painting yourself into a corner, but I suppose you have something up your sleeve. All right – I'll buy it.'

'Have you ever done any photography?'

I resisted the impulse to explode. This man had more ways of talking around a subject than anyone I had ever known. He had been the same in Johannesburg – never talking in a straight line for more than two minutes. 'I've clicked a shutter once or twice,' I said tightly.

'Black-and-white or colour?'

'Both.'

Mackintosh looked pleased. 'When you take colour photographs – transparencies – and send them away for processing, what do you get back?'

I looked appealingly at Mrs Smith and sighed. 'Small pieces of film with pictures on them.' I paused and added, 'They're framed in cardboard mounts.'

'What else do you get?'

'Nothing.'

He wagged his finger. 'Oh yes, you do. You get the distinctive yellow box the things are packed in. Yes, yellow – I suppose it could be described as Kodak yellow. If a man is carrying one of those boxes in his hand you can spot it across a street and you say to yourself, "That man is carrying a box of Kodachrome transparencies."'

I felt a thrill of tension. Mackintosh was coming to the meat of it. 'All right,' he said abruptly 'I'll lay it out for you. I know when a parcel of diamonds is being sent. I know to where it is being sent – I have the accommodation address. Most important of all, I know the packaging and it's unmistakable. All you have to do is to wait near the address and the postman will come up to you with the damn thing in his hand. And that little yellow box will contain one hundred and twenty thousand quid in unset stones which you will take from him.'

'How did you find out all this?' I asked curiously.

'I didn't,' he said. 'Mrs Smith did. The whole thing is her idea. She came up with the concept and did all the research. Exactly *how* she did the research is no concern of yours.'

I looked at her with renewed interest and discovered that her eyes were green. There was a twinkle in them and her lips were curved in a humorous quirk which smoothed out as she said soberly, 'There must be as little violence as possible, Mr Rearden.'

'Yes,' agreed Mackintosh. 'As little violence as possible commensurate with making a getaway. I don't believe in violence; it's bad for business. You'd better bear that in mind.'

I said, 'The postman won't hand it to me. I'll have to take it by force.'

Mackintosh showed his teeth in a savage grin. 'So it will be robbery with violence if you get nabbed. Her Majesty's judges are hard about that kind of thing, especially considering the amount involved. You'll be lucky to get away with ten years.'

'Yes,' I said thoughtfully, and returned his grin with interest.

'Still, we won't make it too easy for the police. The drill is this; I'll be nearby and you'll keep on going. The stones will be out of the country within three hours of the snatch. Mrs Smith, will you attend to the matter of the bank?'

She opened a folder and produced a form which she pushed across the desk. 'Fill that in.'

It was a request to open an account at the *Züricher Ausführen Handelsbank*. Mrs Smith said, 'British politicians may not like the gnomes of Zurich but they come in handy when needed. Your number is very complicated – write it out fully in words in this box.'

Her finger rested on the form so I scribbled the number in the place she indicated. She said, 'That number written on the right cheque form in place of a signature will release to you any amount of money up to forty thousand pounds sterling, or its equivalent in any currency you wish.'

Mackintosh sniggered. 'Of course, you'll have to get the diamonds first.'

I stared at them, 'You're taking two-thirds.'

'I did plan it,' Mrs Smith said coolly.

Mackintosh grinned like a hungry shark. 'She has expensive tastes.'

'Of that I have no doubt,' I said. 'Would your tastes run to a good lunch? You'll have to suggest a restaurant, though; I'm a new boy in London.'

She was about to answer when Mackintosh said sharply, 'You're not here to play footsie with my staff, Rearden. It wouldn't be wise for you to be seen with either of us. Perhaps when it's all over we can have dinner together – the three of us.'

'Thanks,' I said bleakly.

He scribbled on a piece of paper. 'I suggest that after lunch you . . . er . . . "case the joint" – I believe that is the correct expression. Here is the address of the drop.' He pushed the paper across the desk, and scribbled again. 'And this is the address of my tailor. Don't get them mixed up, there's a good chap. That would be disastrous.'

II

I lunched at the Cock in Fleet Street and then set out to look up the address Mackintosh had given me. Of course I walked in the wrong direction – London is the devil of a place to get around in if you don't know it. I didn't want to take a taxi because I always play things very cautiously, perhaps even too cautiously. But that's why I'm a success.

Anyway, I found myself walking up a street called Ludgate Hill before I found I'd gone wrong and, in making my way into Holborn, I passed the Central Criminal Court. I knew it was the Central Criminal Court, because it says so and that surprised me because I always thought it was called the Old Bailey. I recognized it because of the golden figure of Justice on the roof. Even a South African would recognize that – we see Edgar Lustgarten movies, too.

It was all very interesting but I wasn't there as a tourist so I passed up the opportunity of going inside to see if there was a case going on. Instead I pressed on to Leather Lane behind Gamage's and found a street market with people selling all kinds of junk from barrows. I didn't much like the look of that – it's difficult to get away fast in a thick crowd. I'd have to make damned sure there was no hue and cry, which meant slugging the postman pretty hard. I began to feel sorry for him.

Before checking on the address I cruised around the vicinity, identifying all the possible exits from the area. To my surprise I found that Hatton Garden runs parallel with Leather Lane and I knew that the diamond merchants hung out there. On second thoughts it wasn't too surprising; the diamond boys wouldn't want their accommodation address to be too far from the ultimate destination. I looked at the stolid, blank buildings and wondered in which of them were the strongrooms Mackintosh had described.

I spent half an hour pacing out those streets and noting the various types of shop. Shops are very useful to duck into when you want to get off the streets quickly. I decided that Gamage's might be a good place to get lost in and spent another quarter-hour familiarizing myself with the place. That wouldn't be enough but at this stage it wasn't a good thing to decide definitely on firm plans. That's the trouble with a lot of people who slip up on jobs like this; they make detailed plans too early in the game, imagining they're Master Minds, and the whole operation gets hardening of the arteries and becomes stiff and inflexible.

I went back to Leather Lane and found the address Mackintosh had given me. It was on the second floor, so I went up to the third in the creaking lift and walked down one flight of stairs. The Betsy-Lou Dress Manufacturing Co, Ltd, was open for business but I didn't trouble to introduce myself. Instead I checked the approaches and found them reasonably good, although I would have to observe the postman in action before I could make up my mind about the best way of doing the job.

I didn't hang about too long, just enough to take rough bearings, and within ten minutes I was back in Gamage's and in a telephone booth. Mrs Smith must have been literally hanging on to the telephone awaiting my call because the bell rang only once before she answered, 'Anglo-Scottish Holdings.'

'Rearden,' I said.

'I'll put you through to Mr Mackintosh.'

'Wait a minute,' I said. 'What kind of a Smith are you?'

'What do you mean?'

'Don't you have a first name?'

There was a pause before she said, 'Perhaps you'd better call me Lucy.'

'Ouch! I don't believe it.'

'You'd better believe it.'

'Is there a Mr Smith?'

Frost formed on the earpiece of my telephone as she said icily, 'That's no business of yours. I'll put you through to Mr Mackintosh.'

There was a click and the line went dead temporarily and I thought I wasn't much of a success as a great lover. It wasn't surprising really; I couldn't see Lucy Smith – if that was her name – wanting to enter into any kind of close relationship with me until the job was over. I felt depressed.

Mackintosh's voice crackled in my ear. 'Hello, dear boy.'

'I'm ready to talk about it some more.'

'Are you? Well, come and see me tomorrow at the same time.'

'All right,' I said.

'Oh, by the way, have you been to the tailor yet?'

'No.'

'You'd better hurry,' he said. 'There'll be the measurements and at least three fittings. You'll just about have time to get it all in before you get slapped in the nick.'

'Very funny,' I said, and slammed down the phone. It was all right for Mackintosh to make snide comments; he wasn't going to do the hard work. I wondered what else he did in that shabby office apart from arranging diamond robberies.

I took a taxi into the West End and found Austin Reed's, where I bought a very nice reversible weather coat and one of those caps as worn by the English country gent, the kind in which the cloth crown is sewn on to the peak. They wanted to wrap the cap but I rolled it up and put it into the pocket of the coat which I carried out over my arm.

I didn't go near Mackintosh's tailor.

III

'So you think it's practicable,' said Mackintosh.

I nodded. 'I'll want to know a bit more, but it looks all right so far.'

'What do you want to know?'

'Number one – when is the job to be?'

Mackintosh grinned. 'The day after tomorrow,' he said airily.

'Christ!' I said. 'That's not allowing much time.'

He chuckled. 'It'll be all over in less than a week after you've set foot in England.' He winked at Mrs Smith. 'It's not everyone who can make forty thousand quid for a week's not very hard work.'

'I can see at least one other from here,' I said sarcastically. 'I don't see that you're working your fingers to the bone.'

He was undisturbed. 'Organization – that's my forte.'

'It means I've got to spend the rest of today and all tomorrow studying the habits of the British postman,' I said. 'How many deliveries a day?'

Mackintosh cocked his eye at Mrs Smith, who said, 'Two.'

'Have you any snoopers you can recruit? I don't want to spend too much time around Leather Lane myself. I might get picked up for loitering and that would certainly queer the pitch.'

'It's all been done,' said Mrs Smith. 'I have the timetable here.'

While I was studying it, she unrolled a plan on to the desk. 'This is a plan of the entire second floor. We're lucky on this one. In some buildings there's a row of letter-boxes in the entrance hall, but not here. The postman delivers to every office.'

Mackintosh put down his finger with a stabbing motion. 'You'll tackle the postman just about here. He'll have the letters for that damnably named clothing company in his hand ready for delivery and you ought to see whether he's carrying the package or not. If he isn't you pass it up and wait for the next delivery.'

'That's what's worrying me,' I said. 'The waiting bit. If I'm not careful I'll stick out like a sore thumb.'

'Oh, didn't I tell you – I've rented an office on the same floor,' said Mackintosh blandly. 'Mrs Smith went shopping and all home comforts are installed; an electric kettle, tea, coffee, sugar and milk, and a basket of goodies from Fortnum's. You'll live like a king. I hope you like caviare.'

I blew out my breath sharply. 'Don't bother to consult me about anything,' I said sarcastically, but Mackintosh merely smiled and tossed a key-ring on the desk. I picked it up. 'What name am I trading under?'

'Kiddykar Toys, Limited,' said Mrs Smith. 'It's a genuine company.'

Mackintosh laughed. 'I set it up myself – cost all of twenty-five quid.'

We spent the rest of the morning scheming and I didn't find any snags worth losing any sleep over. I found myself liking Lucy Smith more and more; she had a brain as sharp as a razor and nothing escaped her attention, and yet she contrived to retain her femininity and avoid bossiness, something that seems difficult for brainy women. When we had just about got everything wrapped up, I said, 'Come now; Lucy isn't your real name. What is?'

She looked at me with clear eyes. 'I don't think it really matters,' she said evenly.

I sighed. 'No,' I admitted. 'Perhaps not.'

Mackintosh regarded us with interest, then said abruptly, 'I said there was to be no lally-gagging around with the staff, Rearden; you just stick to doing your job.' He looked at his watch. 'You'd better leave now.'

So I left the gloom of his nineteenth-century office and lunched again at the Cock, and the afternoon was spent in the registered office of Kiddykar Toys, Ltd, two doors away from the Betsy-Lou Dress Manufacturing Co, Ltd. Everything was there that Mackintosh had promised, so I made myself a pot of coffee and was pleased to see that Mrs Smith had supplied the real stuff and not the instant powdered muck.

There was a good view of the street and, when I checked on the timetable of the postman, I was able to identify his route. Even without the telephone call Mackintosh was to make I ought to get at least fifteen minutes' notice of his arrival. That point settled, I made a couple of expeditions from the office, pacing the corridor and timing myself. There really was no point in doing it without knowledge of the postman's speed but it was good practice. I timed myself from the office to Gamage's, walking at a fair clip but not so fast as to attract attention. An hour in Gamage's was enough to work out a good confusing route and then work was over for the day and I went back to my hotel.

The next day was pretty much the same except I had the postman to practise on. The first delivery I watched from the office with the door opened a crack and a stopwatch in my hand. That might seem a bit silly; after all, all I had to do was to cosh a man. But there was a hell of a lot at stake so I went through the whole routine.

On the second delivery of the day I did a dummy run on the postman. Sure enough, it was as Mackintosh had predicted; as he approached Betsy-Lou's door the letters for delivery were firmly clutched in hand and any box of Kodachromes should be clearly visible. I hoped Mackintosh was right about the diamonds; we'd look mighty foolish if we ended up with a photographic record of Betsy-Lou's weekend in Brighton.

Before I left I telephoned Mackintosh and he answered the telephone himself. I said, 'I'm as ready as I'll ever be.'

'Good!' He paused. 'You won't see me again – apart from the hand-over of the merchandise tomorrow. Make a neat job of that, for God's sake!'

'What's the matter?' I asked. 'Got the wind up?'

He didn't answer that one. Instead, he said, 'You'll find a present awaiting you at your hotel. Handle with care.' Another pause. 'Good luck.'

I said, 'Give my sincere regards to Mrs Smith.'

He coughed. 'It wouldn't do, you know.'

'Perhaps not; but I like to make my own decisions.'

'Maybe so – but she'll be in Switzerland tomorrow. I'll pass on your message when I next see her.' He rang off.

I went back to the hotel, picked up a small package at the desk, and unwrapped it in my room. Nestling in a small box was a cosh, lead-centred and rubber-padded with a non-skid grip and a neat strap to go round the wrist. A very effective anaesthetic instrument, if a bit more dangerous than most. Also in the box was a scrap of paper with a single line of typescript: HARD ENOUGH AND NO HARDER.

I went to bed early that night. There was work to do next day.

IV

Next morning I went into the City like any other business gent, although I didn't go so far as to wear a bowler and carry the staff of office – the rolled umbrella. I was earlier than most because the first postal delivery of the day was before office hours. I arrived at Kiddykar Toys with half an hour in hand and immediately put on the kettle for coffee before inspecting the view from the window. The stallholders of Leather Lane were getting ready for the day's sales and there was no sign of Mackintosh. I wasn't worried; he'd be around somewhere in the neighbourhood keeping an eye open for the postman.

I had just finished the first cup of coffee when the phone rang. Mackintosh said briefly, 'He's coming.' There was a click as he hung up.

In the interests of his leg muscles the postman had put in a bit of time and motion study on this building. It was his habit to take the lift to the top floor and deliver the letters from the top down on the theory that walking downstairs is easier than climbing them. I put on my coat and hat and opened the door a couple of inches, listening for the whine of the lift. It was ten minutes before I heard it go up, and then I stepped out into the corridor, carefully drawing the office door closed but not quite shut so that the least push would swing it open.

It was very quiet in the building at that hour and, as I heard the postman clattering down the stairs to the second floor, I retreated down the flight of stairs to the first floor. He hit the second floor and turned away from Betsy-Lou's door to deliver the post to other offices. That was his usual routine and so I wasn't worried.

Then I heard him coming back a few steps at a time, the intervals punctuated by the metallic bangs of swinging letterbox flaps. Just at the right time I came up the stairs and headed for the Kiddykar office which brought me facing him. I stared at his hands but there was no little yellow box to be seen.

'Morning,' he said. 'Lovely day, isn't it?' He went past at a quick pace and I fumbled my way into the office, faking the opening of the door with a key. As I closed it behind me I found that I was sweating slightly; not much but enough to show that I was under tension. It was ridiculous, I suppose – I had only to take a little box away from an unsuspecting man, which should have been the easiest thing in the world and no occasion for nerves.

It was the contents of that box which set up the tension. A hundred and twenty thousand quid is a hell of a lot of money to be at stake. It's rather like the man who can walk along a kerbstone unconcernedly and never put a foot wrong, yet let him try the same thing with a two-hundred-foot drop on one side and he'll break into a muck sweat.

I walked over to the window and opened the casement, not so much to get fresh air as to signal to Mackintosh that the first delivery was a bust. I looked down into Leather Lane and saw him in his appointed place. He was standing before a fruit and vegetable stall prodding tomatoes with a nervous forefinger. He flicked his eyes up at the window then swung around and walked away.

I lit a cigarette and settled down with the morning papers. There was quite a while to wait before the second post.

Two hours later the telephone rang again. 'Better luck this time,' said Mackintosh, and hung up.

I went through the same routine as before – there was no harm in it as this would be a different postman. I waited on the landing just below the second floor and listened intently. It would be more difficult now that the building was inhabited and a lot depended on whether I could catch the postman alone in the corridor. If I could then it was easy, but if there was anyone else present I would have to grab the box and run for it.

Steady footsteps warned me that he was coming and I trotted up the stairs at the critical moment. I swung my head back and forwards like someone about to cross a street, and found that all was clear – no one in the corridor except for me and the postman. Then I looked at his hands.

He was carrying a bundle of letters and right on top of the bundle was a little yellow box.

I stepped right in front of him as he drew abreast of the Kiddykar office. 'Have you anything for me?' I asked. 'I'm in there.' I pointed to the door behind him.

He turned his head to look at the name on the door and I hit him behind the ear with the cosh, hoping to God he hadn't an unusually thin skull. He grunted and his knees buckled. I caught him before he fell and pushed him at the door of the office which swung open under his weight, and he fell over the threshold spilling letters before him. The Kodachrome box fell to the floor with a little thump.

I stepped over him and hauled him inside, pushing the door closed with my foot. Then I grabbed the yellow box and dropped it into the innocuous brown box that Mackintosh had had specially tailored to fit it. I had to pass it on to him in the street and we wanted no flash of that conspicuous yellow to be seen.

In less than sixty seconds from the time I greeted the postman I was outside the office and locking the door on him. As I did so someone passed behind me in the corridor and opened the door of the Betsy-Lou office. I turned and went downstairs, not moving too fast but not dawdling. I reckoned the postman wouldn't come round for two or three minutes, and then he still had to get out of the office.

I came out on to the street and saw Mackintosh staring at me. He averted his eyes and half-turned away and I strode across the street among the stalls in his direction. It was easy enough, in the throng, to bump him with my shoulder, and with a muffled 'Sorry!' I passed the packet to him and continued in the direction of Holborn.

I hadn't gone far when I heard the smash of glass behind me and a confused shouting. That postman had been smart; he had wasted no time on the door but had broken the window as a means of drawing attention to himself. Also he hadn't been unconscious for as long as I had hoped – I hadn't hit him nearly hard enough.

But I was safe – far enough away not to be spotted by him and moving farther all the time. It would take at least five minutes to sort out the confusion and by that time I intended to get thoroughly lost – and I hoped Mackintosh was doing the same. He was the hot one now – he had the diamonds.

I ducked into the rear entrance of Gamage's and made my way through the store at an easier pace, looking, I hoped, like a man who knows where he's going. I found the men's room and locked myself into a cubicle. My coat came off and was reversed – that so carefully chosen coat with the nicely contrasting colours. The natty cap came from my pocket and the hat I was wearing was regretfully screwed into a shapeless bundle. It wouldn't do it much good to be jammed into my pocket but I didn't want to leave it lying around.

Clothes make the man and a new man left that men's room. I wandered casually about the store, drifting towards the front entrance, and on the way I bought myself a new tie just to have a legitimate reason for being in Gamage's, but that precaution was unnecessary. I emerged on to the pavement of Holborn and set off to walk west. No taxis for me because taxi-drivers would be questioned about pick-ups in the area at that time.

Half an hour later I was in a pub just off Oxford Street near the Marble Arch and sinking a thankful pint of beer. It had been a good smooth job but it wasn't over yet, not by a hell of a long way. I wondered if I could trust Mackintosh to do his half of the job properly.

V

That evening, as I was preparing to go out on the town, there came a firm knock at the door of my room. I opened it and was confronted by two very large men dressed very conservatively and in the best of taste. The one on the right said, 'Are you Joseph Aloysius Rearden?'

I didn't have to bend my brain too far to realize that these two were coppers. I gave a twisted grin. 'I'd rather forget the Aloysius.'

'We are police officers.' He flipped a wallet in front of me negligently. 'We hope you can assist us in our enquiries.'

'Hey!' I said. 'Is that a warrant card? I've never seen one of those before.'

Reluctantly he flipped open the wallet again and let me read the card. He was Detective-Inspector John M. Brunskill and indubitably the genuine article. I babbled a bit. 'You see these things happening at the bioscope; I never thought it would happen to me.'

'Bioscope?' he said dubiously.

'The films – we call a cinema a bioscope in South Africa. That's where I'm from, you know. I don't know how I can help you in any enquiries, Inspector. I'm a stranger to London – in fact, I'm a stranger to England. I've been here only a week – less than that, really.'

'We know all that, Mr Rearden,' said Brunskill gently.

So they'd checked on me already. These boys moved fast – the British police are wonderful.

'May we come in, Mr Rearden? I think you *will* be able to help us.'

I stood on one side and waved them into the room. 'Come in and take a seat. There's only one chair so one of you will have to sit on the bed. And take your coats off.'

'That won't be necessary,' said Brunskill. 'We won't be staying long. This is Detective-Sergeant Jervis.'

Jervis looked an even harder nut than Brunskill. Brunskill was polished and had the suavity that maturity brings, while Jervis still had his sharp corners and was all young, rock-hard cop. But Brunskill would be the more dangerous – he'd be tricky.

I said, 'Well, what can I do for you?'

'We are making enquiries about the theft of a package from a postman in Leather Lane this morning,' said Brunskill. 'What can you tell us about it, Mr Rearden?'

'Where's Leather Lane?' I asked. 'I'm a stranger here.'

Brunskill looked at Jervis and Jervis looked at Brunskill and then they both looked at me. 'Come, Mr Rearden,' said Brunskill. 'You can do better than that.'

'You've got a record,' said Jervis suddenly.

This was the shot across the bows. I said bitterly, 'And you johns will never let me forget it. Yes, I've got a record; I did eighteen months in Pretoria Central – eighteen months of stone cold jug – and that was a long time ago. I've been straight ever since.'

'Until perhaps this morning,' suggested Brunskill.

I looked him straight in the eye. 'Don't pull the old flannel on me. You tell me what I'm supposed to have done, and I'll tell you if I did it – straight out.'

'Very good of you,' murmured Brunskill. 'Don't you think so, Sergeant?'

Jervis made a nasty noise at the back of his throat. Then he said, 'Mind if we search your room, Rearden?'

'It's Mr Rearden to sergeants,' I said. 'Your boss has better manners than you. And I most certainly do object to you searching my room – unless you have a warrant.'

'Oh, we have that,' said Brunskill calmly. 'Go ahead, Sergeant.' He took a document from his pocket and slapped it into my hand. 'I think you'll find that in order, Mr Rearden.'

I didn't even bother to look at it, but just tossed it on to the dressing-table and watched Jervis do an efficient overhaul of the room. He found nothing – there wasn't anything for him to find. As last he gave up, looked at Brunskill and shook his head.

Brunskill turned to me. 'I must ask you to come to the police station with me.'

I was silent and let the pause lengthen for a long time before I said, 'Well, go ahead and ask.'

'We've got ourselves a joker here, sir,' said Jervis. He looked at me with dislike.

'If you do ask I won't come,' I said. 'You'll have to arrest me to get me anywhere near the nick.'

Brunskill sighed. 'Very well, Mr Rearden; I arrest you on suspicion of being involved in an assault on a postman on premises in Leather Lane at about nine-thirty this morning. Does that satisfy you?'

'It'll do to be going on with,' I said. 'Let's go.'

'Oh, I almost forgot,' he said. 'Anything you say will be noted and may be used in evidence.'

'I know the form,' I said. 'I know it only too well.'

'I'm sure you do,' he said softly.

I expected them to take me to Scotland Yard but I found myself in quite a small police station. Where it was I don't know – I don't know London at all well. They put me into a small room unfurnished except for a deal table and two bentwood chairs. It had the same institutional smell of all police stations anywhere in the world. I sat in a chair and smoked one cigarette after another, watched by a uniformed copper who stood with his back to the door, looking undressed without his helmet.

It was nearly an hour and a half before they got around to doing anything and it was tough boy Jervis who started the attack. He came into the room and waved abruptly at the uniformed john who did a disappearing act, then he sat down at the other side of the table and looked at me for a long time without speaking. I ignored him – I didn't even look at him and it was he who broke first. 'You've been here before, haven't you, Rearden?'

'I've never been here before in my life.'

'You know what I mean. You've sat on hard wooden chairs with a policeman the other side of the table many, many times. You know the drill too well – you're a professional. With another man I might pussyfoot around – use a bit of psychology, maybe – but that wouldn't work with you, would it? So I'm not going to do it. There'll be no tact, no psychology with you. I'm going to crack you like a nut, Rearden.'

'You'd better remember Judges' Rules.'

He gave a sharp bark of laughter. 'See what I mean? An honest man wouldn't know Judges' Rules from Parkinson's Law. But you know, don't you? You're a wrong 'un; you're bent.'

'When you're finished with the insults I'll go,' I said.

'You'll go when I say you can,' he said sharply.

I grinned at him. 'You'd better check with Brunskill first, sonny.'

'Where are the diamonds?'

'What diamonds?'

'That postman is in a bad way. You hit him a bit too hard, Rearden. The chances are he'll cash in his chips – and where will that put you?' He leaned forward. 'You'll be inside for so long that you'll trip over your beard.'

I must say he was trying hard but he was a bad liar. No dying postman could have busted that window in the Kiddykar office. I just looked him in the eye and kept my mouth shut.

'If those diamonds aren't found it'll go hard for you,' said Jervis. 'Maybe if the diamonds turn up the judge will be a bit easier on you.'

'What diamonds?' I asked.

And so it went on for a good half-hour until he got tired and went away and the uniformed man came back and took up his old stance in front of the door. I turned and looked at him. 'Don't you get corns? Isn't this job bad for your feet?' He looked at me with a bland face and expressionless eyes and said exactly nothing.

Presently a bigger gun was brought to bear. Brunskill came in carrying a thick folder bulging with papers which he put on the table. 'I'm sorry to have kept you waiting, Mr Rearden,' he said.

'I wouldn't like to bet on it,' I said.

He gave me a pitying, though understanding, smile. 'We all have our jobs to do, and some are nastier than others.

You mustn't blame me for doing mine.' He opened the folder. 'You have quite a record, Mr Rearden. Interpol have a fat dossier on you.'

'I've been convicted once,' I said. 'Anything else is not official and you can't use it. What anyone might have to say about me isn't proof of a damned thing.' I grinned and, pointing at the folder, quoted: '"What the policeman said isn't evidence."'

'Just so,' said Brunskill. 'But it's interesting all the same.' He mused over the papers for a long time, then said, without looking up, 'Why are you flying to Switzerland tomorrow?'

'I'm a tourist,' I said. 'I've never been there before.'

'It's your first time in England, too, isn't it?'

'You know it is. Look here, I want an attorney.'

He looked up. 'I would suggest a solicitor. Have you anyone in mind?'

From my wallet I took the scrap of paper with the telephone number on it which Mackintosh had given me with this eventuality in mind. 'That'll find him,' I said.

Brunskill's eyebrows lifted when he read it. 'I know this number very well – he's just the man to tackle your type of case. For a man who's been in England less than a week you know your way around the fringes.' He put the paper on one side. 'I'll let him know you're here.'

My throat was dry from smoking too many cigarettes. 'Another thing,' I said. 'I could do with a cup of tea.'

'I'm afraid we can't run to tea,' said Brunskill regretfully. 'Would a glass of water be all right?'

'It'll do.'

He went to the door, gave instructions, and then came back. 'You people seem to think that we spend all our time in police stations drinking tea – running a continuous cafeteria for old lags. I can't think where you get it from unless it's from television.'

'Not me,' I said. 'We have no TV in South Africa.'

'Indeed!' said Brunskill. 'How curious. Now, about those diamonds. I think that . . .'

'What diamonds?' I broke in.

And so it went on. He shook me more than Jervis because he was trickier. He wasn't stupid enough to lie about something I knew to be true, as Jervis had done, and was better at the wearing down process, being as persistent as a buzzing fly. The water came – a carafe and a tumbler. I filled the tumbler and drank thirstily, then refilled it and drank again. Brunskill watched me and said at last, 'Had enough?'

I nodded, so he reached out and took the tumbler delicately in his fingertips and carried it out. When he came back he looked at me sorrowfully. 'I didn't think you'd fall for that chestnut. You know we can't fingerprint you until you're booked. Why did you let us have them?'

'I was tired,' I said.

'Too bad,' he said sympathetically. 'Now, to get back to those diamonds . . .'

Presently Jervis came into the room and beckoned to Brunskill and they stood by the door and talked in low voices. Brunskill turned around. 'Now, look here, Rearden; we've nailed you. We have enough evidence now to send you up for ten years. If you help us to get back those stones it might help you when the judge sentences you.'

'What diamonds?' I asked tiredly.

His mouth shut with a snap. 'All right,' he said curtly. 'Come this way.'

I followed, the meat in a sandwich between Brunskill and Jervis. They escorted me to a large room occupied by a dozen men lined along one wall. Jervis said, 'No need to explain what this is, Rearden; but I will because the law says

I must. It's a line-up – an identification parade. There are three people coming in to see you. You can insert yourself anywhere in that line, and you can change your position in the intervals if you like. Got it?'

I nodded and walked over to the wall, putting myself third in line. There was a pause in the action and then the first witness came in – a little old lady, someone's darling mother. She went along the line and then came straight back to me and pointed at my chest. 'That's the one.' I'd never seen her before.

They took her out, but I didn't bother to change position. There wasn't any point, really; they had me nailed just as Brunskill had said. The next one was a young man of about eighteen. He didn't have to go all the way along the line. He stopped in front of me. 'That's 'im,' he said.' 'E did it.'

The third witness didn't have any trouble either. He took one look at me and yelled, 'This is the boyo. I hope you get life, mate.' He went away rubbing his head. It was the postman – not nearly as dead as Jervis would have me believe.

Then is was over and Jervis and Brunskill took me back. I said to Jervis, 'You'd make a good miracle-worker; you brought that postman back to life pretty smartly.'

He gave me a sharpish look and a slow smile spread over his face. 'And how did you know that was the postman?'

I shrugged. My goose was cooked whichever way I looked at it. I said to Brunskill, 'Who is the bastard of a nark that shopped me?'

His face closed up. 'Let's call it "information received", Rearden. You'll be charged tomorrow morning and you'll go before a magistrate immediately. I'll see that your solicitor is in attendance.'

'Thanks,' I said. 'What's his name?'

'By God!' he said. 'But you're a cool one. Your solicitor is a Mr Maskell.'

'Thanks again,' I said.

Brunskill whistled up a station sergeant who put me in a cell for the night. I had a bite to eat and then stretched out and went to sleep almost immediately.

It had been a tiring day.

TWO

Maskell was a short, stout man with shrewd brown eyes and an immense air of dignity. He was introduced to me just before the charge was laid and did not seem at all perturbed at the prospect of acting for a criminal. The law is a strange profession in which ordinary morality goes by the board; a well liked and generally respected barrister will fight like a tiger for his client, who may well be a murderer or a rapist, and will receive well-merited congratulations on an acquittal. Then he will go home and write a letter to the editor of *The Times* fulminating about the rise in crime. A schizophrenic profession.

I said as much to Maskell once when I knew him better. He said gently, 'Mr Rearden, to me you are neither guilty nor innocent – the people who decide that are the twelve men in the box. I am here to find out the facts in a case and to present them to a barrister who will conduct the argument – and I do it for money.'

We were in court at the time and he waved his hand largely. 'Who says crime doesn't pay?' he asked cynically. 'Taking all in all, from the court ushers to his Lordship up there, there are at least fifty people directly involved in this case, and they're all making a living out of it. Some, such as myself and his Lordship, make a better living than others. We do very well out of people like you, Mr Rearden.'

But at this time I didn't know Maskell at all. It was a hurried introduction, and he said hastily, 'We will talk in more detail later. First we must find what this is all about.'

So I was taken and charged. I won't go into all the legal language but what it all boiled down to was robbery with violence – an assault on the person of John Edward Harte, an employee of the GPO, and the theft of diamonds, the property of Lewis and van Veldenkamp, Ltd, valued at £173,000.

I nearly burst out laughing at that. It had been a bigger haul than Mackintosh had expected, unless Mr Lewis and Meneer van Veldenkamp were trying to sting their insurance company. But I kept a straight face and when it was over I turned to Maskell and asked, 'What now?'

'I'll see you in the Magistrates' Court in about an hour. That will be a mere formality.' He rubbed his chin. 'There's a lot of money involved here. Have the police recovered the diamonds?'

'You'd better ask them. I know nothing about any diamonds.'

'Indeed! I must tell you that if the diamonds are still – shall we say *at large*? – then it will be very difficult for me to get you out on bail. But I will try.'

The proceedings in the Magistrates' Court were brief, lasting for about three minutes. They would have been even briefer but Brunskill got on his hind legs and argued against the granting of bail. 'The diamonds have not yet been recovered, your Honour, and if the prisoner is released on bail I fear they never will be. Further, if the prisoner had not been apprehended last night he would have been in Switzerland this morning.'

The magistrate flapped his hand. 'You think the prisoner will jump bail?'

'I do,' said Brunskill firmly. 'And there is one thing more, the prisoner is in the dock on a charge of violence and he has a police record in which violence figures largely. I fear the intimidation of witnesses.'

He nearly overreached himself. 'You think he will leave the country *and* intimidate witnesses?' asked the magistrate with polite incredulity. 'I doubt if his violent arm would reach so far. However, on the balance of evidence and especially in respect of the missing property I am inclined to agree with you. Bail is denied.'

Brunskill sat down and Maskell shrugged and stuffed some papers back into his briefcase. And so I was remanded for trial at the Central Criminal Court. I was going to see the inside of the Old Bailey, after all.

Maskell had a few words with me before I was taken away. 'Now I can find out the strength of the police case against you. I'll have a word with the prosecution and then you and I can sit down together and discuss this whole thing. If you want anything ask that I be informed, but I shall probably see you tomorrow, anyway.'

A prisoner on remand is theoretically an innocent man. Practically, he is regarded neutrally as neither guilty nor innocent. The food was good, the bed soft and there were no irksome restrictions – except one. I couldn't get out of the nick. Still, you can't have everything.

Maskell came to see me the following afternoon and we sat in one of the interviewing rooms. He regarded me thoughtfully, then said, 'The case against you is very strong, Mr Rearden; very strong, indeed. Unless you can prove conclusively and without equivocation that you could not have committed this crime, then I fear you will be convicted.'

I was about to speak, but he raised his hand. 'But we can go into that later. First things first. Now, have you any money?'

'About a hundred and fifty pounds. But I haven't paid my hotel bill – I wasn't given the chance. I don't want hotel bilking to be added to the charge sheet, so it'll be nearer a hundred pounds I have to play around with.'

Maskell nodded. 'As you may know, my own fee has been taken care of. But I am not the man who will fight your case in court; that will be done by a barrister, and barristers come even more expensive than I do, especially barristers of the calibre needed to win this case. A hundred pounds would come nowhere near the amount necessary.'

I shrugged. 'I'm sorry; it's all I've got.' That wasn't exactly true but I could see that even the best barrister in the business couldn't get me out of this one and there wasn't any point in throwing my money away.

'I see. Well, there is provision for a case like yours. A barrister will be appointed by the Court to act for you. The trouble is that he will be not of your choice; yet I am not with out influence and I will see if I have any strings to pull that will get us the best man.'

He took a folder from his briefcase and opened it. 'I want you to tell me exactly what you did on the morning in question.' He paused. 'I already know you did not have breakfast at your hotel.'

'I didn't sleep well that night,' I said. 'So I got up early and took a walk.'

Maskell sighed. 'And where did you walk to, Mr Rearden?'

I thought it out. 'I went into Hyde Park and walked up as far as the Round Pond. There's a famous building up there – Kensington Palace – but it was closed. It was very early in the morning.'

'I shouldn't imagine there would be many people in Hyde Park or Kensington Gardens so early. Did you speak to anyone – make enquiries – at Kensington Palace? Did you ask the time of opening, for instance?'

'There wasn't anyone around to ask.'

'Very well; what did you do then?'

'I walked back through the park to Hyde Park Corner and over into Green Park. Then up Bond Street into Oxford Street. I was doing a bit of window shopping, you see.'

'And what time would this be?'

'Oh, I don't know. Say, about nine fifteen. I was dawdling a bit. I had a look at a place called Burlington Arcade, then I went on up Bond Street looking at the shops, as I said. It's marvellous – nothing like it in South Africa.'

'And you didn't speak to anyone at all?'

'If I'd known I needed an alibi I would have,' I said bitterly.

'Just so,' said Maskell. 'So you arrived at Oxford Street – what did you do then?'

'Well, I hadn't had breakfast and I felt a bit peckish so I found a pub and had some sandwiches and a pint. I was chatting to the barman, an Irishman. He ought to remember me.'

'And what time was this?'

'It must have been after ten o'clock because the pub was open. Say, half past ten.'

'That alibi comes a little late,' said Maskell. 'It's not relevant.' He consulted a sheet of paper from the folder. 'I must tell you that the police version differs from yours substantially – and they have a great deal of evidence to show.' He looked me in the eye. 'Do I have to point out the dangers of lying to your lawyer?'

'I'm not lying,' I said indignantly.

He spoke gravely. 'Mr Rearden, let me say that you are in deep trouble. I gather you want to enter a plea of not guilty at your trial, but I must warn you that, on the evidence now extant, you are likely to lose the case. Public concern about crimes of violence of this nature has been increasing and this concern is reflected by the heavy sentences imposed by the courts.'

He paused to collect his thoughts and then went on in measured tones. 'Now, as your solicitor I cannot prejudge this case, but I would like to say this: If the diamonds were to be returned, and if you entered a plea of guilty, then the court would be inclined to leniency and, in my opinion, your sentence would be not more than five years and possibly as little as three years. With a remittance of sentence for good behaviour you could be out of prison in as little as two years.

'On the other hand, if the diamonds are *not* returned and if you enter a plea of not guilty then your sentence is going to be very heavy – assuming you are convicted, an assumption which on the evidence I have is very likely. If I may use slang I would say that his Lordship is going to throw the book at you; he'll lock you up and throw away the key. I doubt if you would get away with much under fourteen years, and I assure you that I have great experience in these forecasts and I do not speak lightly.'

He cleared his throat. 'Now, what do you say, Mr Rearden? What shall we do about this?'

'The only diamonds I saw that morning were in the shop windows of Bond Street,' I said distinctly.

He looked at me in silence for a long time then shook his head. 'Very well,' he said quietly. 'I will go about my business – and yours – but with no great hope of success. I ought to warn you that the police have such evidence that will be very difficult for defence counsel to refute.'

'I'm innocent,' I said obstinately.

He said no more but collected his papers and left the room without a backward glance.

II

So there I was in the dock of the Central Criminal Court – the Old Bailey. There was much pomp and circumstance, robes and wigs, deferences and courtesies – and me popping up from the bowels of the earth into the dock like the demon king in a pantomime, the centre of attraction. Of course, I had competition from the Judge. It seems that when a man gets to sit on the Bench he feels that he's entitled to be a licensed jester and he loves nothing more than to have the audience rolling in the aisles at his witticisms. I've seen worse music hall turns than a Criminal Court judge. Still, it does lighten the atmosphere – a court would be a pretty grim place without the comic bits – and the Chief Comic isn't prejudiced; he aims his barbs at prosecution and defence alike. I found that I quite enjoyed it and laughed as much as anyone else.

Maskell was there, of course, but in a minor role; defence counsel was a man called Rollins. Maskell had tried again, just before the trial, to get me to alter my plea of not guilty. He said, 'Mr Rearden, I want you to consider once more the consequences of losing this case. You will not only receive a long sentence but there are certain other implications. Long-term prisoners are invariably regarded as high-risk prisoners, especially those who are regarded as having financial backing. In the absence of diamonds to the value of £173,000 you would undoubtedly come into that category. A high risk prisoner is treated very differently from the ordinary prisoner and I understand that the circumstances can be rather unpleasant. I would think of that if I were you.'

I didn't have to think of it. I hadn't a hope in hell of getting the diamonds back and that was the crux of the matter. Even if I pleaded guilty I'd get a stiff sentence in the absence of the diamonds. The only thing to do was to put on a brave face and make the best of it. It struck me that Mackintosh was a very smart man and that maybe Mrs Smith was even smarter.

I said, 'I'm sorry, Mr Maskell, but I'm innocent.'

He looked puzzled. He didn't believe a word I said but he couldn't figure out why I was keeping my mouth shut. But then a wintry smile came to his face. 'I hope you don't think the investment of so many years of your life is worth the money. Too much time in prison is apt to change a man for the worse.'

I smiled at him. 'I thought you said you wouldn't prejudge the case.'

'I think you are a very foolish young man,' he said. 'But you have my best wishes in your unfortunate future.'

The trial got under way laboriously. First the jury details were settled and then the action began, the prosecution getting first crack. The prosecuting counsel was a tall, thin man with a face like the blade of a hatchet, and he fairly revelled in his job. He led off with a rather skimpy introduction and then began to lay on the prosecution witnesses, while Rollins, my counsel, looked on with a bored expression on his face. I had met Rollins only twice and he had been offhanded on both occasions. He knew this was one he wasn't going to win.

The prosecution witnesses were good – very good, indeed – and I began to see why the prosecuting counsel was looking so cheerful despite the misfortune of his face. Expert police witnesses introduced photographs and drawings of the scene of the crime and, that groundwork laid, the pressure was applied.

There was the motherly old soul who had identified me at the police station line-up. 'I saw him strike the postman,' she testified, the light of honesty shining from her eyes. 'I was standing in the corridor and saw the accused hit the postman with his fist, grab a yellow box from him, and push him into an office. Then the accused ran down the stairs.'

The prosecutor offered her a plan of the second floor. 'Where were you standing?'

She indicated a place in the corridor and looked across the court straight at me as guileless as you please. The sweet old lady was lying like a flatfish, and she knew that I knew she was lying. She couldn't have been standing in the corridor because I'd checked, and the details of her evidence were all wrong, anyway. There wasn't a thing I could do about it, though.

Another highlight was a man from Fortnum and Mason who testified to having sent a packed picnic basket to a certain hotel. The order was telephoned in by a Mr Rearden. Questioned by the defence he said he couldn't be certain that the Mr Rearden who ordered the basket was the accused.

A hotel employee testified that the accused stayed at his hotel and that a basket had been delivered addressed to Mr Rearden. Asked what had happened to it he said he didn't know but presumably the accused had collected it. There was a bit of argument about that and part of his answer was struck out.

A detective produced a picnic basket in court and testified that he had found it in the office of Kiddykars Ltd. It had been identified as coming from Fortnum's. Another police witness testified that the basket was liberally covered with the accused's fingerprints, as were other items in the room; to wit – an electric kettle, a coffee pot and several pieces of crockery and cutlery.

The jury drew its own conclusions.

Then there was the police witness who said he had been interested in tracking down the ownership of Kiddykars Ltd. Apparently it was a genuine company but not doing any business. The lines of ownership were very tangled but he had finally cracked it with the helpful assistance of the South African police. The owner proved to be a Mr Joseph Aloysius Rearden of Johannesburg. No, he had no means of knowing if the Joseph Aloysius Rearden of Kiddykars was the Joseph Aloysius Rearden who stood in the dock. That would be taking him further than he was prepared to go.

Again the jury drew its conclusions.

The postman gave his evidence fairly. I had hit him and he had recovered consciousness in the Kiddykar office. There was nothing in that which contradicted the perjured evidence of Old Mother Hubbard. The third eye-witness was the office boy from Betsy-Lou; he said he saw me lock the office door and run downstairs. I remembered him vaguely as the person who had walked behind me at that time. But I hadn't *run* downstairs – that was his imagination working overtime.

Brunskill was a star witness.

'Acting on information received I went, with Detective-Sergeant Jervis, to see the accused at his hotel. His answers to my questioning were such that I arrested him on suspicion of having been concerned in this crime. Subsequently I obtained his fingerprints which matched prints found in the office of Kiddykars Ltd. Further enquiries were made which resulted in three witnesses coming forward, all of whom identified the accused. More extensive enquiries led to the further evidence that has been presented to the Court relating to the picnic basket and the ownership of Kiddykars Ltd.'

The prosecutor sat down with a grin on his face and Rollins bounced to his feet for cross-examination.

Rollins: You spoke of 'information received', Inspector. How did this information come to you?

Brunskill: (hesitantly) Must I answer that, my Lord? The sources of police information may be prejudicial to . . .

Rollins: (quickly) This goes to the malice of a person or persons unknown which may prejudice the case for the accused, my Lord.

Judge: (in Churchillian tones) Mr Rollins; I don't see how your case *can* deteriorate much further. However, I am inclined to let the question go. I am as interested as anybody. Answer the question, Inspector.

Brunskill: (unwillingly) There was one telephone call and one letter.

Rollins: Both anonymous?

Brunskill: Yes.

Rollins: Did these communications indicate that the accused had committed this crime?

Brunskill: Yes.

Rollins: Did they indicate where he was to be found?

Brunskill: Yes.

Rollins: Did they indicate that the basket found in the Kiddykar office had been purchased by the accused at Fortnum and Mason?

Brunskill: er . . . Yes.

Rollins: Is it a crime to purchase foodstuffs from that eminent firm of retailers?

Brunskill: (sharply) Of course not.

Rollins: Did these anonymous communications indicate that the firm of Kiddykars Ltd was owned by the accused?

Brunskill: (uncomfortably) Yes.

Rollins: Is it a crime to own such a firm as Kiddykars Ltd?

Brunskill: (with ebbing patience) No.

Judge: I am not so sure. Anyone who so maltreats the English language as to arrive at so abominable a name ought to be treated as a criminal.

(Laughter in court)

Rollins: Inspector, would you not say it was true that all your work had been done for you in this case? Would you not say it was true that without these malicious communications the accused would not be standing in the dock at this moment?

Brunskill: I cannot answer that question. He would have been caught.

Rollins: Would he? I admire your certitude.

Brunskill: He would have been caught.

Rollins: But not so speedily.

Brunskill: Perhaps not.

Rollins: Would you not characterize your mysterious communicant as someone who 'had it in' for the accused at worst – or a common informer or stool pigeon at best?

Brunskill: (smiling) I would prefer to think of him as a public-spirited citizen.

Very funny! Mackintosh – a public-spirited citizen! But, by God, the pair of them had been infernally clever. The first time I had laid eyes on that picnic basket had been in the Kiddykars office, and I certainly hadn't telephoned Fortnum's. Mrs Smith had done her shopping to good effect! Nor did I own Kiddykars Ltd – not to my own knowledge; but I'd have a hell of a time proving it. They had delivered me to the law trussed up like a chicken.

There wasn't much after that. I said my piece, futile though it was; the prosecutor tore me into shreds and Rollins half-heartedly tried to sew up the pieces again without much success. The judge summed up and, with one careful eye on the Appeal Court, directed the jury to find me guilty. They were out only for half an hour – just time enough for a much-needed smoke – and the answer was predictable.

Then the judge asked if I had anything to say, so I spoke up with just two words: 'I'm innocent.'

Nobody took much notice of that – they were too busy watching the judge arrange his papers and gleefully anticipating how heavy he'd be. He fussed around for a while, making sure that all attention would be on him, and then he began to speak in portentous and doomladen tones.

'Joseph Aloysius Rearden, you have been found guilty of stealing by force diamonds to the value of £173,000. It falls to me to sentence you for this crime. Before I do so I would like to say a few words concerning your part in this affair.'

I could see what was coming. The old boy couldn't resist the chance of pontificating – it's easy from a safe seat.

'An Englishman is walking the streets in the course of his usual employ when he is suddenly and unexpectedly assaulted – brutally assaulted. He is not aware that he is carrying valuables which, to him, would undoubtedly represent untold wealth, and it is because of these valuables that he is attacked.

'The valuables – the diamonds – are now missing and you, Rearden, have not seen fit to co-operate with the police in their recovery in spite of the fact that you must have known that the court would be inclined to leniency had you done so. Therefore, you cannot expect leniency of this court.

'I have been rather puzzled by your recalcitrant attitude but my puzzlement abated when I made an elementary mathematical calculation. In the normal course of events such a crime as yours, a crime of violence such as is abhorrent in this country, coupled with the loss to the community of property worth £173,000, would be punished by the heavy sentence of fourteen years' imprisonment. My calculation, however, informs me that for those fourteen years you would be receiving an annual income of not less than £12,350 – tax free – being the amount you have stolen divided by fourteen. This, I might add, is considerably more than the stipend of one of Her Majesty's Judges, such as myself – a fact which can be ascertained by anyone who cares to consult Whitaker's Almanack.

'Whether it can be considered that the loss of fourteen years of freedom, and confinement to the hardly pleasant environs of our prisons, is worth such an annual sum is a debatable matter. You evidently think it is worth while. Now, it is not the function of this court to make the fees of crime worth while, so you can hardly blame me for endeavouring to reduce your annual prison income.

'Joseph Aloysius Rearden, I sentence you to twenty years' detention in such prison or prisons as the appropriate authority deems fit.'

I'd bet Mackintosh was laughing fit to bust a gut.

III

The judge was right when he referred to 'the hardly pleasant environs of our prisons'. The one in which I found myself was pretty deadly. The reception block was crowded – the judges must have been working overtime that day – and there was a lot of waiting about apparently pointlessly. I was feeling a bit miserable; no one can stand in front of a judge and receive a twenty-year sentence with complete equanimity.

Twenty years!

I was thirty-four years old. I'd be fifty-four when I came out; perhaps a bit less if I could persuade them I was a good boy, but that would be bloody difficult in view of what the judge had said. Any Review Board I appeared before would read a transcript of the trial and the judge's remarks would hit them like a hammer.

Twenty long years!

I stood by apathetically while the police escort read out the details of my case to the receiving officer. 'All right,' said the receiving officer. He signed his name in a book and tore out a sheet. 'Here's the body receipt.'

So help me – that's what he said. 'Body receipt.' When you're in prison you cease to be a man; you're a body, a zombie, a walking statistic. You're something to be pushed around like the GPO pushed around that little yellow box containing the diamonds; you're a parcel of blood and guts that needs feeding at regular intervals, and you're assumed not to have any brains at all.

'Come on, you,' said the receiving officer. 'In here.' He unlocked a door and stood aside while I walked in. The door slammed behind me and I heard the click of the lock. It was a crowded room filled with men of all types, judging by their clothing. There was everything from blue jeans to a bowler and striped trousers. Nobody was talking – they just stood around and examined the floor minutely as though it was of immense importance. I suppose they all felt like me; they'd had the wind knocked out of them.

We waited in that room for a long time, wondering what was going to happen. Perhaps some of us knew, having been there before. But this was my first time in an English gaol and I felt apprehensive. Maskell's words about the unpleasant circumstances that attend the high-risk prisoner began to worry me.

At last they began to take us out, one at a time and in strict alphabetical order. Rearden comes a long way down the alphabet so I had to wait longer than most, but my turn came and a warder took me down a passage and into an office.

A prisoner is never asked to sit down. I stood before that desk and answered questions while a prison officer took down the answers like the recording angel. He took down my name, birthplace, father's name, mother's maiden name, my age, next-of-kin, occupation. All that time he never looked at me once; to him I wasn't a man, I was a statistics container – he pressed a button and the statistics poured out.

They told me to empty my pockets and the contents were dumped on to the desk and meticulously recorded before being put into a canvas bag. Then my fingerprints were taken. I looked around for something with which to wipe off the ink but there was nothing. I soon found out why. A warder marched me away and into a hot, steamy room where I was told to strip. It was there I lost my clothes. I wouldn't see them again for twenty years and I'd be damned lucky if they'd be in fashion.

After the bath, which wasn't bad, I dressed in the prison clothing – the man in the grey flannel suit. But the cut was terrible and I'd rather have gone to Mackintosh's tailor.

A march up another corridor led to a medical examination, a bit of bureaucratic stupidity. Why they can't have a medical examination while a man is stripped after his bath is beyond me. However, I undressed obligingly and dressed again, and was graded for labour. I was top class – fit for anything.

Then a warder took me away again into an immense hall with tiers of cells lining the walls and with iron stairs like fire escapes. 'I'll tell you once,' said the warder. 'This is "C" Hall.'

We clanked up some stairs and along a landing and he stopped before a cell and unlocked it. 'This is yours.'

I went inside and the door slammed with a cold sound of finality. I stood for some time, not looking at anything in particular. My brain had seized up – gone on strike. After, maybe, fifteen minutes I lay on the bed and damn near cried my eyes out.

After that I felt better and was able to bring some intelligence to bear on the situation. The cell was about twelve feet by seven, and perhaps eight feet high. The walls were distempered – institutional cream and Borstal green – and in one of them was a small barred window set high. The door looked as though it could withstand artillery fire and there was a Judas hole set in it.

The furnishing was sparse; an iron-framed bed, a wooden table and a chair, a washstand with jug, basin and chamberpot, and a bare shelf. Exploring a prison cell is one of the quickest tasks a man can set himself. Within three minutes I had checked everything there was to find – three blankets, two sheets, a lumpy mattress, another shirt, a pair of felt slippers, a thin non-absorbent towel, a spoon and a mug. Hanging on a nail in the wall by a loop of string was a copy of the Rules and Regulations governing HM Prisons together with an informational pamphlet.

Three minutes and I knew practically everything there was to know about that cell. I wondered what I was going to do for the next twenty years. Right there and then I decided I'd have to ration my curiosity – shut down the dampers on thought. There would be too much time and not enough happening, and every new experience would have to be jealously hoarded.

The walls of that prison suddenly had physical meaning. I felt them looming all about me, thick and strong. It was a claustrophobic quarter-hour before the feeling receded and I was able to stop shivering.

I immediately broke my promise about rationing curiosity by beginning to read the informational pamphlet, but that was absolutely necessary. I was a new boy in this school and the sooner I learned the ropes the better. There were too many tricks that could be played on the newcomer by the old hands and I didn't want to fall for any of them.

It was an interesting compilation of data. I discovered that the spare shirt in the cell was to be used as a night shirt, that lights-out was ten-thirty, that the waking call was six-thirty in the morning, that I was to be issued with a razor blade to be returned after shaving. There were other helpful hints even to the point of finding a way out of prison.

For instance, I could refer my case to the Court of Criminal Appeal and, if that failed, I could apply to the Attorney-General to put the case before the House of Lords. At any time I could petition the Home Secretary and I was permitted to write to my Member of Parliament.

I couldn't see myself doing any of those things. I wasn't pally enough with the Home Secretary to enter into any kind of extended correspondence and my Member of Parliament was a shade too far away to do any good – 6,000 miles away.

I read the booklet through and then started on it again from the beginning. I had nothing else to do so I decided to memorize the whole goddamn thing. I was still reading it when the light went out.

IV

The bell clanged and I opened my eyes and was confused until I remembered where I was. I dressed hurriedly and made the bed, then hoisted it up so that it stood on end in a corner of the cell. I sat on the chair and waited. Presently there was a slight metallic sound from the door and I knew someone was watching through the Judas hole.

There was a sharp snap from the lock and the door opened. I stood up and the warder came in. He looked appraisingly around the cell and then fixed me with a hard eye. 'You're new here. You've been reading that thing, haven't you?' He nodded to the booklet on the table.

'Yes, I have.'

'Your bed's in the wrong corner, and the book should be hanging on the wall where you found it. You'll learn. Take a tip from me; do just what you're told and you'll be all right. Now, pick up your chamber-pot and get ready for slopping out.'

'I haven't used it,' I said.

'It gets slopped out whether you've used it or not,' he said curtly. 'Remember what I told you – do as you're told with no arguments. That's lesson number one.'

I picked up the chamber-pot and followed him on to the landing which was full of men, all lined up and each holding his pot. 'All right,' someone shouted. 'Move along.'

There was mephitic stink in the air. I trudged along and found that I was expected to empty the pot into one sink and wash it in another. I went through the motions and returned to my cell, taking my cues from what the others were doing.

The warder came back. 'You can eat in your cell if you like. You'll be served with the others down in the hall, but you can bring your tray up here if you don't feel like joining the party just yet.'

I didn't feel like talking to anyone at all right then. I was too busy trying to keep a firm hold on myself. 'Thanks,' I said, and heard my voice crack.

He was ironic. 'Don't thank me; it's regulations for new prisoners. And another thing, you'll be seeing the Governor this morning. A trusty will take you to his office.'

The trusty came just before ten o'clock and I went with him out of 'C' Hall. 'You're Rearden,' he said. 'I've heard about you.'

'Have you?'

'I'm Simpson.' He nudged me in the ribs with a sharp elbow. 'You're going before the Reception Board. Don't volunteer anything – that's my tip.'

'What happens?'

'Oh, it's just the big boys giving you the once-over. The Governor, the Bible-Slapper, the Senior Screw, the Welfare Officer – people like that. The Governor's not too bad if you keep on the right side of him, but Gawd help you if you don't. Some of the others'll try to feed you a load of old cod's wallop – a crowd of flaming do-gooders. But watch out for Hudson – he's a right bastard.'

'Who's he?'

'The Chief Screw.'

Simpson took me into a waiting room in which half a dozen other prisoners were sitting. They all looked dispirited. Simpson chuckled. '*You* won't have to wait your turn, mate. You're on first; you're someone special.'

I stared at him. 'What's so special about me?'

'You'll see. The Governor'll explain it all very nicely.'

I was about to pursue that a bit further but a warder came into the room. 'Rearden, come this way. Simpson, get back to "C" Hall.'

There were five men seated around a large table, two of them prison officers in uniform. It's a funny thing about prison officers – they never take off their caps, not even when sitting in the Governor's office. Perhaps it's a tradition of the service. One of the civilians wore a dog-collar, so he'd be Simpson's Bible-Slapper – the Prison Chaplain.

The military-looking man in the middle spoke up first. 'Rearden, I'm the Governor of this prison. You are here because you have committed a crime and society has decided that you cannot be allowed to remain at large. How you get on in this prison is your own affair. There are two ways of looking at a prison – as a place of punishment and as a place of rehabilitation. The choice is up to you; we have ample facilities for both modes of operation. Do I make myself clear?'

'Yes, sir.'

He picked up a paper from the table. 'It is normally my practice to treat all prisoners alike. However, I have received notification from the Home Office that you are to be treated as a high-risk prisoner and that entails certain restrictive modifications of your treatment here. For instance, you were brought to this office by a Star Class trusted prisoner, that will never happen again. In future, if you have to move about inside the prison you will be escorted by a prison officer. You will also wear coloured patches upon your clothing. I have prepared a list here of all the other restrictions appertaining to a high-risk prisoner which you will study and to which you will conform.'

He handed me the paper and I folded it and put it into my pocket.

He cleared his throat. 'You must understand, Rearden, that whether you remain in the high-risk category depends entirely upon yourself. The position is reviewed at regular intervals and my recommendations are forwarded to the Home Office. You must also understand that the Home Office is at liberty to disregard my recommendations. The fact that you are a high-risk prisoner is entirely of your own doing, and if there is any way you can convince the police authorities that you are not a risk then I strongly recommend that you do so.'

He meant the diamonds, of course. They still wanted those bloody diamonds. 'Yes, sir,' I said woodenly. 'I'll try to think of something, sir.'

The Governor turned his head. 'Anything from you, Padre?'

The chaplain smiled. 'My name is Clark. I note you claim to have no religion.'

'That's right, sir.'

'I'm not one for pushing religion down a man's throat,' said Clark. 'But do you mind if I come to see you from time to time?'

'No, sir.'

The Governor said, 'This is Mr Anderson, our Welfare Officer. He can do a lot for you if you will let him. Any time you want to see him ask your landing officer. Have you anything you would like to ask him now?'

'Yes, sir. How do I get writing material and books?'

Anderson said easily, 'The writing materials – pens and paper – you will buy in the canteen shop with money you will earn by doing work in the prison. You will be paid a minimum of one shilling and eightpence a day, but you can improve on that if you choose to. Books you can obtain from the prison library.'

'Thank you, sir,' I said. 'Is it possible to get books from outside?' I hesitated. 'I'll be here for a long time – I want to study. I want to improve myself.'

Anderson started to speak but checked himself and looked at the Governor, who said, 'Very commendable, but we'll have to see about that. That will depend upon your general conduct and, as you say, you'll be here a long time.' He nodded to the uniformed officer at the end of the table. 'This is Mr Hudson, the Chief Officer responsible for prison discipline. Have you anything to say, Mr Hudson?'

'Just one thing, sir,' said Hudson. He had a hard face and eyes like chips of glass. 'I don't like high-risk prisoners, Rearden. They upset prison routine and cause trouble among the other prisoners. Don't give me any trouble, that's all. If you do it will be the worse for you.'

I kept my face studiously blank. 'I understand, sir.'

'I sincerely hope you do,' said the Governor. 'You have a visitor – a police officer from Scotland Yard.' He signalled to a warder standing by the door. 'You know where to take him.'

I expected to see Brunskill but it was another detective. 'Detective-Inspector Forbes,' he said. 'Sit down, Rearden.'

I sat down, facing him over the table, and he said pleasantly, 'I expect the Governor has broken the news that you have been classified as a high risk. Do you know what that means?'

I shook my head. 'Not really.'

'You'd better find out,' Forbes advised. 'The Governor must have given you a copy of the high-risk rules. I'll give you five minutes to read it.'

I took the sheet of paper from my pocket and smoothed it out on the table. It was immediately apparent after a cursory reading that life was going to be made quite a bit tougher. The light in my cell was going to be on all night, for one thing. All my clothes, except for shirt and slippers, were to be deposited outside the cell door each night. Any letters I wrote I would have to hand to a prison officer – copies would be made and only photostats would be sent to the ultimate destination, the originals to be filed in the prison. Any conversations with visitors were to be monitored by a prison officer.

I looked up at Forbes. He said, 'Those are only the rules which concern you directly, of course. There are other things. You'll be moved from cell to cell without warning; your cell will be searched – and so will you – at a moment's notice. It will all be very harassing.'

'And what is it to you?' I asked.

He shrugged. 'Nothing really – except that I feel sorry for you. If you weren't so stupid you could get yourself out of this jam.'

'Out of this nick?'

'I'm afraid not,' he said regretfully. 'But the Review Board would look upon you very kindly if you co-operated with us.'

'What sort of co-operation?'

'Come off it, Rearden,' he said tiredly. 'You know what we want. The diamonds, man; the diamonds.'

I looked him in the eye. 'I've never seen any diamonds.' Which was the exact truth – from the start to the finish of the caper. I never saw the diamonds at all.

'Look, Rearden; we know you did it, and we've proved it conclusively. Why try to act the innocent? My God, man; you've been sentenced to a quarter of a lifetime in prison. Do you think you'll be good for anything when you come out? The judge was right – the game isn't worth the candle.'

I said, 'Do I have to sit here and listen to you? Is that part of my punishment?'

'Not if you don't want to,' Forbes said. 'I don't understand you, Rearden. I don't understand why you're taking all this so calmly. All right, let's try another tack. How did you know the drop? How did you know where the diamonds were being sent? That's of some interest, too.'

'I don't know anything about it.'

'You don't know anything about it,' he repeated. 'Do you know – maybe that's true. You could be telling the truth.' He leaned back in his chair, opened his mouth and shut it again and stared at me. After a few moments he began to laugh. 'Oh, no!' he said. 'It couldn't be as simple as that! You couldn't have been double-crossed, could you, Rearden?'

'I don't know what you're talking about.'

Forbes tapped the table. 'You arrive in England out of the blue, and four days later you do the snatch. It must have been set up for you – you couldn't have laid it all on in three days. Then we pick you up and there are no diamonds. So where are they? Obviously, someone else must have them.'

He chuckled. 'Could it be the same someone who made a telephone call and wrote an anonymous letter? You passed on the diamonds and then got shopped, Rearden. Your brainy pal who planned all this made a patsy of you – isn't that the truth?'

I sat mute.

'What!' he said. 'Honour among thieves? Don't be as big a fool as you make out to be. Your friend sold you to the law for a few thousand lousy quid and you're standing for it.' He sounded disgusted. 'Don't think you're going to get out of here to go looking for him; it's not going to be as simple as that. I'm to make recommendations to the Home Office, too, you know; and I'm going to report a total lack of co-operation. And that will mean that you'll be a high-risk prisoner for a hell of a long time – no matter what the Governor may recommend. You can be a good boy in here – you can be the perfect prisoner – but it will cut no ice with the Review Board after they read my report.'

I said hesitantly, 'I'll think about it.'

'You do that,' he said forcibly. 'Any time you want to see me just pass word to the Governor. But don't try to play the fool with me, Rearden. Don't waste my time. You give us what we want and we'll nail your friend for you. We'll crucify him. And *you'll* be off the hook as far as high risk is concerned. What's more, I'll see to it personally that the Review Board gives your case every favourable consideration. I can't do more than that, can I?'

Privately, I doubted if he could do as much. A detective-inspector is pretty small fry at Scotland Yard and if he thought I couldn't see what he was up to he must have thought I was a dumb bunny. All that Forbes wanted was to clear the case and get a good conduct tick on his card – the man who recovered the unrecoverable. And once he'd done it then I could go to hell as far as he was concerned. I wouldn't count; I was just another bent villain, and you don't have to keep promises to crooks. Talk about honour among thieves!

I said slowly, 'Twenty years is a long time. I'll think about it very seriously, Mr Forbes.'

'You won't be sorry,' he said expansively. 'Here, have a cigarette.'

THREE

I suppose a man can get used to anything. They tell me the Jews even got used to living – and dying – in Belsen and Dachau. Well, this was no Dachau, crummy though it was.

At the end of the first week I no longer had my meals in the cell but joined with the others in eating in the Hall. It was then I discovered that I was a personality. There's a very strong caste system in a prison largely based on criminal achievement and, oddly enough, on the lack of achievement which results in a long sentence. Roughly speaking, the long-term prisoners, such as myself, were at the top of the heap with the high-risk boys as the élite. They're looked up to and respected; they hold their little courts and can command the favour of many parasites and hangers-on.

That is one classification. Another is by type of crime. The brainy boys – the con men and professional frauds – are on top with safe breakers running them close. At the bottom of this heap are the sex criminals whom nobody likes. The honest burglar is a much respected man, more for his workmanlike and unassuming ways than anything else.

I was in a position to command a lot of respect, had I so wished it. My status stemmed from the fact that not only was I a long-term man but that I'd diddled the johns and hadn't grassed on my mysterious pal. You can't keep a secret in prison and everyone knew the facts of my case.

Because I kept my mouth shut about the diamonds and because everyone knew what pressure Forbes was exerting I was reckoned to be one of the all right boys; an oddity, but one to be respected.

But I steered clear of all entanglements and alliances. I was being a good boy because I didn't want my high-risk status to continue for any longer than it had to. The time would come when I was going to escape and I had to get rid of the constant surveillance – the singling out of attention on Rearden. Not that I was the only high-risk prisoner – there were others – about half a dozen in all. I steered clear of the lot of them.

Because I was high risk they gave me the job of looking after the tidiness of 'C' Hall where I was under the eye of the Hall screw permanently on duty. Otherwise they would have had to provide a warder to escort me to the workshops instead of going with the others in a gang supervised by a trusty. They were short-staffed and this was a convenient arrangement. I didn't object; I mopped the floors and scrubbed the tables and worked with a will. Anything to be a good boy.

Homosexuals are the bane of prison life. One of them rather fancied me and pursued me to the extent that the only possible way of dissuading him was to give him a thump on the nose which I didn't want to do because that would have been a black mark on my record sheet. It was Smeaton, my landing screw, who got me out of that predicament. He saw what was happening and warned off the queer with a few choice and blasphemous threats, for which I was thankful.

Smeaton was typical of the majority of prison officers. He hadn't interfered because he particularly wanted to prevent my corruption. He'd done it for the sake of a quiet life. The screws looked upon us neutrally for the most part and to them we were just a part of the job. Over the years they had learned a technique – stop it before it starts; keep the temperature down; don't let trouble spread. It was a very effective technique.

So I kept to myself and out of trouble. Not that I didn't mix with the others at all; if I drew attention as a loner then the prison psychiatrist would fix his beady eye on me. So, during the free association periods, I played a few games of cards and improved my chess considerably.

There were others to talk to besides one's fellow criminals. There were the unofficial visitors. Why these were called unofficial I never found out because they had to be authorized by the Governor. They were the prison visitors, the do-gooders and penal reform crowd, and a mixed bag they were. Some of them thought the way to reform a criminal was to moralize at him solemnly by the hour as though a steady drip of predigested religious pap would wash away the canker of the soul. Others were better than that.

Fortunately they weren't obligatory and one could pick and choose to some extent. I discarded a couple before finding a good one. He used to come and chat with me about all sorts of things without ever once trying to fill me up with a lot of guff or trying to convert me. He, also, had lived in South Africa and so we had something in common. Of course, since I was a high-risk prisoner, all these conversations were under the watchful eye and listening ear of a screw. Once I popped in a sentence in Afrikaans to which my visitor replied in the same language. The screw soon put a stop to that and we were both reprimanded by the Governor. But no black mark for Rearden, thank God.

Clark, the Prison Chaplain, also came to see me occasionally. He, also, was no toffee-nose and we got on together quite well. Basically, he was a very religious man and so found himself in a dilemma. He found it hard to reconcile the Christian precept of 'Love thy enemies' with the task of ministering to his flock who were locked up in a big cage. I think it was wearing him down a bit.

The best of the lot was Anderson, the Welfare Officer. He did quite a lot for me and I think his reports to the Governor were encouraging. It was through him that I got the radio, something for which I had worked assiduously. I had been going to the library once a week, as per regulations, and each visit needed the supervision of a screw. I asked Anderson why I couldn't take out a double ration of books and halve the number of library visits, thus taking a bit of strain off the overworked staff.

He saw the point and quickly agreed. I think I managed successfully to give him the notion that I was playing along and trying to help. When I applied for permission to have a radio there was no opposition and, soon after that, I was given permission to start correspondence courses through the prison educational system. After all, if you are doing twenty years' bird you have to fill in the time somehow.

I chose English Literature and Russian. There was a bit of doubt about the Russian but it went through all right in the end. I had no intention of finishing either course if I could help it; it was all a bit of wool-pulling to make them think Rearden was reconciled to his fate. Still, I buckled down and worked hard. It had to look good and, besides, it was something to do.

The only other prisoner I got close to at this time was Johnny Swift who was doing a 'cut' for burglary. In prison jargon a 'sleep' is a sentence of from six months to two years; a 'cut' is from two to four years, and a 'stretch' is anything over four years. Johnny had been sent up for three years for having been found on business premises after closing time, so he was doing a cut and I was doing a stretch.

More shrewd than intelligent, he gave me lots of tips about the minor rackets that go on in prison and the best ways of keeping out of trouble. Once, when I had changed cells for the umpteenth time, I was a bit grouchy about it. He laughed. 'The penalty of being famous,' he said. 'I know one cell you'll never be put in.'

'Which is that?'

'That one over there in the corner. Snooky's cell.'

Snooky was an odd little man with a permanent smile; he also was in for burglary. 'And why shouldn't I go in there?'

Johnny grinned. 'Because the main sewer runs under there – right across the corner of the Hall. It's big enough to crawl through if you could dig down to it.'

'I see,' I said thoughtfully. 'But they'll trust your burglar mate, Snooky.'

'Burglar!' said Johnny in disgust. 'He's no more a burglar than my Aunt Fanny. He's nick-struck – that's what he is. Every time he's discharged tears roll down his cheeks as they push him through the gate. Then he goes and does a job and bungles it so he can get back in here.'

'He *likes* it here!'

'If you'd been brought up like Snooky you'd find this place a home from home,' said Johnny soberly. 'But I agree he's not all there.'

Another time Johnny said, 'Be careful who you talk to in here. I wouldn't trust a bloody soul myself.'

'Even you?'

He chuckled. 'Especially me, mate. But seriously, watch out for Simpson – he's a proper arse-creeper. If you find him hanging around, clip his bloody earhole.'

He pointed out others I should beware of, and some of them surprised me. 'That gang would peach on anyone if they thought it would get them in good with the Governor so he'll put in a good word to the Review Board. But they're wasting their time; he's too fly for them. He knows what goes on in here without those narks helping him.'

Johnny was philosophical about doing time. To him, his work was his profession and prison an occupational hazard. 'I've done two sleeps and a cut,' he said. 'Next time it'll be a stretch.'

'Aren't you worried about that?'

'A bit,' he admitted. Like an economist discussing the effect of government legislation on industrial activity he began to analyse the situation. 'It's these bloody do-gooders,' he said. 'They've knocked out capital punishment and they've got to put something in its place. So you get long terms for murderers. But a bloke serving a long term doesn't like it and wants to get out, so they class him as a high risk.'

He grinned. 'And they've got to find a special place to put him. Nicks like this are no good – you could get out of here with a bent pin – so they're building high-risk nicks special like. But when you've got a place like that there aren't enough killers to fill it – there's a bit of space going to waste – so they begin to get a bit harder on the sentences. That's where you felt the draught, chum.'

I said, 'But why put me in here to do my bird if it isn't safe?'

'Because the special nicks aren't ready yet. You wait until they've built those places on the Isle of Wight that Mountbatten's been going for. You'll be whizzed out of here in no time. In the meantime they spread you high-risk blokes around thin, a few in each nick, so you can be watched easy.'

I looked around 'C' Hall. 'If this place is so easy to get out of why haven't you tried?'

He looked at me incredulously. 'Think I'm a mug, mate? I'm only doing a cut, and that means I'm out of here in just over two years from start to finish – if I don't lose me temper and clobber that bastard, Hudson. You got no idea what it's like when you go over the wall and you know that every bluebottle in England is looking for you. It ain't worth it, chum; not with all those bloody dogs. They use helicopters, too, and radio. It's like a bloody army exercise.'

He tapped my arm. 'Could be different for you, though. You ain't got as much to lose. But it wouldn't be as easy for you to go over the wall as it would be for me, 'cause they're watching you all the time. They're on to you, mate. And if you *did* get over the wall you'd get nowhere without an organization.'

That sounded interesting. 'Organization! What organization?'

'You got to have planning on the outside,' said Johnny. 'You don't want to be like those mugs who find themselves on the Moor running in circles and eating raw turnip and listening for the dogs.' He shuddered slightly. 'Those bloody dogs! No, you got to have an organization that'll get you clean away. How do you suppose Wilson, Biggs, and the others did it?'

'All right,' I said. 'I'll buy it. How did they get away?'

He rubbed the side of his nose. 'Like I said – organization and outside planning. But it takes the shekels; you got to have a lot of money.' He looked around to see if there was anyone within earshot, and lowered his voice. 'You ever hear of the Scarperers?'

'Scarperers?' I shook my head. 'Never heard of them.'

'Well, it's only a rumour and I could be wrong, but the griff is that there's a mob specially set up for it – helping you long-term blokes.' He chuckled. 'Could call it a new kind of crime. But you got to have the bees.'

That didn't need much working out; the bees and honey – the money. 'How do I contact them?'

'You don't,' said Johnny bluntly. 'They contact you. This is a very exclusive mob; very picky and choosy. But I hear on the grapevine that they do a guaranteed job – you get clear away or no pay – barring expenses. Course, they don't bother about blokes like me because they know it ain't worth me while, but you could be different.'

I hesitated. 'Johnny, this isn't my country and I don't know the ropes. I was in England for less than a week before I was picked up. But if you put it out on the grapevine that there's a bloke in this nick who could do with a bit of help it might do me some good. No names, mind!'

'Think I'm a mug?' he asked. 'No names it is.' He looked at me speculatively. 'Can't say that I blame you, chum. Twenty years' bird would send me round the twist. Trouble with you is that you didn't cough up nicely when asked; you slapped 'em in the face with it and they didn't like it.'

He sighed heavily. 'As I said, next time I'm up before the beak it'll be a stretch. Time was when I could reckon on five or seven years, but that was before the beaks got bloody-minded. Now I don't know what they'll do – could be ten, twelve or even fifteen years' bird. I don't know if I could do fifteen years. It unsettles a man, it really does, not having a dependable stretch to rely on.'

I said, 'Maybe you'd better call it a day when you get out of here.'

'What else can I do?' he said despondently. 'I'm not brass-faced enough to go on the con; besides, I ain't got the voice – you need to be la-di-da for that. And I'm too old to learn how to dip. And I hates the protection bit – too soft-hearted to beat anybody up. No, I'm an inside man – up the old drainpipe, that's me.'

'You could turn honest,' I suggested.

He looked at me incredulously. 'That's for peasants. Can you see me as a nine-to-five? Can you see me working in the corner garage getting me hands black?' He was silent for a while. 'Not that I'm *relying* on getting boobed, you understand. I'm not like Snooky, you know. But I know it's in the cards and I got to face it.'

He stared blindly into the middle distance as though seeing a very bleak future. 'And the scarperers won't do nothing for me,' he said softly. 'I ain't got the bees – I never have had.'

As far as I could see there wasn't much difference between Snooky and Johnny Swift – they both faced the same end.

II

The months went by.

I mopped and scrubbed and polished 'C' Hall in a continual round of endeavour; it was like cleaning out the Augean stables because of some of the pigs who lived in it. I had one or two arguments on that score but nothing serious enough to get me a black mark.

Forbes tried to con me a couple of times into narking about the diamonds but when he saw he wasn't getting anywhere he gave it up. I suppose I was written off as incorrigible.

Maskell came to see me a couple of times. The first time he asked if I wanted to appeal against my sentence. I said, 'Is there any point?'

'A technicality,' he said. 'You may remember that the judge told Rollins that he didn't see how your case could deteriorate much further. That was an unfortunate remark and could be construed on appeal as having undue influence on the jury. On the other hand, your attitude about the missing property has not been an encouraging feature.'

I smiled at him. 'Mr Maskell, if I knew nothing about the diamonds then I couldn't help in the way I'm expected to, could I?'

We did nothing about the appeal.

The second time he came I saw him in the Governor's office. The Governor said, 'Your solicitor is asking that you should sign a power of attorney.'

Maskell broke in smoothly. 'Mr Rearden had certain assets in South Africa which have now been liquidated and transferred to England. It is natural that he had an advisor to handle the investment of these funds since he is incapable of doing it himself.'

'How much is involved?' asked the Governor.

'A little over £400,' said Maskell. 'A safe investment in trustee funds should turn it into over £1,000 in twenty years – something for Mr Rearden to look forward to, I hope.' He produced a document. 'I have Home Office approval.'

'Very well,' said the Governor, so I signed the power of attorney. Someone had to pay for the radio I had been granted permission to have – they aren't supplied free of charge. And it was nice to know I hadn't been forgotten. I thanked Maskell warmly.

The time came when I was able to strike day number 365 from my calendar – only another 19 years to go. I had heard nothing from Johnny about the so-called scarperers and was becoming despondent about my chances.

I was still classified as high risk with all the attendant irritants. By now I had got used to sleeping with the light on and it had become an automatic and unthinking reaction to put my clothes outside the cell door before Smeaton locked up for the night. I changed cells irregularly and kept a record, wondering if I could detect a pattern but there were no regularities as far as I could see, either in the timing or in the particular cell I was transferred to next. I think they randomized it by pulling numbers out of a hat or some such method. That kind of thing is unbeatable.

It was about this time that I first met Slade. He was a new boy inside for a first offence and he'd got forty-two years, but I don't believe the First Offenders Act covers espionage. I had heard about him before, of course; the news broadcasts had been full of the Slade Trial. Since most of the juicy bits had been told *in camera* no one really knew what Slade had been up to, but from all accounts he was the biggest catch since Blake.

He was a pallid man and looked as though he had been bigger at one time but had shrunk, so that his skin was baggy and ill-fitting, something like the skin of a bloodhound. He walked with two sticks and I later learned that he'd been shot through the hips and had spent eight months in hospital before being put on trial. A spy leads an interesting life – sometimes too interesting.

At the trial it had come out that he was really Russian but to speak with him you wouldn't think so because his English was perfect, if a little too public school. His forty-two year stretch should have made him the doyen of the prison but it didn't work out that way. Surprisingly, the most hardened criminal can be patriotic and, to a large extent, he was given the cold shoulder.

Not being English that didn't worry me too much. He proved to be a most interesting conversationalist, cultured and knowledgeable, and was instantly prepared to help me with my Russian lessons when I asked him. He looked at me blandly when I put the question. 'Certainly I speak Russian,' he said. 'It would be very odd if I didn't under the circumstances.' A faint smile played about his lips.

My Russian improved spectacularly after Slade's arrival.

It was nearing the end of Johnny's sentence and he had been transferred to the hostel. That meant he was employed on jobs outside the prison, the theory being that it would acclimatize him gradually to the rigours of the outside world – a part of the rehabilitation process. I didn't see it would make much difference to Johnny Swift.

But it meant I didn't see him as often. Sometimes we had a few words in the exercise yard but that was as far as it went. I looked around in 'C' Hall for someone else to chum up with, someone who was a likely prospect for contacting an escape organization – if the damned thing existed. At any moment I could be transferred without notice to another nick – possibly a high security prison – and that didn't suit my book at all.

It was fifteen months to a day before anything happened. I was breathing the lovely smog-laden air in the exercise yard when I saw Johnny Swift signal that he wanted to talk. I drifted over to him and caught the football that he threw, apparently by accident. I bounced it a couple of times and took it to him and handed it over. 'You still want to get out?' he asked, and kicked the ball up the yard.

I felt my stomach muscles tense. 'Had an offer?'

'I been approached,' he admitted. 'If you're still interested it could go further.'

'I'm bloody interested. I've had enough of this.'

'Fifteen months!' he scoffed. 'That's nothing. But have you got the lolly? That's important.'

'How much?'

'Five thousand nicker and that's just a starter,' said Johnny. 'It's to be put up before anything happens – before they even think about getting you out.'

'Christ! That's a lot of money.'

'I been told to tell you that this is the expense money – and it's non-returnable. The real payment will be more than that.'

'How much?'

'I dunno. That's all I been told. They want to know how soon you can spring the five thousand quid.'

'I can get it,' I said. 'I have funds tucked away in South Africa that no one knows about.' I looked along the exercise yard. Hudson was at the bottom end, making his way up slowly. 'I'll want a cheque form on the Standard Bank of South Africa, Hospital Hill Branch, Johannesburg. Got that?'

He repeated it slowly, then nodded. 'I got it.'

'I'll sign it, and they cash it. It'll have to be cashed in South Africa. That shouldn't be too difficult.'

'It'll take some time, mate,' said Johnny.

I laughed humourlessly. 'I've got nineteen years. But tell them to hurry. I'm getting nervous about being moved out of here.'

'Watch it – here's Hudson,' Johnny said. 'You'll be contacted.' He ran forward and intercepted the football and both he and I joined in the game.

The cheque form came ten days later. A new arrival brought it in and it was passed to me surreptitiously. 'I was told to give you this. Pass it to Sherwin when you've done with it.'

'I knew Sherwin; he was due for release, I said quickly, 'Wait a minute; anything else?'

'I don't know nothing else,' the man muttered, and shuffled away.

That night I settled my correspondence course books on the table and started work as usual. I'd been plugging away at the Russian and I reckoned I was pretty good – my pronunciation had improved vastly since Slade's arrival although that makes no difference to the examiner's marks in a correspondence course. I carried on for half an hour and then dug out the cheque form and smoothed it out.

It had been quite a while since I'd seen that familiar sight, and I could almost smell the dust blowing off the Johannesburg mine dumps. The amount had been filled in – R10,000 – Ten Thousand Rand – and I thought the mob was laying it on a bit thick; since devaluation of the value of the pound sterling had deteriorated relative to the Rand, and this cheque was for about £5,650. The payee line was blank – I wasn't supposed to know about that yet, and when I did find out it would be too late to do anything about it.

I filled in the date and added my signature – and it wasn't J. A. Rearden, either – then stuck the cheque between the pages of the Russian grammar, wondering if I was a wise man or the prize chump of all time. Someone could be conning me – it could even be Johnny Swift – and if he was I was over £5,000 in the red and all for nothing. But I had to rely on cupidity; if it was realized that there was more loot where that came from then someone would be back for more, but this time it would be payment by results – after the results had been achieved.

Next morning I passed the cheque on to Sherwin who palmed it expertly and I knew he wouldn't have any trouble in getting it out unseen. Sherwin was a card sharp and no one in 'C' Hall would dream of playing nap with him; he could make a deck of cards sit up and talk, and concealing a cheque would be no trouble at all.

Then I settled down to wait, wondering what expenses the mob would have that could run to five thousand quid.

The weeks went by and again nothing happened. I had figured out the time needed to cash the cheque and get word back to England and had estimated it at just over a week. When five long weeks had gone by without result I began to get edgy.

Then it broke very suddenly.

It was at free association time. Smeaton was giving me a minor dressing down for a small infraction; I'd not been cleaning up as well as I should have done – a sign that I was slipping. Cosgrove came up carrying a chess board. He waited until Smeaton had finished, then said, 'Cheer up, Rearden; what about a game?'

I knew Cosgrove; he'd been the brains behind a hijacking mob – cigarettes and whisky mostly – and someone had squealed on him and he'd been pulled in and got ten years. He was in his sixth year and, with a bit of luck, he'd be out in another two. He was also the 'C' Hall chess champion, a very astute and intelligent man.

I said abstractedly, 'Not today, Cossie.'

He glanced sideways at Smeaton who was standing two paces away. 'Don't you want to win out?'

'Win out?' I said sharply.

'The big tournament.' He held up a box of chessmen. 'I'm sure I can give you a few tips if you play with me.'

We found a table at the other end of the Hall away from Smeaton. As we set out the pieces I said, 'Okay, what is this, Cossie?'

He put down a pawn. 'I'm your go-between. You speak to me and no one else. Understand?' I nodded briefly and he carried on. 'To begin with I'm going to talk money.'

'Then you can stop right now,' I said. 'Your mob already has over five thousand quid of mine, and I've yet to see a result.'

'You're seeing me, aren't you?' He looked around. 'Play chess – it's your first move.' I moved to QP3 and he laughed softly. 'You're a cautious man, Rearden; that's a piano opening.'

'Quit being subtle, Cossie. Say what you have to say.'

'I don't blame you for being cautious,' he said. 'All I'm saying is that it's going to cost you a hell of a lot more.'

'Not before I'm out of here,' I said. 'I'm not that much of a sucker.'

'I don't blame you,' said Cossie. 'It's like taking a jump in the dark. But the fact is we've got to talk money or the deal's off. We've both got to know where we stand.'

'All right. How much?'

He moved his king's knight. 'We're a bit like tax collectors – we take *pro rata*. You made a killing of £173,000. We want half – that's £86,500.'

'Don't be a bloody fool,' I said. 'There are too many things wrong with that calculation and you know it.'

'Such as?'

'There was only supposed to be £120,000 in that parcel. I think the owners were laying it on a bit.'

He nodded. 'Could be. Anything else?'

'Yes. Do you suppose we could sell for the full value? It's not like selling legitimate – you ought to know that more than anyone.'

'Play chess,' he said calmly. 'That screw's watching us. You could sell for full value with uncut diamonds if you were clever enough and I think you are clever. That wasn't a stupid job you pulled. You'd have got clean away if you hadn't been shopped.'

'They *weren't* uncut diamonds,' I said. 'They'd been cut in Amsterdam and were being brought back for setting. Diamonds of that value are X-rayed, photographed and registered. They've been recut and that means a hell of a drop in value. And another thing – I wasn't alone. I had a mate who's in on a fifty-fifty split. He planned it and I did it.'

'The boys were wondering about that,' said Cossie. 'They can't quite make you out. Did your mate shop you? Because if he did you've not got a bean, have you? And that means you're no good to us.'

'It wasn't my mate,' I said, hoping to make it stick.

'The buzz is going around that it was your mate.'

'The buzz couldn't have been started by a busy called Forbes – or another called Brunskill? They have their reasons, you know.'

'Could be,' he said thoughtfully. 'Who is your mate?'

'Nothing doing,' I said firmly. 'I didn't give him to the busies, and I'm not giving him to your mob. That, in itself, ought to prove he didn't shop me. My friend and I move along very quietly; we mind our business and we don't want anyone else minding it for us.'

'We'll let that one lie for a bit,' said Cossie. 'I'll put it to the boys. But that brings us back to the boodle – what was *your* take?'

'We estimated it at forty thousand nicker,' I said calmly. 'And it's out away safely. You get it through me – not my mate.'

He smiled slightly. 'In a Swiss numbered account?'

'That's right. It's quite safe.'

'So it's still half,' he said. 'Twenty years at a thousand a year – cheap at half price. We take you over the wall and deliver you *outside* the United Kingdom, and if you come back that's your trouble. But let me tell you something – you'd better not welsh on us; you'd better have the boodle for us because, if you don't, nobody will ever hear of you again. I hope that's quite clear.'

'It's very clear,' I said. 'You get me out of here and you'll get your money. I'll still be up on the deal, anyway.'

'I'll put it up to the boys,' he said. 'It's up to them whether you're accepted as a client.'

I said, 'Cossie, if your mob is as good as you say it is, what the hell are you doing in here? That puzzles me.'

'I'm just the contact man,' he said. 'I was recruited in here. Besides, I only have another two years' bird, then I'm out, anyway. Why make trouble for myself? I've got a good business waiting for me outside and I'm not going to throw that away.' He looked up. 'It'd be dicey for you if you came back to England.'

'That doesn't trouble me,' I said. 'I was only on the loose for a week in England – I know nothing about the place and I don't care to know any more.'

Cossie moved a piece. 'Check. There's another thing. You've been matey with Slade lately, haven't you? You do a lot of talking together.'

'He's helping me with my Russian,' I said, moving my king.

'That stops,' said Cossie flatly. 'You keep clear of Slade or the deal's off no matter how much money you have.'

I looked up, startled. 'What the hell . . .'

'That's the way it is,' he said equably, and moved his bishop. 'Check!'

'Don't tell me your mob is patriotic,' I said, and laughed. 'What's the idea?'

Cossie gave me a pained look. 'You ought to know better than to ask questions. You just do as you're told.' He turned to Smeaton who was walking past. 'What do you know?' he said. 'Rearden nearly beat me.' And that was a damned lie. 'He's got a good chance in the tournament.'

Smeaton looked at him with expressionless eyes and moved on.

III

So the game was on. I felt the tension rising in me and this time it was the tension of hope and not hopelessness. I even began to sing a bit as I scrubbed the tables in the Hall and I didn't slip up on a thing. Smeaton looked on me with approval, or as near to it as he could show. I was proving to be a model prisoner.

I obeyed Cosgrove's orders and dropped Slade who glanced at me reproachfully from time to time. I didn't know why Cossie wanted me to do that but this wasn't the time to argue it out. All the same, I felt a bit sorry for Slade; he hadn't too many friends in this nick.

I kept my eye on Cosgrove unobtrusively and watched who he talked to and who his pals were. As far as I could see he was as relaxed as usual and there were no changes in his normal pattern, but since I hadn't studied him especially before it was difficult to tell.

After a couple of weeks I went up to him during free association time. 'What about a game of chess, Cossie?'

He looked at me with blank eyes. 'Keep away from me, you silly bastard. I don't want to be involved with you.'

'You *are* involved,' I snapped. 'Smeaton was just asking if I wasn't going to enter the chess tournament, after all. He wanted to know if I'd given up my lessons. He also wanted to know if I'd given up Russian.'

Cosgrove blinked. 'Okay,' he said. 'Let's go over there.'

We set up the board. 'Any news?'

'I'll tell you when there's any news.' He was in a bad temper.

'Look, Cossie; I'm worried,' I said. 'I've just heard that the top security nick is finished – the one on Wight. I'm scared of being transferred. It could happen any time.'

He looked around the Hall. 'These things can't be rushed – it's a complicated set-up. What do you suppose you've paid five thousand quid for? Just a jump over a wall? There's a whole escape line to be laid on.' He moved a chess piece. 'I don't know much about that side of it, but I hear it's a different set-up every time. No pattern, see? You ought to know that, Rearden, of all people.'

I stared at him. 'I see someone's been checking up on me.'

He looked at me with cold eyes. 'What do you think? A part of that five thousand nicker went towards checking you out. The boys are very security-minded. You have an interesting record; I can't see why you slipped up this time.'

'It happens to all of us,' I said. 'I was shopped – same as you, Cossie.'

'But I *know* who shopped me,' he said savagely. 'And the bastard is going to regret it to his dying day once I get out of here.'

'Better have it done before you get out,' I advised. 'You have the perfect alibi – you're in the nick; and enough time has gone by so that the busies aren't likely to think of you.'

He smiled reluctantly. 'You have interesting ideas, Rearden.'

'And what makes you think I don't know who shopped *me?'* I asked. 'Trouble is I don't have contacts on the outside to arrange an accident.'

'I can arrange it,' he offered.

'Forget it. I'll be out myself soon enough if your mob comes up to scratch. So they had me investigated in South Africa, did they? I hope they were satisfied.'

'You passed. You've got some good friends out there.' Smeaton was passing close by. Cossie said, 'Not that move, stupid; it gives me mate in three moves.' He looked up at Smeaton. 'He's not as good as I thought he was; he'll never make it in the tournament.'

Smeaton sneered at him without moving a muscle of his face.

IV

Cossie was right – I didn't make it in the tournament – but it wasn't because of my lousy chess. Two days later he came to me instead of *vice versa*. 'It's set up.'

'They changed my cell yesterday,' I said.

'Doesn't matter. You'll be taken out in daylight – from the exercise yard on Saturday. Three o'clock exactly – remember that.'

There was a sudden tightening in my belly. 'What's the drill?'

'Have you ever seen them putting up the Christmas lights in Regent Street?' Cossie asked. He snapped his fingers in annoyance. 'Of course, you haven't. Anyway, they have this truck, see, with a platform on a long articulated arm – to hoist up the electricians.'

'I know what you mean,' I said. 'They use them at Jan Smuts Airport at Jo'burg to service the big jets. They call them cherry-pickers.'

'Do they?' he said interestedly. 'I see why they might. Anyway, there'll be one of those coming over the wall on Saturday. I'll show you where to stand, and when it comes over you jump in quick. There'll be a bloke on the platform to help you, and you'll be out in two ticks. That's going over the wall in style.'

He turned to survey the Hall, then continued rapidly. 'There'll be a hell of a lot of other things going on at the same time, but you won't take any notice of all that. Just keep your mind on the big platform.'

'Okay,' I said.

'And I've been asked to tell you something – if you're taken out and you can't find the twenty thousand quid, then God help you because no one else will. You'll not live to regret it – and that's not a slip of the tongue. I was specially asked to tell you that in case you want to change your mind.'

'The mob will get its money,' I said shortly.

'All right; I'll see you on Saturday then.' He turned away, then paused and turned back. 'Oh, I nearly forgot,' he said casually. 'Someone else is going with you, and you're going to help him.'

'Who?'

Cosgrove looked at me blandly. 'Slade!'

FOUR

I stared at Cosgrove unbelievingly. 'Are you out of your mind?'

'What's the matter?' he asked. 'Don't you believe in freedom for others?'

'The matter!' My voice rose. 'The man walks with *sticks,* Cossie. He's a bloody cripple.'

'Keep your voice down,' he warned.

In a low voice I said savagely, 'How in hell is Slade supposed to make a break for it? He can't run.'

'You'll be there to help him, won't you?' said Cosgrove smoothly.

'Like hell I will.'

'Well, I'll tell you something, Rearden. Those sticks of his are a bit of a fake – he's been putting it on a bit ever since he came out of hospital. He can run well enough. Oh, I don't say he could break the four-minute mile, but he can toddle along enough for what we want.'

'Then he can bloody well toddle along by himself,' I said forcibly. 'Christ, if he obstructs my escape and I'm nabbed, I'll spend six months in solitary – and I'd certainly be sent to the new nick in Wight or to "E" Wing in Durham. I'd *never* get out of there.'

'The same applies to Slade,' said Cosgrove easily. 'And don't forget he's in for over forty years.' His voice tautened and a rasp entered into it. 'Now you listen to me, Rearden; Slade is a bloody sight more important to us than you are. You wouldn't believe how much money we have riding on him. So you'll bloody well do as you're told. As for going to Durham, you're due to be transferred there on Sunday, anyway.'

'Oh, boy!' I said. 'You play rough.'

'What's the matter? Is it that Slade is a spy? Has a sudden wave of patriotism overcome you?'

'Hell, no! I wouldn't care if he's inside for kidnapping the Queen, the Prime Minister and whole damned Cabinet. It's just that he's going to be a flaming liability.'

Cosgrove assumed a placatory tone. 'Well, now; maybe we can compensate you for that. Our agreement is that when we get you out then you pay us twenty thousand quid. Right?'

I nodded wearily. 'Right.'

'Suppose we cut that in half and make it ten thou'. With the live body of Slade as makeweight for the other ten thou'. How would you feel about that?'

'It has its points,' I conceded.

'I don't think it's at all bad considering you're going to be lumbered with Slade anyway,' said Cosgrove.

'Do you have authority for that offer?' I asked suspiciously.

'Of course I have,' he said, and smiled thinly. 'Of course, it has its converse side. If you get over the wall and Slade doesn't, then you get the chop. That's just so you remember that Slade is more important than you are.'

I said, 'This is just getting him over the wall?'

'That's it. Once the pair of you are on the other side my pals will look after you both.' He shrugged. 'It's a certainty Slade couldn't make it on his own so that's why we're doing it this way. I'll give it to you straight; he *can't* run very well.

Neither could you if you had a stainless steel peg through each hip joint.'

'How is he at climbing?'

'His arms are strong but you might have to give him a bunk up when that platform comes over.'

'All right,' I said. 'I'd better have a talk to him.'

'No!' said Cosgrove. 'You don't go near him. That's part of the deal. He's been talked to already and he knows what to do. I'm the one who tells *you* what to do.' A bell rang stridently signifying the end of free association time. He flipped his hand at me. 'See you in the yard on Saturday.'

Saturday was a long time coming. I was in a muck sweat when they changed my cell again – two changes in three days – and I wondered if someone guessed that an escape was in the wind. It took all my will power to carry on with my studies in the evenings and my Russian suffered and I turned to the course on Eng. Lit. but found *Finnegans Wake* hardly more relaxing in the circumstances.

I kept my eye on Slade and noted with glumness the obvious weakness of his legs. It wasn't going to be at all easy to get him over the wall, cherry-picker or no cherry-picker. Once he saw me watching him and his eyes casually swept past me without a flicker. I didn't see Cosgrove talking to him and came to the conclusion that he might have a different contact. It was possible that the whole damn prison was riddled by the hirelings of the Scarperers.

I scrubbed the tables and swept the Hall during the day and made sure I did a good job – even on the Saturday morning. I wanted no sign of abnormality to appear at all. But I hadn't much appetite for the midday meal and left most of it. At a table across the Hall I saw Slade polishing his tin plate with a slice of bread.

At two-thirty we were marched into the yard for free exercise. Some of the boys were kicking a ball about, but most strolled up and down enjoying the sun and the sky and the air. I drifted over to Cosgrove and we walked the length of the yard. He said, 'I'll tell you where it's coming over and then we walk right past, see? Then I'll take you to the place you have to wait. You stay there and you keep one eye on me and one on the wall – but don't stare at it as though expecting something to happen.'

'I'm not stupid.'

He grunted. 'That's as maybe. All right, we're coming to it now. See that chalk mark?'

'I see it,' I said, and almost laughed. It was a crudely phallic scrawl more likely to be found in a run-down public lavatory.

Cossie wasn't laughing. 'That's where it comes over. Now we carry on to the end of the yard.' We walked on and turned in unison, just like the teachers who supervised the playground at school used to do when I was a kid. 'You might have to jump for it, but there'll be a bloke to help you.'

'Jump!' I said. 'What about Slade?'

'You give him a bunk-up first. There'll be ropes hanging from the platform. He'll be all right once he grabs those – he has strong arms.'

I saw Slade watching the football match with evident appreciation. 'He'll be leaving his sticks behind then.'

'That's obvious,' said Cosgrove impatiently. We strolled back to a point on the other side of the yard facing the chalk mark. Slade was leaning against the wall quite close to the mark and wouldn't have to move more than a few feet when the action started.

Cosgrove said, 'Now you just stay here and wait for it.' He consulted something he held in his fingers and I saw it was a very small ladies' watch. 'Nearly twenty minutes to go.'

The watch vanished. 'Where did you get that?' I asked.

'That doesn't matter,' he said with a sour grin. 'And I won't have it at all in twenty-five minutes. The screws'll act as though someone lit a fire under them when this comes off and they'll turn the whole bloody place upside down. They won't find this watch, though.'

I leaned against the wall and looked at the faint chalk mark on the other side of the yard. I could hear the traffic on the other side of that exterior wall but not much because it was Saturday afternoon and there wasn't much commercial stuff on the roads.

Cosgrove said, 'I'll leave you now, and this is what you do. At two minutes to three a fight will start over in that corner. There'll be a lot of noise. As soon as you hear it you start walking – slowly, mind you – across the yard towards that mark. Don't make a fuss about it and, for God's sake, don't run. Slade will see you move and he'll get ready.'

'I could have done with talking to him about it myself,' I grumbled.

'Too dangerous,' said Cosgrove. 'Now, don't be surprised by anything else that happens around you, no matter what it is. Just keep your mind on your job and head for that mark. By the time you get there the platform will be coming over. You hoist Slade up on your shoulders and then you jump for it yourself. It should be easy.'

'I'll be all right, Cossie.'

'Okay,' he said. 'Good luck, Rearden.' He grinned crookedly. 'Under the circumstances we won't shake hands. I'm going now; I'll be talking to Paddy Colquhoun until this thing's all over.' The watch appeared again. 'Fifteen minutes exactly.'

'Wait a minute,' I said. 'What about the closed-circuit TV outside the wall?'

'That'll be taken care of,' he said patiently. 'Goodbye, Rearden.'

He walked away across the yard leaving me leaning against the wall alone. My hands were sweating and my mouth was suddenly dry as I looked at the barbed wire on top of the exterior wall. God help me if I got snagged on that. I wiped my wet hands on my trousers and squatted down on my heels.

Slade was standing next to the chalk mark and he, too, was alone. Probably everyone had been warned to keep clear of us; they wouldn't know why but they'd obey, especially if the warning had been given by the strong-arm boys. Accidents can be arranged, even in prison, and it's awfully easy to get a broken arm, or worse.

Cosgrove was talking to Paddy and they appeared to be enjoying a huge joke. I hoped the joke wasn't on me. I was taking a hell of a lot on faith, but if Cossie was conning me – if he was pulling a practical joke – I'd have his lights for a necktie. The prison wouldn't be big enough for both of us. But I looked across at Slade and knew, deep in my bones, that this was the real thing.

There were four screws in the yard, walking up and down with set, expressionless faces. And I knew there were two more watching from the high windows above my head. From there they could see into the street outside the exterior wall. God in heaven, surely they'd ring the alarm as soon as they saw that mechanical lift drive into the street. They couldn't be as stupid as all that.

The minutes went by. I found myself losing track of time. Fifteen minutes had already gone by – or was it only five? Again I could feel the sweat on the palms of my hands, and again I rubbed them dry. If I had to jump for a rope I didn't want any chance of slipping.

I looked at Cosgrove again. He was standing with his head cocked on one side listening to what Paddy had to say, and I saw him flick an eye towards me before he burst into a guffaw of laughter and slapped Paddy on the back.

I didn't see him give the signal but suddenly there were raised voices at the other end of the yard, so perhaps the slap on Paddy's back had been the signal. I got to my feet and began to walk slowly forward as though hypnotized by that distant chalk mark. Slade pushed himself away from the wall and came forward, hobbling on his sticks.

The men all around me were looking towards the disturbance which had grown noisier. Some of the prisoners were running in that direction and the screws had begun to converge on the fight. I glanced to my right and saw Hudson, the senior screw, who had apparently sprung from nowhere, making his way across the yard. He wasn't running but walking at a smart pace, and he was on a collision course with me.

Something astonishing happened behind. There was a sharp crack, like a minor explosion, and a billow of dense, white smoke erupted from the ground. I kept going but Hudson turned and stared. There were more explosions in the yard and the smoke grew thick and heavy. Somebody was being liberal with the smoke bombs that were being tossed over the wall.

Hudson was now behind me, and I heard his anguished bellow. 'Escape! Escape! Sound the alarm.'

Frantically he blew on his whistle but I kept going to where Slade was waiting. His face was set in lines of strain and as I approached he said urgently, 'Where the hell is that damned contraption?'

I looked up and saw it coming over through the wreaths of smoke, looming over the wall like the head and neck of a prehistoric monster with slimy weeds dripping from its jaws. As it dipped down I saw that the weeds were four knotted ropes dangling from the platform on which stood a man who was, so help me, talking into a telephone.

I bent down. 'Come on, Slade; up you go!'

He dropped his sticks as I heaved him up and he made a grab at one of the ropes as it came within reach. He was no lightweight and it was not easy for me to hold him up. He caught on to the rope and I was thankful when his weight eased from me.

The man on the platform was looking down at us and when he saw that Slade had a secure hold he spoke urgently into the telephone and the platform began to rise. The only trouble about that was it was leaving me behind. I made a frantic leap and grasped the last knot on the same rope that Slade was climbing. He was going up fast but his legs were flailing about and he caught me under the jaw with the tip of his shoes. I felt dizzy and nearly let go but managed to tighten my grip at the last moment.

Then somebody grabbed my ankle and I looked down and saw it was Hudson, his face contorted with effort. The man had a grip like iron so I lifted my other leg and booted him in the face. I was learning from Slade already. He let go and tumbled to the ground which, by that time, seemed to be a long way down. I carried on up the rope, my shoulder muscles cracking, until I could grasp the edge of the platform.

Slade was sprawled on the steel floor, gasping with the effort he had made, and the man with the telephone bent down. 'Stay there,' he said. 'You'll be all right.' He spoke into the mouthpiece again.

I looked down and saw the barbed wire apparently moving away underneath as the great articulated arm swept me over the wall. Then it began to drop and the man bent down again, directing his words at both of us. 'Do exactly as I do,' he said calmly.

We were swept dizzily over the street and then stopped dead. A small open delivery truck came from nowhere and pulled up beneath the platform. The man swung over the railings of the platform and dropped lightly into the back of the truck and I thankfully let go of the rope and followed him. Slade came after and fell on top of me and I cursed him, but then he was thrown off me by a sudden surge of acceleration as the little truck took off and went round the first corner with a squeal of tyres.

I looked back along the street and saw the big cherry-picker move ponderously into view and the great arm fell forward, completely blocking the street. Men tumbled from the cab and ran, and then we turned another corner and I saw no more of that.

Slade leaned against the side of the truck with his head lolling on one side. His face was grey and he seemed thoroughly exhausted. I remembered that he had been in hospital not long before. The man with us thumped his elbow into my ribs. 'Pay attention!' he said sharply. 'You'll be transferring into a little black mini-van. Get ready to move.'

The truck was moving fast but there was little traffic to hinder us on that Saturday afternoon. Suddenly we swooped to a stop behind a mini-van which stood at the kerb with its rear doors open. 'That's it. Into there – quickly.'

I jumped out of the truck and took a header into the mini-van, and heard the doors slam shut behind. I lifted my head and, looking through the windscreen between two broad-shouldered men in the front seats, saw that the truck I had left was already on the move with Slade still in it. It turned ahead to the right and at high speed.

The mini-van took off more sedately, well within the speed limit, and turned to the left. I felt absolutely breathless. My lungs were strained and my heart was thumping as though it was going to burst in my chest. I lay there panting until I felt better and then raised myself and poked at the passenger in front with my finger. 'Why were we separated?'

He made no answer to that, so I tried again. 'Where are we going?'

'Shut up and keep down,' he said without turning. 'You'll find out soon enough.'

I relaxed as much as I could, sitting there on the hard metal floor of the van. From what I could gather from the brief glimpses I saw from the rear windows we were covering a complicated course among the streets, stopping properly at all the traffic lights and not moving fast enough to excite attention.

The van turned into a side street and swung up an alley. I leaned up on my elbow and looked forward cautiously. Ahead were two big wooden doors which were open, and inside the building was a huge moving-van with the tail-gate down. Without hesitation the driver headed right for it in low gear, bumped up the ramp formed by the tail-gate and drove right inside the pantechnicon. Behind us something came down from the roof, enclosing the van completely, and I heard the slam of the tail-gate as it was closed.

We were in complete darkness when the rear doors of the mini-van were opened. 'You can get out now.' It was a woman's voice.

I scrambled out and bumped into her, steadying myself on a soft arm. The front door of the mini-van slammed. 'For God's sake!' she said. 'Turn on a light.'

A light came on in the roof and I looked around. We were in a cramped compartment just big enough to take the van with a little space left over. The woman was a tall blonde dressed in a white overall and looking like a doctor's receptionist. One of the men pushed past me and bent down; I saw he was attaching a shackle to the rear bumper of the mini-van.

I heard the throb of a heavy diesel engine and the whole compartment lurched. The man straightened up and gave me a grin. He patted the side of the van. 'We don't want this to get loose, do we?'

There was another lurch and a grinding of gears. The big pantechnicon was travelling, taking me to – where?

The blonde smiled at me. 'We haven't much time,' she said practically. 'Take your clothes off.' I must have gaped at her because she said sharply, 'Strip, man! Don't be prudish – you won't be the first man I've seen bollock-naked.'

I took off the grey flannel jacket – the uniform of servitude – and watched her unpack a suitcase, producing underwear, socks, a shirt, a suit and a pair of shoes. 'You can start to get dressed in these,' she said. 'But don't put on the shirt yet.'

I took off the prison uniform and dressed in that lovely soft underwear, then balanced uneasily against the rocking motions of the moving pantechnicon to put on the socks. One of the men said, 'How does it feel to be out, chum?'

'I don't know. I'm not sure I'm out, yet.'

'You are,' he assured me. 'You can bank on it.'

I put on the trousers and then the shoes. Everything was a perfect fit. 'How did you know my measurements?' I asked.

'We know *everything* about you,' the man said. 'Except maybe one thing.'

'And what's that?'

He struck a match and lit his cigarette, then blew a plume of smoke in my face. 'Where you keep your money. But you'll tell us, won't you?'

I zipped up the trousers. 'At the proper time,' I said.

'Come over here,' said the blonde. She had pulled up a stool in front of a basin set on a shelf. 'Sit down. I'm going to give you a shampoo.'

So I sat down and she lathered my hair, digging her fingers deep into my scalp. She rinsed and then shampooed again before giving a final rinse. Then she took me by the chin and tilted my head. 'That'll do. Now for the eyebrows.' She got to work on my eyebrows and when she had finished she handed me a mirror. 'How do you like yourself now?'

I looked at my reflection in the mirror. Gone was the black hair and I was now middling blond. I was surprised at the difference it made; even Mackintosh wouldn't recognize me now. I felt her fingers on my cheek. 'You'll have to shave twice a day. That dark five o'clock shadow would give you away. You'd better shave now – you'll find the kit in your suitcase.'

I opened the case and found it very well fitted out with everything a man would normally travel with. There was a small battery-powered shaver which I put into use immediately. As I shaved she began to lay objects on the shelf. 'Your name is Raymond Cruickshank,' she said. 'Here are your initialled cuff-links.'

'Do I have to be that kind of a man?' I asked lightly.

She wasn't amused. 'Don't be funny,' she said coldly. 'The same initials are on the suitcase. All this is your insurance, Rearden; insurance against getting caught – treat it seriously.'

'Sorry,' I said.

'You've been to Australia, Rearden. You were mixed up in something in Sydney a few years ago, so we've made you an Australian. People over here can't tell the difference between a South African and an Australian accent, so you should get away with it. Here's your passport.'

I picked it up and flipped it open. It had a photograph of a blond-haired me.

She produced a wallet and opened it for my inspection. 'This is all pure Cruickshank; you'd better check it to make sure you know what's in it.'

So I did, and was very surprised. This mob was super-efficient – no wonder Cossie had said it needed time to set up. There were membership cards of Sydney clubs, an odd Australian two-dollar note among the British currency, an Australian AA card together with an Australian driving licence and an International driving licence, a dozen business cards announcing where I lived and what I did – it seemed I was the managing director of a firm importing office machinery. All very efficient, indeed.

I held out a dog-eared photograph. 'What's this?'

'You and the wife and kids,' she said calmly.

I looked at it more closely in the dim light and, by God, she was right! At least, it was a blond-haired me with my arm around a brunette's waist and with a couple of kids in front. A nice tricky photograph.

I put it back into the wallet and felt something else at the bottom of the pocket which I dug out. It was an old theatre stub, dated two months previously – the theatre, naturally enough, was in Sydney. Apparently I had been to see *Fiddler on the Roof*.

I put it back carefully. 'Very nice,' I said admiringly. 'Very nice indeed.' I laid down the wallet and began to put on my shirt. I was just about to fasten the sleeves with the cuff-links when she said, 'Mr Cruickshank, I said all this stuff was your insurance.'

I paused. 'Well?'

'Hold him, boys,' she said sharply, and I was grabbed from behind and held cruelly tight.

'What the hell . . .?'

'Mr Cruickshank,' she said clearly. 'This is *our* insurance.' Her hand came from behind her back holding a hypodermic syringe which she held up to her eyes and squirted professionally. With one movement she rolled up the unfastened shirt sleeve. 'No hard feelings,' she said, and jabbed the needle into my arm.

There wasn't a damned thing I could do about it. I just stood there helplessly and watched her face go all swimmy. And then I didn't know any more about anything.

II

I woke up with the feeling of having been asleep for a long, long time. I didn't know why this should be, but it seemed a hundred years since I had gone to sleep in my cell, the new cell into which I had just been moved. I certainly didn't feel as though I had wakened from a normal night's sleep; after all, by now I had got used to the light being on all night.

And I had a hangover!

Hangovers I don't mind when there has been a cause for them; one takes one's pleasures and pays the consequences. But I strongly object to the consequences when the pleasure has been missed. I hadn't had a drink for eighteen months and to have an unaccountable hangover was abominable.

I lay there in bed with my eyes closed stickily. My head felt as though there was a red-hot iron bar wrapped around it and it throbbed as a blacksmith beat lustily on it with his hammer. I also had the old familiar dehydrated feeling and my mouth tasted, as a friend once inelegantly put it, like the inside of a Greek wrestler's jockstrap.

I turned over slowly and groaned involuntarily as the blacksmith gave an extra hard thump. Then I opened my eyes and looked at the ceiling vacantly. With care I traced the elegant moulding of the cornice which was picked out in gilt, being careful not to go too quickly in case my eyeballs fell out. 'Funny !' I thought. 'They've given me a nice cell this time.'

With grudging movements I leaned up on one elbow just in time to see someone leave. The door closed with a gentle click and there was the sound of a key turning in a lock. That was familiar enough, anyway, which was more than the cell was.

As I stared uncomprehendingly at the dove-grey walls and the gilt rococo panelling, at the Dolly Varden dressing-table and the comfortable armchair standing on the thick-piled carpet, it hit me suddenly. My God, I made it! I got out of the nick!

I looked down at myself. I was dressed in silk pyjamas and the last time I had seen those was in the bottom of a suitcase in a moving-van.

A moving-van?

Slowly and painfully it all came back. The frantic grab at the rope; the wild swing over the barbed-wired wall; the jump into the truck, then into the mini-van, then into the pantechnicon.

The pantechnicon! That was it. There was a blonde who had dyed my hair and who gave me a wallet. My name was Cruickshank and I was an Australian, she said. And then the bitch doped me. I put my hand to my arm and rubbed it where it felt sore. Now, why the hell had she done that?

I threw back the bedclothes and swung out my legs. No sooner was I standing upright than I felt violently ill, and so I staggered to the nearest door which gave at a push and I fell into a bathroom. I lurched to my feet and over to the water-closet where I retched up my guts, but nothing came forth but a thin brown mucus. Still, when it was over I felt fractionally better, so I got to my feet and swayed towards the wash basin which I clutched hard as I stared into the mirror at the unfamiliar face.

She was right, I thought; the five o'clock shadow does give the game away. The blond hair with the black-bearded face looked incongruous and the whole ensemble wasn't improved by eyes which looked like burnt holes in a blanket. I rubbed my arm again and, on impulse, rolled up the pyjama sleeve to see *five* red pinpricks.

Five! How long had I been unconscious? I fingered my beard which rasped uncomfortably. That felt normal for about thirty-six hours, or maybe a bit longer. Unless they'd shaved me when I was dead to the world – which was a distinct possibility.

I turned on the cold tap and ran some water into the basin, then gave my face a thorough dousing, spluttering a bit. There was a clean towel at hand and, as I wiped myself dry, I began to feel better but the feeling tended to ooze away when I caught sight of the bathroom window. There were thick steel bars on the inside and, although the glass was frosted, I could see the outline of similar bars on the outside.

That was going one better than the nick. Even in there they had but one set of bars to a window.

I dropped the towel on to the floor and went back into the bedroom. Sure enough the bedroom window was also barred inside and out, although here the glass was clear. I looked through the window and saw a courtyard surrounded by buildings. Nothing moved except a blackbird foraging for worms on a neatly mown lawn.

I watched the courtyard for five minutes but nothing happened, so I turned my attention to the bedroom. On the dressing table by the window was the toilet case and the shaver that the blonde had provided. I opened the case, took out a comb and combed my hair. Shaving could wait a while. I looked into the mirror and stuck out my tongue at the changed man who faced me. He did the same and I hastily pulled it in again as I saw the coating on the tongue.

Then I stiffened as I looked over his shoulder, and I whirled about to face the room. There were *two* beds; the one I had occupied had rumpled sheets, but the other bed was occupied. I strode over and found Slade breathing heavily through his mouth and totally unconscious. I slapped his cheeks and prised open his eyelids all to no avail; apart from the breathing he was a reasonable facsimile of a dead man.

So I left him to it, principally because I had seen a newspaper lying by the side of the armchair. Whoever had been waiting for me to wake up hadn't taken his *Sunday Times* with him.

We were front page news. The headlines blared in a most uncharacteristic *Sunday Times* manner, but I'd bet the *News of the World* outdid them in that respect. There was a photograph of the outside of the nick with a thick, pecked line to show the course of events – there was a photograph of the cherry-picker with its neck collapsed across the entrance to a street, looking a bit like a dead Disney dinosaur from *Fantasia*; there was a photograph of someone being carried to an ambulance on a stretcher – Senior Prison Officer Hudson had unaccountably broken his leg!

The front page news story was pretty factual and they hadn't got much wrong as far as I could see. I read with interest that the exterior closed-circuit TV cameras had been rendered inoperable by having paint sprayed on to the lenses. That was a nice touch. It was also interesting to read that the small open truck had been found abandoned near Colchester, and the black mini-van near Southampton. Police had established road blocks around both areas.

Slade captured most of the limelight. What was a jewel thief compared with a master spy? But Brunskill had a go at me. 'This man is dangerous,' he said, with a straight face. 'He was convicted for a crime of violence and has a record of violence extending back for many years. The public should be wary of him and should on no account try to tackle him unaided.'

That was the most libellous thing I've ever read. Two convictions for violence over twelve years and I was being described as a Jack the Ripper. All Brunskill was trying to do was to build up the original arrest. I hoped his bosses threw the book at him for talking out of turn.

Insight had nothing to say about it, but they would, they would – I'd have to wait until next week's issue to get the inside story on how we'd escaped. But the editorial went off pop! The escape was described as a colossal piece of impudence and that if criminals were going to use such methods as mortar-fired smoke bombs then it was time that the prison authorities should also use military means to defend the integrity of the prisons.

I thought so, too.

Lord Mountbatten was not available for comment, but lots of other people were, whether they had anything relevant to say or not. One man especially fulminated about it – a Member of Parliament called Charles Wheeler who spoke bitterly about gangsterism in our English streets and swore he'd put a question to the House at the first available opportunity. I wished him luck. The mills of government grind slowly and it takes a hell of a long time to close even a stable door.

I quite enjoyed reading that Sunday paper.

I had just finished when the door clicked open and a man in a white coat wheeled in a trolley on which were several silver-covered dishes. Behind him followed a tall man with a balding head fringed with silvery hair. 'Ah,' he said. 'I'm sure you would relish a light meal.'

I looked at the trolley. 'I might,' I said cautiously. 'If my stomach will stand it.'

He nodded gravely. 'You feel a little ill; that I can understand. You will find two bottles on the table. One contains aspirin and the other a stomach preparation. I had assumed you would find them.'

'I didn't,' I said, and held up the paper. 'I was more interested in this.'

He smiled. 'It does make interesting reading,' he agreed, and tapped the white-coated man on the shoulder. 'You can go now.' He turned back to me. 'You don't mind if I stay for tea?'

'Not at all,' I said magniloquently. 'Be my guest.'

White Coat had laid the table and pushed out the trolley; he closed the door behind him and again I heard the snap of the lock. They weren't taking any chances even with one of their own in the room. I looked with attention at the tall man; there was something incongruous about him which I couldn't put my finger on – and then I had it. He was tall and thin but had a curiously pudgy face, ill-suited to his build. It was as though the face of a fat man had been grafted on to a thin man's body.

He gestured. 'You'll find a dressing-gown behind the bathroom door.'

I crossed to the table and found the two small bottles, then went into the bathroom. The stomach preparation I ignored but the aspirin was very welcome. I put on the dressing-gown and returned to the bedroom to find Fatface in the act of pouring himself a cup of tea. 'You don't mind if I'm Mother?' he asked sardonically.

I sat down and picked up the glass of chilled tomato juice. Fatface pushed over the Worcestershire sauce. This improved it. I laced the juice liberally, added pepper, and drank it quickly. Almost immediately I felt better, but not so much better that I could face the breakfast that faced me when I lifted the silver cover from my plate. I looked down at the yellow eyes of eggs, with sausages for eyebrows and a bacon moustache, and shuddered delicately. Pushing the plate away distastefully I picked up a slice of toast and buttered it sparingly.

I said, 'If you're being Mother you can pour me a cup of tea.'

'Certainly – anything to oblige.' He busied himself with the teapot.

I crunched on the toast and said indistinctly, 'Anything? Then perhaps you can tell me where I am.'

He shook his head regretfully. 'Then you'd know as much as me – and that would never do. No, Mr Rearden; that is one of the things I can't tell you. You realize, of course, that because of that particular restriction your movements must be, shall we say, circumscribed.'

I'd already figured that out; the double bars at the windows weren't there for nothing. I jerked my head at the bed behind me. 'Slade is a bit too circumscribed right now.'

'He'll be all right,' said Fatface. 'He's older than you and takes longer to recover.' He passed me a cup of tea. 'You will be confined to these two rooms until the time comes to move you again.'

'And when will that be?'

'That depends entirely on you. We hope to make your stay here as comfortable as possible. If you have any special preferences at meals – grapefruit juice instead of tomato juice, for instance – we will do our best to please you.' He rose to his feet and crossed to a cabinet which he opened. It was well stocked with bottles. 'You can help yourself to a drink at any time. By the way, what cigarettes do you prefer?'

'Rothmans filter.'

He produced a notebook and made an entry like a conscientious *maître d'hôtel*. 'That we can manage easily.'

I grinned at him. 'I'd like a half-bottle of wine with lunch and dinner. White, and on the dryish side; a hock or moselle, preferably.'

'Very well.' He made another note. 'We try to run a top-class establishment. Of course, our expenses being what they are, our charges are high. In fact, there is a standard charge no matter how long you stay here. In your case I think it has been agreed already – twenty thousand pounds, wasn't it, Mr Rearden?'

I picked up my tea-cup. 'It wasn't,' I said economically. 'Ten thousand pounds is lying on that bed over there. That was the deal.'

'Of course,' said Fatface. 'I forgot.'

'No, you didn't,' I said amiably. 'You were trying it on. Your tea is getting cold.'

He sat down again. 'We would prefer to settle the account as soon as possible. The sooner it is settled the sooner you will be able to go on the next stage of your journey.'

'To where?'

'I think you can leave that to us. I assure you it will be outside the United Kingdom.'

I frowned at that. 'I don't like buying a pig in a poke. I want a better guarantee than that, I want to know where I'm going.'

He spread his hands. 'I'm sorry, Mr Rearden; but our security arrangements preclude your knowing in advance. You must understand the importance of this. We cannot take any chances at all on the penetration of our organization by . . . er . . . undesirable elements.'

I hesitated, and he said impatiently, 'Come, Mr Rearden; you are an intelligent man. You must know that we have a reputation that rests entirely on our ability to keep our promises. Our good faith is our stock-in-trade and it would need but one dissatisfied client to do us irreparable harm.' He tapped gently on the table with his teaspoon. 'In any case, I believe you were informed of what would certainly happen to you if you did not keep your side of the bargain.'

The threat was there again – veiled but unmistakable. I had to play for time, so I said, 'All right; get me a cheque form of the *Züricher Ausführen Handelsbank.*'

Fatface looked pleased. 'And the number – the account number?'

'You'll know that when I put it on the cheque,' I said. 'I have security precautions, too, you know.' I did a quick calculation. 'Make it out for 200,000 Swiss francs. You take your share and let me have the balance in the currency of the country in which I'm being dropped.'

He nodded. 'A wise precaution. The sensible man never leaves himself short of liquid funds,' he said sententiously.

I looked down at myself. 'Do I *have* to live in pyjamas?'

He looked shocked. 'Of course not. I apologize for not telling you sooner. Your clothes are in the wardrobe.'

'Thanks.' I crossed the room and opened the wardrobe. Hanging up was a business suit and, next to it, a more sporty and informal outfit. Underwear was neatly laid out on the shelves and two pairs of highly polished shoes – black and brown – nestled in the shoerack.

I went through the pockets of the suits quickly and found them empty, then I clicked open the suitcase which stood at the bottom of the wardrobe and found it as empty as Mother Hubbard's cupboard. I swung on Fatface, 'No passport,' I said. 'No wallet – no identification.'

'We let you look at those to show our good faith, Mr Rearden – or should I call you Mr Cruickshank? We wanted you to see the lengths to which we would go to ensure a successful outcome of this enterprise. But there is no necessity for you to have them just yet. They will be returned to you prior to the next stage of your journey.' He wagged his finger at me solemnly. 'Security – that's the watchword here.'

That I could well believe. This mob considered all the angles.

Fatface said, 'If you want anything, all you have to do is to press this button – like this.' He waited, looking expectantly at the door, and White Coat arrived within two minutes. 'Taafe will look after you, Mr Rearden; won't you, Taafe?'

White Coat nodded, but said nothing.

'I must be going now,' said Fatface regretfully, as though he desired nothing more in the world than to stay and chat. 'We have to get on with our business.' He looked at me closely. 'I advise you to shave; you look most uncivilized. I daresay that while you are attending to your toilet Taafe will tidy up the room.' He gave me a brief nod and departed.

I looked curiously at Taafe who was busying himself with the breakfast crockery and leaving only his broad back for my inspection. He was a big man with the battered face of a small-time bruiser – small time because good boxers don't get hit about like that. After a while I shrugged and went into the bathroom. It was a good idea, no matter who had suggested it.

I ran a bathful of hot water and settled down to soak and think. The mob was good – there was no doubt about that. Provided I could come up with the money I would undoubtedly be released in some foreign country with adequate, if fraudulent, identification and enough money to see me right. Of course, the converse wasn't too good – if I couldn't provide the funds required then I would probably occupy a cold hole in the ground in an isolated place and my bones would be discovered to mystify some rural copper in the distant future.

I shook my head. No – this mob was too efficient for that. They would leave no bones to be discovered. I would probably be encased in a block of concrete and tipped over the side into the deepest part of the sea available. It would be an act of charity if they killed me *before* pouring the concrete.

I shivered a little in spite of the hot water and thought glumly of the *Züricher Ausführen Handelsbank* and that cold-minded bastard, Mackintosh. I had better begin making plans to break out of this luxurious nick.

That brought me to another question. Where the hell was I? Fatface had played safe on that one, but maybe he had slipped up, after all. I thought about Taafe. That wasn't an English name at all – so could I be already out of England? It hadn't been smart of Fatface to let that name slip out.

As I mused, a little rhyme came into my head:

Taffy was a Welshman,
Taffy was a thief;
Taffy came to my house
And stole a side of beef.

I had learned that one at my mother's knee. Apart from being libellous to Welshmen did it mean that I was somewhere in Wales – still in the United Kingdom?

I sighed and splashed water. Time would tell, but time was something I hadn't much of.

FIVE

They looked after us like an international hotel looks after a couple of Greek shipping magnates. Nothing was too good for Mr Slade and Mr Rearden – nothing except immediate freedom. We asked for newspapers and we got newspapers; I asked for South African brandy and I got it – Oude Meester, too – something I had found unobtainable during my few days in London. Slade looked askance at my South African brandy; his tipple was 15-year-old Glenlivet which was also hospitably provided.

But when we asked for a television set or a radio we drew a blank. I said to Slade, 'Now why is that?'

He turned his heavy face towards me, his lips twisted with contempt for my minuscule intelligence. 'Because the programmes would tell us where we are,' he said patiently.

I acted dumb. 'But we get the newspapers regularly.'

'Oh, God!' he said, and stooped to pick up *The Times*. 'This is dated the fifth,' he said. 'Yesterday we had the issue of the fourth, and tomorrow we'll have the issue of the sixth. But it doesn't follow that today *is* the fifth. We could be in France, for example, and these newspapers are airmail editions.'

'Do you think we are in France?'

He looked from the window. 'It doesn't look like France, and neither does it . . .' He twitched his nose. '. . . smell like France.' He shrugged. 'I don't know where we are.'

'And I don't suppose you care very much,' I said.

He smiled. 'Not really. All I know is that I'm going home.'

'Your people must think you're important,' I said.

'Moderately so,' he said modestly. 'I'll be glad to get home. I haven't seen Russia for twenty-eight years.'

'You must be bloody important if my help in getting you out was worth ten thousand quid.' I turned to him and said seriously, 'As a sort of professional what do you think of this mob?'

He was affronted. 'A *sort* of professional! I'm good in my work.'

'You were caught,' I said coldly,

'After twenty-eight years,' he said. 'And then by sheer chance. I doubt if anyone could have done better.'

'Okay, you're good,' I said. 'Answer my question. What do you think of this crowd?'

'They're good,' he said judiciously. 'They're very good. Their security is first class and their organization impeccable.' He frowned. 'I didn't think ordinary criminals could retain that kind of cohesion.'

That thought had occurred to me and I didn't like it. 'You think they're in your line of work?'

'It's unlikely but just barely possible,' he said. 'To run a network takes a lot of money. The West Germans had the Gehlen *Apparat* just after the war – that was more-or-less private enterprise but it was supported by American money.'

'Who would support this kind of outfit?' I asked.

He grinned at me. 'My people might.'

True enough. It seemed as though Slade was home and dry; instead of growing his beard in the nick he'd be knocking back vodka in the Kremlin with the boss of the KGB before very long, and dictating his memoirs as a highly placed member of British Intelligence. That much had come out at his trial; he'd infiltrated the British Intelligence Service and got himself into quite a high position.

He said, 'What do you think of me?'

'What am I supposed to think?'

'I spied on your country . . .'

'Not my country,' I said. 'I'm from the Republic of South Africa,' I grinned at him. 'And I come of Irish stock.'

'Ah, I had forgotten,' he said.

Taafe looked after us like Bunter looked after Lord Peter Wimsey. The meals were on time and excellently cooked and the room kept immaculately tidy, but never a word could I get out of Taafe. He would obey instructions but when I sought to draw him into conversation he would look at me with his big blue eyes and keep his mouth tightly shut. I didn't hear him say one word the whole time I was imprisoned in that room, and I came to the conclusion he was dumb.

There was always another man outside the bedroom door. Sometimes I would catch a glimpse of him as Taafe came into the room, a dim and shadowy figure in the corridor. I never saw his face. I thought hard about him and came to a swift conclusion. It would be impossible for one man to keep up a twenty-four hour guard duty, so there would be three of them, at least. That meant at least five in the house, and maybe more.

I didn't see any women; it was a purely masculine establishment.

I checked on the bars of the windows, both in the bathroom and the bedroom, and Slade watched me with a sardonic amusement which I ignored. It seemed that to get out that way was impossible; it was the double-barred arrangement, inside and out, that was the trouble. Besides, Taafe checked them, too. I came out of the bathroom once to find him on a tour of inspection, making very thoroughly sure they hadn't been tampered with.

Fatface came to see us from time to time. He was affability itself and spent time by the hour discoursing on world affairs, the situation in Red China and the prospects for South Africa in Test Cricket. He would join us in a drink but took care not to take too much.

That gave me an idea. I took care to appear to drink a lot, both in his presence and out of it. He watched me swig the brandy and made no comment when I became maudlin. Luckily I have a hard head, harder than I allowed to appear, and I took damned good care not to drink too much in Fatface's absence, although I contrived to fool Slade as well. I didn't know that I could trust Slade very much if things came to the crunch. It was with regret that I poured many a half-bottle of good hooch into the lavatory pan before pulling the chain for the night.

I've always found it good policy to appear to be what I'm not, and if Fatface and his mob thought I was a drunk then that might give me a slight edge when I needed it. There was certainly no attempt to stop me drinking. Taafe would take away the dead soldiers every morning and replace them with full bottles, and not a smile would crack his iron features. Slade, however, came to treat me with unreserved contempt.

Slade didn't play chess, but all the same I asked Fatface if he could rustle up a set of chessmen and a board as I wanted to work out chess problems. 'So you play chess,' he said interestedly. 'I'll give you a game, if you like. I'm not a bad player.'

He wasn't a bad player at all, though not as good as Cossie, but Cossie had more time to practise. He was certainly better than me, and after the first couple of games he gave me two pawns' advantage and I still had to battle to beat him.

Once, as we finished a game, he said, 'Alcohol and the type of concentration needed in chess don't mix, Rearden.'

I poured another slug of Oude Meester. 'I don't intend to take it up professionally,' I said indifferently. 'Here's to you . . . er . . . what the hell is your name, anyway?'

He kept a blank face. 'I don't think that matters.'

I giggled drunkenly. 'I think of you as Fatface.'

He was miffed at that and inclined to take umbrage. 'Well, I have to call you *something,*' I pointed out reasonably. 'What do you expect me to do? Whistle or shout "Hey, you!"'

But that crack lost me a chess partner.

The *Zürich Ausführen Handelsbank* cheque came a week after I had woken up in that room, and it was long enough for Slade and I to get on each other's nerves. I thought of the Swiss numbered account, of Mackintosh and of the slim chances of escape. What Slade thought about I don't know but he also became increasingly restless.

Once he was taken out of the room under guard, and when he returned an hour later, I said, 'What was that about?'

'A business conference,' he said enigmatically, and lapsed into silence.

My turn came the next day. I was taken downstairs and into a pleasant room which had just one fault – the curtains were drawn. The Scarperers were too bloody efficient for my own good; even here they were taking no chances of me finding out where I was.

Fatface came in and laid a cheque on the table. He unscrewed the cap of a fountain pen and put the pen down next to the cheque. 'The account number,' he said briefly.

I sat down and picked up the pen – and hesitated. Numbered accounts are funny things, and the number is something you guard as jealously as the combination of your safe.

I had to make this look good because he would be expecting it. I put down the pen, and said, 'Look, Fatface; any jiggery-pokery with this account and you'll wish you'd never been born. You take out of the account exactly the amount set out on this cheque – 200,000 Swiss francs and not a centime more. If you clean out this account I'll find you and break your back.'

'Finding me might prove impossible,' he said suavely.

'Don't bank on it, buster, don't bank on it.' I stared at him. 'You've had me checked pretty thoroughly so you know my record. People have tried things on before, you know; and I have a reputation which you ought to know about by now. The word has got about that it's unprofitable to cross Rearden.' I put a lot of finality in my voice. 'You'd get found.'

If he was nervous, he didn't show it, except that he swallowed before speaking. 'We have a reputation to keep up, too. There'll be no tampering with your account.'

'All right,' I said gruffly, and picked up the pen again. 'Just so we understand each other.' Carefully I wrote the number – that long sequence of digits and letters which I had memorized at Mrs Smith's insistence – and put a stroke on the uprights of the sevens in the continental manner. 'How long will it take?'

He picked up the cheque and peered at it, then flapped it in the air to dry the ink. 'Another week.'

I watched the cheque fluttering in his hand and suddenly felt cold. Now I was totally committed.

II

Three days later they took Slade away and he didn't come back. I missed him. He had become an irritant but once he had gone I felt lonely and oddly apprehensive. I did not like at all the idea of us being separated and I had assumed that we would be going along the escape route together.

Fatface had taken a dislike to me and had stopped his social visits so I spent long hours at the window, screening my face behind the pot plants, and watched the courtyard through rain and sunshine. There wasn't much to see; just the unused gravel drive to the house and the trim lawn, much blackbird-pecked.

There was one peculiar thing that happened every morning at about the same time. I would hear the *clip-clip* of hooves; not the heavy *clip-clop* of a horse, but the lighter sound as of a pony, and accompanied by a musical clinking noise. It would stop and there would be more clinks and clanks and sometimes the faint piping whistle of a man pleased with himself. Then the *clip-clip* would begin again and fade away into the distance. And once, at this time, I saw the shadow of a man fall athwart the entrance to the courtyard, although I did not see him.

On an occasion when Fatface made a rare appearance I tried to talk my way out. 'Christ, I wish I could get some exercise,' I said. 'What about letting me stretch my legs in the courtyard?'

He shook his head.

'You can have a couple of your goons watching me,' I said, but then gave up as I saw I was making no impression. 'I should have stayed in the nick,' I grumbled. 'At least there was an exercise yard.'

Fatface laughed. 'And look what happened when you used it,' he pointed out. 'You got away. No, Rearden; if you want exercise do some physical jerks in this room.'

I shrugged and poured another drink. Fatface looked at me contemptuously. 'You'll rot your liver, Rearden. You'd better do some exercise if only to sweat the booze out of your system.'

'There's damn-all to do except drink,' I said sullenly, and took a swallow of brandy. I was glad he'd fallen for the line I was feeding him, even though it was becoming a strain to keep up. Reckoning by the dead soldiers Fatface would think I was getting through a bottle and a half a day, and when he was in the room I had to drink heavily in order to keep up the pretence. On this occasion I had drunk a quarter of a bottle in under an hour, I'm a fair drinker but my head was beginning to spin.

'What's the matter?' he asked. 'Getting edgy?' He smiled mirthlessly. 'Could it be there's nothing in that bank account? Could it be there is no bank account at all?' He stretched out his legs and looked at me thoughtfully. 'We know you were shopped, Rearden; and the story is that it was your partner who shopped you. I know you deny it, but it won't do you any good at all if your partner has skipped with all the loot leaving you holding the bag. I had my doubts about you when I heard Cosgrove's report.'

'You'll get your money,' I said. 'My mate will have seen me right.'

'I sincerely hope so,' he said. 'For your sake.'

But Fatface was right – I *was* getting edgy. I snapped at Taafe irritably when he brought my meals. It made no difference; he just looked at me with those baby blue eyes set in that battered face, said nothing and went about his business leaving me to pace the room and ignore the food.

The hours and days slipped by. Every morning I heard the *clip-clip of* the pony and the pleasantly fluting whistle; every day my chances became slimmer.

At last it happened.

Fatface came into the room. 'Well,' he said in an unusually jovial voice. 'You've surprised me, Rearden.'

'I have?'

'Yes. I rather think you've been playing fast and loose. We cashed your cheque.'

'I'm glad to hear it,' I said. 'I hope there was enough in the account to cover it.'

'Quite enough,' he said. 'You've been trying to lead me up the garden path, haven't you?'

'My God!' I said. 'I *told* you the money would be there.' I laughed a little uncertainly. 'You're like the man in Moscow who said, "Schmuel, you told me you were going to Minsk so I would think you were going to Pinsk, and you fooled me by going to Minsk, anyway. I can't believe a thing you say."'

'A very interesting illustration,' said Fatface drily. 'Anyway, the money was there – all we needed.'

'Good!' I said. 'When do I leave?'

He gestured. 'Sit down. There's something we have to discuss.'

I walked around him to the liquor cabinet and poured a drink. This time I really needed it – I never *had* been absolutely sure of Mackintosh. I splashed water into the glass and sat down at the table. 'I'll be bloody glad to get out of this room.'

'I daresay you will,' said Fatface. He regarded me in silence for a long time, then said at last, 'There's just one snag. It's only a small detail, but it may prove to be an insuperable obstacle. Still, if you can explain it satisfactorily – and I don't mean explain it *away* – I see no reason why we can't carry on as planned.'

'I don't know what in hell you're talking about,' I said bluntly.

He lifted his eyebrows. 'Don't you? I'm sure you do. Think hard.'

'Don't play games, Fatface. If you've got anything to say, then spit it out.'

'All right,' he said. 'But *I'm* not playing games.' He leaned forward. 'Now, I know you're not Rearden but, for the record, I would like to know who the devil you are.'

It was as though a giant had gripped me hard and squeezed me in the belly, but I think I kept my face straight. 'Are you crazy?' I said.

'You know I'm not.'

I took a deep breath. 'Well, I think you are. What is this? Are you trying to welsh now you've got the loot?' I stuck my finger under his nose. 'I wouldn't try that, my friend; you'll come unstuck so bloody fast.'

'You're at a disadvantage,' said Fatface calmly. 'You're in no position to threaten anyone about anything. And I'd stop playing the innocent if I were you. You're not Rearden and we know it.'

'I'd like to see you prove it,' I said tightly.

'Don't be a damned fool – we *have* proved it.' He leaned back in his chair. 'You surely didn't think we pass a man on the escape line without checking him thoroughly – turning him inside out? We had you checked in South Africa and you failed the test. No police force is incorruptible – not the British police and not the South African police. If you are Rearden you must know John Vorster Square – you've been bounced in and out of there often enough.'

'But they never could prove anything,' I said.

'Yes, it's police headquarters in Johannesburg, isn't it?' He waved his hand. 'Oh, I'm sure you know the geography of Johannesburg well enough – but that doesn't prove that you are Rearden.'

'You haven't proved otherwise yet.'

'We have a friend in John Vorster Square, a brave policeman who does occasional odd jobs for us. He checked the files on Rearden and sent us a copy of Rearden's fingerprints. You've had it, chum, because they certainly don't match your dabs – and don't think we haven't tried over and over again, just to make sure.' He pointed to the glass I was holding. 'We've had plenty of chances to get your prints, you know.'

I stared at him for a long time. 'I know what a John Vorster Square dab-sheet looks like,' I said. 'I ought to – I've seen enough of them. You bring yours to me and I'll put my dabs anywhere you like for comparison.'

A veiled look filmed his eyes. 'All right,' he said abruptly. 'We'll do that. But I'll tell you something – you'll not leave this house alive until we know exactly who you are and what the hell you're doing here.'

'You know what I'm doing here,' I said tiredly. 'You bloody well brought me here. You've got your boodle, now keep your side of the bargain.'

He stood up. 'I'll be back tomorrow bright and early. That will give you plenty time to think up a good story.' He pressed the service button. 'It had better be a true story.'

The door clicked unlocked and he stalked out.

I sat and looked at the amber liquid in the glass before me. Fatface was full of good ideas. Perhaps it would be better to think up not one story but two – the true story and a plausible false one. It would be difficult; I'm a pretty good liar when the need arises, but I never was much good at sustained fiction.

III

Where does a thing like this begin? I suppose one might be logical and say it began at birth, but that's the trouble with logic – it leads to silly conclusions. Again, one might say it began in Johannesburg but it was only because of who I was – and what I was – that led to me being chosen, and so the roots go further back. Anyway, Johannesburg seemed to be a convenient point to begin, so I started to think of Jo'burg, that overgrown mining camp where the streets are paved with gold.

It was a bright sunny morning with not a cloud in the sky, something which might lighten the spirits of an Englishman but doesn't do a damn thing for a South African because most mornings are bright and sunny and clouds in winter are as rare as hens' teeth. I lived in Hillbrow in a flat in one of the towering blocks of concrete overlooking the city – the city which, at that moment, was covered with its usual layer of greasy smog. On and off, for twenty years, the City Fathers have been thinking of introducing the smokeless zone system, but they haven't got round to it yet.

A man living on his own either lives like a pig or develops certain labour-saving knacks, short-cuts like the egg in the coffee percolator. Within twenty minutes of getting up I was on my way down to the street. In the foyer I opened my personal letter-box and collected the day's mail – three of those nasty envelopes with windows in them which I stuck into my pocket unopened – and a letter from Lucy.

I looked at it a little blankly. I hadn't heard from Lucy for over six years – six slow and uneventful years – and I couldn't really believe it at first. I read the letter again. It was just a quickly scrawled note really; green ink on expensive, deckle-edged writing paper.

> Darling,
>
> I'm in Johannesburg for a quick visit. Could I see you again for old time's sake? I'll be at the Zoo Lake restaurant at midday. I've changed, darling, I really have – so I'll be wearing a white gardenia. I don't want you to put your foot in it by accosting the wrong girl.
>
> Please come, darling; I'm looking forward to seeing you so much.
>
> Ever yours,
> Lucy.

I sniffed the sheet of paper and caught a delicate fragrance. Lucy was up to her old tricks again. I put the note into my breast pocket and went back to my flat to telephone the office. I forget what excuse I used but I really couldn't tell the boss I wanted the day off to see an old girl friend. Then

I took the car for servicing; it could be I would need it in a hurry and it had better be in good shape.

At a quarter to twelve I was drifting along the road towards the Zoo Lake. The expanses of winter-yellowed grass were dotted with black nannies looking after their young charges and, in the distance, the lake twinkled under the hot sun. I put the car in the restaurant car park and wandered slowly down to the water's edge where people were feeding the birds.

There was nobody around who looked like Lucy. At least no one was wearing a gardenia. I looked across the lake at the people boating inexpertly, then turned to go back to the restaurant where, just outside, a sand-coloured man sat on a bench fanning himself with his hat. He wore a white gardenia.

I walked over and sat beside him. 'Lucy?'

He turned and looked at me with curiously naked eyes. 'Lucy!' he said venomously. 'Ever since that Russian operation in Switzerland during the war the security clots have gone nuts on the name.' He put on his hat. 'I know who you are – I'm Mackintosh.'

'Glad to know you,' I said formally.

He cast a speculative eye at the lake. 'If I happened to be a crackerjack secret service man I'd suggest that we hire a boat and row into the middle of that bit of water so we could talk privately. But that's nonsense, of course. What I suggest is that we have an early lunch here. We'll be just as private, providing we don't shout, we'll be a bloody sight more comfortable, and I won't run the risk of making a damned fool of myself in a boat.'

'Suits me,' I said. 'I didn't have much breakfast.'

He arose and took the gardenia from his lapel to drop it into a convenient waste basket. 'Why people have this fetish for the sexual organs of vegetables is beyond me,' he said. 'Come on.'

We found a table in a corner in the outside court where a vine-covered trellis protected us from the heat of the sun. Mackintosh looked around and said appreciatively. 'This is a nice place. You South Africans know how to live well.'

I said, 'If you know who I am then you know I'm not a South African.'

Of course,' he said, and took a notebook from his pocket. 'Let me see – ah, yes; Owen Edward Stannard, born in Hong Kong in 1934, educated in Australia.' He reeled off a string of schools. 'At university specialized in the study of Asiatic languages. Was recruited by a department that it is better not to mention while still at university. Worked in the field in Cambodia, Vietnam, Malaysia and Indonesia under a variety of covers. Was captured in Indonesia during the upheaval which disposed of Sukarno and cover badly blown.'

He looked up. 'I understand you had a nasty time there.'

I smiled. 'There are no scars.' That was true – no scars that were visible.

'Umph!' he said, and returned to his notebook. 'It was considered that your usefulness was at an end in the Far East so you were pulled out and sent to South Africa as a sleeper. That was seven years ago.' He snapped the notebook closed and put it back into his pocket. 'That would be while South Africa was still in the Commonwealth.'

'That's right,' I said.

'Our masters are not very trusting folk, are they? Anyway, you're here as a sleeper; you say nothing and do nothing until you're called upon – is that right?' He wagged a finger. 'Forgive the recapitulation but I'm from a different department. All this secret service stuff strikes me as being a bit comic opera, and I want to see if I've got it right.'

'You've got it right,' I assured him.

Serious conversation stopped then because a waiter came to take our order. I ordered crayfish cardinal because it wasn't often that someone stood me a lunch, while Mackintosh had something with a salad. We shared a bottle of wine.

When the dishes were on the table and it was safe to talk again Mackintosh said, 'Now I want to get this absolutely straight. Are you known to the police here – or to the security forces?'

'Not that I know of,' I said. 'I think my cover is safe.'

'So you've never had a prison sentence?'

'No.'

'What about civil cases?'

I considered. 'Just the usual things. I've had a couple of parking tickets. And a couple of years ago I had a legal barney with a man who owed me money; it came to a court case.'

'Who won?'

'He did, damn it!' I said feelingly.

Mackintosh smiled. 'I've been reading your record so I know most of these things. I just wanted to see your reactions. So what it comes to is that you have a clean record here as far as the local coppers are concerned.'

I nodded. 'That sums it up.'

'Good,' he said. 'Because you are going to be working with the South African police and it would never do if they knew you to be a British plant. I couldn't see them co-operating in those circumstances.' He nibbled on a lettuce leaf. 'Have you ever been to England?'

'Never,' I said, and hesitated, 'You ought to know that I've built up my cover with a slightly anti-British bias. It's a quite common thing here for even English-speaking people to be anti-British – especially since Rhodesia blew up. In the circumstances I thought it inadvisable to take a holiday in England.'

'I think we can forget your cover for a moment,' said Mackintosh. 'I'm authorized to pull you out if I find it necessary. The job I'm considering you for will be in England.'

It was very strange. All my adult life had been spent in the service of Britain and I'd never even seen the place. 'I'd like that,' I said.

'You might not like it when you hear what the job is,' said Mackintosh grimly. He sampled the wine. 'Very nice,' he said appreciatively, 'if a touch acid.' He put down the glass. 'What do you know about the British prison system?'

'Nothing.'

'I'll let you have a copy of the Mountbatten Report,' he said. 'You'll find it fascinating reading. But I'll give you the gist of it now. Lord Mountbatten found that the British prisons are as full of holes as a Swiss cheese. Do you know how many escapes there are each year?'

'No. There was something about it in the papers a couple of years ago, but I didn't read it up closely.'

'More than five hundred. If it's any less than that they think they've had a good year. Of course, most of the escapees are picked up quite soon, but a small percentage get clean away – and that small percentage is rising. It's a troublesome situation.'

'I can imagine it would be,' I said. I couldn't see his point; there was nothing in this to concern me.

Mackintosh wasn't a man to miss a nuance in a tone of voice. He looked me in the eye and said quietly, 'I don't give a damn how many murderers or rapists, homicidal maniacs or ordinary small-time thieves get out of gaol. That's the worry of the prison officers and the police. My field is state security and, as far as I'm concerned, the situation is getting out of hand. The Prime Minister thinks likewise and he's told me to do something about it.'

'Oh!' I said uncertainly.

'Oh!' he echoed disgustedly. 'Look at it this way. We put Blake away for forty-two years, not altogether as a punishment but to keep him out of the hands of the Russians.

Within five years he flies the coop and pops up in Moscow where he chirps his head off.'

He looked broodingly into his glass. 'Suppose Blake hadn't got clean away – suppose he'd been picked up in a month. The police would be happy and so would the prison officers, but damn it all to hell, I wouldn't! I'd want to know what the devil he'd been doing that month – who he'd been talking to. See my point?'

I nodded. 'If that happened the major reason for gaoling him would disappear. To slap him back in chokey for another forty years would be like closing the stable door after the horse has gone.'

'The horse being the information in Blake's head – not the man himself.' Mackintosh moved restlessly. 'They're building a high-security prison on the Isle of Wight. Mountbatten wants to call it Vectis which shows that, among other things, he's had a classical education. A very able man, Mountbatten. He took one look at the plans of this high class chicken coop and demonstrated how easy it would be to get a man out.'

He looked at me expectantly as though he wanted me to say something, so I obliged. 'To *get* a man out?'

He grinned. 'I'm pleased to see you live up to the good things your dossier records of you.' He held out his glass. 'I rather like this wine.'

I gave him a refill. 'It's nice to know I'm appreciated.'

'If you read the Mountbatten Report – particularly the bits towards the end where he discusses this new prison – you'll find yourself wondering if you haven't come across a major work of science fiction. Closed-circuit television with delay lines and electronic logic circuits which trigger an alarm if anything moves in the field of vision is one nice idea – that's for the defence, of course. For the attack there are helicopters and rocket-powered jump suits, for God's sake! Very James Bondery. Do you get the drift of it?'

'Yes,' I said slowly. 'Organization.'

'Right!' said Mackintosh. 'For the first time in years someone has come up with a brand new crime. Crime is just like any other business – it's conducted only for profit – and someone has figured a way to make a profit out of getting people out of prison. I suppose it started with the Great Train Robbery; those boys were given exceptionally heavy sentences – Biggs and Wilson got thirty years each – but they had money and were able to buy an organization.'

He sighed. 'Sometimes I wonder if the judges know what the devil they're doing. A murderer can be out in ten years or less, but watch your step if you commit a crime against property. Anyway, an organization was set up, dedicated to springing long-term prisoners who could pay enough, and you'd be surprised how many of those there are. And once such an organization gets going, like any other business it tends to expand, and whoever is running it has gone looking for custom – and he doesn't care where the money comes from, either.'

'The Russians?'

'Who else,' said Mackintosh sourly. 'I don't care if all the train robbers fly the coop and live the life of Riley on the Riviera, but when it comes to state security then something must be done.' He frowned. 'If I had my way such security risks would be collected together in a special prison and guarded by the army – military police empower to kill if necessary. But our masters prefer not to do it that way.'

I said curiously, 'Where do I come into all this?'

'I haven't finished putting you in the picture,' he said irritably. 'The PM wanted something done about it – so something was done. The police had a crack at it, and so did the Special Branch and the more shady and esoteric counter-intelligence units. They all got nowhere. There was one occasion when they did get a bit close to it; a prisoner already in gaol expressed a willingness to talk. Guess what happened to him.'

I'm a realist, so I said flatly, 'He died suddenly.'

'Oh, he was killed, all right,' said Mackintosh. 'But this gang sprung him from prison to do it. Can't you see the flaming impudence of it? This organization is so bloody sure of itself that it can take a man out of one of Her Majesty's prisons who doesn't want to go. One cheep from him and he'd still be alive – but they were still able to spring him. His body was found three days later; he'd been shot through the back of the head.'

'I didn't see any reports on that,' I said.

'It was put under security wraps immediately,' said Mackintosh a little tiredly. 'Nobody wanted a thing like *that* to be aired publicly. There's a veiled reference to it in the Mountbatten Report – look at paragraph 260.'

'Where do I come in?' I asked again.

'I'll come to you when I'm good and ready. Now, my business is state security, and you can put out of your head any guff about counter-intelligence cloak-and-dagger stuff. I work on a quite different plane, at Cabinet level, in fact – responsible and reporting to only the Prime Minister. Since everybody else has fallen down on this job he has given me the sole and total responsibility of getting the job done in my own peculiar way – but not in my own time.' He rubbed the top of his head. 'Of course, time is a relative thing, as I explained to the PM and he agreed. But let's hope there are no more security escapes while I'm in charge, because it's my head that's on the block.'

He looked around and waved at a waiter. 'Let's have coffee – and I think I'll have a van der Hum; I believe in sampling the wine of the country. Will you join me?'

'I'll have a Drambuie,' I said drily.

He ordered the coffee and the liqueurs, then said abruptly, 'Ever heard of a man called Rearden – Joseph Rearden?'

I thought about it for a while. 'No.'

'I didn't think you would. Rearden is – or was – a criminal. A very good one, too. Clever, intelligent and resourceful; somewhat like you, I'd say.'

'Thanks for the compliment,' I said. 'He's dead?'

'He was killed three weeks ago in South-West Africa. No funny business suspected – just a plain ordinary car crash. The God of Motorists sacrifices good and bad alike. The point is that no one knows he's dead, except you, me and a few highly placed South African coppers. When the PM gave me this Godawful job certain facilities were placed at my disposal, and I immediately began to look for someone like Rearden – a newly dead rotten egg whose death could be hushed up. He could have been found in Canada, Australia, New Zealand, the States or, even, South Africa. The fact is that he turned up in South Africa. Here's his photograph.'

I laid it face down on the table as the waiter served the coffee and only turned it up when we were alone again. Mackintosh watched me approvingly as I scanned the picture. He said, 'As soon as I had Rearden I began to look for someone who looked like Rearden, someone who could pass for a South African. Computers are marvellous gadgets – one came up with you in twenty minutes.'

'So it's going to be a substitution,' I said. 'I've done that kind of thing before, but it's risky. I could be spotted very easily.'

'I don't think so,' said Mackintosh confidently. 'To begin with, you'll be in England where Rearden has never been and, even so, you won't be moving about England much so it's unlikely you'll bump into any of his old pals.'

I said, 'What happened to Rearden's body?'

'He was buried under another name. I pulled some strings.'

'Tough luck on his family,' I said. 'Did he have a wife?'

'No wife – and his parents will get along without him.'

I looked at this spare man with the thinning sandy hair and the colourless eyelashes and thought that he was a pretty ruthless bastard. I wondered how I would get along with him in this peculiar arrangement he was planning. 'So I'm Rearden,' I said. 'And I'm in England. What then?'

'Not so fast,' said Mackintosh. 'Although Rearden was clever he lost – once only. He served a prison sentence in Pretoria quite a while ago. Do you know anything about South African prisons?'

'Not a thing, thank God!'

'You'd better learn. I'll have a man give you a course on prison conditions and the slang – especially the slang.' He offered me a twisted smile. 'It might be a good idea if you did time for a month to get the right idea. I can arrange that.' I could see him turning the idea over in his mind and rejecting it. He shook his head. 'No, that won't do. It's too risky.'

I was glad of that; I don't particularly like gaols. He drained his coffee cup. 'Let's leave here; the place is filling up and I'd like to discuss the rest of it in greater privacy.' He paid the bill and we left the restaurant and strolled into the middle distance to sit under a gum tree where there were no ears within fifty yards.

He took out a pipe and started to fill it. 'All the people who have tried to crack this organization have failed. They've tried it from the outside and failed, and they've tried penetration and failed. They've tried to ring in fake gaolbirds – and failed. The organization has fantastically good security because we know as much now as we did at the beginning – and that's only one thing. The organization is known to the underworld as the Scarperers, and that doesn't get us very far.'

He struck a match. 'Stannard, this is a volunteer's job, and I'll have to ask you to make up your mind now. I can't tell you anything more – I've already told you too much. I suppose I must tell you that if anything goes wrong it'll go badly for you – and your death may not be the worst thing that can happen. Not in my book, at any rate. It's a tricky and dangerous task and, I don't mind telling you, I wouldn't volunteer for it myself. I can't be more honest than that.'

I lay back on the grass and looked up at the sky, leaf-dappled through the branches of the gum tree. My life in South Africa had been calm and uneventful. Seven years before I had been in pretty bad shape and I'd sworn I'd never do that kind of thing again. I suppose my bosses had seen that frame of mind and had given me the job of a sleeper in South Africa as a sort of sinecure – a reward for past services. God knows, I had done nothing to earn the retainer that was piling up quite nicely in that British bank account and which I had never touched.

But time heals everything and of late I had been restless, wishing that something would happen – an earthquake – anything. And here was my earthquake in the person of this insignificant-looking man, Mackintosh – a man who hob-nobbed with the Cabinet, who chit-chatted about security with the Prime Minister. I had a vague idea of what he was getting at and it didn't seem difficult. Risky, perhaps; but not too difficult. I wasn't afraid of a gang of English crooks; they couldn't be worse than the boys I'd been up against in Indonesia. I'd seen whole towns full of corpses there.

I sat up. 'All right; I volunteer.'

Mackintosh looked at me a little sadly and thumped me gently on the arm. 'You're a lunatic,' he said. 'But I'm glad to have you. Perhaps we need a little lunacy on this job; orthodox methods haven't got us anywhere.'

He pointed at me with the stem of his pipe. 'This is top-secret. From now on only three people will know about it; you, me and one other – not even the PM knows.' He chuckled sardonically. 'I tried to tell him but he didn't want to know. He knows how my mind works and he said he wanted to keep his hands clean – he said he might have to answer questions in the House and he didn't want to be put in the position of lying.'

I said, 'What about the South African police?'

'They know nothing,' said Mackintosh flatly. 'It's a *quid pro quo* – a favour returned. They might do a bit of digging into your background, though. Can it stand it?'

'It should,' I said. 'It was designed by experts.'

Mackintosh drew gently on his pipe and blew out a plume of smoke. 'Other people have tried to penetrate this damned organization and they've failed – so we start from there and ask, "Why did they fail? " One of the more promising gambits was to ring in a fake prisoner and wait for advances to be made. At one time there were no less than eight of these decoys scattered through the British prisons. Not one of them was contacted. What does that suggest to you?'

'The Scarperers have a good intelligence service,' I said. 'I'll bet they do a preliminary check before contact.'

'I agree – and that means that our bait, which is Rearden, must stand up to rigorous scrutiny. There must be no cracks in the cover at all. Anything else?'

'Not that I can think of off-hand.'

'Use your loaf,' said Mackintosh with an air of disgust. 'The crime, man; the crime! Rearden – or, rather, you – is going to commit a crime in England. You'll be caught – I'll see to that – you'll be tried and you'll be jugged. And it has to be a particular form of crime; a crime which involves a lot of money and where the money isn't recovered. The Scarperers have to be convinced that you can pay hard cash for your escape. Now, what does that suggest to you – in view of what I've already told you?'

'Nothing much,' I said. 'It shouldn't be too difficult to arrange.'

'No, it shouldn't be too difficult,' said Mackintosh in an odd voice. 'Look here, Stannard; this is going to be a genuine crime – don't you understand that? Nothing else will do. I am going to plan, and you are going to execute, a crime of some magnitude. We are going to steal a considerable sum of money from some inoffensive British citizen who will scream to high heaven. There's going to be no fake about it because . . .' He spaced his words very distinctly. '. . . I . . . will . . . not . . . risk . . . breaking . . . security.'

He turned and said very earnestly, 'If this is so then when you are tried and gaoled you will be in the jug for a perfectly genuine crime, and if anything goes wrong there will be nothing that I, or anyone else, can do about it. If you get fourteen years then you'll rot in prison for your sentence if the Scarperers don't contact you. And the reason for that is because I *cannot* compromise security on this operation. Are you willing to risk it?'

I took a deep breath. 'Christ! You're asking a hell of a lot, aren't you?'

'It's the way it's got to be,' he said doggedly. 'A trained man like you should be able to get out of any leaky British prison without half trying. But you won't, damn you! You'll sit on your backside and wait for the Scarperers to get you, no matter how long they take to make up their minds. You'll bloody well wait, do you hear?'

I looked into his fanatical eyes and said very gently, 'I hear. Don't worry; I'm not going to back out now. I gave you my word.'

He took a deep breath and relaxed. 'Thanks, Stannard.' He grinned at me. 'I wasn't worried about you – not *too* worried.'

'I've been wondering about something,' I said. 'Mountbatten investigated the prisons when Blake flew the coop. That was quite a long time ago. Why all the sudden rush now?'

Mackintosh reached out and knocked out his pipe on the trunk of the tree. 'A good question,' he agreed. 'Well, for one thing, the effect of Mountbatten is wearing off. When the Report came out and the prisons tightened security every sociologist and prison reformer in Britain let out an outraged howl – and I'm not saying they were wrong, either. There are two ways of regarding prisons – as places of punishment and as places of rehabilitation. The suddenly tightened security knocked rehabilitation right out of the window and the penal reformers say it did ten years of damage in six months.'

He shrugged. 'They're probably right, but that's outside my field. I'm not interested in civil prisoners – it's the Blakes and Lonsdales of this world who are my meat. When you catch them you can either put them up against a wall and shoot them, or you can put them in chokey. But you imprison them not to punish and not to rehabilitate, but to keep them out of circulation because of what they know.'

There was nothing in this to explain the question I had asked, so I prompted him. 'So what now?'

'There's a big fish coming down the line,' he said. 'The biggest we've caught yet. God knows, Blake was big enough, but this man is a shark to Blake's tiddler – and he must not escape. I've pleaded with the PM to establish a special prison for this type of prisoner but he says it's against policy, and so Slade goes into the general prison system, admittedly as a high-risk man.'

'Slade!' I said thoughtfully. 'Never heard of him.'

'He's in hospital,' said Mackintosh. 'He was shot through the hips when he was caught. When he's fit he'll stand trial, and if we handed out sentences like the Texans he'd get five thousand years. As it is, we must keep him secure for the next twenty – after that it won't matter very much.'

'Twenty years! He must know a hell of a lot.'

Mackintosh turned a disgusted face towards me. 'Can you imagine that a Russian – and Slade is a Russian – could get to be second-in-command of an important department of British Intelligence concerned with counter-espionage in Scandinavia? Well, it happened, and Sir David Taggart, the damned fool who put him there, has been kicked upstairs – he's now Lord Taggart with a life peerage.' He snorted. 'But he won't be making any speeches or doing any voting. If he knows what's good for him he'll keep his mouth permanently shut.'

He blinked his colourless eyelashes and said in a passionately suppressed voice, 'The man who caught Slade was a man whom Taggart had fired for inefficiency, for God's sake!' He rapped his pipe against the tree with such force that I thought it would break. 'Amateurs!' he said in a scathing voice. 'These bloody amateurs running their piddling private armies. They make me sick.'

'How do I relate to Slade?' I asked.

'I'm going to try to put you next to him,' he said. 'And that will mean breaking the law. What Slade knows is sheer dynamite and I'd break every law in Britain, from sodomy upwards, to keep that bastard inside where he belongs.' He chuckled and thumped my arm. 'We're not just going to bend the laws of England, Stannard; we're going to smash them.'

I said a little shakily, 'Now I *know* why the Prime Minister wouldn't listen to you.'

'Oh, yes,' said Mackintosh matter-of-factly. 'It would make him accessory to the crime, and he's too much the gentleman to get his hands dirty. Besides, it would lie heavily on his conscience.' He looked up at the sky and said musingly, 'Funny animals, politicians.'

I said, 'Do you know what kind of a tree this is?'

He turned and looked at it. 'No, I don't.'

'It's a gum tree,' I said. 'The thing I'll be up if this operation doesn't pan out. Take a good look at it.'

IV

I suppose you could call Mackintosh a patriot – of sorts. There don't seem to be many avowed patriots around these days; it has become the fashion to sneer at patriotism – the TV satire programmes jeer at it, and to the with-it, swinging set it's a dead issue. So with patriots so few on the ground you can't pick and choose too freely. Certainly, to a casual eye Mackintosh bore a remarkable resemblance to a dyed-in-the-wool fascist; his God was Britain – not the Britain of green fields and pleasant country lanes, of stately buildings and busy towns, but the *idea* of Britain incorporated in the State. He took his views directly from Plato, Machiavelli and Cromwell who, if you think about it, aren't all that different from Mussolini, Hitler and Stalin.

But there was more to him than that as I found out later – much later.

There was a lot of work to be done and not a great deal of time in which to do it. I studied South African prison conditions with a prison officer, temporarily donning the guise of a sociologist for the occasion. He advised me to read the works of Herman Charles Bosman which was a superfluity as I had already done so. Bosman, possibly the best writer in English South Africa has produced, knew all about prison conditions – he had done a stretch for killing his step-brother and he wrote illuminatingly about his experiences in Pretoria Central Prison – Pretoria Tronk, in the vernacular – which conveniently was where Rearden had served his sentence.

I also studied Rearden's record, culled from the files of John Vorster Square. There was not much fact and a hell of a lot of conjecture in that file. Rearden had been imprisoned only once and that for a comparatively minor offence, but the conjecture was lurid. He was suspected of practically every crime in the book from burglary to drug-smuggling, from armed robbery to illicit gold buying. He was a many-faceted character, all nerve and intelligence, whose erratic and unexpected switches in criminal activity had kept him out of trouble. He would have made a good intelligence agent.

I smiled at that. Perhaps Mackintosh had been right when he said that Rearden was like me. I had no illusions about myself or my job. It was a dirty business with no holds barred and precious little honour, and I was good at it, as would have been Rearden if anyone had had the sense to recruit him. So there we were – birds of a feather – Mackintosh, Rearden and Stannard.

Mackintosh was busy on the upper levels of the job in South Africa – pulling strings. From the way people danced to his tune like marionettes I judged he had been right when he said the Prime Minister had given him 'certain facilities'. This was counter-espionage work at diplomatic level and I wondered what was the *quid pro quo* – what the hell had we done for the South Africans that we should be given this VIP treatment with no questions asked?

Gradually I was transformed into Rearden. A different style of haircut made a lot of difference and I took much trouble with the Transvaal accent, the accent of the Reef towns. I studied photographs of Rearden and copied his way of dress and his stance. It was a pity we had no films of him in action; the way a man moves means a lot. But that I would have to chance.

I said to Mackintosh once, 'You say I'm not likely to run into any of Rearden's pals in England because I'm not going to be at large for very long. That's all very well, but I'm a hell of a lot more likely to run into his mates when I'm in the nick than when I'm walking up Oxford Street.'

Mackintosh looked thoughtful. 'That's true. What I can do is this; I'll have a check done on the inhabitants of the prison you're in, and any that have been to South Africa I'll have transferred. There shouldn't be too many and it will minimize your risk. The reason for transfer shouldn't become apparent – prisoners are being transferred all the time.'

He drilled me unmercifully.

'What's your father's name?'

'Joseph Rearden.'

'Occupation?'

'Miner – retired.'

'Mother's name?'

'Magrit.'

'Maiden name?'

'Van der Oosthuizen.'

'Where were you born?'

'Brakpan.'

'The date?'

'28th May, 1934.'

'Where were you in June, 1968?'

'. . . er . . . in Cape Town.'

'Which hotel did you use?'

'Arthur's Seat.'

Mackintosh stuck his finger under my nose. 'Wrong! That was in November of the same year. You'll have to do better than that.'

'I could get away with it if I had to,' I said.

'Maybe. But this has to be a seamless job – no cracks which need papering over. You'd better get down to studying again.'

Again I pushed my nose into the files, if a little resentfully. My God, a man wasn't supposed to remember and account for every minute of his life. But I knew Mackintosh was right. The more I knew about Rearden, the safer I'd be.

At last it was over and Mackintosh was due to return to England. He said, 'The local coppers are a bit worried about you; they're wondering why you've been picked for this job. They're wondering how I was able to lay my hands on an Australian immigrant to impersonate Rearden. I don't think you'll be able to come back here.'

'Will they talk?'

'There'll be no talk,' he said positively. 'There are only a few of the top brass who know about you, and they don't know *why* – that's why they're becoming curious. But it's all top-secret, diplomatic-level, hush-hush stuff and that's something the South Africans are good at. They understand security. As far as the middle and lower levels of the police are concerned – well, they'll be a bit surprised when Rearden gets nabbed in England, but they'll just heave a sigh of relief and cross him off the books for a few years.'

I said, 'If you're right about the Scarperers they'll be doing some extensive checking here in South Africa.'

'It'll stand up,' he said with certainty. 'You've done a good job on this, Stannard.' He smiled. 'When it's all over you'll probably get a medal. There'll be a few private words with the people concerned – insurance company, whoever we rob, and so on. The Home Secretary will probably issue a free pardon and you won't have a stain on your character.'

'If it comes off,' I said. 'If it doesn't, I'll be up that bloody gum tree.' I looked straight at him. 'I want a bit of insurance on this. I know you're nuts on security – and rightly so. As you've organized it there'll be only three people who know about this operation – you, me and one other. I'd like to know who this "other" is, just in case anything happens to you. I'd be in a hell of a mess if you got run over by a bus.'

He thought about that. 'Fair enough,' he said. 'It's my secretary.'

'Your secretary,' I said expressionlessly.

'Oh, Mrs Smith is a very good secretary,' he said. 'Very efficient. She's hard at work on this case now.'

I nodded. 'There's something else,' I said. 'I've been going over possible eventualities. What happens if I'm sprung and Slade isn't?'

'Then you go for the Scarperers, of course.'

'And if Slade is sprung and I'm not?'

Mackintosh shrugged. 'That wouldn't be your fault. We'd have to leave it to the ordinary authorities. Not that I'd like it very much.'

'Try this on for size,' I said. 'Supposing both Slade and I are sprung. What then?'

'Ah,' he said. 'I see what you mean.'

'Yes; I thought you would. Which is the more important? To smash the Scarperers or to take Slade back to the jug?'

He was silent for a moment. 'Slade is obviously the more important, although ideally I'd like you to pull off both jobs should that eventuality arise. As far as taking Slade back to prison goes you may use your own discretion. If he turned up dead I wouldn't shed a single tear. The important thing about Slade is that he must not get loose – he must not communicate any information to a third party.' He flicked his pale blue eyes in my direction. 'Dead men tell no tales.'

So that was it. Orders to kill Slade – at my discretion. I began to understand the Prime Minister's reservations about Mackintosh. A tame hatchet man must be an uncomfortable asset to have around the house. He went to England next day and I followed two months later in response to another letter from Lucy. The crime had been set up.

SIX

I stared at the brandy in the glass. I had been thinking for a long time and I hadn't touched a drop. The time for drinking had gone and the time for thinking had arrived. And I had a hell of a lot to think about.

Everything had gone as Mackintosh had planned. The crime, the trial, the nick, Slade – and the Scarperers. Then things turned sour. They were a clever mob and as keen on security as any professional espionage ring. Here I was, injected into their organization like a drug, and I was no nearer to cracking it than I had been in South Africa.

It was that damned hypodermic syringe in the moving-van that had turned the trick in their favour. I hadn't expected that, nor had I expected this imprisonment. Still, I could see their point; they worked on the 'need to know' principle, and an escapee didn't need to know how he had escaped – just that he had done so. This mob was too bloody professional to be true.

And I had lost Slade.

That was the worst bit, and Mackintosh would rip open my guts for it if ever I got past Fatface. His instructions had been oblique but clear; if there was any possibility of Slade getting clear then I was to kill him. I could have cut his throat with a blunt table knife while he slept, or strangled him with a length of electrical wire from the table lamp. I had done neither.

Of course, if I had killed Slade one night then next morning I would have been a dead man, but that wasn't why I'd refrained. I had weighed the odds and made a number of assumptions – that Slade and I would be going out together; that I still had a chance of escape, taking Slade with me; that my cover was still secure. Not one of those assumptions had proved valid and now things were in one hell of a mess.

I lay on the bed with my hands clasped behind my head and wondered how they had tumbled to the substitution. Fatface was trying to convince me that he knew I wasn't Rearden because of Rearden's fingerprints extracted from his file at John Vorster Square. I knew that to be a damned lie because I had personally substituted my own fingerprints for Rearden's in that very file, with Mackintosh looking on, and any prints coming from that file would match mine.

If Fatface knew I wasn't Rearden it certainly wasn't on account of fingerprints – so why in hell was he trying to kid me?

I thought hard, trying one hypothesis after another. For instance supposing Fatface only suspected I wasn't Rearden – he might try to pull a bluff in the hope that I'd crack. I hadn't cracked, and I'd put him in the position of having to produce those fingerprints which I knew damned well he hadn't got or, if he had, would certainly match mine.

That was one hypothesis among many, but they all boiled down to the same thing – that either Fatface knew for a certainty I wasn't Rearden, or he merely suspected it. And in both cases the problem was how the devil had he done it? Where had I slipped up?

I went back over my actions since my arrival in England and found no flaw. I had done nothing, in either word or deed, to break my cover, and that led me to the nasty suspicion that there had been a leak – a flaw in security.

I thought about Mackintosh. Now there was a tough, ruthless, conniving bastard who would sell his grandmother to boil down for soap if that soap would grease the runway of the Ship of State. I shook my head irritably. That was straining a metaphor pretty far which showed I was tired – but it was true, all the same. If Mackintosh thought it would serve his purpose to break security on me he would do it without hesitation.

I thought about it hard then rejected the possibility for the time being because I could see no purpose to it. And that left the super-efficient Lucy Smith whom Mackintosh trusted so much and about whom I knew damn-all. There were other possibilities, of course; either of them could have inadvertently broken security, his office could have been bugged by an interested third party, and so on.

I went into the bathroom and doused my face in cold water. To hell with Mackintosh's devious ways! What I had to do now was to find a way out of this trap. There must be less thinking of how I had got into it and more on how to get out.

I wiped my face dry, went back into the bedroom, and sat at the table to review my armoury of weapons. A trained man in my position assembles his weapons as and when he can from the materials at hand. For instance, I had three meals a day at which pepper was on the table. In my pocket was a twist of paper containing enough pepper to blind a man, which could come in useful on an appropriate occasion.

After a few minutes' thought I went to the wardrobe and took out a sock which I half-filled with earth from the row of pot plants on the window ledge, taking a little from each. I hefted the sock, whirled it, and swung it against the palm of my hand. It made a satisfying thump. It wasn't as good as a sandbag – it wasn't all that heavy – but it would do.

There are many ways of getting out of a locked room. You can shoot your way out – if you have a gun. You can set fire to the place, but that's risky; there's no guarantee you'll get out, and it can have disastrous consequences – I've always kept in mind Charles Lamb's story of burnt pig. You can use deception in its many forms but I didn't think these boys would be deceived easily; I'd already tried to con Fatface into letting me walk in the courtyard and he hadn't fallen for it.

That led me to think of Fatface and what he did when he came into the room. He was very careful; the door would click open and he would walk in, closing it behind him and always facing into the room with his back to the door. The man outside would then lock it. Fatface always kept his front to me. I had experimented a bit – trying to get behind him – but he'd never let me. He also carried a gun. When your life may depend on it you notice little details like that, and, no matter how carefully tailored the suit, the bulge shows.

So I had to get behind Fatface and club him with a sockful of wet leaf mould. And that involved a conjuror's trick – he had to believe I was in front of him when I was really behind him. Short of hypnosis I didn't see how I could do it but I tackled the problem.

Presently I went into the bathroom and flushed the water closet. It had no chain, being one of those low cistern contraptions operated by a short lever. Then I hunted around for a cord. What I really needed was a ball of string, but that I hadn't got, so I had to improvise.

The light switch in the bathroom was operated, as good buildings regulations insist, by a ceiling pull-switch from which a strong cord hung to a convenient hand level. That gave me four feet. The bedside lamp was wired to a plug on the skirting board behind the bed, and the wire was two-strand, plastic coated, the strands spiralling around each other. When I separated the strands I had a good bit more cord.

There was another lamp on the dressing table which contributed more, but still not enough, so I was forced to consider other sources. My dressing-gown was of terry-towelling and had a cord which went around the waist. This cord unravelled into several strands which I plaited and, at last, I had enough. In fact, there was enough wire to make a garrotting loop – not as efficient as piano wire, it's true – but I was in no position to complain.

I made a loop on the end of my long cord and slipped it over the lever of the cistern, then ran the cord from the bathroom, around the walls of the bedroom and right up to the door. I could have done with some small pulleys but, instead, I used the insulated staples which had held down the electric wiring and hoped they would hold.

They didn't.

A gentle tug and nothing happened. A harder tug gave the same result. A very hard tug and a staple sprang from the skirting board.

This wasn't working at all.

I went back to the bathroom and flushed the water closet again, using as little pressure on the lever as possible. It was obviously too stiff to be pulled down by my improvised cord, so I had to think of something else. I studied the cistern for a while, and then removed the top, revealing its guts – the ball valve and associated gimmickry invented by that unsung genius, Thomas Crapper. The action of the lever downwards resulted in the movement of a plunger upwards, and I figured it was the friction involved in this mechanism that stiffened the lever action. If I could disconnect the lever and work on the plunger directly I thought I could do it.

Half an hour later I was ready to try again. I had lengthened my cord by means of a strip torn from the sheet; it would show, but that didn't matter in the bathroom. I left the bathroom door ajar and returned to my post at the other end of the cord. I picked it up, crossed my fingers, and pulled with a steady pressure.

The toilet flushed with a welcome and loud squirt of water.

I dropped the cord and carefully surveyed the room, making sure that nothing was out of place, that nothing would give the game away to Fatface when he entered. Everything was neat and tidy except for the bed I had stripped. I took the sheet I had ripped and tore it into long lengths. I would have a use for those. Then I remade the bed.

There still remained a few things to do. I opened the wardrobe and considered the contents. There was a suit of a decent dark grey, and there was a sports coat with non-matching trousers and brown shoes. I didn't know where I was – country or town – and if I emerged into a town then the suit would be more appropriate; but if I was in the heart of the country the suit would stick out a mile whereas the more informal dress would not be out of place in a town. So I plumped for the sports coat and associated trimmings. I'd also take the hat and the raincoat.

I'd been on the run before and I knew that one of the most difficult things to do is the apparently simple act of washing and the general idea of keeping clean. If my beard grew out a different colour than my hair I'd be an object of attention – that blonde had warned me to shave twice a day. This question of cleanliness is something of which the police are well aware, and in searching for a man on the run a check is routinely made on all public washrooms in railway stations and large hotels.

So I was taking the shaver, a tablet of soap, a face cloth and a hand towel – all of which would fit conveniently into the pockets of the raincoat without bulging too much. I coiled my garrotting wire loosely and fitted it into the sweatband of the hat. Any copper worthy of the name knows one of those when he sees it, and if I was searched I didn't want it to be obvious – I'd be thrown in the nick immediately if it were found.

That also went for the gun – if I could get hold of Fatface's artillery. Which brought me to another question. How far was I justified in using a gun if the occasion arose?

The cult of James Bond has given rise to a lot of nonsense. There are no double-o numbers and there is no 'licence to kill'. As far as I knew I didn't have a number at all, except perhaps a file number like any other employee; certainly no one ever referred to me as number 56, or whatever it was – or even 0056. And agents don't kill just for the hell of it. That doesn't mean that agents never kill, but they kill strictly to order under carefully specified conditions. Elimination by death is regarded with distaste; it's messy and irretrievable, and there are usually other ways of silencing a man which are almost as effective.

Yet sometimes it has to be done and an agent is detailed to do it. Whether this constitutes a licence to kill I wouldn't know; it certainly doesn't grant a general licence to commit unrestricted mayhem. You leave too many unexplained bodies lying around and the secret service stops being secret.

Now, Mackintosh hadn't told me to kill anyone apart from Slade and that meant, generally speaking, no killing. Such unordered deaths are known in the trade as 'accidental' and any agent who is crass enough to cause such an accidental death quickly gets the chop as being unreliable and inept. For an agent to leave a trail of corpses in his wake would cause untold consternation in those little hole-in-the-corner offices in Whitehall which have the innocuous and deceptive names on the doors.

In fact, it came back to the old moral problem – when is a man justified in killing another man? I resolved it by quoting the phrase – 'Kill or be killed!' If I were in danger of being killed then I would kill in self-defence – and not until then. I had killed only one man in my life and that had made me sick to my stomach for two days afterwards.

That settled in my mind, I began planning arson. An inspection of the liquor cabinet showed a bottle and a half of South African brandy, the best part of a bottle of Scotch, ditto gin, and a half-bottle of Drambuie. A few tests showed the brandy and the Drambuie as being most flammable, although not as fiery as I would have wished. I was sorry I hadn't developed a taste for rum – there's some nice 100° stuff on the market which would have suited me fine – although God knows what it does to the lining of the stomach.

Then I went to bed and slept the sleep of the morally just.

II

There was no breakfast next morning. Instead of Taafe trundling his trolley before him he came in empty-handed and jerked his thumb at the door. I shrugged and walked out. It seemed as though the party was over.

I was taken downstairs and across the hall into the closely curtained room where I had signed the cheque. In the hall I passed an elderly couple, Darby and Joan types, who were sitting nervously on the edges of their chairs as though they thought it was a dentist's waiting room. They looked at me incuriously as I walked past them into the room where Fatface was waiting for me.

There was a bleak look on his face. 'You've had a night to think about it,' he said. 'Your story had better be very good, Mr Whoever-you-are.'

I went on the attack. 'Where's that dab-sheet?'

'We don't keep it here,' he said shortly. 'In any case, it isn't necessary.'

'I still don't know what you're talking about,' I said. 'And if you think I've spent all night cooking up a cock-and-bull story just to satisfy you then you're crazy. I don't have much to do with my time, but I've better things to do than that.' I was telling him the exact truth.

He made a noise expressive of disgust. 'You're a liar. Can't you get it into your thick skull that the gaff has been blown? There's just one little detail missing – your identity.' He shook his head pityingly. 'We *know* you're not Rearden. All we want to know is who the devil you really are.'

Now, why did he want to know that? I had a fair idea, and I didn't like it at all. If I wasn't Rearden then he'd want to know if I'd be seriously missed. That's an important thing to know if you're contemplating murdering anyone. Was I important? Did I have important connections? For whom was I working? And why? All those were questions he would want answering.

And he was too damned certain that I wasn't Rearden, which was faintly alarming. I heaved a deep sigh. 'I'm Joseph Rearden. From what Cosgrove told me before you got me out of the nick you've done a thorough check on me. Why this sudden switch, Fatface? Are you trying to slip out of your obligations?'

'Don't call me Fatface,' he snapped. 'I don't need fingerprints to tell me you're not Rearden because you've just proved it yourself. Out there in the hall you passed a couple of old people, Mr and Mrs Rearden from Brakpan, South Africa. Your dear old father and your sainted old mother, you son of a bitch. You didn't recognize them and they didn't recognize you.'

There wasn't much to say to that, so I kept my mouth shut. But my stomach did a back flip.

Fatface showed his teeth in a savage grin. 'I said the gaff has been blown, and I meant it. We know about Mackintosh, and there's no point in you denying you know him. We know all about that tricky little set-up, so you'd better get ready to tell the truth for a change.'

This time I really was jolted – and badly. I felt as though I'd just grabbed a live wire and I hoped it didn't show on my face. For my cover to be blown could have meant any number of things; for Mackintosh's cover to be blown sky-high was bloody serious.

I said, 'For God's sake – who is Mackintosh?'

'Very funny,' said Fatface acidly. He looked at his watch. 'I can see we'll have to take stronger measures but, unfortunately, I have an appointment and I don't have the time now. I'll give you two hours to think about those stronger measures; I can assure you they will be most unpleasant.'

Depressed as I was I nearly laughed in his face. He was acting like the villain in a 'B' picture. He had no appointment and the two hours were intended to break me down thinking of very imaginable tortures. And he wouldn't be away for two hours, either; he'd be back in an hour, or possibly three hours. It was supposed to add to the uncertainty of the situation. Fatface was an amateur who seemed to get his ideas from watching TV. I think he was too soft-centred to get down to the torture bit and he was hoping I'd break down more-or-less spontaneously.

'All right,' I said. 'If you want me to cook up a story, then I'll cook up a story. It will take me two hours to think it up.'

'We don't want a story – as you put it. We want the truth.'

'But you've got the truth, damn it!'

He merely shrugged and waved to the man behind me who took me upstairs again. The Reardens – if that's who they were – had vanished from the hall. It struck me that

Fatface might very well have been bluffing about them. But he still knew about Mackintosh.

Once locked in the bedroom I got on with what I had to do. I shaved quickly and put the shaver and the rest of the stuff into the pockets of the raincoat. I dressed and put on the tweed sports coat, grabbed my weighted sock and took up position behind the door, the end of the improvised cord held in my fingers.

It was a long wait and it seemed to be hours, but I had to stay there, exactly in that place, because in this thing timing was everything. I looked about the bedroom, checking to see that all was in order, and found it good. The bathroom door was ajar, but looked closed; the cord going around the room was invisible and wouldn't be noticed by the casual eye. All I had to do was to stay behind that door and wait.

Although it seemed a long time he was back on the hour – I'd been right in predicting that. I heard the murmur of voices on the other side of the door and tightened my fingers on the cord. As soon as I heard the key in the lock I began to pull, exerting a steady and growing pressure on the piston in the cistern.

As the door opened the cistern flushed noisily.

Fatface came into the room alone and cautiously, but relaxed visibly as he heard the noise from the bathroom. He took a step forward, pushing the door closed behind him, and I heard the key turn as the outside guard locked it. He took another step forward without looking behind him. He could easily have seen me by a half turn of his head but the thought never came to him. After all, wasn't I in the bathroom?

I wasn't! I hit him with the weighted sock very hard, much harder than I'd hit the postman in the Kiddykar office. He gasped and his knees buckled but he kept his feet and he twisted his head slightly so that I could see his mouth was open and he was gasping for air and struggling to shout. I knew the sock wasn't too efficient – not like a proper sandbag – so I hit him even harder, and then again, pounding unconsciousness into his skull.

I caught him as he fell. I didn't want him thumping on the floor with a noise which might be heard outside. Even then, the repeated thud of the sock hitting his head had seemed to echo around the room and I paused for a moment, holding him in my arms, and waited to see if anything would happen.

Nothing did, so with a sigh of relief I lowered him to the floor. The first thing I did was to go for his gun. It was a neat flat automatic with nine rounds in the magazine but nothing in the chamber. I had been right; the man was an amateur, after all! To carry a gun with nothing up the spout is to carry a piece of junk metal. What's the use of a gun which can't be fired at a split second's notice?

I put back the magazine, worked the action to jump a round into the breech, saw the gun was on safety, and put it into my pocket. And all the time I was talking aloud. The guard outside must not hear dead silence.

I stripped off Fatface's jacket and took off the shoulder holster he wore. Then I trussed him like a fowl, using the strips of sheeting I had prepared, and not forgetting to stuff his mouth with a gag. He was breathing heavily through his mouth and I wondered for a moment if the gag would suffocate him, but he began to breathe through his nose rather noisily and I knew I hadn't hit him too hard. Apart from the moral aspect of murder I wanted him alive. I had a use for him.

Swiftly, I went through the pockets of his jacket. There was a wallet, which, when flicked open briefly, displayed the edges of many bank notes. That was very good – I'd need money. I didn't investigate it further, but stowed it away, together with a small notebook I found, and got on with the search. I found a handful of loose change which went into my pocket and a couple of spare magazines for the pistol, also well worth confiscating. Everything else I left, except for a penknife and a fountain pen, both of which could prove handy to have.

Then I went about the next part of the plan. I tossed the mattress on to the floor just by the door and ripped open the ticking, using Fatface's useful penknife. There was a lot of beautifully inflammable cotton wadding which I piled in a heap ready for the conflagration, and I set the bottles of brandy and Drambuie close to hand.

Then I turned my attention to Fatface who was just coming round. He stirred a little and a heavy snoring noise came from his nose which would have been a groan if he hadn't been gagged. I went into the bathroom, filled the tooth glass with cold water, went back and dumped the lot on his face. He snorted again and his eyes flickered open.

It must have been quite a shock for him to see the muzzle of his own gun held not a foot from his head. I waited until full comprehension came to him, then said casually, 'If you think there isn't one up the spout, you're wrong. If I want to blow your brains out all I have to do is pull the trigger.'

He flinched and arched his neck, trying to pull his head away, while muffled noises came from behind the gag. 'Take it easy,' I counselled. 'That way you won't get hurt.' I could see the muscles of his arms working as he tested the bindings on his wrists which were pinioned behind his back. When he had finished struggling, I said, 'I'm going out of here – and you are going to help me. You can help voluntarily or involuntarily; take your pick. I have to warn you that one mistaken move on your part might mean your death. You'll be in the middle and if any shooting starts you'll probably stop a bullet.'

I didn't wait to see his reaction to that – it didn't really matter – but took the raincoat and hat and put them on, and checked the pockets to see if I had everything. Then I doused the mattress wadding with the spirits, pouring liberally until the room smelled like a distillery.

I returned to Fatface and cut his ankles free. 'Get up – slowly!'

He staggered to his feet, hampered by the bonds on his arms. He stood quite passively, just looking at me, and I could read no expression in his eyes. I jerked the gun. 'Walk forward to the door and stop a yard in front of it. I wouldn't kick it, though; that could be fatal.'

He shuffled forward obediently, and I took his jacket and draped it across his shoulders so that the empty sleeves hung loose. Apart from the gag and the lack of hands he looked quite normal – normal enough to give me a fraction of a second's advantage when that door opened. The trick is to keep the opposition off balance, and the guard would have other things to do with his eyes just at that moment.

I struck a match and dropped it on the pile of wadding, and blue flames ran over the surface. It wasn't much of a fire but it was the best I could do under the circumstances. I kept an eye on it until the first yellow flames appeared, then pressed the bell-push – the signal that Fatface wanted to be let out.

When the lock snapped I was right behind him, prodding him with the pistol to make sure he understood the spot he was in. The door swung open and I pushed him forward, the flat of my hand in the middle of his back, and yelled at the top of my voice. 'Fire!'

I followed up fast as he staggered into the corridor and, over his shoulder, saw the startled face of the guard who was slow in reacting. He had some kind of a weapon in his hand, but he dithered as he saw Fatface lurch towards him and the flickering glow of the flames from the room. With the opening of the door a draught had swept into the bedroom and the fire really got going. I don't think the guard saw me at all.

I gave Fatface another mighty push so that he collided heavily with the guard and they both went down in a tangled heap. A gun went off and someone screamed; it must have been the guard because Fatface had a gag in his mouth.

I jumped over the sprawl of wriggling bodies and ran down the corridor, the pistol in my hand with the safety catch off. The corridor was wood-panelled with doors on either side which I ignored. At the end was a stair landing with stairs going both up and down. I went *up*. I had made my decision on that one the previous evening. It's a curious thing, but people escaping from a house always try to get immediately to the ground floor – which is why they're usually caught. I suppose it's an instinctive reaction, but the department that trained me worked hard to eradicate it.

The floor above was not so fancy – no wood-panelled walls – so I figured I was in the servants' quarters, which meant I had to look out for Taafe, if he was that kind of servant, which I doubted. I moved fast, trying to make no noise, and heard an increasing uproar from downstairs. It was becoming too dangerous to stay in the corridors so I ducked into the nearest room – gun first.

It was empty of occupants, thank God, and I'd done it just in time because someone ran down the corridor with a heavy thumping tread. I shot the bolt and crossed to the window and found I was on the other side of the house away from the courtyard. For the first time I could see the surrounding country and it was very pleasant to view – rolling fields and areas of woodland with blue-green mountains beyond. About half a mile away a car sped along a road. There lay freedom.

For over a year and a half I had seen nothing but stone walls and my eyes had focused on nothing further away than a few yards. This glimpse of countryside caused a sudden lump to come to my throat and my heart thumped in my chest. It didn't matter that dark clouds were lowering and that a sudden shift of wind sent a spatter of raindrops against the window. Out there I would be free and nobody was going to stop me.

I returned to the door and listened. There was a slice of chaos downstairs and it seemed that the fire I had started had got out of hand. I unbolted the door and opened it a crack, to hear Fatface shout, 'To hell with the fire – I want Rearden. Taafe, get downstairs to the front door; Dillon, you take the back door. The rest of us will search the house.'

A deep voice said, 'He's not upstairs. I've just come down.'

'All right,' said Fatface impatiently. 'That leaves just this floor. Taafe was at the bottom of the stairs and didn't see him. Get moving.'

Someone else said, 'Mother of God, will you look at it! It'll burn the house down.'

'Let it burn. We're done for here, anyway, if Rearden escapes.'

I stepped out into the corridor and hastened away from the staircase and, turning a corner, came upon the back stairs. I trotted down quickly, depending on speed to get to the ground floor before the searchers spread out. And I made it, too, only to find the back door wide open and a man standing before it. That would be Dillon.

Fortunately, he was not looking in my direction as I came down the back stairs, but was staring up the wide passage which led to the front of the house. I oozed my way into a side passage and out of his line of sight and then let out my breath inaudibly. No doubt I could have overcome Dillon, but not without noise, and noise would have brought the lot on top of me.

The first door I opened led into a broom closet – useless because it had no window. But the second door led into a well-stocked larder and there was a sash window. I closed the door gently and tackled the window which evidently hadn't been opened for years because it was very tight. As I forced it open it groaned and rattled alarmingly and I stopped to see if Dillon had heard it. But there was no sound apart from a few heavy thumps upstairs.

I attacked the window again and got it open at last, a mere nine inches or so, but enough to take me. I went through head first and landed in a bed of nettles, but fortunately screened from the back door by a large water-butt. As I rubbed my stinging hands I looked about and felt a bit depressed as I noted the high stone wall which seemed to encircle the house. The only gate within view was directly opposite the open back door and if I tried to leave that way Dillon would certainly spot me.

A trickle of water ran down my neck. It was beginning to rain really hard, which was in my favour. The wind was strong and blowing sheets of rain across the kitchen garden. If I could get into the open countryside I stood a chance of getting clean away because the low visibility was in my favour. But it wasn't as low as that – Dillon could certainly see from the back door to the garden gate.

The water-butt wasn't going to collect much rain; it was rotten and useless, and a stave had come away from the hoops. I picked it up and hefted it thoughtfully. No one, least of all Dillon, would expect me to go back *into* the house, and one of the major arts of warfare is the attack from the unexpected direction. I grasped the stave in both hands, sidled up to the back door, and then stepped through boldly.

Dillon heard me coming and must have noticed the dimming of the light as I blocked the entrance. But he was very slow in turning his head. 'Found him?' he asked, and then his eyes widened as he saw who it was. He didn't have time to do much about it because I swung the stave at him and caught him on the side of the head. His head was harder than the stave which, rotten as it was, splintered in two – but it was hard enough to lay Dillon out.

Even as he fell I turned and ran for the gate, dropping the remnant of the stave as I went. The gate wasn't locked and within seconds I was through and walking in a dampish country lane. That wasn't good enough because it was too open, so I ran to the left until I found a gate leading into a field, over which I jumped and then sheltered in the lee of a hedgerow.

Rain dripped on to my face from the brim of my hat as I looked across the field, trying to remember the layout of the land as I had seen it from that upstairs window. If I went across that field I would come to a wood beyond which was the road I had seen. I set off at a brisk pace and didn't look back.

Only when I was sheltered in the wood did I stop to check on my tracks. There was no sign of pursuit and, over the house, I thought I saw an eddying streamer of black smoke, although I could have been wrong because of the wind-driven rain.

I reached the other side of the wood and left by a gate and came out on to the road. But before I got to the gate I heard again the light *clip-clip* of hooves, together with a clinking sound and that pleasant fluting whistle. I opened the gate and looked up the road. A flat cart was just passing, drawn by a donkey, and a man was sitting holding the reins and whistling like a blackbird. A couple of cans which might have held milk clinked behind him on the cart.

I watched it go and tried to figure out which country I was in. The donkey cart looked as though it could be Spanish but, surely to God, it never rained like this in Spain except, maybe, in the plain. I watched the cart recede into the distance and found I couldn't even tell which side of the road he was supposed to be on because he drove dead centre.

I turned and looked up the road the other way. In the distance I could see an approaching bus and, on the other side, a man was waiting by a bus stop. I noted that the bus was coming up on the left of the road so it was pretty certain I was still in England. I was surer of it still when I crossed the road and the man turned a shining red countryman's face towards me, and said, ' 'Tis a grand, soft morning.'

I nodded, and the rain dripped from the brim of my hat. 'Yes.'

Then my self-confidence received a sudden jolt because when I looked up at the sign above my head I found it was written in two languages, English and another, and the second wasn't even in Roman script but in some weird characters I had never seen before, although they were vaguely familiar.

The bus was coming along the road very slowly. From where I was standing I could see the roof and the top storey of the house, from which a column of black smoke was rising. I switched my gaze back to the bus and wished the bloody thing would get a move on. I felt terribly vulnerable.

On impulse I put my hand into my pocket and fished out some of the loose change I had looted from Fatface. The first coin I examined was apparently a penny, but certainly not an English one. It depicted a hen and chickens and underneath was a single word in that odd script – a word I couldn't even read. I turned the coin over in my fingers and nearly dropped it in surprise.

On this side was a harp and the inscription in the strange script, but this time it was readable. It said: 'Eire – 1964.'

My God, I was in Ireland!

SEVEN

The bus drew up and because I was now screened from the house, some of the tension left me. However, so preoccupied had I been with my discovery, I had neglected to look at the destination board of the bus. Damn silly omissions of that kind can be the death of one, and I felt a bit of a fool as I sat down. I took Fatface's wallet from my breast pocket and riffled through the bank notes. Most of them were British Bank of England fivers but there were some Irish pound notes, so I took one of those as I didn't know if British currency was acceptable in Ireland.

The conductor came up and I held out a pound note. 'All the way,' I said casually.

'Right you are,' he said. 'That'll be two-and-tuppence.' He gave me the ticket and counted the change into my hand. I hung on to it until he had moved away and then examined it. It was interesting to see that half the coinage was British, so it seemed as though all the currency in Fatface's wallet would be readily negotiable.

So here I was, going 'all the way' and with not a notion in my head about where I was going. It was bloody ridiculous! I looked at the passing scene and found nothing to tell me where the devil I was. Ireland! What did I know about Ireland?

The answer came without much thought – practically nothing! Ireland was a page in the atlas I hadn't bothered to study, and Irishmen were comic characters given to fighting. There were also vague ideas of revolution and civil war – the Black and Tans and armed insurrection – but that had been a long time ago, although I had read of recent trouble in Northern Ireland.

The bus stopped to take on passengers and before it started again a fire engine went by with a clanging bell, going the other way at a hell of a clip. Necks were craned to follow its passage and I smiled. During my getaway a gun had gone off and someone had screamed, so there was probably someone in the house with a gunshot wound, a circumstance which Fatface might have difficulty in explaining away.

The bus trundled on, going God knows where. We passed a place called Cratloe which didn't sound particularly Irish, but there was a sign pointing the other way to Bunratty, which did. A big jet came over – a commercial air liner, not a military job – and circled widely, losing altitude and obviously intending to land somewhere nearby. From nowhere a name clicked in my mind – *Shannon Airport*. That was the Irish international airport, but I hadn't a clue where in Ireland it was.

I mentally added an item to the list of things urgently required – maps.

We pressed on and the sun came out, shining through the rain to make a rainbow. There were more houses here, and a racecourse – and then a magic word – Limerick. So that's where I was! It didn't make a great deal of difference; all I knew of Limerick was the one about the girl from Khartoum. But it was a big, busy city and that was something to be thankful for; I could get lost in a town of this size.

I got off the bus before it reached the centre of town and the conductor looked at me in a puzzled way – but that might have been my imagination. The reason I dropped off was that I had seen a biggish bookshop which could give me what I wanted most of all – information. I walked back the hundred yards to the shop and went inside, drifting casually from counter to counter until I found what I wanted.

It was there in plenty. There were a score of guidebooks to choose from, and any number of maps from folded sheets to bound volumes. I disregarded the antiquarian and literary guides and settled for a closely printed compendium of information. I also bought a single sheet motoring map which would fold for the pocket, a writing pad, a packet of envelopes and a newspaper, paying with one of Fatface's fivers. I took this booty into a tea-shop next door and settled to examine it over a pot of weak tea and a few stale buns – it was that kind of tea-shop.

The map told me that Limerick was at the head of the Shannon estuary and, as I had suspected, not very far from Shannon Airport. The house from which I had escaped was to the north of Limerick, somewhere between Sixmilebridge and Cratloe, very handily placed for Fatface and his crew, a mere fifteen minutes' drive from the airport.

I poured another cup of lukewarm tea and opened the newspaper to find that Slade and Rearden were still very much in the news and even on the front page, but that might have been because Detective-Inspector Brunskill had arrived in Dublin, which would make for local interest. There was a photograph showing him getting off the aircraft and when questioned about what he expected to find, he said, tight-lipped, 'No comment.' Detective-Inspector Forbes was just back in London from Brussels where he reported, 'No joy!'

Of course, Slade made the running in the newspaper much more than I did; a spy has more glamour than a jewel thief. But, from the way Brunskill and Forbes were running around, I wasn't being neglected. Those two had been picked because they could identify me by sight, and it seemed they had a lot of travelling still to do because Rearden had been seen in the Isle of Man, Jersey, the Côte d'Azure, Ostend, Manchester, Wolverhampton, Regent Street, Bergen and Middle Wallop. I wondered if Detective-Sergeant Jervis was just as busy.

The tea-shop was empty so I pulled out the wallet and opened it. First I counted the money; it was important and I couldn't get far without it. There was a total of £78, mostly in British fivers, which was most welcome. There was also a British driving licence which was even more welcome. I wanted to be mobile which meant hiring a car, something I couldn't do without producing a driving licence. It was made out in the name of Richard Allen Jones, which sounded phoney on the face of it, although the name could have been genuine. There *are* a few Joneses around; there must be for the rest of us to keep up with.

There was a letter which made no sense at all because it was written in an unknown language. I tasted the words on my tongue and thought I detected faintly Slavic overtones but I could have been wrong; eastern languages are my strong point. I pondered over it for some time then carefully put it away without becoming any the wiser.

The thin notebook was of more interest because it contained a few addresses scattered through the pages – some in Ireland, some in England and others in France, Italy and Spain. It gave me a jolt to find the address of Anglo-Scottish Holdings Ltd, in London; Mackintosh's cover was blown wide open.

There were two Irish addresses, one in the Irish Republic at a place called Clonglass in Connemara, and the other in Belfast. Both places were a hell of a long way from Limerick, and Belfast was across the frontier in Northern Ireland. It was thin stuff to work on but it was all I had and it would have to do.

I paid for the tea and asked for, and got, a handful of loose change; then I went to look for a telephone box, which I found difficult until I discovered that the Irish paint them green. I didn't make a call from the first box I found but took a note of the number and then went in search of another from which I put a call through to Anglo-Scottish in London. It was only a few minutes before I heard the voice of Mrs Smith: 'Anglo-Scottish Holdings Limited.' Her voice was warm and friendly, but that might have been an illusion on my part – I hadn't spoken to a woman for a year and a half, apart from the one who doped me.

I said, 'Your telephone might be tapped – I think it is. Find a safe phone and ring this number as soon as possible.' I gave her the number of the other box and rang off before she could answer.

Ultra-cautious maybe, but I'm still around to prove it's the best method. Besides, if she rang me I wouldn't have to keep stuffing small coins in the slot during what might be a lengthy conversation. I trudged back to the first telephone kiosk and found it occupied, so I sneered at the woman through the glass until she went away, then I went inside and fiddled with the directory while waiting for the ring.

All things considered she was prompt; the bell rang within ten minutes. I picked up the telephone, and said, 'Stannard.'

'What are you doing in Limerick?' Her voice wasn't as warm as it had been.

'What the hell do you think I'm doing?' I said grumpily. 'I want to speak to Mackintosh.'

'He's not available.'

'Make him available,' I snapped.

There was a pause. 'He's in hospital,' she said. 'He was in a car accident.'

'Oh! How serious?'

'The doctors don't expect him to live,' she said flatly.

A yawning cavity opened in the pit of my stomach. 'Christ!' I said. 'That's bad. When did it happen?'

'The day before yesterday. It was a hit-and-run.'

Bits of a deadly jigsaw began to fall into place. That was about the time that Fatface Jones had become so certain I wasn't Rearden – and he'd had Mackintosh's address in his notebook. 'That was no accident,' I said. 'His cover was blown.'

Mrs Smith's voice sharpened. 'Impossible!'

'What's so impossible about it?' I demanded.

'Only the three of us knew.'

'That's not so,' I contradicted. 'I've just hammered one of the Scarperers and he had the Anglo-Scottish address written down in a notebook. That's why I thought you might have a tap on your phone.' I took a deep breath. 'Take very good care of yourself, Mrs Smith.'

I had every reason for saying that, even apart from natural humanity. If Mackintosh died and the Scarperers also killed Mrs Smith then I'd be well and truly up that gum tree. The very best that could happen was that I'd be taken back to gaol to serve the rest of the sentence.

And there would be more. They would nail me for an assault on a prison officer; I had kicked the Chief Screw in the face and caused him to break his leg and they'd put me away for another five years because of that.

With Mackintosh and Mrs Smith gone I wouldn't have a hope of proving anything. Mackintosh's tight security system had just blown up in my face. I had lowered the telephone and a quacking noise came from the ear piece. I raised it again, and said, 'What was that?'

'How *could* they have known the address?'

'That doesn't matter right now,' I said. 'This whole operation has gone sour on us and the best we can do is to cut our losses.'

Her voice sharpened. 'What happened to Slade?'

'He got away,' I said wearily. 'God knows where he is now. Probably stowed away in the hold of a Russian freighter bound for Leningrad. It's a bust, Mrs Smith.'

'Wait a minute,' she said, and there was an abrupt silence which lasted a full five minutes. I became aware of a man standing outside the kiosk tapping his foot impatiently and glaring at me. I gave him the stony stare and turned my back on him.

Mrs Smith came back on the line. 'I can be at Shannon Airport within three hours. Is there anything you need.'

'By God there is,' I said. 'I need money – lots of it; and a new identity.'

'There's no reason why you shouldn't resume your real identity,' she said. 'I have your suitcase here with your clothing and passport. I'll bring them with me.'

'Stay away from the Anglo-Scottish office,' I warned her. 'And watch out for strange men on your tail. Do you know how to shake surveillance?'

Her voice was cold. 'I wasn't born yesterday. Meet me at Shannon in three hours.'

'That's not on. Airports aren't for men on the run. They're apt to be full of men in my line of business. Don't forget I'm on the run from the police and that Brunskill has just arrived in Ireland.' I turned and looked past the queue that was forming. Take a taxi to the St George Hotel – I'll meet you outside. I might even have a car.'

'All right – and I'll bring the money. How much do you want?'

'As much as you can lay your hands on conveniently. Can you really make it in three hours?'

'If I'm not held up talking to you,' she said acidly, and rang off.

I put down the telephone and pushed open the door. The first man in the queue said sarcastically, 'And where would it be you'd be telephoning to? Australia?'

'No,' I assured him blandly. 'Peking.' I pushed past him and walked up the street.

II

Hiring a car proved to be easy – the British licence was good enough. A hired car is not notoriously speedy but I managed to get a Cortina 1500 which would be enough to get me out of trouble – or into it – reasonably quickly.

I arrived at the St George Hotel early and parked on the other side of the road and about a hundred yards along. Several taxis drew up but no Mrs Smith appeared but finally she arrived and only fifteen minuses late. She stood on the pavement when the taxi departed with two suitcases at her side and the hall porter from the hotel dashed out to succour her. I saw her shake her head and he went back into the hotel, a disappointed man, while she looked uncertainly about her. I let her stew for a while because I was more than curious to see if anyone was taking an undue interest in her.

After ten minutes I came to the conclusion that if I didn't pick her up then someone else would because she looked too damned fetching in stretch pants, open-neck shirt and short jacket, so I entered the traffic stream and swung around to pull up in front of the hotel. I wound down the nearside window, and said, 'Give you a lift, ma'am?'

She leaned down to look into the car, and her green eyes were snapping. 'Where have you been?' she said curtly. 'I've been standing here like a fool. I've already slapped down three passes.'

'It's the Irish,' I said. 'They can't resist a pretty girl. Get in; I'll put the bags into the boot.'

'Three minutes later we were rolling on our way out of Limerick and towards Cratloe. I said, 'You made good time. You must have just caught the plane at the right moment.'

She stared ahead through the windscreen. 'I flew in my own plane.'

'Well, well!' I said. 'The intrepid aviatrix. That might prove useful – but for what, I don't know.'

'I didn't like something you said on the telephone,' she said.

'What was that?'

'You were talking about cutting losses. I didn't like that at all.'

'I don't like it much,' I said. 'But there are precious few leads to follow and I have no great hopes.'

'Why did you let Slade get away?'

'I didn't,' I said. 'He was taken.'

'There must have been *something* you could have done.'

I glanced sideways at her. 'Would you have relished cutting his throat while he slept?'

She gave me a startled glance. 'Why, I . . .' She fell into silence.

I said, 'It's easy criticizing from the sidelines. These Scarperers are efficient – more efficient than any of us realized. Slade thought they might be a Russian outfit – Russian subsidized, anyway; possibly Russian trained. One thing is certain; they're no gang of ordinary criminals.'

'You'd better tell me about it,' she said. 'But first tell me where we're going now.'

'I want to have a look at the house in which we were incarcerated. We may be able to pick up something, but I doubt it; the last I heard the boss man was shouting about abandoning the place. Anyway, this is the way it went.'

One thing about Irish roads is that they're traffic free and we made good time, so much so that I was only halfway through my tale of woe by the time I saw the first fire engine. 'This is it,' I said, and pulled off the road well away from the scene of action.

It was a shambles. Mrs Smith took one look at the smoking shell of the house, and said, 'I don't know about the boss abandoning the house, it looks as though it abandoned him. Why should he burn it down?'

'He didn't,' I said immodestly. 'I did.' I stuck my head out of the window and hailed a passing cyclist coming from the scene of the crime. 'What's happened here?'

The cyclist, a gnarled old man, wobbled across the road and lurched to a halt. 'A wee bit of a fire,' he said, and gave me a gap-toothed grin. 'Reminds me of the Troubles, it does.'

'Anyone hurt?'

'Indeed there was. They found a poor gentleman in the middle of it all – burnt to a crisp.'

'That's dreadful,' I said.

The old man leaned forward and peered at me. 'A friend of yours, could he be?'

'Oh, no,' I said. 'I was just passing and saw the fire engines.'

'A natural curiosity,' he agreed. 'But there's a mystery going on, there is. There were other men in that house and they've all run away. The *garda* are wondering why.'

'The *garda*?'

'The natural enemies of good men,' said the ancient. 'The men in blue.' He pointed up the road. 'In England you call them the police.'

About a hundred yards away was a police car – they're unmistakable – with a policeman walking towards it. I glanced at Mrs Smith. 'Should we be on our way, darling? We have to be in Roscommon tonight.'

'Roscommon, is it?' said the old man. 'But it's on the wrong road you are.'

'We're calling in to see friends in Ennis,' I said. The man was as sharp as a tack.

'Ah, then it's straight ahead.' He took his hand from the side of the car. 'May you have luck in Ireland – you and your beautiful lady.'

I smiled at him and let out the clutch and we drove slowly past the police car. I looked at the mirror and checked that it showed no inclination to follow before I said, 'If they do a thorough autopsy of that corpse they're likely to find a bullet.'

'Did you kill him?' asked Mrs Smith. Her voice was as cool and level as though she had asked if I had slept well.

'Not me. It was an accident, more-or-less; he shot himself in a scuffle.' I checked the mirror again. 'He was right, you know.'

'Who was?'

'The old man. You *are* beautiful.' I gave her no time to worry about it but went straight on. 'How's Mackintosh?'

'I telephoned the hospital just before I left London,' she said. 'There was no change.' She turned to me. 'You don't think it was an accident?'

'How did it happen?'

'He was crossing a street in the City late at night. A man found him by the side of the road. Whoever hit him didn't stop.'

'The man Jones knew I wasn't Rearden about the same time,' I said. 'I don't think it was an accident'

'But how did they know?'

'I didn't tell them so it must have been either you or Mackintosh,' I said.

'It wasn't me,' she said quickly. 'And why should it have been him?' I shrugged and she was silent for a while before she said slowly, 'He's always been a good judge of men but . . .' She stopped.

'But what?'

'But there was £40,000 in that Swiss numbered account and you had the number.'

I glanced at her. She was staring straight ahead, her body held rigid, and a pink spot glowed on her cheek. 'That's all we need,' I said. 'So you think I sold out to the Scarperers, is that it?'

'Can you think of any other explanation?'

'Not many,' I admitted. 'Talking about money – how much did you bring?'

'You're taking this too damned coolly.' Her voice had an edge to it.

I sighed and drew the car to a halt by the roadside. I put my hand beneath my jacket and brought out the gun I had taken from Jones – butt first. I offered it to her on the palm of my hand. 'If you're so certain I sold out then we may as well get it over with quickly,' I said. 'So take this and let me have it.'

Her face whitened when she first saw the pistol, but now she flushed pink and lowered her eyelids to avoid my gaze. 'I'm sorry,' she said quietly. 'I shouldn't have said that.'

'It's just as well you did,' I said. 'Or you might be still thinking it. There are only the two of us, and if we can't trust each other we'll get nowhere. Now, you're sure you couldn't have let fall even a hint of the operation?'

'I'm positive,' she said.

I put away the gun. 'I didn't,' I said. 'So that leaves Mackintosh.'

'I don't believe it,' she said.

'Who did he see just before this so-called accident?'

She thought about it. 'He saw the Prime Minister and the Leader of the Opposition. They were both worried about the lack of news of Slade. There's an election coming up and the PM thought the Leader of the Opposition should be informed of developments.'

'Or the lack of them,' I said. 'I suppose he might do that – it's not a party issue. Anyone else?'

'Yes; Lord Taggart and Charles Wheeler. Wheeler is a Member of Parliament.'

'I know of Taggart,' I said. 'He was Slade's boss at one time.' The name, Wheeler, rang a faint bell. 'What did he talk to Wheeler about?'

'I don't know,' she said.

'If Mackintosh were to tell anyone of the operation would you expect him to inform you?'

'He never kept anything from me that I know of.' She paused, then said, 'But he had the accident before he could get to me.'

I mulled it over and got nowhere. I sighed, and said, 'I'm damned if I'm going to keep calling you Mrs Smith and neither am I going to call you Lucy. What *is* your name?'

'All right,' she said resignedly. 'You may call me Alison.'

'What do we do now, Alison?'

She said decisively, 'We check on the Irish addresses you found in Jones's notebook. First, at Clonglass, and then at Belfast if necessary.'

'That might not be too easy. The Clonglass reference wasn't as much an address as a mention – just a scribbled memorandum; "Send Taafe to the House at Clonglass".'

'We'll try it anyway,' she said. 'It's not far.'

III

We booked in for the night at a hotel in Galway, but pushed on immediately to Clonglass which was about 25 miles further west along the coast. From the bare look of the map there didn't seem to be any likelihood of finding an hotel west of Galway, especially late at night, so we played safe.

Clonglass proved to be a wide place in the road overlooking a small inlet from the main bay. The houses were scattered, each with its thatched roof tied down against the advent of the western gales, and each with its peat stack handy to the door. It didn't look too promising.

I drew the car to a halt. 'What do we do now? I wouldn't know where to start in a place like this.'

She smiled. 'I do,' she said, and got out of the car. An old woman was toiling up the road, swathed in black from head to foot and with a face like a frost-bitten crab apple. Alison hailed her and damned if she didn't proceed to jabber away in a strange language.

As always when one eavesdrops on a conversation in a foreign language it seemed as though they were discussing everything from the current price of potatoes to the state of the war in Vietnam and it seemed to go on interminably, but presently Alison stepped back and the old woman resumed her trudge up the road.

I said, 'I didn't know you could speak Irish.'

'Oh, yes, I have the Gaelic,' she said casually. 'Come on.'

I fell into step. 'Where are we going?'

'To the place where the gossip is,' she said. 'The local shop.'

The shop was instantly familiar. I had seen many like it in the back-blocks of Australia and the more remote parts of the African veld. It was what I used to call as a child an 'anything shop' selling anything and everything in minute quantities to a small population. This shop had an added attraction; it had a bar.

Alison went into her Irish routine again and the words washed around my ears without penetrating, and then she turned to me, and asked, 'Do you drink whiskey?'

'Indeed I do.'

I watched with fascination as the bartender did his best to empty the bottle into a glass. In Ireland a glass of whiskey is a tenth of a bottle and the men are noble drinkers. Alison said, 'One of them is for him – his name is Sean O'Donovan. You talk to him and I'll join the ladies at the other end of the shop. Men can talk to each other better over a drink.'

'Talk to him!' I said. 'That's easy, but what do I do when he talks back?'

'Oh, Sean O'Donovan speaks English,' she said, and drifted away.

'Yes,' said O'Donovan in a soft voice. 'I have the English. I was in the British army during the war.' He put the glasses on the counter. 'You'll be here for a bit of a holiday?'

'Yes,' I said. 'Having a look around – a travelling holiday. You have a beautiful country, Mr O'Donovan.'

He cracked a grin. 'You English have always shown a fancy, for it,' he said sardonically. He lifted his glass and said something in Irish which I didn't catch but the action was obvious so I returned the toast in English.

We talked for a while about the things a man talks about to a bartender in bars, and finally I got down to the meat of it. 'All over Ireland I've been crossing the tracks of a friend of mine,' I said casually. 'But I haven't caught up with him. I was wondering if he's been here. His name is Jones.' That sounded silly, but I said it all the same.

'Would he be a Welshman?' asked O'Donovan.

I smiled. 'I doubt it. He's English.'

O'Donovan shook his head. 'I have not heard of the man. He may be at the Big House, but they keep to themselves entirely.' He shook his head. 'They buy their provisions in Dublin and not a thought do they give to the local trader. My father, now, who had this place before me, supplied the Big House all his days.'

That sounded promising. I said sympathetically, 'Standoffish, are they?'

He shrugged. 'Not that Himself is here often. He comes only once or twice a year – from the Other Island, you know.'

It took me a good twenty seconds to realize that O'Donovan meant England. 'So the owner is English?'

O'Donovan gave me a sidelong glance. 'It would seem he is another Englishman who has taken a fancy to a piece of Ireland.' I looked at O'Donovan's tough face and wondered if he was an active member of the IRA; he appeared to like Englishmen only in so far as they stayed in England, although he chatted pleasantly enough to me.

He held up his hand. 'I said "seems" and that is what I meant, for I was reading in the paper only the other day that the man is not English at all.'

'So he gets his name into the newspapers?'

'And why wouldn't he? He speaks in the Parliament of the Other Island. Now isn't that a strange thing, and him not an Englishman.'

'It is, indeed,' I said. My acquaintanceship with members of the British Parliament was limited, to say the least of it, and I didn't know the rules of entry. 'So what is he if he isn't English?'

'Ah, now; that I forget entirely. Some small place far away in Europe he comes from. But it's a rich man he is. He has all the money in the world that the American Kennedys haven't laid their fists on already. He comes here in his big yacht which is now anchored in the bay and it's as big as the British royal yacht, if not bigger. Such a pleasure boat has never been seen in these waters before.'

A wealthy and foreign Member of Parliament! It wasn't as promising as I had thought, although it had its curiosity value.

O'Donovan shook his head. 'Maybe Mr Wheeler is richer than the Kennedys, after all.'

Wheeler!

Every nerve cell in my cerebrum sprang to attention simultaneously. That was the name of the MP Mackintosh had seen the day before being hit by the car. I put down my glass slowly. 'I think we'll have another, Mr O'Donovan.'

'And that's a kindly thought,' he said. 'I'm thinking you'll be from the newspapers yourself.' I opened my mouth to speak, and he winked at me. 'Hush, now; you've no need to fear I'll give you away. We've had other London reporters here – ay, and one American – all trying to find out things about the Wheeler man to publish in their papers but not one of them had the wit that you have – to bring an Irish girl with you to do a bit of talking in the Gaelic.'

'I thought it might smooth the way,' I said prevaricatingly.

He leaned over the counter and looked into the shop where Alison was talking animatedly to a group of black-shawled women. 'Ah, but she did not learn her tongue in the West; in Waterford, maybe.'

'I believe she mentioned that she lived there,' I said guardedly. 'But she lives in Dublin now.'

O'Donovan nodded in satisfaction, pleased to have been proved right. He picked up the glasses, and then paused, looking over my shoulder. 'Look, now; here comes Seamas Lynch from the Big House. I'll not tell him what you are.'

I turned and looked at the man who was walking up to the bar. He was a black Irishman, dark as a Spaniard, and tall, lean and muscular. O'Donovan put our whiskey on the counter, and said, 'And what will you have, Seamas?'

'I'll have a half,' said Lynch.

O'Donovan picked up a glass and turned to fill it, throwing a question over his shoulder. 'Seamas, when is Himself leaving in his big boat?'

Lynch shrugged. 'When he takes it into his head to do so, Sean O'Donovan.'

O'Donovan put the glass in front of Lynch. I observed that half an Irish single whiskey was about as big as an English double. 'Ah, it's nice to be rich,' he said. 'And have all the time in the world.'

I said, 'Maybe the House of Commons isn't sitting.'

'Then he should be talking to his constituents – and he has none here,' said O'Donovan. He turned to Lynch. 'This gentleman is having a fine time seeing Ireland.'

Lynch looked at me. 'So you think Ireland is a fine place, do you?'

It wasn't what he said but the way he said it that made my hackles rise; his tone of voice held a thinly veiled contempt. I said, 'Yes; I think it's a very nice country.'

'And where are you going next?' asked O'Donovan.

I had an inspiration and told a true story. 'I believe my grandfather on my mother's side was harbour master at Sligo many years ago. I'm going up there to see if I can trace the family.'

'Ach,' said Lynch. 'Every Englishman I meet tells me of his Irish ancestry.' His contempt was now open. 'And they all claim to be proud of it. You'd think from the way of it that the British Parliament ought to be in Dublin.'

I nearly lost my temper but kept my voice even. 'Maybe it's true. Maybe it's because your Irish girls can't find good husbands at home so they have to cross the Irish sea,' I said coolly.

Lynch's face darkened and his hand tightened on his glass. As he straightened up from leaning on the counter O'Donovan said sharply, 'Seamas, that's enough, now. You've got as good as you've given, which does not happen too often, so put your glass back in your mouth or on to the counter. I'll have no breakages in my house unless it's your head with a bottle I'll be holding.'

Lynch sneered at me and turned his back. O'Donovan said, not very apologetically, 'You'll understand the English are not well liked hereabouts.'

I nodded. 'And with good reason, from some of the things I've heard. As it happens, I'm not English – I'm Australian.'

O'Donovan's face lightened. 'Are you, now? I ought to have known from your pleasant ways and your good manners in the face, of provocation. That's a great country – it is, indeed.'

I finished my drink as I saw Alison giving me a come-hither look. O'Donovan watched approvingly as I sank the full Irish measure in four seconds flat. I put down the empty glass. 'It's been nice talking to you, Mr O'Donovan,' I said. 'I'll be back.'

'And you'll be welcome,' he said.

I went to join Alison at the door. As I passed Lynch he stuck his foot out backwards but I neatly evaded it and carried on. I wasn't looking for a fight. Alison opened the door and went outside. I was about to follow her but stood aside as a big man entered. He walked past me and then paused uncertainly.

I ran for it. It was Taafe, and while his thought processes might have been slow they hadn't stopped altogether. While he was making up his minuscule mind about what action to take I dashed outside and grabbed Alison's arm. 'Run for the car!' I said urgently. 'We've found trouble.'

What I liked about Alison was her quick comprehension. She wasted no time insisting on having an explanation, but immediately took to her heels and ran. She must have been in superb physical condition because she could cover the ground faster than I, and within a hundred yards she was ten yards ahead.

Behind I heard boots thumping the ground as someone chased behind and I reckoned the someone was Taafe. It was now dusk and the light was ebbing from the western sky which is why I didn't see the fishing net spread out to dry about twenty yards from where we had left the car. I got my feet tangled in the netting and pitched forward to the ground.

That made it easy for Taafe. I heard the crunch of his boots as he ran up, and then the rasp of the engine as Alison started the car. The next thing I knew was Taafe had put the boot into me good and solid. He had boots like a skinhead, probably steel-tipped, and one of them crunched into my side with terrifying force. He made no sound apart from a heavy breathing.

I rolled over, desperately trying to free my feet, and his foot whistled past my head so closely that I felt the draught. If he kicked me in the head it would be lights-out for Stannard – maybe permanently. The engine of the car roared and then we were illuminated as Alison switched on the headlights.

I looked up and saw Taafe loom over me, his teeth drawn back over his lips in a snarl as he manoeuvred for another kick. I rolled frantically and saw a stab of light from the direction of the car, and heard a report as from a dud firecracker. Taafe made a gargling sound in his throat and suddenly collapsed on top of me. He made horrible noises as I heaved him off and then he writhed on the ground clutching his left knee.

I ripped the netting from my feet and ran to the car. The passenger door was open and Alison was revving the engine impatiently. As I tumbled in she was putting a small pistol into the glove compartment and, before I got the door closed, she was away, swinging the car around and barely avoiding Taafe who still wriggled on the ground.

I gasped, 'Where did you shoot him?'

'In the kneecap,' she said. Her voice was as steady and cool as though she was discussing a shot on the target range. 'It seemed the best thing to do. He was going to kill you.'

I turned and looked back. Although it was dark I could see someone bending over Taafe. It was someone tall and lean and it could very well have been Seamas Lynch.

IV

'Wheeler,' I said thoughtfully. 'What can you tell me about him?'

It was next morning and we were having breakfast in my bedroom. If the management thought this an irregular procedure they showed no sign of it, and, in view of the previous evening's brouhaha, I didn't feel like being pinned down to a static and open position in the public dining room.

She spread marmalade on toast. 'MP for Harlingsdon East, very wealthy, not too popular with fellow Commons members, so I understand.'

'And a foreigner?'

She wrinkled her brow. 'I believe he is. But he must have arrived in England a long time ago. He'll be naturalized, of course.'

'Can a foreign-born person become an MP?'

'Oh, yes; there have been quite a few,' Alison said indistinctly past the toast

'An American President must be American born,' I said. 'What about an English Prime Minister?'

'I don't think there's any rule about it,' she said. 'We'd have to look it up in Erskine May.'

'What's his standing? In politics, I mean? Is he a Minister or anything like that?'

'He's a very vociferous back-bencher.'

I snapped my fingers. 'That's where I saw his name before. He was blowing off steam after Slade and I escaped. Going on about "gangsters in our English streets". I read about him in the *Sunday Times*.'

'Yes,' said Alison. 'He made quite a noise about it in the House. The PM put him down quite firmly.'

I said, 'If what I'm thinking is correct then he's got a hell of a nerve. Try this on for size. Mackintosh sees Wheeler and he's hit by a car – a hit-and-run car. I take a notebook from Jones which mentioned Clonglass. In Clonglass we run across Wheeler; we also ran into Taafe – and too bloody hard, if I might say so – and I know that Taafe is one of the Scarperers. Wouldn't you think it would be too much of a coincidence for Wheeler *not* to be implicated with the Scarperers?'

Alison buttered another piece of toast; the girl had a healthy appetite. 'I'd say he's in it up to his neck,' she said concisely. She paused. 'What I don't understand is why Taafe didn't shout; he didn't make a sound even when I shot him.'

'I don't think he *can* shout,' I said. 'I think he's dumb. I've never heard him speak. Let me have a look at that pistol of yours.'

She leaned over, picked up her bag, and produced the pistol. It was a very natty little weapon, only .22 in calibre and with a total length of less than four inches – hardly the gun for accurate shooting in uncertain light at any range over twenty feet. I said, 'Did you intend to hit Taafe in the kneecap?'

'Well,' she said. 'He had one foot off the ground but even then these bullets are so small that if I'd hit him anywhere else it wouldn't bring him down. I could have gone for a head shot, of course, but I didn't want to kill him.'

I looked at her with respect. As I had thought, Mackintosh gathered around him people with talents. 'So you *did* intend to hit him where you did.'

'Oh, yes,' she said, and put the ridiculous little gun away.

I said, 'Let's get back to Wheeler. What kind of a foreigner is he? Or was he? Where did he come from?'

'I don't know. I haven't taken much interest in him. But the details ought to be in *Who's Who.*'

'I'm thinking of Slade,' I said. 'He was taken out of the house near Limerick four days ago. That yacht is very convenient. If it has been anchored at Clonglass for more than four days *and* Wheeler decides to take off on a Baltic cruise this summer then there'll be a bloody good chance that Slade is on board. It's just a hypothesis, mind you.'

'I like it.'

'I've got a few more. What about this one? Let's say there's a man called X who is either a Russian or favours the Russian philosophy; and let's say he devotes his time to springing Russian spies from British gaols. He'd need assistance and where would he get it?' Alison opened her mouth to answer but I ploughed on. 'There's a fair amount of anti-British feeling in Ireland, especially now that Northern Ireland has blown up, and the IRA is still an active force. I detected a bit of that ill feeling last night.'

'Was that the man you were talking to at the bar?'

'He was Seamas Lynch and he seemed to hate my guts on principle. What's more, he works for Wheeler and I think I saw him helping Taafe when we left last night. But I digress. Let's say Mr X organizes the Scarperers from elements of the IRA. He has the money to get it started but from then on it's self-financing because the Scarperers don't confine their attention to spies. The IRA need the money and it's a better way of getting it than holding up banks, so they're happy. Mr X is also happy because the IRA are doing a good job for him. How does that strike you?'

She raised her eyebrows. 'Mr X being Wheeler?' She shook her head sadly. 'Self-made millionaires aren't usually enthusiastic communists.'

'How did he make his money?'

'I think he made his first fortune in the property boom of the 1950s and early '60s. Then he got into the property market in the United States and made another fortune. *Time* had a front cover article about him; they called him "Wheeler-Dealer." Since then he's diversified into nearly everything you can think of that makes money.'

'And he still has time to be a Member of Parliament! He's a busy little man.'

'Too busy to be a Russian spy,' said Alison.

'Maybe.' I had my own reservations about that. I said, 'I'd like to know how Mackintosh is getting on. Will you telephone?'

'I was going to,' she said. 'I think we ought to get rid of the car. It will have been seen at Clonglass.' She hesitated. 'I'll go out and get another. I don't think you ought to walk the streets of Galway just now.'

'But . . .'

'They're not likely to know much about me yet,' she said. 'We weren't conspicuously together last night.'

'Providing Sean O'Donovan has kept his mouth shut,' I said.

'I'll have to chance it,' she said, and picked up the telephone.

She put a call through to London and talked to someone at the hospital. Her words were brief and she did more listening than talking but I knew what was happening by the expression of her face. She put down the handset and said bleakly, 'Still no change. He's fighting hard – but he would.'

I lit a cigarette. 'Have you known him long?'

'All my life,' she said. 'He's my father.'

V

That led to an argument. My immediate reaction was to say that I'd get on with the job myself while she went back to London.

'Damn it!' I said. 'You *ought* to be there. You'll never forgive yourself if he dies in your absence.'

'And he'd never forgive me if Slade gets away because I'm too damned sentimental,' she said. 'You don't know my father very well, Owen, if you think he'd want that. He's a hard man.'

'And you're a hard woman,' I said. 'A chip off the old block.'

She said tautly, 'An unnatural daughter?'

'I think you ought to go back,' I said stubbornly.

'And I'm staying,' she said, equally stubbornly. 'I have two jobs to do here. One is to help you to get Slade. You can't run up against this crowd by yourself.'

'And the other?'

'To stop you getting yourself killed, you damned fool!'

I was turning that over in my mind while she opened her suitcase and impatiently ripped open a brown-paper parcel, revealing more money than I've seen anywhere outside a bank. For a moment that diverted me. 'How much have you got there, for God's sake?'

'Five thousand pounds,' she said, and tossed me a bundle of fivers. 'There's five hundred. We might get separated and you'll need the money.'

I said drily, 'Her Majesty's Treasury is becoming unreasonably reckless. Do I sign a receipt?'

'I'm going to find out what I can about Wheeler,' she said. 'Don't move out of this room.'

She stuffed the rest of the money into one of those oversized bags women carry and stormed out of the room before I could say another word. I sat down bonelessly on the bed and looked at the bundle of notes, one hundred sheets thick, and the only thought in my head was the irrelevancy that she had called me by my given name for the first time.

She was away for two hours and came back with news – Wheeler's yacht was on the move, heading south. She didn't know if Wheeler was on board or not.

She pulled a piece of paper from her pocket, a printed page from a book. 'I bought an old copy of *Who's Who.* It was a bit too big to lug around so I tore out the relevant page.'

She passed it to me and pointed out the paragraph. Charles George Wheeler, aged 46, was born in Argyrokastro, Albania. *Albania!* He was a Member of Parliament with three honorary doctorates, a member of this, an associate of that, a fellow of the other. A flat in London, a country house in Herefordshire; clubs so-and-so and such-and-such – my eye skipped down the page until I was suddenly arrested by an entry – Interests – penal reform, for God's sake!

I said, 'How does he come by the name of Charles George Wheeler?'

'He probably changed it by deed poll.'

'Do you know when he arrived in England from Albania?'

'I know nothing about him,' said Alison. 'I've had no occasion to study him.'

'And his yacht has gone south. I'd have thought he'd have gone north – to the Baltic.'

'You're still assuming that Slade is aboard.'

'I have to,' I said grimly.

Alison frowned. 'He might be going to the Mediterranean. If so, he'll refuel somewhere in the south, perhaps Cork. I have a friend in Cork: an old lady – an honorary aunt. We can fly to Cork from Shannon.'

'There'll be more coppers than tourists at Shannon Airport,' I said. 'I can't risk it.'

'Airports are big places. I can get you through,' Alison said confidently.

'And how will you account for me to your old aunt?'

Alison smiled. 'I could always twist Maeve O'Sullivan around my little finger.'

VI

We sneaked into Shannon Airport quite easily and unobtrusively. It seemed to me that their security was lousy, but the places are so big and the perimeters so extensive that to make them leakproof would swallow all the profits. Within fifteen minutes, after a bit of radio natter, we were in the air heading for Cork while I watched Alison's expert handling of the controls. She flew the plane – a Piper Apache – like she did everything else – with an economy of movement and a total lack of showmanship. I wondered what it was like to have Mackintosh as a father. Some girls might have found it a traumatic experience.

Maeve O'Sullivan lived in Glanmire on the outskirts of Cork. She was very old, but still quick and sharp-eyed and shrewd as the proverbial barrel-load of monkeys. She crowed with delight as she saw Alison and gave me a glance which stripped me to the bone in two seconds. 'You've been away too long, Alison Mackintosh.'

Alison smiled. 'Smith,' she said.

'And so it is – so it is. A sassenach name for a Celt, more's the pity.'

'This is Owen Stannard,' said Alison. 'He's working for my father.'

The wise old eyes regarded me with renewed interest. 'Is he, now? And what devil's business is that young rip up to now?'

The idea of a man as hard-bitten as Mackintosh being referred to as a young rip made me want to smile, but I manfully repressed it. Alison gave me a warning glance. 'Nothing that should concern you,' she said tartly. 'He sends you his love.' I mentally agreed with her that it would not be a kindness to tell the old lady of his condition.

'You're just in time for your tea,' said Mrs O'Sullivan, and went off in a bustle into the kitchen with Alison close behind her. I sat down in a big armchair which swallowed me in comfort, and looked at my watch. It was six-thirty – early evening – less than twenty-four hours had passed since Alison had punctured Taafe in the kneecap.

'Tea' proved to be an enormous meal with many dishes thrust upon us, interspersed with brisk and depreciatory comments on the poor appetites of young folk these days. When I called the old lady Mrs O'Sullivan she laughed and said, 'You call me by my name, young man, and I'll feel easier,' so I called her Maeve, but Alison called her Aunt Maeve.

'There's something I must tell you, Aunt Maeve,' said Alison. 'Owen, here, is wanted by the *garda* , so no one must know he's here.'

'The *garda,* is it?' cried Maeve. 'It'll not be dishonest, I know; but is this Alec's doing?'

'In a way,' said Alison. 'It *is* important.'

'I've held my tongue about more things than you've ever spoken in your life, girl,' said Maeve. 'You don't know what it was like here in the old days, and now the crazy men are at it again in the North.' She looked up with sharp black-button eyes. 'It's nothing to do with that, is it, now?'

'No,' I said. 'Nothing to do with Ireland at all, really.'

'Then I'll keep my peace,' she said. 'You are welcome in this house, Owen Stannard.'

After tea we washed up and Maeve said, 'I'm an old woman and I'm wanting my bed. Make yourselves easy, the pair of you.'

'I'd like to use the telephone,' said Alison.

'It's there when you want it. Put your sixpences in the box – I'm saving up for my old age.' Maeve shouted with laughter.

'It'll be more than sixpences, Aunt Maeve,' said Alison. 'I'll be telephoning to England and more than once.'

'Rest easy, girl. If you talk to Alec, ask him why he never comes to Ireland these days.'

'He's a busy man, Aunt Maeve.'

'Aye,' said Maeve. 'And when men like Alec Mackintosh get busy it's time for normal folk to find a deep hole. But give him my love, and tell him he doesn't deserve it.'

She went off and I said, 'She's quite a character.'

'I could tell you stories about Maeve O'Sullivan that would make your hair curl,' said Alison. 'She was very active during the Troubles.' She picked up the telephone. 'Let's hear what the Harbourmaster has to say.'

The Harbourmaster was most obliging. Yes, *Artina* was expected. Mr Wheeler had arranged for refuelling. No, he didn't really know when she would arrive but if previous visits by Mr Wheeler were anything to go by then *Artina* would be staying in Cork for a couple of days.

As Alison put down the telephone I said, 'Now I have to think of a way of getting aboard. I wish I knew more about Wheeler's craft.'

'Give me a few hours and I'll have all you need to know,' said Alison. 'The telephone is a wonderful invention. But first I must ring the hospital.'

It was a time for rejoicing because Alec Mackintosh was fighting his way through to life again. Alison was radiant. 'He's better! The doctor said he was better! His condition has improved and they think there's a chance now.'

'Is he conscious? Is he able to speak?'

'No, he's still unconscious.'

I thought back. If Mackintosh had been unconscious all this time it would be quite a while before the doctors let him speak to anyone, even if he was able and willing. I'd have given a lot to be able to hear what he'd said to Wheeler the day before the hit-and-run.

'I'm glad he's better,' I said sincerely.

Alison picked up the telephone again, suddenly all businesslike. 'And now to work.'

I left her to it, only answering her questions from time to time. I was busily engaged in developing my hypothesis which was beginning to blossom into a very strange shape indeed. If I was right then Wheeler was a most odd fish and a very dangerous man – more dangerous to state security, even, than Slade.

I was deep in thought when Alison said, 'I've done all I can now; the rest will have to wait for morning.'

She flipped open the notebook which was full of shorthand notes, page after page. 'What do you want first – Wheeler or the yacht?'

'Let's have the yacht.'

She leafed through the pages. 'Here we are. Name – *Artina;* designed by Parker, built by Clelands on the Tyneside; she was two years old when Wheeler bought her. She's a standard design known as a Parker-Clelands which is important for reasons I'll come to later. Overall length – 111 feet, beam – 22 feet, cruising speed – 12 knots, speed flat out – 13 knots. She has two Rolls-Royce diesel engines of 350 horse-power each. Is this the sort of stuff you want?'

'Just right.' I could begin to build up a picture. 'What's her range?'

'I haven't got that yet, but it's coming. A crew of seven – skipper, engineer, cook, steward and three seamen. Accommodation for a maximum of eight passengers.'

'How is the accommodation arranged?'

'That will be coming tomorrow. The plans of her sister ship were published a few years ago. They're being photographed and sent by wire to the Cork *Examiner* where we can pick them up tomorrow, together with some photographs of the ship.'

I regarded Alison with admiration. 'Wow! Now that's something I wouldn't have thought of doing.'

'The newspaper is a very efficient information gatherer and transmitter. I told you I could pull strings.'

'What about Wheeler?'

'There's a detailed account coming to the *Examiner* on the telex, but this is the meat of it. He fought the Italians when they moved into Albania before the war.' She looked up. 'He'd be about 14 years old then. He fled with his family into Jugoslavia and again fought against the Italians and the Germans during the war both in Jugoslavia and Albania towards the end of the war. He left Albania in 1946 when he was somewhere in his early twenties and settled in England. Was naturalized in 1950. Started to deal in property just about that time and that was the beginning of his fortune.'

'What kind of property?'

'Offices. That was about the time they first began to put up the big office blocks.' She wrinkled her brow. 'I talked to a financial editor; he said there was something funny about the first deals Wheeler made.'

'That's interesting,' I said. 'Tell me more.'

'According to this editor it wasn't easy to see how Wheeler had made a profit. He evidently had made a profit because he suddenly had the money to go bigger and better, and he never looked back right from the early days.'

'I wonder how he paid his taxes,' I said. 'It's a pity we can't subpoena his tax inspector. I'm beginning to see the light. Tell me, when he was fighting in the war – did he fight for the Cetniks or the Partisans? The Nationalists or the Communists?'

'I don't have that here,' said Alison. 'It will be coming by telex, if it's known at all.'

'When did he enter politics?'

She consulted her notes. 'He fought a by-election in 1962 and lost. He fought in the general election of 1964 and got in by a fair margin.'

'And I suppose he lashed out generously for party funds,' I said. 'He'd do that, of course. Any known connections at present with Albania.'

'Nothing known.'

'Russia? Any communist country?'

Alison shook her head. 'He's a dinkum capitalist, mate. I don't see it, Owen. He's always popping off with anti-communist speeches in the House.'

'He's also against prisoners escaping from gaol, if you remember. What about this prison reform bit?'

'He used to be a prison visitor, but I suppose he's got too big for that now. He's generous in his subscription to various prison reform societies, and he's a member of a House committee studying prison reform.'

'My God, that would come in useful,' I said. 'Did he visit prisons in that capacity?'

'I suppose he might.' She put down the notebook. 'Owen, you're building up quite a structure on a weak foundation.'

'I know.' I stood up and paced the room restlessly. 'But I'll add another layer on my hypothesis. I once talked to a multimillionaire, one of the South African variety; he told me that the first quarter-million is the hardest. It took him fifteen years to make £250,000, three years to bring it up to the round million, and in the next six years he reached the five million mark. The mathematicians would say he was riding an exponential curve.'

Alison was getting a little impatient. 'So what?'

'The first quarter-million is hardest because our potential millionaire has to make all his own decisions and has to do his own research, but once he has money he can afford to hire regiments of accountants and platoons of lawyers and that makes decision making a lot easier. It's the starting of the process that's the snag. Go back to your financial editor – the one who smelled something funny in Wheeler's first deals.'

Alison picked up her notes again. 'I haven't anything more than I've already told you.'

'Let's take our man X,' I said. 'He's not a Russian – let's call him an Albanian – but he still favours the Russians. He comes to England in 1946 and is naturalized in 1950. About that time he starts dealing in property and makes money at it, but at least one man can't see how he did it. Let's assume the money was fed to him from outside – perhaps as much as half a million. X is a sharp boy – as sharp as any other potential millionaire – and money makes money. So he begins to roll in the time-honoured capitalistic way.'

I swung around. 'In 1964 he entered politics and got himself a seat in the Commons where he's now an enthusiastic and keen back-bencher. He's forty-six years old and still has another twenty-five years of political life in him.'

I stared at Alison. 'What would happen if he were to attain high position in the Government? Say, Chancellor or Minister of Defence – or even Prime Minister – in 1984, which seems to me to be an appropriate date? The boys in the Kremlin would be laughing their heads off!'

EIGHT

I slept badly that night. In the dark hours my hypothesis began to seem damned silly and more and more unlikely. A millionaire and an MP could not possibly be associated with the Russians – it was a contradiction in terms. Certainly Alison found she could not accept it. And yet Wheeler was associated with the Scarperers, unless the whole series of assumed links was pure coincidence – and that possibility could not be eliminated. I had seen too many cases of apparent cause and effect which turned out to be coincidence.

I turned over restlessly in bed. Yet assume it was so – that Wheeler actually was controlling the Scarperers. Why would he do it? Certainly not to make money; he had plenty of that. The answer came out again that it was political, which again led to Wheeler as a Member of Parliament and the dangers inherent in that situation.

I fell asleep and had dire dreams full of looming menace.

At breakfast I was still tired and a shade bad-tempered. My temper worsened rapidly when Alison made the first phone call of the day and was told by the Harbourmaster that *Artina* had arrived during the night, refuelled quickly, and left for Gibraltar in the early hours.

'We've lost the bastard again,' I said.

'We know where he is,' said Alison consolingly. 'And we know where he'll be in four days.'

'There are too many things wrong with that,' I said glumly. 'Just because he has clearance for Gibraltar doesn't mean he's going there, for one thing. For another, what's to prevent him from transferring Slade to a Russian trawler heading the other way through the Baltic? He could do it easily once he's over the horizon. And we don't even know if Slade is aboard *Artina*. We're just guessing.'

After breakfast Alison went out to collect the stuff from the *Examiner.* I didn't go with her; I wasn't going anywhere near a newspaper office – those reporters had filled up their columns with too much about Rearden and too many photographs. A sharp-eyed reporter was the last person I wanted to encounter.

So I stayed in the house while Maeve tactfully busied herself with the housework and left me alone to brood. Alison was away for an hour and a half, and she brought back a large envelope. 'Photographs and telex sheets,' she said, as she plopped the envelope in front of me.

I looked at the photographs first. There were three of Wheeler, one an official photograph for publicity use and the others news shots of him caught with his mouth open as the news photographers like to catch politicians. In one of them he looked like a predatory shark and I'd bet some editor had chortled over that one.

He was a big man, broad-shouldered and tall, with fair hair. The photographs were black-and-white so it was difficult to judge, but I'd say his hair was ash-blond. His nose was prominent and had a twist in it as though it had been thumped at some time or other, and the cartoonists would have no trouble taking the mickey if he ever attained a position of eminence. I put the photographs of Wheeler aside – I would recognize him if I saw him.

The other photographs were of the *Artina,* and one was a reproduction of the plans of her sister ship. Sean O'Donovan had exaggerated – she was not nearly as big as the royal yacht, but she was a fair size for all that, and it would take a millionaire to buy her and to run her. There was an owner's double cabin forward of the engine room and aft were three double cabins for six guests. The crew lived forward, excepting the skipper who had the master's cabin just behind the wheelhouse.

I studied that plan until I had memorized every passage and door. If I had to board her I would want to know my way around and to know the best places to hide. I checked off the aft peak and the room which held the air conditioning equipment as likely places for a stowaway.

Alison was immersed in reading the telex sheets. 'Any joy there?'

She looked up. 'There's not much more than I told you last night. It's expanded a bit, that's all. Wheeler fought for the Partisans in Jugoslavia.'

'The communists,' I said. 'Another strand in the web.'

I began to read and found that Alison was right; there wasn't much more solid information. The picture was of a bright young man who became a tycoon by the usual clapper-clawing methods and who now had a solid base in society built up by saying the right things at the right times and by contributing largely to the right causes. The picture of a successful man now looking for new worlds to conquer – hence the politics.

'He's not married,' I said. 'He must be the most eligible bachelor in England.'

Alison smiled wryly. 'I've heard a couple of rumours. He runs a mistress who is changed regularly, and the story goes that he's bisexual. But no one in his right mind would put that on the telex – that would be publishing a libel.'

'If Wheeler knew what was in my mind libel would be the least of his worries,' I said.

Alison shrugged unenthusiastically. 'What do we do?'

'We go to Gibraltar,' I said. 'Will your plane take us there?'

'Of course.'

'Then let's chase the wild goose. There's nothing else to do.'

II

We had time to spare and in plenty. An inspection of the plans of *Artina's* sister ship and a reading of the description that went with it made it quite certain that she was no high speed craft and she certainly couldn't get to Gibraltar in less than four days. We decided to play it safe and to be in Gibraltar in three days so we would be there when she came in.

That gave Alison time to fly back to London to see how Mackintosh was managing to survive and to dig up more dirt on Wheeler. We decided it would be most unwise for me to go back to London. Ducking in and out of Cork airport was one thing – Gatwick or Heathrow was quite another. Every time I smuggled myself incognito through the airport barriers I took an added risk.

So I spent two days cooped up in a suburban house in Cork with no one to speak to but an old Irishwoman. I must say that Maeve was most tactful; she didn't push and she didn't question, and she respected my silences. Once she said, 'Och, I know how it is with you, Owen. I went through it myself in 1918. It's a terrible thing to have the hand of every man against you, and you hiding like an animal. But you'll rest easy in this house.'

I said, 'So you had your excitement in the Troubles.'

'I had,' she said. 'And I didn't like it much. But there are always troubles – if not here then somewhere else – and there'll always be men running and men chasing.' She gave me a sidelong glance. 'Especially men like Alec Mackintosh and whoever concerns himself with that man.'

I smiled. 'Don't you approve of him?'

She lifted her chin. 'Who am I to approve or disapprove? I know nothing of his business other than that it is hard and dangerous. More dangerous for the men he orders than for him, I'm thinking.'

I thought of Mackintosh lying in hospital. That was enough to disprove that particular statement. I said, 'What about the women he commands?'

Maeve looked at me sharply. 'You'll be thinking of Alison,' she said flatly. 'Now that's a bad thing. He wanted a son and he got Alison, so he did the best with what he had and made her to his pattern; and it's a strong pattern and a hard pattern, enough to make a girl break under the burden of it.'

'He's a hard man,' I said. 'What about Alison's mother? Didn't she have a say in the matter?'

Maeve's tone was a little scornful, but the scorn was intermingled with pity. 'That poor woman! She married the wrong man. She didn't understand a man the like of Alec Mackintosh. The marriage never went well and she left Alec before Alison was born and came to live here in Ireland. She died in Waterford when Alison was ten.'

'And that's when Mackintosh took over Alison's education.'

'It is so,' said Maeve.

I said, 'What about Smith?'

'Has Alison not told you about him?'

'No,' I said.

'Then I'll not be telling,' said Maeve decidedly. 'I've gossiped enough already. When – and if – Alison wants you to know, then she'll tell you herself.' She turned away, and then paused, looking over her shoulder at me. 'I'm thinking you're a hard man yourself, Owen Stannard. I doubt if you'll be the one for Alison.'

And I was left to make of that what I could.

* * *

Alison rang up late the first night. 'I flew out to sea when I left,' she said. '*Artina* was on course for Gibraltar.'

'You didn't make the inspection too obvious, I hope.'

'I overtook her flying at five thousand feet and climbing. I didn't turn until I was out of sight.'

'How is Mackintosh?' I still called him that, even to her.

'He's better, but still unconscious. I was allowed to see him for two minutes.'

That wasn't too good. I could have done with Mackintosh being awake and talkative; he wasn't alive enough yet for my liking. Which brought me to another and delicate subject. 'You might be under observation in London.'

'No one followed me. I didn't see anyone I know, either, except one man.'

'Who was that?'

'The Prime Minister sent his secretary to the hospital. I saw him there. He said the PM is worried.'

I thought of Wheeler and the man who had been taken out of prison to be killed, and then I thought of Mackintosh lying helpless in a hospital bed. 'You'd better do something,' I said. 'Ring the secretary chap and ask him to spread the word around that Mackintosh is dying – that he's cashing in his chips.'

She caught on. 'You think they might attack Father in hospital?'

'They might if they think he's going to recover. Ask the PM's secretary to drop the unobtrusive word, especially to any of Wheeler's known associates in the House. If Wheeler rings London to have a chat with one of his mates the news might get through – and that could save your father's life.'

'I'll do that,' she said.

'Anything on Wheeler?'

'Not yet; not what we want, anyway. He lives a blameless public life.'

'It's not his public life we're interested in,' I said. 'But do your best.'

Alison came back two days later, arriving in a taxi in mid-afternoon. She looked tired as though she had not had much sleep, and Maeve clucked at the sight of her but relaxed as Alison said, 'Too much damned night-clubbing.'

Maeve went away and I raised my eyebrows. 'Been living it up?'

She shrugged. 'I had to talk to people and the kind of people I had to talk to are in the night club set.' She sighed. 'But it was a waste of time.'

'No further dirt?'

'Nothing of consequence, except maybe one thing. I checked the servant situation.'

'The *what* situation!'

She smiled tiredly. 'I checked on Wheeler's servants. The days of glory are past and servants are hard to come by, but Wheeler does all right even though he needs a large staff.' She took her notebook from her pocket. 'All his staff are British and have British passports excepting the chauffeur who is an Irish national. Do you find that interesting?'

'His contact with Ireland,' I said. 'It's very interesting.'

'It gets better,' she said. 'As I said, the rest of his servants are British, but every last one of them is naturalized and they've all had their names changed by deed poll. And what do you think was their country of origin?'

I grinned. 'Albania.'

'You've just won a cigar. But there's an exception here too. One of them didn't take a British name because it would be peculiar if he did. Wheeler has taken a fancy to Chinese cooking and has a Chinese cook on the premises. His name is Chang Pi-wu.'

'I see what you mean,' I said. 'It would seem bloody funny if he changed his name to McTavish. Where does he hail from?'

'Hong Kong.'

A Hong Kong Chinese! It didn't mean much. I suppose it was quite reasonable that if a multi-millionaire had a taste for Chinese food then he'd have a Chinese cook; millionaires think differently from the common ruck of folk and that would be part of the small change of his life. But I felt a tickle at the back of my mind.

I said carefully, 'It may be that Wheeler is doing the charitable bit. Maybe all these British Albanians are his cousins and his cousins' cousins, nieces and nephews he's supporting in a tactful sort of way.'

Alison looked up at the ceiling. 'The problem with servants is keeping them. They want four nights a week off, television in their rooms and a lie-in every morning, otherwise they become mobile and leave. The turnover is high, and Wheeler's turnover in servants is just as high as anyone else's.'

'Is it, by God?' I leaned forward and peered at Alison closely. 'You've got something, damn it! Spit it out.'

She grinned cheerfully and opened her notebook. 'He has thirteen British Albanians working for him – gardeners, butler, housekeeper, maids and so on. Not one had been with him longer than three years. The last one to arrive pitched up last month. They come and go just like ordinary servants.'

'And they take holidays in Albania,' I said. 'He's got a courier service.'

'Not only that,' said Alison. 'But someone is supplying him with a regular intake.' She consulted her notebook again. 'I did a check with the local branch of the Ministry of Social Security in Herefordshire; in the last ten years he's had fifty of them through his hands. I can't prove they were all Albanians because they had British names, but I'll take a bet they were.'

'Jesus!' I said. 'Hasn't anyone tumbled to it? What the hell is the Special Branch doing?'

Alison spread her hands. 'They're all British. If it's come to anyone's attention – which I doubt – then he's doing the charitable bit, as you said – rescuing his compatriots from the communist oppressors.'

'Fifty!' I said. 'Where do they all go when he's done with them?'

'I don't know about the fifty – I've only had time to check on two. Both are now in the service of other MPs.'

I began to laugh because I couldn't help it. 'The cheek of it,' I said. 'The brazen nerve! Don't you see what he's doing? He's getting these fellows in, giving them a crash course on British mores and customs as well as the finer points of being a gentleman's gentleman, and then planting them as spies. Can't you imagine him talking to one of his mates in the Commons? "Having servant trouble, dear boy? It just happens that one of mine is leaving. Oh, no trouble like that – he just wants to live in Town. Perhaps I can persuade . . ." It beats anything I've ever heard.'

'It certainly shows he has present connections with Albania,' said Alison. 'I wasn't convinced before – it seemed too ridiculous. But I am now.'

I said, 'Do you remember the Cicero case during the war. The valet of the British Ambassador to Turkey was a German spy. Wheeler has been in the money for twenty years – he could have planted a hundred Ciceros. And not only at the political end. I wonder how many of our industrial chieftains have Wheeler-trained servants in their households?'

'All with English names and all speaking impeccable English,' said Alison. 'Wheeler would see to that.' She ticked off the steps on her fingers. 'They come to England and while they're waiting for naturalization they learn the language thoroughly and study the British in their native habitat. When they're British they go to Wheeler for a final gloss and then he plants them.' She shook her head doubtfully. 'It's a very long-term project.'

'Wheeler himself is a long-term project. I don't see him packing his bags and returning to his native land. Look at Slade, for God's sake! He was worming his way in for *twenty-eight* years! These people take the long view.' I paused. 'When do we leave for Gibraltar?'

'Tomorrow morning.'

'Good,' I said. 'I want to catch up with this incredible bastard.'

III

I went into Cork airport the hard way, as usual. I was beginning to forget what it was like to use the front door. Maeve O'Sullivan had been uncharacteristically emotional when we left. 'Come back soon, girl,' she said to Alison. 'It's an old woman I am, and there's no telling.' There were tears in her eyes but she rubbed them away as she turned to me. 'And you, Owen Stannard; take care of yourself and Alec Mackintosh's daughter.'

I grinned. 'She's been taking care of me so far.'

'Then you're not the man I thought you were to let her,' replied Maeve with asperity. 'But go carefully, and watch for the *garda*.'

So we went carefully and it was with relief that I watched the city of Cork pass under the wings of the Apache as we circled to find our course south. Alison snapped switches and set dials, then took her hands from the control column. 'It will be nearly six hours,' she said. 'Depending on the wind and the rain.'

'You're not expecting bad weather?'

She smiled. 'It was just a manner of speaking. As a matter of fact, the weather report is good. The wind is northerly at 24,000 feet.'

'Will we be flying that high? I didn't think these things did that.'

'The engines are supercharged, so it's more economical to fly high. But this cabin isn't pressurized, so we'll have to go on oxygen soon – as soon as we reach 10,000 feet. You'll find the mask by your side.'

The last time I had seen the Apache it had been a six-seater but in Alison's absence in London the two rearmost seats had been removed and had been replaced by a big plastic box. I jerked my thumb over my shoulder, and said, 'What's that?'

'An extra fuel tank – another seventy gallons of spirit. It increases the range to 2,000 miles at the most economical flying speed. I thought we might need it.'

The capable Alison Smith thought of everything. I remembered what Maeve had said: *Made to a hard pattern, enough to break a girl under the burden of it.* I studied Alison; her face was calm as she checked the instruments and then tested the oxygen flow, and there were no lines of stress to substantiate Maeve's remark. Alison glanced sideways and caught me looking at her. 'What's the matter?'

'A cat may look at a king,' I said. 'So a dog may look at a queen. I was just thinking that you're lovely, that's all.'

She grinned and jerked her thumb backwards. 'The Blarney Stone is back there, and I know for a fact you never went near it. You must have Irish in your ancestry.'

'And Welsh,' I said. 'Hence the Owen. It's the Celt coming out in me.'

'Put on your mask,' she said. 'Then you'll look as beautiful as me.'

It was a long and boring flight. Although the masks had built-in microphones we didn't do much talking, and presently I put down the back of the seat to a reclining position. We flew south at 200 miles an hour – fifteen times faster than Wheeler in *Artina* – and I slept.

Or, rather, I dozed. I woke up from time to time and found Alison alert, scanning the sky or checking the instruments or making a fine adjustment. I would touch her shoulder and she would turn with a smile in her eyes and then resume her work. After nearly four hours had passed she nudged me and pointed ahead. 'The Spanish coast.'

There was a haze of heat below and a crinkled sea, and ahead the white line of surf. 'We won't overfly Spain,' she said. 'Not if we're landing at Gibraltar. It's politically inadvisable. We'll fly down the Portuguese coast.'

She took out a map on a board and worked out the new course, handling the protractor with smoothly efficient movements, then switched off the auto-pilot and swung the aircraft around gently. 'That's Cape Ortegal,' she said. 'When we sight Finisterre I'll alter course again.'

'When did you learn to fly?' I asked.

'When I was sixteen.'

'And to shoot a pistol?'

She paused before answering. 'When I was fourteen – pistol and rifle and shotgun. Why?'

'Just wondering.' Mackintosh believed in teaching them young. I found it hard to imagine a little girl of fourteen looking past the sights of a rifle. I bet she knew the Morse code, too, and all the flag semaphore signals, to say nothing of programming a computer and lighting a fire without matches. 'Were you a Girl Guide?'

She shook her head. 'I was too busy.'

Too busy to be a Girl Guide! She'd have her head down at her books studying languages when she wasn't practising in the air or banging away on the target range. I wouldn't have put it past Mackintosh to make certain that she was at home in a submarine. What a hell of a life!

'Did you have any friends in those days?' I asked. 'Girls of your own age?'

'Not many.' She twisted in her seat. 'What are you getting at, Owen?'

I shrugged. 'Just the idle thoughts of an idle man.'

'Has Maeve O'Sullivan been filling you up with horror stories? Is that it? I might have known.'

'She didn't say a word out of place,' I said. 'But you can't help a man thinking.'

'Then you'd do better to keep your thoughts to yourself.' She turned back to the controls and lapsed into silence, and I thought it would be as well if I kept my big mouth shut, too.

As we turned the corner and flew up the Strait of Gibraltar Alison took the controls and we began to descend. At 10,000 feet she took off her oxygen mask and I was glad to do the same. And then, in the distance, I saw the Rock for the first time, rising sheer from the blue water. We circled and I saw the artificial harbour and the airstrip jutting into Algeciras Bay like the deck of an aircraft carrier. Apparently, to Alison who was busy on the radio, it was all old hat.

We landed from the east and our small aircraft did not need all that enormous runway. We rolled to a halt and then taxied to the airport buildings. I looked at the military aircraft parked all around, and said grimly, 'This is one airport which will have good security.' How was I going to smuggle myself through this one?

'I have something for you,' said Alison, and took a folder from the map pocket from which she extracted a passport. I nicked it open and saw my own face staring up from the page. It was a diplomatic passport. She said, 'It will get us through customs in a hurry, but it won't save you if you are recognized as Rearden.'

'It's good enough.' Even if I was recognized as Rearden the sight of that diplomatic passport would be enough to give my challenger cause to wonder if he could possibly be right. I said, 'My God, you must have pull.'

'Just enough,' she said calmly.

The passport officer smiled as he took the passport, and the civilian with the hard face who was standing next to him ceased to study me and relaxed. We went right through within three minutes of entering the hall. Alison said, 'We're staying at the Rock Hotel; whistle up a taxi, will you?'

If Wheeler's trained Albanians made the perfect servants then Alison Smith was a God-given secretary. I hadn't thought for one moment of where we were going to lay our heads that night, but she had. Alec Mackintosh was a lucky man – but, perhaps, it wasn't luck. He'd trained her, hadn't he?

We had adjoining rooms at the Rock Hotel and agreed to meet in the bar after cleaning up. I was down first. Alison Smith was no different in that respect than any other woman, I was glad to observe; the female takes fifty per cent longer to prink than the male. It *is* only fifty per cent even though it seems twice as long. I had sunk my first cold beer by the time she joined me.

I ordered her a dry Martini and another beer for myself. She said, 'What will you do when Wheeler arrives?'

'I have to find if Slade is aboard *Artina* and that will mean a bit of pirate work.' I grinned. 'I promise not to have a knife in my teeth when I go over the bulwarks.'

'And if he is on board?'

'I do my best to bring him off.'

'And if you can't?'

I shrugged. 'I have orders covering that eventuality.'

She nodded coolly, and I wondered briefly if Mackintosh had ever given his own daughter similar instructions. She said, 'Wheeler being what he is and who he is will probably anchor off the Royal Gibraltar Yacht Club. I wouldn't be surprised if he's a member – he comes here often enough.'

'Where is it?'

'About half a mile from here.'

'We'd better take a look at it.'

We finished our drinks and strolled into the sunshine. The yacht basin was full of craft, sail and power, big and small. I stood looking at the boats and then turned. 'There's a convenient terrace over there where they serve cooling drinks. That will be a nice place to wait.'

'I'm just going to make a telephone call,' said Alison, and slipped away. I looked at the yachts and the sea and tried to figure how I could get aboard *Artina* but without much success because I didn't know where she would be lying. Alison came back. 'Wheeler is expected at eleven tomorrow morning. He radioed through.'

'That's nice,' I said, and turned my face up to the sun. 'What do we do until then?'

She said unexpectedly, 'What about a swim?'

'I forgot to pack trunks; I didn't expect a semi-tropical holiday.'

'There *are* shops,' she said gently. So we went shopping and I bought trunks and a towel, and a pair of German duty-free binoculars, smooth, sleek and powerful.

We went across the peninsula and swam at Catalan Bay which was very nice. That night we went night-clubbing, which was even nicer. Mrs Smith seemed to be human and made of the same mortal clay as the rest of us.

IV

At ten o'clock next morning we were sitting on the terrace overlooking the yacht basin and imbibing something long, cold and not too alcoholic. We both wore sun-glasses, not as much to shade our eyes as to join the anonymous throng just as the film stars do. The binoculars were to hand and all that was lacking was *Artina* and Wheeler, and, possibly, Slade.

We didn't talk much because there wasn't anything to talk about; we couldn't plot and plan in the absence of *Artina*. And Alison had loosened the strings of her personality the previous night as near as she had ever got to letting her hair down, and possibly she was regretting it. Not that she had let me get too close; I had made the expected pass and she evaded it with practised ease. But now she had returned to her habitual wariness – we were working and personal relationships didn't matter.

I soaked up the sun. It was the thing I had missed in England, especially in prison, and now I let it penetrate to warm my bones. Time went on and presently Alison picked up the binoculars and focused them on a boat making its way to harbour between the North Mole and the Detached Mole. 'I think this is *Artina.*'

I had a glass to my lips when she said it, and I swallowed the wrong way and came up for air spluttering and choking. Alison looked at me with alarm. 'What's the matter?'

'The impudence of it!' I gasped with laughter. '*Artina* is an anagram of Tirana – and that's the capital of Albania. The bastard's laughing at us all. It just clicked when you said it.'

Alison smiled and proffered the binoculars. I looked at the boat coming in with the dying bow wave at her forefoot and compared what I saw with the drawings and photographs of her sister ship. 'She could be *Artina,*' I said. 'We'll know for sure within the next five minutes.'

The big motor yacht came closer and I saw the man standing at the stern – big and with blond hair. '*Artina* it is – and Wheeler.' I swept the glasses over her length. 'No sign of Slade, but that's to be expected. He wouldn't parade himself.'

She anchored off-shore and lay quietly in the water and I checked every man who walked on deck, identifying five for certain without Wheeler. There was a crew of seven apart from an unknown number of guests, but the men I saw didn't seem to be guests. Two were on the foredeck by a winch and another was watching the anchor chain. Two more were lowering a boat into the water.

I said, 'Count the number of men who come ashore. That might be useful to know.'

The two men by the winch moved amidships and unshipped the folding companionway and rigged it at the side of the yacht. One of them went down the steps and tethered the boat. Presently Wheeler appeared with a man in a peaked cap and they both descended the companionway into the waiting boat. The engine started and it took off in a wide curve and then straightened, heading for the yacht club.

Alison said, 'Wheeler and the skipper, I think. The man at the wheel is a crewman.'

They stepped ashore at the club and then the tender took off again and returned to *Artina* where the crewman tethered it to the bottom of the companionway and climbed up on board again. Alison nudged me. 'Look!'

I turned my head in the direction her finger indicated. A big work boat was ploughing across the water towards *Artina*. 'So!'

'It's a fueller,' she said. '*Artina* is taking on diesel fuel and water already. It seems that Wheeler isn't going to waste much time here.'

'Damn!' I said. 'I was hoping he'd stay the night. I'd much rather go aboard in darkness.'

'He doesn't seem to have any guests,' she said. 'And he's in a hurry. From our point of view those are encouraging signs. Slade might very well be on board.'

'And a fat lot of use that is if I can't go aboard to find him. How long do you think refuelling will take?'

'An hour, maybe.'

'Time enough to hire a boat,' I said. 'Let's go.'

We bickered with a Gibraltan longshoreman for the hire of a motor launch and got away with him charging not more than twice the normal rate, and then launched out into the harbour. The fueller and *Artina* were now close-coupled on the port side, with hoses linking them. Another crew member in a peak cap was supervising – that could be the engineer.

I throttled down as we approached and we drifted by about fifty yards from the starboard side. Someone came into view, looked at us incuriously and then lifted his head to look up at the Rock. He was Chinese.

I said, 'That, presumably, is Chang Pi-wu. Wheeler must like Chinese cooking if he takes his Chinese chef to sea. I hope the crew like Chinese food.'

'Maybe they have their own cook.'

'Maybe.' I studied the Chinese covertly. Many occidentals claim that all Chinese look alike. They're wrong – the Chinese physiognomy is as varied as any other and I knew I'd recognize this man if I saw him again. But I'd had practice; I'd lived in the East.

We drifted to the stern of *Artina*. The ports of the rearmost guest cabin were curtained in broad daylight, and I had a good idea of where Slade was lying low. It was exasperating to be so close and not be able to get at him.

Even as I opened the throttle and headed back to the shore I saw a crewman drop into the boat moored at the bottom of *Artina's* companionway and take off. He was faster than we were and as we handed our launch to the owner I looked out and saw him returning with Wheeler and the skipper. They climbed aboard and the companionway was unshipped and stowed.

An hour later I was burning with a sense of futility as *Artina* moved off and headed out to sea. 'Where the hell is she going now?' I demanded.

'If he's going east into the Mediterranean to the Greek islands he'll refuel at Malta,' said Alison. 'It would be the logical thing to do. Let's go and find out where he's cleared for.'

So we did, and Alison was right – not that it made me feel any better. 'Another four days?' I asked despondently.

'Another four days,' she agreed. 'But we might have better luck at Valletta.'

'I'd like that yacht to have an accident,' I said. 'Just enough to delay her for one night. You don't happen to have any limpet mines about you?'

'Sorry.'

I stared moodily at the white speck disappearing into the distance. 'That Chinese worries me,' I said. 'He ought to worry Slade even more.'

'Why ever should he?'

'Communist Albania has ceased to hew to the Moscow line. Enver Hoxha, the Albanian party boss, has read the Little Red Book and thinks the thoughts of Mao. I wonder if Slade knows he's in the hands of an Albanian?'

Alison wore a half-smile. 'I was wondering when you'd get there,' she said.

'I got there a long time ago – probably before you did. It would be very nice for the Chinese if they could get hold of Slade – a top British intelligence man and a top Russian intelligence man in the same package. They'd squeeze him dry in a month and they wouldn't care how they did it.'

I shrugged. 'And the damned fool thinks he's going home to Moscow.'

NINE

Limpet mines we didn't have but, in the event, I got hold of something just as good and a lot simpler. That was in the Grand Harbour of Valletta and four days later. In the meantime we paid the bill at the Rock Hotel and flew to Malta where that diplomatic passport got me through the barriers at Luqa Airport just as easily as it had done at Gibraltar.

With nearly four days to wait we suddenly found ourselves in holiday mood. The sky was blue, the sun was hot and the sea inviting, and there were cafés with seafood and cool wine for the days, and moderately good restaurants with dance floors for the nights. Alison unbent more than she had ever done.

I found there was something I could do better than she, which did my mauled ego a bit of good. We hired scuba equipment and went diving in the clear water of the Mediterranean and I found I could out-perform her at that. Probably it was because I had lived in Australia and South Africa where the ambient waters are warmer and skin-diving is a luxury and not a penance as it is in England.

We swam and lazed the days away and danced the nights away for three days and three nights until, on the morrow, Wheeler was due to arrive. It was nearly midnight when I brought up the subject of Mr Smith. Alison took no umbrage this time but, perhaps, it was because I had been plying her with the demon alcohol. Had it been the opposition tipping the bottle she would have been wary but the hand that filled her glass was the hand of a friend and she was taken unaware. Sneaky!

She held up the wine glass and smiled at me through liquid amber. 'What do you want to know about him?'

'Is he still around?'

She put down the glass and a little wine spilled. 'No,' she said. 'He's not around any more.' She seemed sad.

I lit a cigarette and said through the smoke, 'Divorce?'

She shook her head violently and her long hair flowed in heavy waves. 'Nothing like that. Give me a cigarette.'

I lit her cigarette and she said, 'I married a man called John Smith. There *are* people called John Smith, you know. Was he an intelligence agent? No. Was he even a policeman? No. He was an accountant and a very nice man – and Alec was horrified. It seemed I hadn't been designed to marry an accountant.' Her voice was bitter.

'Go on,' I said gently.

'But I married him, anyway; and we were very happy.'

'Had you been with your father before then?'

'With Alec? Where else? But I didn't stay on – I couldn't, could I? John and I lived in a house near Maidenhead – in the Stockbroker Belt – and we were very happy. I was happy just being married to John, and happy being a housewife and doing all the things which housewives do, and not having to think about things I didn't want to think about. Alec was disappointed, of course; he'd lost his robot secretary.'

I thought of John Smith, the accountant; the nine-to-fiver who had married Alison Mackintosh. I wondered how he had regarded the situation – if he ever knew about it. I couldn't see Alison cuddling up on his knee, and saying, 'Darling, you're married to a girl who can shoot a man in the kneecap in impossible light, who can drive a car and fly a plane and kill a man with one karate chop. Don't you think we're going to have a delightful married life? Look how handy it will be when we're bringing up the children.'

I said, 'And then?'

'And then – nothing. Just a stupid, silly motorway accident on the M4.' Her face was still and unsmiling and she spoke through stiff lips. 'I thought I'd die, too; I really did. I loved John, you see.'

'I'm sorry,' I said inadequately.

She shrugged and held out her glass for more wine. 'Wanting to die didn't help, of course. I brooded and moped for a while, then I went back to Alec. There wasn't anything else to do.' She sipped the wine and looked at me. 'Was there, Owen?'

I said very carefully and noncommittally, 'Perhaps not.'

She gave me a wry look, and said, 'You're pussyfooting, Owen. You don't want to hurt my feelings by saying what you think. Well, that's commendable, I suppose.'

'I'm not one to make casual judgments.'

'Without knowing the facts – is that it? I'll give you some. Alec and my mother never got on very well. I suppose they were basically incompatible, but he was away so often, and she didn't understand his work.'

'Was he in the same work as now?'

'Always, Owen; always. So there was a legal separation just before I was born, and I was born in Waterford where I lived until I was ten when my mother died.'

'Were you happy in Waterford?'

Alison became pensive. 'I don't really know. I can't seem to remember much about those days; there has been so much overlaid on top since.' She stubbed out her cigarette. 'I don't know if anyone would ever call Alec an ideal father. Unorthodox, maybe, but not ideal. I was a bit of a tomboy – never one for frilly frocks and playing with dolls – and I suppose he took advantage.'

I said slowly, 'You're a woman now.'

'I sometimes wonder about that.' She plucked at the tablecloth with tapering fingers. 'So Alec trained me to be – I didn't know what. It was fun at the time. I learned to ride a horse, to ski on snow and water, to shoot, to fly – I'm qualified on jets, did you know that?'

I shook my head.

'It was damned good fun, every bit of it – even grinding at the languages and mathematics – until he took me into the office and I learned what it was all for. Then it wasn't fun any more.'

'Did he send you out on field jobs?'

'I've been on three,' she said evenly. 'All very successful – and most of the time I was sick to my stomach. But that wasn't the worst of it. The worst was being in the office and sending others out into the field, and watching what happened to them. I planned too many operations, Owen. I planned yours.'

'I know,' I said. 'Mackintosh . . . Alec told me.'

'I became the one person whom he could trust absolutely,' she said. 'A very valuable consideration in the profession.'

I took her hand. 'Alison,' I said. 'What do you really think of Alec?'

'I love him,' she said. 'And I hate him. It's as simple as that.' Her fingers tightened on mine. 'Let's dance, Owen.' There was a hint of desperation in her voice. 'Let's dance.'

So we went on to the dimly lit floor and danced to the sort of music that's usually played in the early hours of the morning. She came very close and rested her head on my shoulder so that her lips were by my ear. 'Do you know what I am, Owen?'

'You're a lovely woman, Alison.'

'No, I'm a Venus Fly Trap. Vegetables – like women – are supposed to be placid; they're not supposed to be equipped with snapped jaws and sharp teeth. Have you ever watched a fly alight on a Venus Fly Trap? The poor beastie thinks it's just another vegetable plant until the jaws snap closed. Most unnatural, don't you think?'

I tightened my arm about her. 'Take it easy.'

She danced two more steps and then a deep shudder went through her body. 'Oh, God!' she said. 'Let's go back to the hotel.'

I paid the bill and joined her at the door of the restaurant and we walked the two hundred yards to our hotel. We were both silent as we went up in the lift and along the corridor, but she held my hand tightly as we came to the door of her room. She was trembling a little as she held out her key.

She made love like a maniac, like a savage, and I had the deep scratches on my back to prove it next morning. It seemed as though all the pent-up frustrations of a warped life were loosed on that night-time bed. But when it was over she was relaxed and calm, and we talked for a long time – maybe two hours. What we talked about I'll never remember; just inconsequentialities too meaningless to take note of – she had had time for few trivialities in her serious life.

The second time was better and she was all woman and, when it was over, she fell asleep. I had sense enough to go to my own room before she woke; I thought she would not be too pleased with herself in the sober light of day.

II

Wheeler was due that morning and we had plans to make. When she came down to breakfast I was on my first cup of coffee and rose from the table to greet her. She was a little self-conscious as she came up and tended to avoid my eye. I sat down, and said, 'What do we use instead of a limpet?'

When I leaned against the back of the chair I felt the pain as the pressure impinged on the scratches she had inflicted. Hastily I leaned forward again and took a piece of toast.

I looked up and saw she had snapped back into professionalism as she took in what I said; personal relationships were one thing and the job was quite another. 'I'll check with the Port Captain when *Artina* is due.'

'We don't want to have a repetition of Gibraltar,' I said. 'One jump from here and Wheeler and Slade will be in Albania – home and dry. What do we do if *Artina* arrives in daylight and leaves in daylight?'

'I don't know,' she said.

'There's one thing certain,' I said. 'I can't invade her in the middle of the Grand Harbour in daylight and take Slade off. So what remains?' I answered the question myself. 'We have to make sure she stays all night.'

'But how?'

'I've thought of a way. We'll go shopping after breakfast. Can I butter some toast for you?'

So the pair of us ate a hearty breakfast and sallied forth into the hot streets of Valletta, a heat seemingly intensified by the warm golden limestone of the buildings. The Port Captain expected *Artina* at midday and that was sad news. Sadder still was the information that the fuelling ship had been booked in advance and was to go alongside as soon as *Artina* anchored.

We went away, and I said, 'That does it. Let's do my bit of shopping.'

We found a ship's chandlery and went inside to find all the usual expensive bits and pieces that go towards the upkeep of a yacht. I found what I was looking for – some light, tough nylon line with a high breaking strain. I bought two hundred feet of it and had it coiled and parcelled.

Alison said, 'I suppose you know what you're doing.'

'It was the scuba gear we've been using that gave me the idea.' I pointed towards the harbour. 'How would you get to the middle of there without being seen?'

She nodded. 'Underwater. That's all very well, but doesn't help you to get aboard.'

'It will – eventually. You're included in this operation. Come and get the gear. We want to be back on the spot when *Artina* arrives.'

We went to the place we had hired the scuba gear and I made absolutely certain we were issued with full bottles. Then, after a brief test in the swimming pool of the hotel, we went back to the harbour. At the swimming pool Alison suddenly drew in her breath and I turned to find that she was blushing deeply. She was looking at my back.

I chuckled. 'They ought to issue a bottle of Dettol with you,' I said. 'You're quite a woman.'

Unaccountably she became angry. 'Stannard, you're a . . . a . . .'

'Buck up,' I said sharply. 'We have a job to do.'

That brought her back fast and the awkward moment was over. We went down to the harbour and settled down to wait for *Artina*. Alison said, 'What's the plan?'

'If you've read my record you'll know I was in Indonesia,' I said. 'One of the diciest moments I ever had out there was when I was in a small launch being chased by a fast patrol boat which was popping off with a 20mm cannon. There was a mangrove swamp nearby so I nipped in there for shelter – that was a big mistake. There was too much seaweed and it got wrapped around the propeller shaft and the launch came to a dead stop. That seaweed was nearly the end of me.'

'What happened then?'

'That doesn't matter.' I nodded towards the harbour. '*Artina* is a lot bigger than the launch I had, but this nylon line is a hell of a lot stronger than strands of seaweed. When she comes in we're going to swim out and wrap the lot around both propeller shafts. It might immobilize her and it might not, but I'm betting it will. And the beauty of it is that even when they find it there'll be no suggestion of foul play. It's something that could happen to any boat. Anyway, they'll have a devil of a job freeing it once the engines have tightened it up, and I'm hoping it will take all night.'

'It could work,' agreed Alison, and then continued evenly, 'I'll do something for those scratches. This water is dirty and they might become infected.'

I looked at her and she met my eye without a tremor. 'Good enough,' I said, and took great pains not to laugh.

She went away briefly and returned with a bottle of something-or-other which she applied to my back. Then we sat and waited patiently for *Artina* to show up.

It was a long hot day. *Artina* was late and I began to wonder if she hadn't by-passed Malta and headed straight for Albania. She came in at two-thirty and dropped anchor well off-shore. Again she lowered a boat but this time only the skipper came ashore. Wheeler wasn't to be seen.

I stubbed out my cigarette. 'This is it,' I said, and tightened the straps of the scuba gear. 'Can you swim as far as that?'

Alison splashed water into her mask. 'Easily.'

'Just stick close to me.' I pointed. 'We're not going to swim right for it. We'll pass by about twenty yards from the stern and then come in from the other side. The fueller might be there – I hope it is – so keep your head down.'

I had the skein of nylon rope strapped to my thigh; I tested to see if it was secure and then slipped into the water. I doubt if skin-divers are encouraged in the Grand Harbour, not that they would want to make a habit of swimming there – the water is none too clean and decapitation by the churning propellers of passing traffic a constant hazard. I had chosen a quiet spot where we could go into the water unobserved.

We went deep right from the start, going down to about twenty-five feet before heading on course. I knew my speed and I had estimated the distance so I kept a steady count of the seconds and minutes. The problem in this sort of exercise was to keep swimming in a straight line. Occasionally I looked back and saw Alison swimming strongly in echelon, behind and to the left.

When I estimated we had arrived at the point I had chosen I waved Alison to a halt and we swam lazily in circles while I looked about. There was an oncoming rumble and a shadow overhead as a vessel passed, her propellers flailing the water and causing eddies which jerked us about. The propellers stopped and presently there was an audible clang transmitted through the water. That would be the fueller coupling to *Artina*.

I waved to Alison and we went on in the new direction. As we went on towards the two boats I hoped that no one was looking over the side to see the line of bubbles breaking on the surface. But we were coming in at the side of the fueller and all the action would be where they were coupling up the fuel and water lines. If anyone had time to look over the side then that fueller was overmanned.

The light diminished as we swam underneath the two boats and I paused again before heading aft and rising to trail my fingers along *Artina's* keel. We came to the stern and I stopped with my left hand on one blade of the port phosphor-bronze propeller, hoping that no damned fool in the engine room would punch the wrong button and start the engine. If those three blades started to move I'd be chopped into bloody mincemeat.

Alison swam up on the starboard side as I fumbled with the strap holding the rope to my thigh. I got it free and began to uncoil it with care. The propeller was about four feet in diameter, and the shaft was supported by struts before it entered the stern gland in the hull. I slipped the end of the rope in between the strut and the hull and coiled it around the shaft and then passed a loop around the shaft in between the propeller and the strut. When I tugged gently it held firm, so that was a start.

That rope was the damnedest stuff. At times it was like wrestling with a sea serpent – the coils floated around in the water dangerously, threatening to strangle us or bind our legs, and Alison and I must have closely resembled that remarkable piece of antique statuary, the Laocoön.

But we finally did it. We entangled those two propellers in such a cat's cradle that when the engines started and the ropes began to tighten all hell would break loose. Most probably everything would grind to a sudden halt, but a shaft could bend and, at worst, one of the engines might slam a piston through the cylinder casing. It was a good job.

We slipped away and swam back to shore, emerging from the water quite a distance from where we had gone in. My sense of direction had become warped, but then it always does underwater. An unshaven character leaning on the rail of a tramp steamer looked at us with some astonishment as we climbed up to the quay, but I ignored him and Alison and I walked away, our back packs bumping heavily.

We went back to our original position and I lit a cigarette and looked across at *Artina*. The fueller had finished and was just casting off, and the skipper was returning in the tender. It seemed as though they intended a faster turnaround than Gibraltar. I wondered where the skipper had cleared for – it wouldn't be Durazzo, the port for Tirana, although I'd be willing to bet that was where he intended to go.

The skipper climbed aboard and the companionway was unshipped immediately. There was a lot of movement on deck and even as the tender was hoisted clear of the water someone was at the winch on the foredeck ready to lift anchor.

Alison said, 'They're very much in a hurry.'

'It seems so.'

'I wonder why.'

'I don't know – but I expect they'll be very annoyed within the next few minutes.'

The anchor came up and *Artina* moved off slowly. I hadn't expected her to move at all and it came as a shock. Apparently 700 horse-power was more than a match for a few coils of nylon line. Alison drew in her breath. 'It isn't working!'

Artina turned and headed for the open sea, picking up speed so that a bow wave showed white. I lowered the binoculars, and said, 'It was a good try.' I felt gloomy. Albania was only 450 miles away and *Artina* could be there in less than two days. The only way I could think of stopping her was by a kamekazi attack in the Apache.

Alison was still watching through her monocular. 'Wait!' she said urgently. 'Look now!'

Artina had swerved suddenly and unnaturally as though someone had spun the wheel fast, and she was now heading straight for the shore. She slowed and water boiled at her stern as the engines were put into reverse. Then the bubble of white water stopped and she drifted helplessly, right into the path of a big Italian cruise liner which was leaving harbour.

There was a deep *booom* as the liner peremptorily demanded right of way but *Artina* did not react. The liner altered course fractionally at the last moment and her sheer side might have scraped *Artina s* paintwork. From the bridge of the liner an officer in whites was looking down and I guessed that a string of choice Italian imprecations was being directed down at the hapless skipper of *Artina.*

The liner went on her way and *Artina* bobbed inertly in the waves raised by her wake. Presently a little tug put out and went to her aid and she was towed back to where she had come from and dropped anchor again.

I grinned at Alison. 'For a moment there I thought. . . . Well, it's done and she'll be staying the night. When they find out what's happened they'll be cursing the idiot who carelessly dropped a line in the water.'

'There's no chance they'll guess it was done deliberately?'

'I shouldn't think so.' I looked over the water at *Artina.* The skipper was at the stern looking down. 'They'll soon find out what it is, and they'll send down a diver to cut it free. It'll take a hell of a lot longer for him to free it than it did for us to tangle it – those engines will have tightened the tangle considerably.' I laughed. 'It'll be like trying to unscramble an omelette.'

Alison picked up her gear. 'And what now?'

'Now we wait for nightfall. I'm going to board her.'

III

We went into Marsamxett Harbour from Ta'Xbiex to where *Artina* was anchored in Lazzaretto Creek. A tug had moved her during the afternoon and put her with the rest of the yachts. We went out in a fibreglass object that resembled a bathtub more than a boat, but Alison seemed to find no difficulty in handling it and she used the oars as though she'd been trained as stroke for Oxford. More of Mackintosh's training coming to the surface.

It was a moonless night but the sky was clear so that it was not absolutely pitch-black. Ahead loomed Manoel Island and beyond a light flashed at Dragutt Point. To our left Valletta rose, clifflike and impregnable, festooned with lights. There were no lights on *Artina,* though, apart from the obligatory riding lights; since it was 2.30 a.m. this was not surprising. I hoped everyone on board was in the habit of sleeping soundly.

Alison stopped sculling as we approached and we drifted silently to *Artina's* stern. The rope ladder which the diver had been using was not there but I hadn't been counting on it even though it was nine feet from the water to the stern rail. What I wanted was a grapnel, but those are hard to come by at a moment's notice, so I had improvised. A shark hook is shaped like a grapnel, being three big fish-hooks welded together. I had wrapped it in many layers of insulating tape, not only to prevent myself from being nastily hooked but also for the sake of silence.

I looked up and saw the ensign-staff silhouetted against the sky and used that to mark the position of the rail. Holding a coil of the rope I threw up my grapnel so it went over the rail. There was a soft thud as it landed on the deck and, as I drew the line back, I hoped it would hold. It did; it caught on the rail and a steady pull told me it would be not unreasonable to climb the rope.

I bent down and whispered, 'Well, this is it. I may come back with Slade or I may not. I may come over the side in a bloody hurry so stick around to fish me out of the drink.' I paused. 'If I don't come back then you're on your own and the best of British luck to you.'

I swarmed up the rope and managed to hook my arm round the ensign-staff, taking the strain off the shark hook. The pistol thrust into the waist of my trousers didn't help much; as I twisted like a contortionist to get a foot on deck the muzzle dug into my groin agonizingly and I was thankful that I'd made sure there wasn't a bullet in front of the firing pin.

I made it at last and in silence. At least nobody took a shot at me as I looked back at the water. Alison was nowhere to be seen and there was just a suspicious looking ripple where no ripple should have been. I stayed there quietly for a moment and strained my ears listening to the loud silence.

If there was a man, on watch he was being quiet in his watching. I hazarded a guess that anyone on watch would stay up forward, perhaps in the wheelhouse or comfortably in the dining saloon. To get to the stern cabins I didn't have to go forward; the entrance to the cabin deck was by a staircase in the deck lounge, and the door to the lounge was just in front of me if the ship plans I had studied were correct.

I took out a pen-light and risked a flash. It was lucky I did so because the deck immediately in front of me was cluttered with diver's gear – I could have made a Godawful clatter if I hadn't seen that. I managed to navigate the booby traps safely until I got to the deck lounge door and was thankful to find it unlocked; which was just as expected because who locks doors on a ship?

The lounge was in darkness but I saw light gleaming through a glass-panelled door on the starboard side. There was just enough light spilling through to illumine the hazards of furniture so I stepped over to look through the door and I froze as I saw movement at the end of a long passage. A man came out of the dining saloon and turned into the galley and out of sight. I opened the door gently and listened; there was the slam of something heavy followed by the clink of crockery. The man on watch was enlivening the night hours by raiding the refrigerator, which suited me very well.

I crossed the lounge again and went below to the cabin deck. There were three cabins down there, all for guests. Wheeler's master cabin was 'midships', the other side of the engine room, so I didn't have to worry about him. The problem that faced me was if he had any guests, apart from Slade, occupying any of the three guest cabins.

The cabin that had been curtained in broad daylight at Gibraltar was the big stern cabin, and that was my first objective. This time the door *was* locked, and this raised my hopes because Slade would certainly be kept under lock and key. I inspected the lock with a guarded flash of the light. It wasn't much of a problem; no one installs Chubb triple-throw locks on a cabin door and I could have opened one of those if I had to – it would have taken longer, that's all.

As it was I was inside the cabin inside two minutes and with the door locked again behind me. I heard the heavy breathing of a sleeping man and flicked my light towards the port side, hoping to God it was Slade. If it wasn't I was well and truly up that gum tree I had shown Mackintosh.

I needn't have worried because it was Slade all right and I cheered internally at the sight of that heavy face with the slightly yellowish skin. I took the gun from my waist and pushed a bullet up the spout. At the metallic sound Slade stirred and moaned slightly in his sleep. I stepped forward and, keeping the light on him, I pressed gently with my finger at the corner of his jaw just below the ear. It's the best way to awaken a man quietly.

He moaned again and his eyelids flickered open, and he screwed up his eyes at the sudden flood of light. I moved the pen-light so that it illumined the gun I held. 'If you shout it'll be the last sound you make on earth,' I said quietly.

He shuddered violently and his adam's apple bobbed convulsively as he swallowed. At last he managed to whisper, 'Who the hell are you?'

'Your old pal, Rearden,' I said. 'I've come to take you home.'

It took some time to sink in, and then he said, 'You're mad.'

'Probably,' I admitted. 'Anyone who wants to save your life must be mad.'

He was getting over the shock. The blood was returning to his face and the self-possession to his soul – if he had one. 'How did you get here?' he demanded.

I let the light wander to the nearest port. It wasn't curtained, after all; plates of sheet metal had been roughly welded over the oval scuttles so that it was absolutely impossible for Slade to see outside – more security expertise on the part of the Scarperers. I grinned at Slade, and asked softly, 'Where is here?'

'Why – on board this ship,' he said, but his voice was uncertain.

'I've been following you.' I watched with interest as his eyes shifted sideways to look at a bell-push by the side of his berth, and I hefted the gun so that it came into prominence again. 'I wouldn't,' I warned. 'Not if you value your health.'

'Who are you?' he whispered.

'I suppose you could say that I'm in the same business as yourself, but in the other corner. I'm in counter-espionage.'

The breath came from him in a long, wavering sigh. 'The executioner,' he said flatly. He nodded towards the gun. 'You won't get away with it. You have no silencer. Kill me with that thing and you're dead, too.'

I'm expendable,' I said lightly, and hoped I wouldn't have to make that statement stick. 'Use your brains, Slade. I could have slid into this cabin and cut your throat in your sleep. It would have been messy, but silent. A better way would have been to stick a steel knitting needle through the nape of your neck and into the medulla oblongata – there's not much blood. The fact that we're talking now means I want to take you out alive.'

He frowned slightly and I could almost see the wheels spinning as he thought it out. I said, 'But don't have any misconceptions. I either take you out alive or you stay here dead. It's your choice.'

He had recovered enough to smile slightly. 'You're taking a big chance. You can't keep me under the gun all the time. I could win yet.'

'You won't want to,' I said. 'Not when you've heard what I have to say. My guess is that you were taken from that room we shared, given a shot of dope, and woke up in this cabin where you've been ever since. Where do you think you are?'

That set the wheels going round again, but to no effect. At last he said, 'There's been no temperature change, so I couldn't have been taken very much north or south.'

'This hooker has a very efficient air-conditioning plant,' I said. 'You wouldn't know the difference. Do you like Chinese food?'

The switch confused him. 'What the hell! I can take it or leave it.'

'Have you had any lately?'

He was bemused. 'Why, yes – only yesterday I . . .'

I cut in. 'The ship has a Chinese cook. Do you know whose ship it is?' He shook his head in silence, and I said, 'It belongs to a man called Wheeler, a British MP. I take it you haven't seen him.'

'No, I haven't,' said Slade. 'I'd have recognized him. I met him a couple of times in . . . in the old days. What the devil is all this about?'

'Do you still think you are going to Moscow?'

'I see no reason to doubt it,' he said stiffly.

'Wheeler was born an Albanian,' I said. 'And his Chinese cook does more than rustle up sweet and sour pork. They're not your brand of communist, Slade. Right now you're in Malta and the next scheduled stop is Durazzo in Albania; from there I guess you'll be shipped by cargo plane straight to Peking. You'd better acquire a real taste for Chinese cooking – always assuming they give you any food at all.'

He stared at me. 'You're crazy.'

'What's so crazy about the Chinese wanting to get hold of you? What you have locked up inside that skull of yours would interest them very much – the secrets of two top intelligence services. And they'd get it out of you, Slade – even if they had to do it by acupuncture. The Chinese *invented* the term " brainwashing".'

'But *Wheeler?*'

'What's so odd about Wheeler? You got away with it for over a quarter of a century – why shouldn't someone else be as smart as you? Or smarter? Wheeler hasn't been caught – yet.'

He fell silent and I let him think it out. Yet I hadn't much time to waste so I prodded him again. 'It seems to me that your choice is simple. You come with me willingly or I kill you right now. I think I'd be doing you a favour if I killed you because I'd hate to see you after you'd been in the hands of the Chinese for a month. I think you'd better come with me and retire to a nice, safe, top-security wing in one of Her Majesty's nicks. At least you won't be having your brains pulled out through your ears.'

He shook his head stubbornly. 'I don't know if I believe you.'

'For God's sake! If Wheeler wanted you to go to Moscow then why didn't he transfer you to one of those ubiquitous Russian trawlers? In the Atlantic they're as thick as fleas on a mangy dog. Why bring you to the Mediterranean?'

Slade looked at me cunningly. 'I've only your word for that, too.'

I sighed, and lifted the gun. 'You don't have much of a choice, do you?' I was getting mad at him. 'If ever I saw a man looking a gift horse in the mouth it's you. I haven't followed you from Ireland to . . .'

He cut in. 'Ireland?'

'That's where we were held together.'

'Lynch is Irish,' he said thoughtfully.

'Seaman Lynch? He works for Wheeler – he's an IRA thug with a dislike of the English.'

'He looks after me here,' said Slade. 'He's my guard.' He looked up and I saw that the strain of uncertainty was beginning to tell. 'Where are we now – exactly?'

'Anchored in Marsamxett Harbour.'

He made up his mind. 'All right, but if I get on deck and I don't recognize it then you might be in big trouble. You'll be wanting silence and I might take my chances on the gun in the darkness. Remember that.'

'How long is it since you've been in Malta?'

'Five years.'

I smiled humourlessly, 'Then I hope to God you have a good memory.'

Slade threw back the bedclothes and then paused, looking at me questioningly. There had been a creak which was not one of the usual shipboard noises. I listened and it came again.

Slade whipped the covers back over his chest. 'Someone's coming,' he whispered.

I held up the gun before his eyes. 'Remember this!' I backed off and opened the door of the lavatory and even as I did so I heard a key snap metallically at the cabin door. I closed the lavatory door gently and used my pen-light in a quick flash to see what I'd got into. As usual in lavatories there was no back door, just the usual paraphernalia of toilet, wash basin, medicine cabinet and shower. The shower was screened off by a semi-transparent plastic curtain.

I switched off the light, held my breath, and listened. Lynch's voice was unmistakable. 'I heard voices – who the devil were you talking to?'

This was the crunch. If Slade was going to give me away he'd do it now, so I listened with care to what was arguably the most important conversation I was ever likely to hear.

'I must have been talking in my sleep,' said Slade, and my heartbeat slowed down to a mere gallop. 'I've been having bad dreams and I've got the makings of a headache.'

'Ach, it's no wonder, and you being cooped up in here all this while,' said Lynch. 'But rest easy, you'll soon be home.'

'Why have we been stopped all this time?'

'Something's gone wrong with the propellers,' said Lynch. 'But I didn't get the exact hang of it.'

'Where are we?'

'Now you know better than to ask that, Mr Slade. That's top secret.'

'Well, when will we be moving again and when do I get my feet on dry land?'

'As to the first,' said Lynch, 'maybe it'll be tomorrow. As to the last, I couldn't rightly tell you. I'm not one of the bosses, you know; they don't tell me everything.' He paused. 'But you're looking so white and peaky, Mr Slade. Could I get you the aspirin?'

The hairs on the nape of my neck stood up and did a fandango as Slade answered. 'No, don't worry; I'll be all right.' It was borne heavily upon me that although I could hear Slade's voice I couldn't see what he was doing with his hands. He might be saying one thing and pointing out to Lynch that he had an unwanted visitor.

Lynch said solicitously, 'Ach, it's no trouble at all. We promise to get you home in good condition; that's part of the deal. I'll get the aspirin for you.'

I ducked into the shower stall and drew the plastic curtain just as Lynch opened the lavatory door. He switched on the light and I saw his outline quite clearly through the curtain as he stepped forward to open the medicine cabinet. I had the gun trained on him all the time and I thought that I could dispose of him and Slade, too, if it came to the push. Getting out would be another matter.

I heard the rattle of pills in a bottle and then the rush of water as a tap was turned on. It was a relief to know that Lynch actually was getting aspirin and that Slade had not sold me out. Lynch filled the glass and turned to leave – he was so close that I could have touched him by only half-extending my arm and only the curtain was between us. Fortunately he was back-lit and I wasn't or he would have seen me had he glanced my way.

He went out, switching off the light and closing the door. 'Here, you are,' he said. 'This should clear up your headache.'

'Thanks,' said Slade, and I heard the clink of the glass.

'Man, but you're sweating,' said Lynch. 'Are you sure it's not the fever you've got?'

'I'll be all right,' said Slade. 'You can leave the light on. I think I'll read for a while.'

'Surely,' said Lynch. 'Have a quiet night, mind.' I heard the cabin door open and close, and then the snap of the lock as the key was turned.

I was doing a fair amount of sweating myself as I waited for the trembling of my hands to stop. My stomach felt all churned up as the adrenalin sped on its appointed rounds gingering up my muscle tone and twanging my nerves like harp strings. At last I stepped out of the shower and gently opened the lavatory door.

Whether his sweating was due to a fright or fever Slade had used his wits when he had asked Lynch to leave on the main cabin light. It meant that I could see at a glance if the place was safe. Slade certainly didn't want to be shot by accident.

He lay in bed with a book held between slack fingers and his face was the yellow colour of old newsprint. 'Why didn't he see you?' he whispered.

I flapped a hand at him to keep him quiet and went to the door, still keeping the gun pointing in his general direction. I heard nothing so presently I turned and strode over to Slade. 'Where does Lynch live? Do you know?'

He shook his head and tugged at my sleeve. 'How the hell did he miss you?'

He found it difficult to believe that in a narrow space the size of two telephone booths one man could miss seeing another. I found it hard to believe myself. 'I was taking a shower,' I said. 'How was Lynch dressed?'

'Dressing-gown.'

That meant he hadn't come far and he probably had been allocated one of the cabins next door to be conveniently close to his charge. 'Have you any clothes?' Slade nodded. 'All right; get dressed – quietly.'

I watched Slade carefully while he dressed, principally to make sure he didn't slip a blunt instrument into his pocket. When he had finished I said, 'Now get back into bed.' He was about to expostulate but I shut him up fast with a jab of the gun. 'I want to give Lynch time to get back to sleep.'

Slade got back into bed and I retreated into the lavatory, leaving the door ajar. Slade had pulled the sheet up high and was lying on his side apparently reading his book. Everything would appear normal if Lynch took it into his head to come back. I gave him half an hour by my watch and during that time heard nothing out of the ordinary.

I stepped into the cabin and signalled Slade to rise. While he was disentangling himself from the bedclothes – it's really surprising how difficult it is to get out of bed when fully dressed because the sheet wraps itself round one's shoes – I jimmied the lock on the door. I had to turn my back on Slade at this point but it couldn't be helped.

I turned and found him walking towards me slowly. When he approached he put his mouth to my ear and whispered, 'When I get on deck I'd better see Valletta.'

I nodded my head impatiently, switched off the light, and opened the door on to the darkness of the passage. The staircase was immediately to the left and I prodded Slade up it with the gun in his back, holding his right arm. I stopped him before we got to the top and cautiously surveyed the deck lounge. All was quiet so I urged him on his way and we went out on to the after deck.

I shone the light to give Slade some idea of the obstacle race he must run to get the twenty feet to the stern rail, and off we went again. Half-way across the afterdeck he stopped and looked around. 'You are right,' he whispered. 'It *is* Valletta.'

'Quit chattering.' I was edgy as I always am on the last lap. Once ashore I could turn Slade in to the Maltese Constabulary and the job was done, apart from wrapping up Wheeler and his mob, but we still had to get ashore.

We got as far as the stern rail and no further. I groped for the grapnel alongside the ensign-staff and couldn't find it. Then shockingly a blaze of light split the darkness as the beam of a powerful lamp shone vertically down on us from the boat deck above, and a voice said, 'That's far enough.'

I dug my elbow into Slade's ribs. 'Jump!' I yelled, but neither of us was quick enough. There was a rapid tattoo of feet on the deck as a small army of men rushed us and we were both grabbed and held. There wasn't a damned thing I could do – two of the three men who tackled me were trying to tear my arms off so they could use them as clubs to beat me over the head, and the other was using my stomach as a bass drum and his fists weren't padded as drumsticks are.

As I sagged and gasped for breath I was vaguely aware of Slade being dragged forward, hauled by two seamen with his feet trailing along the deck. Someone shouted and I was also hustled forward and thrust headlong through the doorway of the deck lounge. A burly black-bearded man whom I recognized as the skipper issued orders in a language whose flavour I couldn't catch. I was unceremoniously dropped to the deck and my assailants began to draw the curtains to the windows.

Before the last of them was drawn I saw a searchlight from the bridge forward begin to search the water around *Artina* and I hoped Alison had got clear. Someone handed my pistol to the skipper; he looked at it with interest, made sure it was cocked, and pointed it at me. 'Who are you?' His English was accented, but with what I didn't know.

I pushed myself up with wobbly arms. 'Does it matter?' I asked wearily.

The skipper swung his eyes to Slade who sagged against a chair, and then beyond him to the staircase which led below. 'Ah, Lynch!' he said, rumbling like a volcano about to explode. 'What kind of a guard are you?'

I turned my head. Lynch was looking at Slade with shocked amazement. 'How did he get here? I was with him not half an hour ago, and I made sure the door was locked.'

'The door was locked,' mimicked the skipper. *'Te keni kujdes;* how could the door be locked?' He pointed to me. 'And this man – he brought Slade out of the cabin.'

Lynch looked at me. 'By God, it's Rearden. But he *couldn't* have been in the cabin,' he said stubbornly. 'I'd have seen him.'

'I was in the shower, standing right next to you, you silly bastard.' I turned to the skipper. 'He nearly got himself killed. Not much of a guard, is he?'

Lynch made for me with blood in his eye, but the skipper got to me first, warding off Lynch with an arm like an iron bar. He dragged my head up by my hair and stuck the gun in my face. 'So you are Rearden,' he said, caressing my cheek with the barrel. 'We're very interested in you, Rearden.'

A cool voice said, 'He's not Rearden, of course.'

The skipper swung away and I saw the Chinese, Chang Pi-wu, who looked at me expressionlessly. Next to him stood a tall man with ash-blond hair, who, at that moment, was fitting a cigarette into a long holder. He dipped his hand into the pocket of his elegant dressing-gown, produced a lighter and flicked it into flame.

'Stannard is the name, I believe,' said Wheeler. 'Owen Stannard.' He lit his cigarette. 'So thoughtful of you to join us, Mr Stannard. It saves me the trouble of looking for you.'

TEN

'How did you get hold of him?' Wheeler asked the skipper.

'Mehmet found a hook on the stern rail and a rope leading to the water. He removed it and told me. I set up a watch.'

Wheeler nodded. 'You didn't know whether someone was going to come on board or leave,' he commented.

The skipper waved his hand at me and Slade. 'We caught these two leaving. This idiot . . .' He stabbed his finger at Lynch. . . . let them go.'

Wheeler regarded Lynch frostily. 'I'll talk to you later. Now get below.'

Lynch looked as though he was about to expostulate but he caught the cold glare from Wheeler's eye and promptly turned on his heel and went away, giving me a look of dislike as he went. I was beginning to improve physically; my shoulders no longer felt totally dislocated and although my belly was one massive ache I could now breathe more or less normally.

Wheeler said, 'Well, Mr Stannard; how did you expect to take Slade ashore? By boat? Where is it?'

'I swam out,' I said.

'And you were going to swim back,' he said incredulously. With Slade a cripple? I don't believe you.' He swung around to the skipper. 'Make a search for the boat.'

The skipper didn't move. 'It's being done.'

Wheeler nodded approvingly and crossed to Slade who had now sagged into a chair. 'My dear chap,' he said anxiously. 'What possessed you to leave with this man? Do you know who he is? If you had left the ship he would have put you in the hands of the police. And you know what that would mean – forty years in a British gaol. What sort of tale could he have told you?'

Slade wearily lifted up his head. 'I know you,' he said, 'we've met before.'

'Yes – in happier circumstances,' said Wheeler. 'Once at an EFTA conference and again, if my memory is correct, at a dinner given by some industrial organization or other – I forget which.'

'Your name is Wheeler, you're a member of Parliament. Why should you want to help *me*?'

'A good question,' I said. 'Answer him, Wheeler. Tell Slade why you are willing to commit treason.' I rubbed my sore stomach tentatively. 'As far as I know treason still carries the death penalty – it isn't covered by the Act of Parliament which abolished hanging for murder.' I grinned at him. 'But who should know that better than you?'

Wheeler didn't rile easily. He smiled, and said coolly, 'I am helping you because I don't recognize British law; because, like you, I'm fighting for a better world.' He put his hand on Slade's shoulder. 'Because, also like you, I'm a good communist.'

'Then why didn't I know about you?' asked Slade. 'I should have known.'

'Why should you have known? You didn't *need to* know, and therefore you weren't told. It was safer that way.' Wheeler smiled. 'You might have been important, Slade, but you were never as important as I am.'

I corrected him. 'As important as you *were*. You're finished, Wheeler.'

Apart from gently shaking his head he ignored me. With his eyes fixed on Slade, he said, 'What nonsense has Stannard been filling you up with? You're a fool if you believe the enemy.'

Slade said, 'What are we doing here in Malta?'

Wheeler straightened and laughed. 'So that's the maggot he's put in your mind. I'm taking you home, of course. I spend my annual holiday in the Mediterranean; it would have looked damned suspicious if I'd gone to the Baltic this year. Even for you I wouldn't risk that.'

I said to Slade, 'Ask him if he's read any good thoughts lately – from the Little Red Book.'

'You're an Albanian,' said Slade flatly. 'I don't trust you.'

'So that's it,' said Wheeler softly. 'Does it make any difference?'

Slade nodded towards the silent Chinese who stood behind Wheeler. 'He does.'

I chipped in again. 'He makes a hell of a difference. Wheeler says he's taking you home. Home is where the heart is, and his heart is in Peking.'

That got to Wheeler. He said venomously, 'I think I'll have to shut you up – permanently.' He relaxed again and struck his hands lightly together. 'Not that it makes much difference whether you know or not, Slade. It made things easier as long as you believed you were going to Moscow – a willing prisoner is easier to handle. But we've got you and you'll still get to your destination intact.'

From the look in Slade's eyes I doubted it. It wouldn't be beyond his capabilities to commit suicide somewhere along the way, and death would be far preferable to the information-extracting process awaiting him in China. Besides, under the circumstances it was his duty to commit suicide. Any man in his position knew that when it came to this sort of crunch he was expendable.

But Wheeler was ahead of us on that one. 'Your confinement will be more rigorous, of course. We can't have you hanging yourself by your braces.'

'Do I get to go along?' I asked.

Wheeler looked at me reflectively. 'You?' He shook his head. 'I don't think my friends would be interested in you. You've been out of the game too long to know much about recent developments in British Intelligence. A South African sleeper is of no consequence.' He half turned his head and said over his shoulder. 'What do you think?'

The Chinese spoke for the first time. 'He is of no use, but he is dangerous because of what he knows,' he said dispassionately. 'Kill him.'

I said something indescribably rude in Mandarin, and he opened his mouth in surprise. Orientals aren't all that inscrutable.

'Yes, Stannard; we must kill you. But how to do it?' Wheeler asked himself pensively. 'I have it. We discover a stowaway on board – an armed stowaway. There is a scuffle on his discovery and a shot is fired – the stowaway is killed with his own gun. We notify the police here and he turns out to be none other than Rearden, the British gaol-breaker.' He smiled. 'That would do a lot for my image; think of the headlines in the British press. What do you think of it?'

'Not much,' I said. 'If you turn me in to the police they'll want to know about Slade, too. He's a hell of a sight more important than I am. They'll want to search this ship, and they'll take it apart. You wouldn't want them to do that with Slade still aboard.'

Wheeler nodded. 'True. I'm afraid I must forgo that charming theatricality; my image must do without it. Besides, before you die there are some questions to be answered, such as what accomplices you have. That reminds me.' He turned to the skipper. 'What result of the search for his boat?'

'I'll find out,' said the skipper, and left the lounge.

I sighed. 'I came aboard alone.'

Wheeler nodded. 'You were alone at the beginning – I know that. But you might have picked up someone along the way. You realize that I must be certain.' He indicated the Chinese. 'My friend has ways of making sure, but you won't want to hear about that.'

I looked about the lounge casually. The departure of the skipper had reduced the odds against me, but not by much. There were two seamen behind me, one covering me with my own gun, and Wheeler and the Chinese were in front. The Chinese held his hand in his pocket and I was certain he also had a gun. I looked at Slade and wondered if he'd join me if it came to putting up a fight.

I said, 'I'd like to know how you got on to Mackintosh and me so fast. You seem to know all about me – including my South African history.'

Wheeler chuckled. 'You British are a nation of amateurs – and that goes for your intelligence services. I was told about you, of course.'

I was genuinely bewildered. 'Who could have told you? There was only Mackintosh and me.'

'Precisely. And you didn't tell me.'

My jaw dropped and I stared at Wheeler incredulously. 'Mackintosh?'

'Who else could – as you point out. He was a little drunk and very indiscreet. I had no difficulty in flattering the fool. Towards the end he realized he was saying too much and shut up, but I got enough out of him.' He laughed. 'We were having a discussion on prison reform at the time.'

I was bewildered. Wheeler's description didn't fit the Mackintosh I knew, who was not a fool and certainly not susceptible to flattery. What in hell had Mackintosh been doing to blow things like that?

'He's dead, of course,' said Wheeler casually. 'I saw to that immediately as soon as I was certain we had you safe in Ireland. But we didn't have you safe, did we? Those IRA clowns are also amateurs. Never mind; here you are and all is well, after all.'

I felt chilled to my bones. Whether Mackintosh was dead or not – and that was a moot point because I had told Alison to spread the word of his impending demise – I felt betrayed and utterly alone. Like a man who treads on a stair that isn't there. I felt jolted. I had to believe Wheeler because nothing else made sense, and yet Mackintosh's betrayal didn't make sense, either. Unless . . .

The skipper returned, breaking my chain of thought. 'No boat found,' he said.

Wheeler was fitting another cigarette into his holder. 'You may have been telling the truth, after all,' he said. He turned his head to the skipper. 'I want safe places for these two separately. What do you suggest?'

'Slade can go back to the cabin,' said the skipper.

'After what has just happened?' Wheeler lifted his eyebrows.

The Chinese said, 'He must be manacled to the bed, and a man must stay *in* the cabin all the time. He must not be permitted to make noise.'

Wheeler thought about it. 'All right; what about Stannard?'

'The forepeak; there's a steel bulkhead with a watertight door. He won't get out of there.'

Wheeler nodded curtly, then said to me, 'I'm afraid your interrogation will have to be postponed until we're away from land. The sound of a man screaming travels a long way.' He waved his hand and I found my arm held. 'By the way, were you responsible for what happened to our screws?'

'What's happened to your screws?' I managed to grin. 'Are they loose?'

'Very stiff-upper-lipped,' commented Wheeler. 'A quip in the face of death – very British. Take him away.'

I was hustled out of the lounge, a man on each side of me. I passed Slade whose face was yellowy-grey and who looked absolutely defeated and then I was thrust out on to the stern deck. There were now lights aboard *Artina* and, as we went forward along the side-deck, I saw that the man on my right still carried my gun. I didn't like the sound of that forepeak; from what I had seen of it on the plans of *Artina's* sister ship it was only four feet high – a hermetically-sealed steel box. The odds were I'd die of heat-stroke or suffocation.

But relish the prospect or not, the man next to me had a gun. The fact that he wasn't pointing it directly at me made not a ha'porth of difference – not while he gripped my arm and the man on the other side held me in a hammer-lock.

They pushed me along the deck until we were amidships and then there was a noise like a dud firecracker and the man with a gun gave a yelp and dropped it on to the deck. He stopped and looked at the blood oozing from the hole in the back of his hand, and let go of me. I'd heard that dud firecracker go off before.

I heard it go off again and saw a brief flash of light from the top of the deckhouse. The seaman who had me in the hammer-lock stumbled slightly and his grip loosened. He went down in apparent slow motion and I saw there was a dark red spot in the middle of his forehead.

'Jump, you damned fool,' yelled Alison, and I went over the side in an inelegant dive, arms and legs going every which way. I landed in the water with a hell of a splash and heard, two seconds later, another neater and more ladylike splash as Alison joined me.

I wasted no time in getting under the surface and swam in a circle searching for her. My hand touched her leg and she twisted in the water and grabbed my wrist. I pulled, leading her, and we swam deep and under *Artina*. It would be natural for anyone to look for us from the side of the ship from which we had jumped and I wanted to get away from there.

Matters were complicated by the fact that I was running out of air. Things had happened so fast that I hadn't had time to prepare myself by taking a good lungful of air, and that wasn't so good. I didn't want to come up within shooting distance of the ship. I compromised by coming up for air under *Artina's* stern, hanging on to her rudder with just my nose and mouth above water. Alison joined me.

I took a few deep breaths and then allowed an ear out of the water. Things were going pop on deck; men ran along the deck in a seemingly confused way and the deep rumble of the skipper's voice held a note of menace. I prodded Alison under the chin so that her head came out of the water and whispered into her ear. 'Swim to Ta'Xbiex – under water as far as possible. I'll meet you at the place we left.'

She wasted no time in answering but sank under water and vanished. I took a last breath and followed her. Normally I like swimming but this was getting to be a bit too much; I like to swim in water I know to be clean. I took it easy, letting the air dribble from my mouth as the strain grew intolerable. When it finally became impossible to stay under any longer I surfaced face upwards, letting only my nose and mouth break the surface.

I cleared my lungs in four breaths and then risked a glance back at *Artina. A* searchlight was probing the water again but not in my direction. As I was about to go under again I heard a roar and ducked under just in time as a fast launch came hurtling in my direction. I struck out strongly to gain depth and the launch passed directly overhead, the disturbance of the wake buffeting me in the water.

Three times I had to surface before I came to the shore or, rather to the long line of yachts moored stern on to the wharf of the Lazzaretto Creek Marina. I came up under the bows of a floating gin palace, puffing and panting in an attempt to get my breath back, but I soon stopped that when I heard the pad of naked feet on the deck above.

Whoever it was seemed irritable. 'More uproar – everyone rushin' about in the middle of the night. What the hell do they think they're doin'?'

A woman said, 'I thought I heard fireworks earlier.'

'Fireworks be damned – they're tomorrow night. And who the hell lets off fireworks at this time in the mornin'?'

The launch came by again, going at a hell of a clip, and the boat I was holding on to rocked heavily in the swell of its passage. This provoked an outburst of rage from above. 'What the hell do you think you're doin'?' the man screamed, and I pictured him as a peppery, curry-voiced retired colonel.

His wife said, 'You're making more noise than anyone else, George. Come back to bed!'

There was the slap of bare feet on the deck as they padded away. 'All right; but a fat lot of sleep I'll get,' he grumbled. 'I'll see the manager tomorrow. We can't have this happenin' at night.'

I grinned and swam a couple of boats down the line before climbing ashore. Then I dog-trotted towards the place I'd assigned to meet Alison, hoping that she'd made it. I was worried about Alison for a number of reasons. Back in Ireland she had been distrustful of me and had wondered out loud if I hadn't sold out to the Scarperers. Now I was distrustful of her.

If what Wheeler had said was true – that Mackintosh had blown the gaff – then I was really in trouble because Mackintosh wouldn't do a thing like that unheedingly. But why should I believe Wheeler? What incentive did he have to tell me the truth? In that case there was only one other person who could have sold out – Alison!

What brought that line of thought up short with a jerk was the recent episode on *Artina*. If Alison had sold out then why did she rescue me? Why did she pop off with that natty pistol of hers to wound one man, kill another, and get Stannard off the hot spot? That made even less sense. But I determined to keep a careful eye on Mrs Alison Smith in the future – providing she hadn't been run down by that launch.

II

I waited for fifteen minutes before she arrived. She was exhausted – so weary she couldn't pull herself from the water. I hauled her out and waited for a while until she recovered sufficiently to speak. Her first words were, 'That damned boat – nearly ran me down twice.'

'Did they see you?'

She shook her head slowly. 'I don't think so – they were just lucky.'

'They nearly got me,' I said. 'What happened to our boat?'

'I saw a man find the grapnel,' she said. 'And I knew you'd be in trouble. I went to the bows and climbed the anchor cable, and just let the boat drift.'

'Lucky for me you did. You're pretty handy with that popgun.'

'Six yards – no more. Anyone could do that.'

'Anyone wasn't there,' I said. 'You were.'

She looked about her. 'We'd better move. We could be picked up if we stay here.'

I shook my head. 'We're pretty safe. This harbour has so many inlets and creeks that Wheeler and his boys would have to search ten miles of coastline. But you're right – we'd better move on. It's a long walk back to the hotel and I want to get there before it's light. Do you feel fit?'

Alison got to her feet. 'I'm ready.'

It would take us, I estimated, a good hour to walk back to the hotel. We walked silently; I don't know what Alison was thinking but I was busy wondering what the hell to do next. At last I said, 'Well, I've fallen down on this one – my instructions were to bring Slade back or to kill him. I've done neither.'

'I can't see that you could have done differently,' said Alison.

'Yes, I could – I could have killed Slade on that yacht but I tried to bring him out.'

'It isn't easy to kill a sleeping man,' she said, and shivered. 'It isn't easy to kill anyone.'

I gave her a sideways glance and wondered about her. All that training must have produced something. 'How many men have you killed?'

'One,' she said, and her voice caught. 'To . . . night.' She started to shake violently.

I put my arm around her. 'Take it easy. It's a bad reaction, but it wears off in time. I know.' I damned Mackintosh for what he had done to his daughter. Yet at least he had made her into a professional and she would respond to the right stimulus just like one of Pavlov's dogs. To take her mind off what she had just done I said, 'We must leave the hotel.'

'Of course,' she said. 'But what then?'

'I'm damned if I know,' I admitted. 'It all depends on how much damage we've done to Wheeler's yacht. If she moves we're finished.'

'And if she doesn't?'

'We have another chance.'

'You can't go on board again – that won't work twice.'

'I know,' I said. 'I must think of something else.' We fell into a dispirited silence as we trudged along. We were both wet and it was cold in the early hours of the morning. We were also tired, and none of this helped us to think straight.

The sun was rising as we came into Floriana and there were a few people stirring in the streets. During our long walk our clothes had pretty well dried out and we didn't attract undue attention. Presently we passed workmen with ladders who were stringing up rows of gay bunting across the street. 'Those boys have started early,' I said. 'What's the celebration?'

'There's a *festa* today,' said Alison. 'They're always having them here.'

I remembered the disgruntled man who had complained about noise in the harbour. 'They'll be having fireworks tonight, then.'

'Inevitably. The two go together in Malta.'

Something prickled at the back of my mind – the first stirrings of an idea. I left it alone to grow in its own good time. 'How much money have we got?'

'About three thousand pounds – including the five hundred I gave you.'

At least we were well equipped with the sinews of war. The idea burgeoned a little more, but I'd have to study the plans of *Artina's* sister ship a little more closely before I could bring it into the open.

A sleepy porter gave us our keys at the hotel and we went up to our rooms. At my door, I said, 'Come in here for a minute.' When we were inside I poured a big lump of scotch into a tooth-glass and gave it to Alison. 'Put that inside you and you'll feel better. Get yourself a hot shower and a change of clothing, but make it fast. We're evacuating – I want us to be out of here within a half-hour.'

She gave a wan smile. 'Where are we going?'

'We're going to ground – just where I don't know. But Wheeler will have his men checking the hotels; he might have started already. Just bring essentials – the money, passport and aircraft documents.'

When she had gone I followed my own advice. I knocked back a fast scotch and took a three-minute hot shower which chased away some of the aches and put some warmth in my bones again. My stomach was black with bruises. I dressed quickly and began to assemble the things I needed, not that there was much.

Then I sat down and began to study the ship plan. Fortunately it was scaled and I was able to measure distances fairly accurately. Not only was the idea burgeoning but blossoms were appearing. It all depended on whether Wheeler was immobilized in Marsamxett Harbour for another night.

Alison came back carrying one of those big bags which magically hold about six times more than they appear to. We left the hotel by a rear entrance and five minutes later we were at Kingsgate boarding a bus for Senglea.

Alison seemed brighter and said, 'Where are we going – and why?'

I paid the fare. 'I'll tell you when we get there.' The bus was crowded and I didn't want to talk about how I was going to kill Slade and Wheeler in public. The driver of the bus laboured under the misapprehension that his name was Jack Brabham, or perhaps he thought that the little shrine to the Virgin, so gaily decked in flowers, was a reasonable substitute for brakes. We got to Senglea in a remarkably short time.

Senglea is a peninsula jutting out into the Grand Harbour between Dockyard Creek and French Creek. Since the rundown of the Royal Navy and the demilitarization of the Naval Dockyard in Malta it seemed to be a reasonable place to find what I wanted – a boatshed, preferably with its own slipway.

It was still too early to do anything about that but the cafés were already open so we had breakfast, and very welcome it was. Over the bacon and eggs I said, 'Were you seen last night – seen to be recognized again?'

Alison shook her head. 'I don't think so.'

'Wheeler appeared to be uncertain about whether I had assistance,' I said. 'Of course, he knows now – but he doesn't know who. I think you're elected to do the shopping; it might not be safe for me on the streets.'

'What do you want?' she asked concisely.

'I want a boatshed. I only want it for twelve hours but we can't say so – we'll probably have to take it on three months' lease. I'm a boat designer and I'm working on a new type of . . . er . . . hydrofoil. I don't want anyone – my rivals, for instance – looking over my shoulder while I'm doing it, so I want discretion and security. That's the story.'

'Then what?'

'Then you push off and buy us a boat. Something about twenty feet overall and hellish fast, with big engines.'

'Outboard or inboard?'

'Doesn't matter. Outboards will be cheaper, but they must be powerful. You bring the boat round to the shed.' I looked through the window of the cafe. 'Over there is a scrap metal yard; I should be able to get most of what I want over there, including the hire of a welding outfit.'

Alison's brow wrinkled. 'So you have a fast boat and a welding outfit.' She waited patiently.

'Then you hire a truck. Can you drive a truck?' She gave me a look of silent contempt, and I grinned. She had probably passed her driving test with flying colours – in a Chieftain tank. I said, 'You take the truck and you buy enough fireworks to fill the boat.'

Now I had got her attention. 'Fireworks!'

'Big ones – especially the ones that go bang and throw out a shower of pretty lights. None of your paltry penny bangers; I want the big professional stuff. If they're so keen on fireworks here there should be quite a stock somewhere in this island. Think you can do that?'

'I can do it,' she said. 'Now tell me why the hell I should.'

I pulled out the ship plan and laid it on the table. 'I've been on board *Artina* and everything I saw fitted in with this plan, so I think we can trust it.' I tapped with my finger.

'The engine room, containing two 350 hp Rolls-Royce diesels which gulp a hell of a lot of fuel. Under the engine room a supply of fresh water and the ready use fuel tank which holds 1,200 gallons.'

My finger moved on the plan. 'Forward of the engine room is Wheeler's cabin, and farther forward are the crew's quarters. Under that, extending for twenty feet, is a double bottom containing the main fuel supply – 5,350 gallons of fuel oil. We know she's just taken on fuel so the tanks are full.'

I did a bit of measuring with my finger nail. 'To penetrate that tank we have to ram a hole at least three feet below the water line – preferably deeper. Her plating is mild steel, five-sixteenths of an inch thick – to punch a hole through that will need a hell of a lot of power.'

I looked up. 'I'm going to build a ram on the boat you're going to get me. At one time ramming was an orthodox naval tactic – all naval vessels had rams. But this is going to be a little different; it's going to be a combination ram and fireship. The boat will be full of fireworks. When we ram the tank we let out the oil. It floats. The fireworks go off pop and set the oil on fire.'

'So you're going to smoke out Wheeler?'

I looked at her in silence for a moment, then I said, 'Don't be silly, I'm going to burn the bastard out.'

III

It all took time, and we had little enough of that. I was right in thinking that I could get a suitable boatshed in Senglea, but moving in quickly was something else again. A few enquiries made in the district soon turned up just what I wanted but the dickering promised to be protracted and it was ten-thirty that morning before the deal went through and only then because of the production of a hundred pounds in crisp, British fivers.

As time was getting short I sent Alison off to buy the boat, which I hoped wouldn't prove to be as difficult and time-consuming as renting the shed. In the meantime I went to the scrap metal yard and rummaged about until I found what I wanted. I selected a few lengths of angle-iron, a lot of nuts and bolts and a steel bar, eight feet long and an inch and a half in diameter. I was also able to hire a welding outfit there, together with two full bottles of oxygen and acetylene and a pair of goggles.

As I paid out for this lot I reflected that the expense account for this lark was going to raise some Treasury official's hair. I could imagine him querying the purchase of perhaps a quarter of a ton of fireworks and acidly scratching out a memo asking Mrs Smith for further verification. But perhaps Mrs Smith also had training in cooking the swindle sheet.

I got all my equipment to the shed and waited around for Alison. I stared across the Grand Harbour to Valletta and wished I could see through it and into Marsamxett Harbour where *Artina* was still anchored – I hoped. At one-thirty I was still waiting and coming to a slow boil. Time was wasting and I had a hell of a lot to do.

It was nearly two o'clock before she arrived and the steam was blowing out of my ears. I caught the painter she tossed, and said curtly, 'What kept you?'

'I had to go to Sliema. Is she what you wanted?'

I studied the boat. She was a sleek, Italian-built job with two 100 hp Kiekhaefer Mercury outboard motors. Her lines looked good and those big engines would push her along at a fair lick. Alison said, 'I got more than thirty knots out of her on the way here.'

'You brought her from Sliema? You must have passed *Artina*.'

'She's still there.' I sagged a little in relief. 'They're doing a lot of work on her stern. When I passed they were hoisting out one of the propellers.'

'Were they, by God?' I laughed. 'Then it will be an all day job.' I jerked my thumb at the shed. 'There's a cradle in there. Help me get this thing up the slip and out of sight.'

We ran the cradle down the slip, floated the boat into it, and then winched the lot into the shed. Alison looked at her watch. 'I've arranged for the fireworks, too. They'll be ready to be picked up at three.'

'Then you'd better push off.'

She hesitated. 'Can you manage alone?'

'I should be able to. There's a block and tackle up there – I can use that to take the engines out.'

'There's a flask of coffee and a packet of sandwiches in the boat. And a bottle of whisky. I'll be back as soon as I can.'

She turned to go, and I said, 'Alison, there's just one more thing; see if you can get a big axe. A felling axe used for cutting down trees.'

She looked puzzled and then doubtful. 'I'm not sure they use those on Malta – there are not too many trees.'

'Do your best.' She left and I rescued the victuals before the bottle got broken, and then I uncoupled the steering cables on the boat and hoisted out the engines. I also used the block and tackle to turn the boat out of the cradle so that it lay upside down on trestles. I ate the sandwiches and drank the coffee while studying the problem; the whisky I left strictly alone because there was a job to be done, although I'd probably be glad of a stiff jolt before I set out.

I proceeded to get my hands dirty. The hull was of glass fibre and I began to ruin it by drilling holes in carefully selected places. The idea was to position the ram so that it was at least three feet below the water line when the boat was planing at speed, and it had to be fixed to the hull firmly enough so that it wouldn't come adrift on impact. If that happened then the momentum given by those big engines would be lost and the ram wouldn't penetrate *Artina's* steel shell.

I cut up lengths of angle-iron and bolted them to the hull and through to steel cross-members which ran athwartship. Then I started to weld it up. It wasn't pretty welding and would have won no prizes at a craft school but, by God, it was strong – I made sure of that. When I had got that far there were two steel triangles built into the hull, the apexes of which were a little over three feet below the bottom. I took the long steel bar and welded it to the apexes of my steel triangles so that it was parallel to the bottom of the hull and projecting two feet in front.

Alison was back long before I had got that far and gave me a hand. It was hot and sweaty work and it took time. It was seven in the evening when I put the finishing touch to it. 'Did you get the axe?'

She produced just what I needed – a long-handled felling axe. I didn't need the handle and wasted no time in fiddling but cut it off with the welding torch. Then I took the blade and welded it vertically to the end of the steel bar – that was the cutting edge of my ram.

I stood back and looked at what I had done. Oddly enough it did look like a weird kind of hydrofoil, but I didn't like to think of what all that heavy ironmongery hung under the boat would do to her planing characteristics. I began to worry about the speed I was going to lose and if I could get her to plane at all.

'I could use a drink,' I said.

Alison poured some whisky into the cup from the vacuum flask and gave it to me. She looked at the boat, and said. 'It's going to be dangerous. I was wondering . . .'

'Wondering what?'

She turned to face me. 'I was wondering if this can't be done more simply – by the police.'

'That's a great idea,' I said sardonically. 'Can you imagine the local coppers believing us? Christ, Wheeler comes here every year and he's a respected figure, a British MP and an eminent capitalist. He's probably given prizes to the yacht club and I wouldn't be surprised if he's the sole support of a local orphanage. By the time we managed to convince anyone both he and Slade would have flown the coop.'

'There's still a body on *Artina,*' said Alison. 'That would take a lot of explaining away.'

'Same objection,' I said. 'Forget it. Let's have a look at the fireworks.'

There were a lot of them and they were big; rockets that would go up under their own power and maroons designed to be fired from mortars. 'This lot should add to the festivities,' I said in satisfaction. 'We must get the boat on to the cradle,'

I had to cut bits away from the cradle to accommodate our strange craft and it was forever ruined for handling normal boats. More expense for the Treasury. I installed the engines and hooked up the steering cables and tested them. When I jumped to the ground the boat, now right way up, looked a bit more practicable.

'How much did you pay for her?' I asked curiously.

'Fifteen hundred pounds,' said Alison.

I grinned. 'Guided missiles always are expensive. Let's put the cargo aboard.'

We filled up every spare inch of the hull with the big fireworks. Alison, as foreseeing as ever, had brought along a jerrican full of petrol and, after topping up the tanks, there was still half a gallon left, more than enough to start a fire to get things going. I now had a new worry; I had drilled a dozen holes in the hull to take bolts and had caulked them with putty, and I was wondering if I had sealed her tight. That couldn't be tested until we put her in the water and that wouldn't be until it was good and dark.

'When do they start shooting off the fireworks for the *festa*?' I asked.

'Two hours after sunset.'

'I'd like to ram *Artina* when the official fireworks are going full blast. It'll help to confuse the issue.' I sat down wearily and pulled out my ship plan; it was becoming worn and tatty and dirty at the creases, but it was still legible. 'The trouble is that I might hit one of the main frames,' I said. 'In that case I doubt if I'll get enough penetration.'

The frames were about two feet apart; statistically I had a good chance of missing – the odds were on my side.

Alison said, 'If we're going to do more underwater swimming we might as well do it comfortably.' She got up and dragged some scuba gear from the corner. 'I took the precaution of hiring this.'

'That slipped my mind.' I wondered what else I'd forgotten. I looked at the gear – there were two sets. 'I'm going to do the swimming,' I said. 'Not you.'

'But I'm coming with you,' she expostulated.

'For what? I don't need you.'

She flinched as though I had slapped her face. I said, 'You're right – it's a dangerous operation, and there's no point in both of us going. Besides, I need you for something else.' I thumped the side of the boat. 'Whether this works or not there's going to be ructions when these fireworks explode. If I don't get back someone must be around to have another crack at Wheeler – and you're elected.'

I reached out for the bottle and poured some more whisky. 'You can try going to the police; they might be interested enough by then to take you seriously.'

She saw the point, but she didn't like it. She set her face in a stubborn mould and prepared to argue. I forestalled her. 'All right; this is what you do. You wait here until nightfall and help me to get the boat into the water. Then you hop over to Ta'Xbiex and hire another boat – if you can get anyone to trust you.' I smiled. 'Looking as you do now I wouldn't trust you with a kid's bath toy.'

She rubbed her smudged face and distastefully inspected her fingertips, 'Thanks,' she said. 'I'll clean up.'

'If you can't hire a boat, steal one. There are plenty of loose boats at the Marina. Meet me at the seaward point of Manoel Island and then follow me in, but not too closely. When the balloon goes up watch out for Slade and Wheeler – they should be doing their best to jump overboard if all goes well. See they don't get ashore.'

'I lost the gun last night,' she said.

'Well, bat them over the head with an oar,' I said. 'I'll be around somewhere so keep your oar away from me.' I looked at my watch. 'It'll be dark enough for launching in about an hour.'

That hour seemed to stretch out interminably rather like I'm told it does in an LSD trip; I wouldn't know about that – I haven't tried it. We didn't talk much and when we did it was of inconsequentialities. The sun set and the light slowly ebbed from the sky until at last it was dark enough to take the boat down the slip without anyone seeing it. Once it was in the water it wouldn't appear too abnormal.

I patted the wickedly gleaming steel axe-head which formed the tip of the ram and went to open the big double doors of the shed, and we steered the cradle down the slip and into the water. I released the boat and we took the cradle away and I turned to see how my handiwork had turned out.

It wasn't too bad; she was down by the head but not by too much considering the weight of iron under her bows, and she appeared quite normal apart from the bits of angle-iron which showed above water on each side of the hull. In another ten minutes it would be too dark to see even that, but even if I was picked up by a light in the harbour I doubt if anyone would notice anything particularly odd about her.

'That's it,' I said wearily. I was bone-tired; no sleep, a beating-up and a hard day's work did nothing to improve me.

'I'll go now,' said Alison quietly. 'Good luck, Owen.' She didn't kiss me, or even touch me. She just walked away, picking up her coat as she went.

I climbed into the boat and rearranged a few of the fireworks to make myself more comfortable. I put the scuba gear handy and checked my primitive system of fuses. Then there was nothing to do but wait another hour before I was due to move off.

Again it was a long wait.

ELEVEN

I checked my watch for the twentieth time in fifteen minutes and decided that time had come. I put on the scuba gear, tightened the weighted belt around my waist, and hung the mask around my neck. Then I started the engines and the boat quivered in the water. I cast off the painter and pushed the boat away with one hand and then tentatively opened the throttles a notch, not knowing what to expect.

At a slow speed she didn't handle too badly although there seemed to be something a little soggy about her response to the wheel. I switched on the lights because I didn't want the harbour patrol to pick me up for running illegally, and went down French Creek into the Grand Harbour. Here, in time past, the British Battle Fleet had lain, line upon line of dreadnoughts and battle cruisers. Now, there was another, but odder, naval craft putting to sea, but this one was in an earlier tradition – more like one of Drake's fireships.

Across the harbour Valletta was all lit up and there were strings of coloured lights spangling Floriana. Tinny music floated across the quiet water punctuated by the thumping of a bass drum. The merry-making was well under way.

I rounded the head of Senglea and steered to the harbour mouth. Nothing was coming my way so I decided to open up and see what the boat would do. The note of the engines deepened as I opened the throttles and I felt the surge of acceleration as 200 hp kicked her through the water. In terms of horse-power per ton of displacement this little boat was perhaps forty times as powerful as *Artina;* that's where the speed came from.

The steering was worse than bad – it was dreadful. The wheel kicked in my hands violently and my course was erratic, to say the least, and I went down the Grand Harbour doing a pretty good imitation of a water boatman, those jerky insects that run across the surface of ponds.

The damned boat wouldn't get on the step and plane and I don't suppose her speed was more than twelve knots, and that wasn't going to be enough. All the power going into the screws was doing nothing more than raising waves and I wasn't supposed to be in the wave-raising business. In desperation I slammed the throttles hard open and she suddenly rose in the water and took off, picking up at least an extra ten knots in as many seconds. But the steering was worse and there was a definite lag between hauling the wheel around and the corresponding reaction.

I throttled down again and she sagged into the water, and her speed dropped as though she'd run into a wall. This was going to be a dicey business. At a pinch I could get the speed, provided the engines didn't blow up, but I didn't know if I could steer her straight enough to hit my target. In spite of the flow of cooling night air I found I was sweating profusely.

If the only way to get her to plane was to run the engines at full bore I'd better not try that again. There would be no more trial speed runs because I was scared of the engines packing up, and next time this boat would be at speed again would be the last time. As for the steering, I'd have to handle that as best I could.

I dropped speed even further and plugged on towards St Elmo's Point. Fort St Elmo reared up starkly against the night sky as I passed between the point and the breakwater. Now I was in the open sea and the boat wallowed sickeningly. That heavy steel bar slung three feet under the water was acting as a pendulum. This lubberly craft was enough to give any self-respecting boat designer the screaming meemies.

I rounded the point and turned into Marsamxett Harbour, glad to get into sheltered waters again, and headed towards Manoel Island. Valletta was now to my left and I wondered from where they shot their fireworks. I checked the time and found I had little to spare.

As I approached Manoel Island I closed the throttles until the engines were barely ticking over, just enough to give me steerage way. Not far away a light flickered and I saw that Alison was in position; she had struck a match and held it so that it illuminated her face. I steered in that direction and made contact.

She was in what seemed to be a small runabout driven by a little outboard motor. 'That's nice,' I said. 'Where did you get it?'

'I took your advice; I stole it,' she said, and laughed quietly. I grinned in the darkness. 'It's our duty to save government money,' I said virtuously.

'How did you get on?' she asked.

'She's a bitch,' I said. 'As cranky as the devil.'

'She was all right when I brought her from Sliema.'

'That was a different boat. She's damned near uncontrollable at speed. How much time have we got?'

'About ten minutes.'

I looked about. 'I'd better get in position. We don't want to stay here or we'll be run down by the Sliema ferry – she's coming now. Is *Artina* in the same place?'

'Yes.'

'Then I'll be on my way. I'll go right down Lazzaretto Creek and turn around so as to get a good run up. You keep clear on the other side of *Artina?'* I paused. 'The steering is so bloody bad I might even miss her on the first pass. In that case I'll turn around and have a go on the other side. Don't be in my way or you'll get run over.'

'Good luck again,' said Alison.

I said, 'If you see Wheeler give him a good clout with my compliments. He was looking forward to seeing his Chinese friend operate on me. If things work out I'll see you in Ta'Xbiex – at the same place as last night.'

Gently I eased the throttles forward and moved off. I passed *Artina* quite closely; there were three men on deck – Wheeler, the Skipper and the Chinese, Chang Pi-wu. I could see them quite clearly because they were illuminated, but I was low on the water in the dark and there was no chance of them recognizing me. I was just another ship passing in the night

Mentally I made a cross on the place on the hull I intended to hit, and then I carried on down Lazzaretto Creek. At the bottom, near the Manoel Island bridge I turned with idling engines. I switched on the air from the scuba bottle and checked the demand-valve, and then bit on the mouthpiece and put on the mask. If things went well I wouldn't have time to do any of that later.

Behind me traffic passed on the road and presently a procession came by with a band of pounding drums and off-key brass. I ignored it and looked across to Valletta and the forthcoming firework display. There was what I thought to be a heavier thump on a drum but it was a mortar banging off. A maroon burst over Valletta in a yellow sunburst and in the echoing reflection from the water of the harbour I saw *Artina* clearly for a brief moment. The fireworks had begun and it was time for me to add my share to the festivities.

I advanced the throttles and moved off slowly as a rocket soared up and exploded in a shower of red and green fiery rain. I steered with one hand and with the other liberally doused my cargo with petrol from an open can, hoping to God that the sparks from the fireworks were totally extinguished by the time they reached water level. It only needed one of those in the boat and I'd go up in a cloud of glory.

Then I pushed open the throttles wider and by the time I was making any kind of speed the sky was alive with lights as the Maltese spent their fireworks with reckless abandon. *Artina* was clearly silhouetted as, with equal abandon, I jammed the throttles wide open.

The engines roared and the boat reared up in the water almost uncontrollably as she began to plane. The wheel kicked in my hands as I strove to keep her on course and I zigzagged dangerously close to the line of yachts moored at the marina. I swung the wheel hard over but the bitch was late in responding and there was an outraged cry from the bow of one of the yachts. It sounded like the curry-voiced colonel who must have got the fright of his life as I scraped his paint at twenty knots.

Then I was past him and heading out into the harbour, bucking and twisting and steering a course which would have brought tears to the eyes of any self-respecting helmsman. The fireworks banged and flashed overhead striking dazzling reflections from the water and my heart jumped into my mouth as a small runabout came out of nowhere and cut across my bows. I cursed him and swung the wheel and missed him by a whisker. That made two damned fools at large in Marsamxett Harbour.

As I swung the wheel hard over the other way I looked for *Artina* and I saw that I was going to miss her by a sizeable margin. I cursed again at the thought of having to make another mad sortie. It occurred to me that with the steering being as crazy as it was then I'd better aim at anything but *Artina* and then I might have a chance of hitting her.

I estimated I was going to shoot under her stern but just then the hard-pressed port engine blew up and, with a nasty flailing rattle of a broken connecting rod, it expired. The boat checked a little in the water and her bow came over to aim directly at *Artina.* I hung on as she loomed over me and then, with a satisfying smash, my underwater ram struck her amidships.

I was thrown forward and bruised my ribs on the wheel but it saved me from going into the water. I still had one last thing to do. As I groped for my cigarette lighter I heard a shout on deck and I looked up into the eye-straining alternation of light and darkness and saw a movement as someone peered over the side to see what the hell had happened now. I couldn't see much of him but I must have been clearly visible as another batch of rockets went up.

I flicked the lighter and it sparked but there was no flame. In the rocket's red glare I saw that the boat's bow was smashed and broken with the impact against *Artina's* side. The ram must have been deeply embedded because she showed no sign of wanting to drift away.

Desperately I flicked the lighter again but again there was no flame. There was a bang from above and a bullet smashed into the instrument panel next to my elbow, ruining the rev counter. I leaned forward and put the lighter right next to a bunch of petrol-soaked fireworks. The boat was making water and I had to start a fire before she went under.

I flicked again and the whole damned lot went up in a brilliant sheet of flame. It was only because I was fully equipped in scuba gear that I wasn't instantly incinerated. It went up, as suddenly ignited petrol does, in a soft explosion – a great *whooof* of flame that blew me overboard. And as I went something hit me in the shoulder very hard.

Whether or not I was actually on fire for a moment I don't know. When I hit the water I was dazed, but the sudden shock brought a reflex into action and I struck for the depths. It was then I found that my right arm was totally useless. Not that it mattered very much; in scuba diving the flippered feet do most of the work. But it worried me because I didn't know what could be wrong with it.

I swam under water for a short while, then stopped because I didn't know where I was going. I was absolutely disoriented and, for all I knew, I could have been swimming out to sea. So I surfaced cautiously and looked around to get my bearings and to see what was happening to *Artina*.

I had not swum as far as I thought – she was about a hundred yards away, too close for comfort, especially in view of the little piece of hellfire that I had established amidships. My fireship was going great guns. With the ram stabbed into *Artina's* side like a narwhal's tusk she was securely fixed, and the fireworks were exploding like an artillery barrage, showering multi-coloured sparks and great gouts of flame which licked up her side. Already a canvas deck awning was on fire and men were running about the deck every which way.

A big maroon went off like a howitzer shell, sending out a burst of green flame and sparks which reached out to patter on the surface of the water about me, hissing viciously as they were extinguished. I was close enough to be seen if anyone had the time to look, so I sank beneath the surface again after a last glance around, and struck out for the shore.

I had not done a dozen strokes before I knew something was wrong. I felt curiously weak and light-headed and my right shoulder had developed a dull throb which was rapidly sharpening up into a stabbing pain. I eased off and felt my shoulder with my left hand and the pain jabbed me with such intensity that I nearly yelled aloud which is a good way of getting oneself drowned.

So I surfaced again and drifted, becoming more light-headed and feeling the strength ebbing from my legs more swiftly every minute. The fire by *Artina* was still going strong but it all seemed blurred as though seen through a rain-washed window. It was then I knew that I was probably going to die, that I no longer had the strength to swim to the shore which was so close, and that I was drifting out to sea where I would drown.

I think I passed out for a moment because the next thing I knew there was a light flashing in my eyes from very close and an urgent whisper, 'Owen; grab this!'

Something fell across my face and floated in the water next to my head and I put out my left hand and found a rope. 'Can you hold on?' I knew it was Alison.

An engine throbbed and the rope tightened and I was being drawn through the water. Desperately I concentrated all my attention on to holding on to that rope. Whatever strength I had left must be marshalled and pushed into the fingers of my left hand so that they would not relinquish their grip. The water lapped about my head, creating a miniature bow wave as I was towed behind Alison's boat and, even in that extremity, I paid tribute to the efficiency of Alison Smith and Mackintosh's training. She knew she could not haul an almost unconscious man into the boat without either capsizing or, worse, attracting attention.

It was a ridiculously short distance to the shore and Alison brought up at a slipway. She rammed the boat up it, careless of the consequences, and jumped overboard into two feet of water and hauled me out bodily. 'What's wrong, Owen?'

I flopped down and sat into the shallow water. 'I think I was shot,' I said carefully, and my voice seemed to come from miles away. 'In the shoulder – the right shoulder.'

The pain washed over me as her fingers probed, and then I heard the rip of cloth and she bandaged the wound roughly but effectively. I wouldn't have been surprised if she had operated there and then, using a penknife and a hairpin to extract the bullet. I was becoming used to her surprising range of talents.

I said tiredly, 'What's happening to *Artina!*'

She moved away and I saw *Artina* in the harbour beyond. All the sea was on fire about her and above the yellow flames rose the roiling cloud of greasy black smoke that could only come from oil. The ram had done its work. Even as I watched there was a red flash just under the wheelhouse and then the wheelhouse vanished as an oil tank exploded in her vitals and blasted through the deck. A deep boom came across the water, echoed and re-echoed from the cliff-like fortifications of Valletta.

'That's it, then,' I said abstractedly.

Alison leaned over me. 'Can you walk?'

'I don't know. I can try.'

She put her hand under my left arm. 'You've been leaking blood like a stuck pig. You need a hospital.'

I nodded. 'All right.' It didn't really matter now. The job had been done. Even if Slade or Wheeler had survived they were done for. I would be asked why I had destroyed *Artina* and I would tell the truth, and I would be listened to very carefully. People don't wander around blowing up millionaires' yachts for nothing and what I had to say would be heard. Whether it was believed or not would be another matter, but enough mud would stick to Wheeler to make sure that hard, professional eyes would be on him for ever more. As for Slade, I had escaped from prison with him and if I was on Malta and said that Slade was around then he would be picked up in jig time. It's a small island and strangers can't hide easily.

As for myself I didn't know what would happen. Alison might give evidence *in camera* as to my part in the affair, but if Mackintosh was dead I didn't know how much weight that would carry. There was a strong possibility that I would spend the rest of my life in the maximum security wing of Durham Gaol. Right at that moment I was past caring.

Alison helped me to my feet and I staggered like a drunken sailor up the slipway, hanging on to her arm with a flabby grip. We had just reached the top when I paused and stared at the man who was waiting. He looked remarkably like that tough, young copper, Sergeant Jervis, who had taken such a strong dislike to me because I had stolen some diamonds and had not the grace to tell him where they were.

I turned my head and looked in the other direction. Brunskill was there with Forbes just behind him. Already they were striding out and coming towards us.

I said to Alison, 'The end of the line, I think,' and turned to face Brunskill.

He stood in front of me and surveyed me with expressionless eyes, noting every detail of my disarray and the bandage on my shoulder. He flicked his eyes at Alison, and then nodded towards the harbour where *Artina* was going down in flames. 'Did you do that?'

'Me?' I shook my head. 'It must have been caused by a spark from the fireworks.'

He smiled grimly. 'I must caution you that anything you say may be taken down in writing and used in evidence.' He looked at Alison. 'That applies to you, too.'

'I don't think Malta is within your jurisdiction,' she said coolly.

'Not to worry about that,' said Brunskill. 'I have a platoon of the local constabulary on call.' He turned to me. 'If you had as many lives as a cat you'd spend them all inside. I'm going to wrap you up so tight this time that they'll have to build a prison just for you.'

I could see him mentally formulating the list of charges. Arson, murder, grievous bodily harm, carrying weapons – and worse – using them, driving a horse and cart through the Explosives Act. Maybe, with a bit of twisting, he could toss in piracy and setting fire to the Queen's shipyards. Those last two are still capital offences.

He said, 'What in hell did you think you were doing?' There was wonder in his voice.

I swayed on my feet. 'I'll tell you after I've seen a doctor.'

He caught me as I fell.

II

I woke up in the nick. It was the prison hospital, to be sure, but still inside thick walls, and they build walls thicker in Malta than anywhere else. But I had a private room and came to the conclusion that the local coppers didn't want the simple, uncomplicated Maltese criminals to be corrupted by contact with such a hard case as myself. This proved to be a wrong assumption.

An uncommunicative doctor performed a simple operation on my shoulder under local anaesthetic and then I lay waiting for the arrival of Brunskill and his inevitable questions. I spent the time thinking out ingenious lies to tell him; there are certain aspects of HM Government it is better for the ordinary copper not to know.

But it was a stranger and not Brunskill who was ushered into the room. He was a tall, middle-aged man with a smooth, unlined face and an air of quiet authority who introduced himself as Armitage. His credentials were impressive; I read a letter of introduction from the Prime Minister and pushed back the rest of the bumf unread.

He pulled up a chair to the bedside and sat down. 'Well, Mr Stannard; how are you feeling?'

I said, 'If you know my name is Stannard then you know most of the story. Did Alec Mackintosh send you?'

'I'm afraid not,' he said regretfully. 'Mackintosh is dead.'

I felt a cold lump settle in my stomach. 'So he never came out of hospital.'

'He died without recovering consciousness,' said Armitage.

I thought of Alison and wondered how she'd take it. The love-hate relationship she had with her father made it difficult to estimate her reaction. I said, 'Has Mrs Smith been told?'

Armitage nodded. 'She took it quite well.'

How would you know? I thought.

'This is all going to be difficult,' said Armitage. 'Your activities – particularly in the Irish Republic – could put the Government into an awkward position.' He paused. 'Should they be fully disclosed.'

I could imagine that they could. Relations were already strained over what was happening in Ulster and the Press would have a field day with garbled stories of a British agent on the rampage in the sovereign State of Ireland.

I said ironically, 'Not to mention my own awkward position.'

'Just so,' said Armitage.

We stared at each other. 'All right,' I said at last. 'Who blew the gaff? This operation had the tightest security of any I've been on. How did it fall apart?'

Armitage sighed. 'It fell apart *because* of the tight security. It fell apart because Mackintosh was constitutionally unable to trust anyone.' He held me with his eye. 'He didn't even trust you.'

I nodded, and Armitage snorted. 'He didn't even trust the Prime Minister. All through he played a lone hand and deceived everyone regarding his motives.'

I said quietly, 'I have a big stake in this. I think you'd better tell me the story.'

It all started with the spate of prison escapes which worried the people at the top. Mountbatten investigated the prison service and security was tightened, but the vague rumours of the Scarperers' organization kept the worries on the boil and Mackintosh was put in charge of doing something about it.

'I didn't like that,' said Armitage disapprovingly. 'And I said so at the time. It ought to have been left to the Special Branch.'

'Mackintosh told me they'd tried and failed,' I said.

Armitage nodded impatiently. 'I know – but they could have tried again. Mackintosh was too much the lone wolf – too secretive.'

I could see what stuck in Armitage's craw. He was a top-level civil servant – a Whitehall mandarin – and he liked things to go through channels in an orderly way. In particular, he didn't like the idea of the Prime Minister having a private hatchet man. It offended his sense of what was fitting.

He leaned forward. 'Unknown to anybody Mackintosh already had his eye on Wheeler but he kept his suspicions to himself. He didn't even tell the PM. We'll never know what went through his mind, but perhaps he thought he wouldn't be believed. Wheeler was coming up fast in popularity and influence; in fact, the Prime Minister was on the point of making him a Junior Minister in the Government.'

'Yes,' I said. 'I can see Alec's problem. How did he get on to Wheeler?'

Armitage shook his head. 'I don't know. I believe the Prime Minister reposed full confidence in Mackintosh regarding certain measures of top-level security.' He sounded even more disapproving.

So Mackintosh was running security checks on the élite. That was one answer to the question: *Quis custodiet ipsos custodes?* I could imagine the Prime Minister might expect Mackintosh to turn up some member of the radical Left or Right as a potential risk, but who would suspect a bourgeois capitalist who firmly trod the middle road of being a Maoist? The idea was laughable.

'So Mackintosh had unprovable suspicions,' I said. 'He didn't want them getting back to Wheeler so he kept his mouth shut until he could catch Wheeler in the act.'

'That must have been the size of it,' conceded Armitage. 'He brought you in and put you next to Slade by means of the diamond robbery.' A slight smile mitigated his severe expression. 'Most ingenious. But he didn't tell you about Wheeler.'

'I wouldn't expect him to,' I said flatly. 'At that stage I didn't need to know.' I rubbed my chin. 'But I'd expect him to tell Mrs Smith.'

'He didn't – but I'll come to that later.' Armitage leaned forward. 'When you and Slade escaped Mackintosh went to see Wheeler. We have established that he saw Wheeler at his club. They had a conversation in the course of which Mackintosh disclosed who you were. That's how . . . er . . . the gaff was blown.'

I blinked, then closed my eyes and lay back on the pillow. 'He did it deliberately?' I asked softly.

'Oh, yes. He wanted to stampede Wheeler into ill-advised action. He wanted to catch him *in flagrante delicto*. Apparently you were expendable.'

I opened my eyes and looked at Armitage. 'I always was. It's an occupational hazard.' All the same I thought that Alec Mackintosh was a ruthless son of a bitch.

'Wheeler was stampeded, all right, but I'm not sure that Wheeler's action was ill-advised,' said Armitage reflectively. 'Mackintosh was run down by a car the same day. We've impounded all Wheeler's cars for forensic examination and I'm pretty sure we'll turn up some evidence even at this late date. I think the job was done by his Irish chauffeur.'

'Or his Chinese cook.'

Armitage shrugged. 'So Mackintosh was unconscious in hospital. He was run down on his way to his office where Mrs Smith was awaiting him. Whether he was going to tell her what he'd done we'll never know. At all events, at this time no one in the Government knew about Wheeler. Do you see what I mean about the security of the operation being too tight?'

I said, 'A top-rank Whitehall man, such as yourself, doesn't turn up in Malta out of the blue so opportunely. Something must have come up.'

'It did. Mackintosh died. He'd taken out insurance. He wrote out a full account of his actions and posted them to his lawyer just before he saw Wheeler. The snag about that was that the sealed envelope was inscribed, "Only to be opened in the event of my death."'

Armitage stared at me. 'And Mackintosh was in the hands of the doctors. He wasn't dead, but you'd hardly call him alive although in the legal sense he was. He was a vegetable maintained by modern medical techniques and the doctors' duty by the Hippocratic Oath, and that was something he hadn't calculated for. That damned envelope was in the lawyer's hands for two weeks before Mackintosh died and by then it was nearly too late. It would have been too late were it not for your actions.'

'That's all very well,' I said. 'But how did that lead you to me? Mackintosh didn't know where I was.'

'We went straight for Wheeler,' said Armitage. 'We were just wondering how to tackle him when you took the problem out of our hands.' He smiled slightly. 'Your methods are direct, to say the least. It was thought that you might be around, so we brought along people who could recognize you.'

'Brunskill and company,' I said. 'So you've got Wheeler.'

He shook his head. 'No; Wheeler is dead, and so is Slade. You saw to that very effectively, if I may say so. The Special Branch is working on the ramifications of Wheeler's organizations – those that are legal and those that are not. I think it will be a lengthy task, but that is none of your concern.' He leaned back in his chair. 'However, you do present a problem to the Government, which is why I am here.'

I couldn't suppress the smile. 'I bet I am.'

'It's no laughing matter, Mr Stannard,' said Armitage severely. 'Already the Press has become alerted to the fact that there is something in the wind.' He stood up and wandered over to the window. 'Fortunately, the worst of your . . . er . . . crimes were committed outside the United Kingdom and to those we can turn a blind eye. But there is the matter of a diamond robbery which may well prove awkward to handle.'

I said, 'Were the diamond merchants paid out by their insurance company?'

Armitage turned and nodded. 'I should think so.'

'Well, why not leave it at that.'

He was affronted. 'Her Majesty's Government cannot connive in the cheating of an insurance company.'

'Why not?' I asked reasonably. 'Her Majesty's Government is conniving in the murder of Wheeler and Slade. What the hell's so sacred about a few thousand quid?'

That didn't sit well with him. Property rights come before human rights in British law. He harrumphed embarrassedly, and said, 'What is your suggestion?'

'Wheeler is dead and Slade is dead. Why shouldn't Rearden be dead, too? He can be killed while evading arrest – it shouldn't be too difficult to stage manage. But you'll have to gag Brunskill, Forbes and Jervis, and you can do that under the Official Secrets Act. Or you can throw the fear of God into them; I don't think any of that gang would relish being transferred to the Orkneys for the rest of his days.'

'And Mr Stannard comes to life again?' he queried.

'Precisely.'

'I suppose it could be arranged. And how do we explain the spectacular death of Wheeler?'

'It must have been those rockets they were shooting over the harbour,' I said. 'One of them must have gone out of whack and hit the ship. It was being repaired at the time – I'll bet there was some fuel open on deck. I think the

Maltese Government ought to be ticked off for not keeping proper control.'

'Very ingenious,' said Armitage, and took out a notebook. 'I'll suggest that the Navy offer a ship and a diver to help lift the wreck. We'll choose the diver, of course.' He made a note with a silver pen.

'You'd better,' I said, thinking of that ram which was probably still embedded in *Artina's* side. 'A sad end to a popular MP. Most regrettable.'

Armitage's lips twitched and he put away the notebook. 'The organization for which you worked before Mackintosh pulled you out of South Africa apparently thinks highly of you. I am asked to inform you that someone called Lucy will be getting in touch.'

I nodded. How Mackintosh would have sneered at that.

'And the Prime Minister has asked me to pass on his sincere thanks for the part you have played in the affair and for the way you have brought it to a conclusion. He regrets that thanks are all he has to offer under the circumstances.'

'Oh, well; you can't eat medals,' I said philosophically,

III

I sat in the lounge of the Hotel Phoenicia waiting for Alison. She had been whisked to England by the powers-that-be in order to attend Alec's funeral. I would have liked to have paid my respects, too, but my face had been splashed in the pages of the British newspapers with the name of Rearden underneath and it was considered unwise for me to put in an appearance until Rearden had been forgotten in the short-lived public memory. Meanwhile I was growing a beard.

I was deriving much amusement from an intensive reading of an air mail edition of *The Times*. There was an obituary of Wheeler which should put him well on the road to canonization; his public-spiritedness was praised, his financial acumen lauded and his well-known charitableness eulogized. The first leader said that in view of Wheeler's work for the prisons his death was a blow to enlightened penology unequalled since the Mountbatten Report. I choked over that one.

The Prime Minister, in a speech to the Commons, said that British politics would be so much the worse for the loss of such a valued colleague. The Commons rose and stood in silence for two minutes. That man ought to have had his mouth washed out with soap.

Only the Financial Editor of *The Times* caught a whiff of something rotten. Commenting on the fall of share prices in the companies of Wheeler's empire he worried at the question of why it was thought necessary for the auditors to move in before Wheeler's body was cold. Apart from that quibble Wheeler had a rousing send-off on his journey to hell.

Rearden came off worse. Condemned as a vicious desperado, his death in a gun battle was hailed as a salutary lesson to others of his kidney. Brunskill was commended for his perseverance on the trail of the villainous Rearden and for his fortitude in the face of almost certain death. 'It was nothing,' said Brunskill modestly. 'I was only doing my duty as a police officer.'

It was hoped that Slade would soon be caught. There were full security wraps on Slade's death and I had no doubt that in another ten or twenty years any number of criminologically inclined writers would make a fair living churning out books about the Slade Mystery.

I looked up to see Alison coming into the lounge. She looked pale and tired but she smiled when she saw me. I rose to my feet as she approached and she stopped for a moment to survey me, taking in the cast on my arm and the unshaven stubble on my cheeks. 'You look awful,' she said.

'I'm not feeling too bad; I can still bend my left elbow. What will you have?'

'A Campari.' She sat down and I whistled up a waiter. 'I see you've been reading all about it.'

I grinned. 'Don't believe everything you read in the papers.'

She leaned back in the chair. 'Well, Owen; it's over. It's all over.'

'Yes,' I said. 'I'm sorry about Alec.'

'Are you?' she asked in a flat voice. 'He nearly got you killed.'

I shrugged. 'He miscalculated the speed and direction of Wheeler's reaction. But for that it was a good ploy.'

'Even though he was selling you out?' Her tone was incredulous.

'God damn it!' I said. 'We weren't playing pat-a-cake. The stakes were too great. Wheeler *had* to be nailed down and if the way to do it was to sacrifice a man in the field then there was no choice. Wheeler was striking at the heart of the State. The Prime Minister was considering him for a ministerial position, and God knows where he could have gone on from there.'

'If all statesmen are like Alec then God help Britain,' said Alison in a low voice.

'Don't be bitter,' I said. 'He's dead. He killed himself, not me. Never forget that.'

The waiter came with the drinks and we were silent until he had gone, then Alison said, 'What are you going to do now?'

I said, 'I had a visit from Lucy. Of course I can't do much until the shoulder heals – say a month to six weeks.'

'Are you going back to South Africa?'

I shook my head. 'I think I'm being considered for the active list.' I sipped my drink. 'What about you?'

'I haven't had time to think yet. There was a lot to do in London apart from the funeral. Alec's personal affairs had to be wound up; I spent a lot of time with his solicitor.'

I leaned forward. 'Alison, will you marry me?'

Her hand jerked so that she spilled a few drops of red Campari on to the table. She looked at me a little oddly, as though I were a stranger, then said, 'Oh, no, Owen.'

I said, 'I love you very much.'

'And I think I love you.' Her lower lip trembled.

'Then what's the matter? We're very well suited.'

'I'll tell you,' she said. 'You're another Alec. In twenty years – if you survive – you'll be sitting in a little, obscure office pulling strings and making men jump around, just like Alec. You won't be doing it because you like it but because you think it's your duty. And you'll hate the job and you'll hate yourself – just as Alec did. But you'll go on doing it.'

I said, 'Someone has to do it.'

'But not the man I marry,' said Alison. 'I told you once that I was like a Venus Fly Trap. I want to be a cabbage of a housewife, living, perhaps on the green outskirts of an English country town, all tweedy and *Country Life*.'

'There's no reason why you shouldn't have that, too,' I said.

'And stay behind and be alone when you went on a job?' She shook her head. 'It wouldn't work, Owen.'

I felt a sudden resentment, and said abruptly, 'Then why did you come back here – to Malta?'

A look of consternation crossed her face. 'Oh, Owen; I'm sorry. You thought . . .'

'You didn't say goodbye and Armitage told me you'd be coming back after the funeral. What was I supposed to think?'

'I was flown to England in an RAF transport,' she said quietly. 'I've come back to pick up my plane . . . and to say goodbye.'

'To say goodbye – just like that?'

'No,' she flared. 'Not just like that.' Her eyes filled with tears. 'Owen, it's all going wrong.'

I took her hand in mine. 'Have you ever been to Morocco?'

She looked at me warily, taken wrong-footed by the sudden change of subject. 'Yes; I know it quite well.'

'Could that aircraft of yours fly to Tangier from here?'

'It *could,*' she said uncertainly. 'But . . .'

'I need a holiday,' I said. 'And I have a year and a half of back pay which I need help in spending. I'm sure you'd make an efficient guide to Morocco. I need one – I've never been there.'

'You're trying the blarney again,' she said, and there was laughter in her voice. 'Maeve O'Sullivan warned me about that.'

Maeve had also told me that I wasn't the man for Alison Smith. She could be right, but I had to try.

'No strings and no promises,' said Alison.

I smiled. Six weeks together was all the promise I needed. A lot could happen in six weeks.

A MATTER OF MONTHS

I

Mrs Matthews entered John Franklin's study and said, 'Mr Richard is here to see you.'

Franklin raised his eyes from the papers on the desk. 'Good! I've been expecting him. Ask him to come in here, will you?'

Mrs Matthews nodded and, as she turned away, Franklin asked, 'Going to your whist drive this evening?'

'Yes, sir.'

Franklin's eyes twinkled. 'You're a compulsive gambler, Mrs M. I don't know what you'd do if you were turned loose in Monte Carlo. You'd probably break the bank and I'd lose a good housekeeper.'

'No fear of that,' said Mrs Matthews. 'My sister, Mary, is always on at me about going to Majorca with her and Jim, but I've always refused. I don't like foreign parts.' She sniffed. 'Not that I'm likely to be asked this year, am I? I'll send Mr Richard in.'

'Have a good game,' said Franklin. 'And don't win too much from the vicar. His stipend won't stand it.' As the door closed he gazed at it blankly for a moment and the laughter wrinkles around his eyes changed fractionally, rearranging into a pattern of weariness before he dropped his head to look again at the papers, those damned pages covered with columns of damned figures, the most important of which were in red.

The door opened again and he said without looking up, 'Good evening, Jason.' At the sound of an ill-suppressed snort he raised his head to regard his nephew. 'Sorry; I know you prefer to be called Richard. I tend to forget.'

Richard Denham dropped into the armchair near the fire. 'Why my mother saddled me with such a damnfool name I've never found out,' he said somewhat querulously.

'My sister was a romantic and had an odd belief in the magical properties of names. She wanted her little boy to grow up and bring back the Golden Fleece.' Franklin's lips quirked sardonically. 'Well, you've not done too badly in that direction if what I read in the City pages is true. Started on your second million yet?'

'Don't believe everything you read,' said Denham. 'This bloody depression isn't helping any of us.'

Franklin nodded and glanced at the balance sheet before him. 'True. If it wasn't for your timely offer of last year I don't know . . .' He broke off abruptly and gathered the papers together then put them in the desk drawer.

'Uncle, that's what I've come about.' Denham hesitated, then said rapidly, 'I want the money back.'

'I see.' Franklin's forehead creased in a puzzled frown because he did not see at all. 'But you said that repayment in three years would be . . .'

'What I said last year and what I'm saying now are two different things. Circumstances have changed since then – and for the worse.'

'But not for you, surely? Thirty thousand to you is small change.'

'I told you not to believe everything you read in the papers. I need every penny I can lay my hands on.'

Franklin took a deep breath. 'I'm sorry, Richard.' He spread his hands. 'I'd help you if I could but I can't. I don't have that kind of money.'

Denham stood up and said in a hard voice. 'Then you'll have to get it, won't you?'

'For God's sake, Richard!' Franklin opened the drawer and took out the balance sheet which he tossed on to the desk. 'Take a look at that. In this state of the economy I'm damned lucky to keep the business afloat at all. If it wasn't for your loan we'd have sunk already.'

'I don't care about your piddling little business; I have bigger things to look after – much bigger. I want my money.'

'And I don't think you'll get it,' said Franklin sharply. 'I have a document signed by both of us which sets out the terms and it calls for payment of the principal three years from the date of signature.'

'Oh, yes.' said Denham. 'I remember all about that document. You were bloody insistent on it, weren't you? I wondered why at the time. Now I know.'

Franklin said stiffly, 'You know very well why I insisted on it. Business transactions between relatives should follow normal business practice, otherwise ill feeling could result.'

'Jesus!' exploded Denham. 'What the hell do you think is happening here and now?'

Franklin sighed. 'Richard, if I had the money you could have it tomorrow, but I don't have that much liquidity.' He pushed the balance sheet forward. 'See for yourself.'

Denham ignored it. Instead he looked around the study with its warm Jacobean linenfold panelling. 'You could sell this place for fifty thousand.'

'Sell my house!?' Franklin was affronted. 'I'll do no such thing.' He was silent for a while, then he said quietly, 'Sit down, Richard, and tell me about the trouble you're in.'

Denham did not sit down, but he did begin to talk, pacing jerkily up and down the room. 'I was in a deal with that shark, Everhart; the biggest thing I've handled yet. If it comes off I'll make three million at a minimum. I pulled a bluff on Everhart – and he called it. As a result I have to find half a million sharpish and I'm scraping the bottom of the barrel.'

'What about the banks?'

'They'll lend me a maximum of a quarter of a million and I can raise another hundred and fifty thousand myself. That leaves me a hundred thousand short. I need that thirty thousand of mine which you've got.'

'You don't *need* it,' said Franklin. 'You just suggested I sell this house. Why don't you sell your own? That's worth a hundred thousand if a penny. And you have a Rolls-Royce which would bring fifteen thousand, not to mention a string of race horses.'

'Good God, I couldn't do that! If it got about that I was selling my personal property I'd really be in trouble. You don't understand big business, uncle.'

'Evidently not,' said Franklin drily. He did not think much of his nephew. To 'pull a bluff' on Everhart was evidently a euphemism for cheating, and Everhart had not fallen for it; and the much prized house and car and race horses were part of the façade, the false front Denham used instead of firm financial foundations. 'How much time do you have?'

Denham shrugged. 'Not much. Perhaps three months at the most. Everhart may even prolong it a bit and watch me squirm. He's like that – a sadistic bastard.'

'And lawyers are very good at stretching things out,' said Franklin contemplatively. 'Do you think it could run to as much as six months?'

'What difference would it make?' said Denham savagely. 'I'd still be on the hook.'

'A lot can happen in six months.' Franklin pulled the balance sheet towards him. 'For instance, I could possibly raise your thirty thousand.'

'You could?'

'It'll leave me an inch this side of bankruptcy but it might be done. It will need some close figuring.' He raised his head. 'I suggest you let me get on with it, Richard. And I suggest you moderate your life style for the next few months. Sell your car; if you need to put on a front you can always hire one for the occasion. And sell a couple of horses – those that will bring a good price. No one will notice the sale of a couple of horses.'

Denham seemed suddenly subdued. 'Yes, uncle; that's a good idea.' He looked at his watch. 'I'll have to hurry if I'm to catch the 7:45 back to town.'

'You didn't come by car?'

'It's in for servicing. Well, goodbye. I didn't mean to quarrel, you know. It's just that I'm screwed up tight. The fact is that if I don't come up with the cash I'll be hammered right into the ground. I'll lose the lot.'

'I'll do my best,' said Franklin quietly. He watched Denham leave the room and heard the murmur of voices just outside the door, then Mrs Matthews' head popped into sight.

'I'm going now, sir. There's some milk on the stove ready for warming if you want it, but please don't leave the lid off this time. That cat is too fat already.'

'I'll remember,' said Franklin, and returned to the balance sheet. The lines on his face were deeper cut as he went yet again through the figures.

The front door slammed.

II

Mrs Matthews was a sensible and level-headed woman. She screamed once in shock but thereafter behaved with commendable good sense. She closed the study door and locked it, took an indeterminate time for tears and restorative brandy, then telephoned the police. After that cried a little more, tidied up the kitchen and made a pot of tea, and was sitting there when the police arrived. Twenty minutes later the house was crawling with them.

Detective Inspector Howell said, 'You found the body, left it undisturbed and notified the police; is that it?'

'Yes,' said Mrs Matthews.

'And you didn't touch anything in the study at all?'

'Just the key. I had to take that from the inside of the door to lock it from the outside.'

Howell nodded. 'You did very well, Mrs Matthews,' he said warmly. 'Now, when did you last see Mr Franklin alive?'

'It would be nearly half-past-seven, just before I went to the whist drive.' Her eyes filled as she gestured to the stove. 'I told him there was milk ready to be warmed.'

Howell stepped over to the stove and, using a ballpoint pen, he put it through the handle of the lid and delicately lifted. 'Did he have any of the milk?'

Mrs Matthews looked into the pan. 'No.'

As he replaced the lid Howell asked, 'Did Mr Franklin have any visitors today?'

'Mr Richard came this evening. He's Mr Franklin's nephew.'

'Richard? Is that his surname?'

'Oh, no; he's Richard Denham.'

The sergeant standing behind Howell uttered a strangled cough. Howell said without turning, 'Well, what is it, sergeant?'

'Would that be Richard Denham, the financier? You know, the whiz-kid wheeler-dealer.'

Howell winced at the sergeant's choice of expression. He turned his head. 'You've been seeing too many American films, Parker.' He returned his gaze to Mrs Matthews. 'Well, is he?'

'I suppose he is,' said Mrs Matthews. 'I know he gets his name in the papers a lot. Not that I see it there myself; I don't read those money pages.'

'When was he here?'

'He came just before I left for the whist drive.'

'And you left him here with Mr Franklin?'

'Oh, no; sir. We left together. He didn't stay long. We walked into the town together.'

'Where was he going?'

'To catch a train to London. He was a bit early – he bought me a sherry in the Station Hotel.'

'What did you talk about?'

Mrs Matthews looked surprised. 'Nothing much. I asked why he hadn't come by car as usual; he has a big car with a chauffeur. He said it was being serviced. He asked if I thought his uncle was unwell; he said he thought Mr Franklin was under a strain. I said I hadn't noticed anything like that; not beyond the ordinary. He asked after my sister and her husband. It was just small talk.'

'And what was the last you saw of him?'

'When the train was leaving. He waved to me out of the window.'

Howell was interested. 'You actually saw him leave on the train? And the train was moving?'

'That's right. When we left the hotel he asked me to walk with him into the station – that's when he asked about his uncle's health. He left me to go on the platform when the train came in. I was about to leave when Meg Anderson, a friend of mine, came up to me and began chatting. She'd just got off the train. We talked for a few minutes and it was during that time that the train left. Mr Richard waved to me and I waved back.' Mrs Matthews paused. 'Proper old gossip is that Meg Anderson. I couldn't get away. I was late for the whist drive,' she said resentfully.

'You make a very good witness, Mrs Matthews,' said Howell. 'One more thing. What was Mr Denham wearing?'

'A dark suit with a white shirt and blue tie. And he had a checked overcoat – a Burberry, I think.'

'Thank you. Now I want you to go through the house to see if anything is missing and to report anything you find – or don't find – to the constable who'll be with you. Later I'd like you to do the same in the study.'

Howell jerked his head at the sergeant and they left the kitchen. In the hall he said conversationally, 'How's your garden, Parker?'

'Terrible,' said Parker in an unsurprised voice. He had worked with Howell before and was becoming acquainted with the inspector's quirks of thought. 'It's burnt to a crisp – very brown at the edges. We could do with some rain.'

'Yes, it has all the promise of being a long, hot, dry summer. So what was Denham doing with an overcoat? Check with the railway police; I want to know where Denham got off that train. I think you'll find he was travelling first-class; that should help. Now tell me about Franklin.'

Parker drew in his breath. 'John Henry Franklin, age about sixty-five; a widower – his wife died five years ago. Ran a small engineering firm – toolmakers making specialist jigs and fixtures for the car industry, mostly expensive one-off stuff. Highly thought of in the trade and the local community.'

'Any financial trouble?'

'Not known, sir. We'll know more tomorrow when we get on to the bank and his lawyer.'

'All right; start your enquiries and join me in the study.'

III

The study seemed overcrowded with large purposeful men. As Howell opened the door the intolerable brightness of an electronic flash smote his eyes leaving a strong after image. Three men were busy with insufflators and fine powder, seeking fingerprints; another man was chalking a small square on the wall behind the desk. Dr Mansell, the police surgeon, was bending over the body but straightened as Howell approached.

'Evening, doctor; what's the verdict?'

'He's dead. As far as I'm concerned he can be removed to the mortuary.'

'Not so fast.' Howell studied the body which sat in the chair, the upper part of the torso slumped over the desk. The back of the head was indescribable. 'What's your analysis?'

'He was shot. The bullet entered the middle of the forehead and passed straight through leaving the usual large hole on exit.'

'Range?'

Mansell shrugged. 'Not more than the width of the room – that's obvious – but I'd say much closer. Say, about six feet.'

'Then it's not suicide,' said Howell grimly.

'That it's not. There's no gun here.'

'Where's the bullet?'

Mansell indicated the police officer at the wall behind the desk. 'Detective Constable Ames has just found it in the wall.'

Howell went around the desk to where Ames was standing. 'How deep is it?'

'Not very, sir. Just embedded in the plaster.'

Howell regarded the small hole and the slimy bits of grey matter around it. 'Don't dig it out with your penknife, Ames. Take out a whole section of plaster, leaving the bullet in it, and send it to the forensic laboratory. But have it photographed first and measure its position to a fare-thee-well.'

He turned and approached the body from the rear. Franklin was lying with his left arm outflung across the desk and his right arm doubled under his chest. 'Time of death, doctor?'

'Anything from four this afternoon to an hour ago. I'll be able to narrow it down after the necropsy. I'll need to know when he ate last and what he ate.'

'We'll get that from the housekeeper.'

'And the sooner I can do the necropsy the more accurate I'll be,' said Mansell. 'The digestive process doesn't stop on death, you know.'

'I'll be as quick as I can.' Howell took the sleeve of Franklin's shirt betwixt thumb and forefinger and slowly lifted the left arm. He slid out the folded sheet of paper from beneath it and let the arm drop again. Presently he said, 'Know anything about balance sheets and profit and loss accounts, doctor?'

'Not much. I didn't train as an accountant.'

'Neither did I; but the amount of red ink on this one doesn't look too healthy.' Howell looked up as Parker entered the room. 'Take this, Parker; put it in a plastic envelope. All right, doctor; you can take the body now.'

Mansell nodded to the ambulance man who stood by the door, and the man went out to return with his mate and a stretcher. As Mansell carefully eased the torso to an upright position Howell said sharply, 'Hold it!' His finger stabbed out and pointed at the desk. 'What's that?'

Franklin's right hand, which had been concealed, held a fountain pen, the point of which was driven through a sheet of paper. Howell bent forward and read:

JASON D

From the terminal 'D' a line was scrawled to the right ending in a jagged tear in the paper where the pen nib had been driven with such force that it had penetrated into the wooden desk top.

'Now who the hell is Jason?' said Howell.

Parker looked up from the balance sheet he had been reading. 'I know, sir,' he said diffidently.

'Do you? Well, are you going to keep it to yourself?'

'It's Denham, sir. His full name is Jason Richard Denham.'

'You're a mine of information about our financial wizard, Parker.'

'I keep a keen eye on the financial pages, sir,' said Parker smugly. He paused, and added, 'Protecting my investments.' Tapping the balance sheet he proceeded further. 'I'm glad I don't have money invested in Franklin's firm. This doesn't read at all well.'

Howell studied him in silence for a moment. 'You can tell me about that later.' He turned to Mansell. 'What do you make of it?'

Mansell gestured to the ambulance man to hold the body upright, then stepped around the desk. He stood about six feet away and pointed his forefinger at Franklin, sighting it like the barrel of a gun.

'Bang!' said Parker, but *sotto voce*.

Mansell went forward and bent over the desk, looking at the paper and the fountain pen, held firmly in the death grip. 'As I reconstruct it, Franklin was sitting there when the bullet hit him. The impact would throw his head back, but not all that much because the bullet would be in and out again very quickly. That's when he made that involuntary scrawl going off to the right. As the bullet progressed through the brain there'd be an intense nervous spasm, and that's when he drove the point of the pen through the paper and into the wood. The upper half of his body then collapsed forward, covering the pen and paper.'

'He was shot from the front from a distance of six feet,' mused Howell. 'That argues it was someone well known to him.'

Mansell kept his mouth firmly shut.

'And when he was shot he was writing what is on that paper?'

At the direct question Mansell nodded a little reluctantly. He could see that he would have to give court evidence on this point. 'I would say so. Yes.'

'And he was writing the name of his murderer?'

Mansell shook his head and smiled. 'That is not within my professional competence to answer,' he said thankfully.

Headlights flared at the French window as a car came up the drive. Parker said, 'That'll be Superintendent Whitlow, sir.'

'No doubt,' said Howell sourly. 'The brass always arrives late.'

But that last observation he said to himself out of a regard for the morale and discipline of the force.

IV

At 11:30 next morning there was a conference in Whitlow's office. 'So Franklin was writing Denham's name at the very moment of the murder!' said Whitlow unbelievingly.

'That's the medical evidence,' said Howell.

'Seems too good to be true.'

Chief Inspector Hammond stirred. 'I think it is. Denham was seen on to the train by Mrs Matthews and we know he got off that same train in London. We know that nearly for certain.'

Howell said, 'Funny he had that fainting fit at the London terminus.'

'Maybe,' said Hammond. 'But he gave a cheque to the St John's Ambulance Unit as soon as he recovered; said it was only fair. I've asked the Metropolitan Police to authenticate it.'

'Where did he go from there?' asked Whitlow.

'According to the Railway Police he took a taxi to his flat. The Met are looking into that, too.'

Whitlow stared at Howell. 'And what do you think they'll find?'

Howell sighed. 'The cheque will be authentic and he did go to his flat,' he said glumly.

'Well, then; he couldn't be here killing Franklin, could he?'

'Not on the evidence, sir.'

'But you have doubts, Inspector?' said Hammond quietly.

'It's as though he *wanted* to be noticed when he got back to town.' Howell seemed to be arguing with himself. 'I have a report on Franklin. His business was in a bad way; he owed Denham thirty thousand pounds. Denham is next-of-kin according to Franklin's will.'

Whitlow snorted. 'Thirty thousand!' he said derisively. 'From what I hear of Denham anything under half a million is small change. You're not suggesting he killed Franklin to get his own money back?'

'I'm not suggesting anything, sir,' said Howell colourlessly. 'I'm just putting facts together.' He glanced at Hammond. 'I'd like permission to carry on with the case.'

Whitlow frowned. 'A murder case involving a man like Denham is rich meat for a mere inspector,' he observed.

'I have complete confidence in Inspector Howell,' said Hammond. 'I think he's done very well so far.'

Howell waited for Whitlow's answer which was a long time coming, but he was relieved when Whitlow said, 'All right. You'll be in liaison with the Met for the interview, I suppose.'

Howell shook his head. 'Denham will be here at midday. I'd much prefer to interview him on my own patch instead of in his London office.'

'Using psychology, are you?' said Whitlow sardonically. 'Don't let it get out of hand. We need hard evidence for the court, not a lot of psychological froth,'

'Yes, sir. And I'd like to keep Sergeant Parker on the case. He's clued up on City affairs, and he read Franklin's balance sheet like I read my morning newspaper. He also collated all the stuff we got from the bank and Franklin's lawyer.'

'A budding tycoon, eh!' said Whitlow genially. 'All right. But you don't *do* anything without referring back to me. Understood?'

'Yes, sir.'

V

'So we've still got it,' said Parker with satisfaction. 'If we crack this one it won't do our promotion prospects one little bit of harm.'

'Yes, we've got it,' said Howell sourly. 'But with the Super breathing down my neck. When Denham comes . . .'

'He's here, sir; in your office.'

Howell grunted. 'Not alone, I hope. Right; I'll see him. You get on to the Met and see what's come up.'

Denham was younger than Howell expected; somehow he associated great wealth with age, and the idea that so young a man should deal in millions obscurely offended him. Nothing of that appeared in his voice as he sat behind his desk, nodded to the shorthand writer in the corner, and said, 'Sorry to have kept you, sir; but we've been busy. May I offer my condolences on your uncle's death?'

'Thank you,' said Denham softly.

'And I'm sorry to hear you were taken ill last night.'

'You got on to that pretty fast,' said Denham in a surprised voice.

Howell ignored that and opened a folder. 'I understand you were the last to see your uncle alive.'

'Not at all,' said Denham smoothly. 'Mrs Matthews spoke to him in the study after I left the room. Something about milk.' He paused. 'And then there was the murderer, of course.'

'Of course. Why did you see your uncle last night? What did you talk about?'

'Mostly financial matters. My uncle had asked to see me to discuss the repayment of some money he owed me.'

Howell turned over a paper. 'Yes, thirty thousand pounds, wasn't it? To be repaid in about two years from now. Why would he want to jump the gun on the repayment?'

Denham shrugged. 'I don't know. He'd pay less interest, of course.'

'But you lent the money at a *nominal* rate of interest. If he had thirty thousand spare it would pay him better to put it in a deposit account, accept bank interest for the next two years, and pocket the difference.'

'It was a family matter, Inspector. My uncle was old-fashioned in many respects and believed in paying his debts – especially to the family. In fact, from something he said, I believe it was *because* the interest was nominal that he wanted to repay the loan as quickly as possible. He had high standards of probity and fair play.'

'And where was he getting this thirty thousand? Have you any idea?'

'I really don't know. Perhaps the business. . .'

'The business was nearly broke,' said Howell flatly.

Denham said acidly, 'I was about to say before you interrupted that perhaps the business was being wound up. He did talk about that, and about the chance of selling out. He was talking in terms of repaying the debt in six months.'

'Not immediately?'

Denham shook his head. 'There was no question of that. It didn't worry me, of course; the repayment of so small a sum was of no consequence.'

Behind Denham the door opened and Parker appeared. He jerked his head at Howell who stood up. 'Excuse me for a moment, sir,' he said, and left the room. Denham leaned back in his chair, lit a cigarette, and smiled at the shorthand writer.

'A message from the Met,' said Parker. 'The cheque he signed holds up, sir; and he *did* go back to his flat in the taxi. His man says he didn't go out and went to bed at midnight.' He shook his head. 'That's after we saw the body.'

'Damn!' said Howell energetically. 'Anything else?'

'Yes, his Rolls-Royce was in for its normal service. What's he like, sir?'

'I think he's telling me a pack of lies. I can smell it on him. You can't be a jack as long as I have without developing a nose for it. But he's a bloody smooth article.'

'He has to be that in his job,' commented Parker. 'I've been using my own nose, sir; asking questions of a couple of stockbrokers I know. Seems there's a fishy smell in the City concerning a property deal going on between Denham and a chap called Everhart. Denham and Everhart were pretty chummy until recently but now there's a noticeable coolness, and the City boys don't like it. They think there's something funny going on.'

'Such as?'

'Nothing to put a finger on, sir; but the City operates on rumours.' Parker grinned. 'Did you ever hear the crack that the Stock Exchange is the only barometer that creates its own weather?' He sobered under Howell's glare. 'Have you tackled him about why Franklin was writing his name when he was shot?'

'No,' said Howell. 'But I bloody well will. Come on; you can sit in.'

As Howell sat again at his desk he said, 'Sorry about that, sir. This is Sergeant Parker. There's not much more to discuss, so we won't keep you long.' He bent his head to the folder. 'Mrs Matthews says you wore an overcoat last night, sir.'

Denham appeared mildly surprised. 'Yes, I did.'

'Strange for such a warm evening.'

'Oh, Inspector; we City men are ultra-careful,' said Denham, laughing. 'You must have heard the jokes about our rolled umbrellas.'

'Mrs Matthews says it was a checked coat. Perhaps it was something like mine, hanging there behind the door.'

Denham turned. 'Yes, it's something like that – but the check is not as pronounced.'

'That's a Burberry,' said Howell conversationally. 'My wife gave it to me for Christmas two years ago. No hat?'

'No hat, Inspector. But I don't see . . .'

'You do know your uncle was shot to death?'

'That's what I've been told.'

'But do you know that when he was shot he was in the very act of writing your name?'

Denham sat very still and was suddenly pale. 'No, I didn't know that. I don't believe it. Could I see . . .'

'No, sir; you can't see it. But I'll show you a photocopy of it.' He took a sheet of paper from the folder and laid it before Denham. 'The dark marks at the top are splashes of blood, but *this* is the matter of interest.' He laid his finger on the line of lettering:

JASON D

Howell observed Denham keenly and noted the fine film of sweat on his face. He said, 'He might have been writing, "Jason Denham", or possibly "Jason did it", or something of that nature.'

'An unwarranted and foul accusation, Inspector. I shall see that this goes right up to the Chief Constable.'

'That's your privilege, sir,' said Howell, unmoved. 'But I would be interested in your explanation.'

'I wasn't aware I had to give an explanation. I am not responsible for what my uncle wrote at any time. Of course, there *is* an explanation – which any fool ought to see.'

'Indeed, sir,' said Howell blandly. 'I'd be very interested to hear it.'

Denham sighed. 'I told you that my uncle was discussing the payment of his debt, and that he expected to pay it off in six months. I expect that when I left he began to do some figuring as to how this should be done. We are now in the middle of June, Inspector. What more natural that my uncle should want to put his thoughts on to paper in an orderly manner. In fact, he was going about it in the way I would have myself.'

'Which is?' Howell was expressionless.

'I would have listed the months and then calculated how much I could raise in each month.' Denham tapped the paper before him. 'These letters are the initial letters of the next six months – July, August, September, October, November and December.'

Howell felt a sudden hollow feeling in the pit of his stomach. He glanced at Parker who refused to meet his eye, and then back at Denham. Very softly he said, 'I told you it wouldn't take long, sir. I think that will be all for now.'

'I should think so,' said Denham coldly. 'I must say I don't appreciate being practically accused of murder. I assure you this will not stop here. May I leave now?'

'Of course, sir. Parker – the door.'

As Parker closed the door behind Denham he said, 'As you said, sir; a very smooth article.'

Howell blew out his cheeks expressively and picked up the photocopy. 'What do you think?'

'I think the defending counsel will have a field day if this thing gets as far as court.'

'I agree with you.' Howell studied the lettering. 'Do you believe all that bull about the months?'

'It sounds reasonable,' said Parker reasonably.

'Oh, he weaselled out of it very nicely – he's a fast thinker – but he's lying like a flatfish.' Howell tossed the paper on to the desk. 'Take a look at that. If you were going to make a listing under months would you put them so close together? Where's the room for any figures to squeeze in?'

'Um!' said Parker, laying his finger down. 'And why the extra big gap between the "N" and the "D"?' He shook his head. 'All very nice, sir; but not what you'd call hard evidence.'

'Then we'll get some hard evidence.'

Parker hesitated. 'You seem very sure he did it, sir. I mean, we wouldn't want to . . . er . . . to . . .'

Howell smiled grimly. 'Manufacture evidence? You know better than that, Parker. Yes, I'm sure he did it. I was watching him carefully and he came out in a muck sweat.' He jabbed a straight forefinger at Parker. 'But no one can commit a murder without leaving evidence somewhere, and we are going to find it.'

'Where, sir?'

'You can start off by handing me my coat.' Parker raised his eyebrows but obediently took the coat from the hook. As he came forward holding it Howell waggled his hand. 'No – look at it. Tell me what you think.'

After a brief inspection Parker said appreciatively, 'Nice coat.'

'Damn it, *what else?'*

The light dawned. 'It's reversible!'

'Precisely. Waterproof on one side – tweed on the other.' Howell scrabbled in his drawer. 'Now let's look at the railway timetable.' He flicked pages then settled down to a concentrated study. After a few minutes he looked up. 'The 7:45 is the slow train; it stops at every bloody station and siding between here and London. If Denham had waited ten minutes and caught the 7:55 he'd have been in London nearly half an hour earlier. Now why wouldn't he wait that ten minutes to catch the fast train?'

'You mean that's how he established his alibi?'

Howell tented his fingers. 'He made sure that Mrs Matthews saw him on to the train here. One, two or, possibly, three stations down the line he gets off, first having reversed the coat. My bet is he'd also have a hat – one of those natty gents' flat caps which could be rolled up and put in his pocket. Also he might have had a pair of horn-rimmed glasses or even a false moustache; anything to change his appearance. He has a car handy, drives back here and shoots Franklin, knowing that Mrs Matthews is out, then drives to a station near London and picks up the slow train again. He arrives in London and fakes his fainting fit to draw attention to himself and to establish his alibi.'

'That lot will take some proving,' said Parker glumly.

'Nonsense! He'll have tripped up. He had to acquire a car, and that should be traceable. He wouldn't leave the car on the street – too dangerous – so my bet is he'd got himself two lock-up garages; one near a station close to here, and another nearer to London. We'll have to get on to the estate agents, Parker. I want a complete rundown on all lock-up garages all along that bloody railway. And you can get a look at that Burberry of his and check on the reverse colour, then talk to porters at every station to try to get an identi . . .'

The telephone shrilled loudly.

VI

Howell's interview with Superintendent Whitlow was uncomfortable and prickly. 'For God's sake!' said Whitlow. 'Don't you have any bloody tact at all?'

Howell moved fractionally in the chair which was the only outward concession he made to writhing. Mentally he was writhing better than a pit full of snakes.

'I said you *do* nothing without referring to me. So what happens? You accuse a suspect – and what a suspect! of murder. I've just had my ears pierced by the Chief Constable,' Whitlow bellowed in a whisper.

'I accused no one of murder,' said Howell stolidly.

'Denham says you accused *him* of murder.'

'I merely put forward certain hypotheses.'

'Did you?' Whitlow leaned back in his chair. 'I take it you have an accurate transcript of the interview?'

'Yes, sir.'

'I want it on my desk this afternoon. Then I will tell you what you did or did not do. In the meantime you will turn your notes over to Chief Inspector Hammond. You will *not* go near Denham again. You are *off* this case – permanently. Is that understood?'

'Yes, sir,' said Howell unhappily.

Whitlow looked at Howell steadily for perhaps thirty seconds, then waved his hand tiredly. 'You may go.'

VII

That, of course, did not do Howell's career prospects any good at all, and he knew it. He knew it so well that he applied for a posting as far away from Whitlow as possible, and Whitlow did not stand in his way. It was not the Orkneys, but not very far short. Deliberately he refrained from taking an interest in the Franklin case or, as he mentally called it to himself, the Denham case.

So it was that he parted from Parker and it was not until six years later that they met again. Howell, by now miraculously a chief inspector, was passing through London, and in a hotel foyer walked into Sergeant Parker. 'Well, by God!' said Parker. 'This deserves a drink.' They repaired to the bar.

Parker was a little more paunchy, jowly and prosperous looking. He bought the drinks – double Scotches – and they sat at a quiet table. 'Mud in your eye!' said Parker expansively. 'How are you doing these days?'

'Not bad,' said Howell quietly.

'You know I left the force?'

'No, I didn't know,' said Howell. 'What are you doing?'

'Oh, I left about four years ago – went into the City. I'm doing quite well.'

Howell smiled slightly. 'You always seemed cut out for that sort of thing. On your own?'

'Oh, no,' said Parker. 'I'm with Denham Holdings Ltd.'

Howell put down his glass a little too quickly and whisky slopped on to the table. *'What!?'*

'I thought that might surprise you,' said Parker gaily.

'For God's sake! Would you work for *that* man?' His voice rose.

Parker's hand was on his arm. 'Take it easy, sir.' The respectful addendum slipped out unconsciously.

'You – of all people – tell me to take it easy?' Howell whispered savagely. 'Denham was as guilty as all hell – and we both know it. We both watched him sweat like a pig.' He threw off Parker's hand. 'It was all very well for Whitlow to read the bloody transcript but that was just words. We *saw* Denham.'

'Would you like to hear what happened?'

'If I must.' Howell took a drink. 'Yes, of course I would.'

'All right, then. You turned the case over to Hammond together with all your notes. At that time I was as convinced as you that Denham had killed Franklin. I passed on to Hammond all your thinking about the coat, the train, the car and everything. So we worked on it – by Christ, how we worked on it! And Denham came out as clean as a whistle. No car, no lock-up garages – nothing.'

Howell thumped the table. 'So how the hell did he do it? I could smell it on the man.'

Parker sighed. 'The fainting fit as he got off the train was quite genuine. He's a diabetic; stress and diabetes don't go too well together. And, by God, did he have stress then? – I've talked to him about it since. The position he was in was that he'd either make three million quid or lose everything he had – and it largely depended on Franklin. He spent the train journey back to town in the shakes and passed out at the end of it.'

A sense of outrage grew in Howell. 'If I ever heard of the perfect motive for murder that's it.'

Parker said gently, 'Denham didn't do it. There was no way.'

'Did Franklin's death get Denham out of the hole he was in?'

'It did. He's riding high now.'

Howell swore violently, obscenely and at length. 'I'm not a bad jack, Parker; I *know* he did it. Damn it, you were there at the interview. Couldn't you see it?'

'I saw something,' said Parker. 'When you told him that Franklin had written his name at the moment of his death you gave him the biggest shock he'd ever had in his life. Given his medical condition I'm surprised he didn't pass out there and then.'

'But, Parker, it all hung together,' said Howell desperately. 'What about the train? Why did he take the slow train?'

Parker was silent for a moment, then spoke slowly. 'The rich aren't the same as us, only richer – they're different. Denham only took the train because his Rolls was out of action, and he hadn't travelled by train for years. He wasn't used to them, and to him, any train back to London was as good as the next.'

Howell was silent for a while. 'Then if not Denham – who? There was no one else, damn it!'

Matter-of-factly Parker said, 'I'd put my money on Mrs Matthews.' As Howell gaped he said, 'She was killed eighteen months later, you know. Fell under a train.' He blinked, and added sadly, 'It was the 7:45 as it happens.'

'I didn't know.' Howell became alert. 'Suicide? Did she leave a note?'

'Not suicide. Mansell cut her up and found she didn't have enough blood in her alcohol stream. She was pretty far gone on the booze by then. She always did like her nip, and it got out of control after Franklin was killed. Did you know that Franklin fired her brother-in-law the week before he was shot?'

Howell shook his head dumbly.

'We all thought of how perfect a witness she was; of how keen she was to establish an alibi for Denham. When she hopped her twig I did a bit of checking back and found that her sister's husband worked for Franklin and had got the push during an economy drive. Remember the red ink on that balance sheet? Then I found a few bits and pieces – you're a jack, you know the kind of thing. I passed it all over to Hammond and he put it in the dead file.'

'What sort of bits and pieces? How did she fiddle the time?'

Parker said meditatively, 'Hammond thought it was the milk. You remember that Mansell established the time of death by the contents of the stomach, and that depended on the time of the last meal. Franklin had a bad ulcer and he was on a bland diet, including warm milk. Mrs Matthews said he had a glass of warm milk with added glucose about every two hours, that's why she left the milk out for him ready for warming. She said he didn't drink it – but what if he did? What if she shot him, waited a while, cleaned up the evidence and then put out more milk? That would confuse the time of death considerably.'

'I see,' said Howell blankly.

Parker drained his glass and stood up. 'It was about that time I decided to quit the force. Denham made me an offer I couldn't refuse. I've never regretted it.'

'Haven't you?' said Howell in a dull voice.

'Look, I have an appointment,' said Parker. 'I must love and leave you. Here's my card – give me a ring some time.'

Insincere sincerity lapped about Howell. He watched Parker stride away, Savile Row clad, a man of the new world, but made no attempt to pick up the card. Instead he went to the bar and ordered another drink, which was most unusual because he was normally abstemious.

And he thought of many things.

He thought of a lowly sergeant who, even then, had investments to protect, a sergeant whose knowledge of accountancy and financial acumen should rightly have brought him a job in the Fraud Squad. A sergeant who, under Hammond, had done the routine legwork in checking Denham's alibi. A quondam sergeant who now, in the Denham organisation, was riding on Denham's coat-tails.

He swore bitterly and assessed his chances of reviving the Denham case from Hammond's dead file as less than nil.

Howell got quite drunk that night, and to his dying day he never believed that Franklin had not written the name of his murderer at the time of his death.

He could very well have been right.

And, of course, he could have been wrong.

DESMOND BAGLEY

'Sizzling adventure.' *Evening Standard*

THE TIGHTROPE MEN

When Giles Denison of Hampstead wakes up in an Oslo hotel room and finds the face looking back at him in the mirror is not his own, things could surely get no more bizarre. But it is only the beginning of a hair-raising adventure in which Denison finds himself trapped with no way to escape. One false move and the whole delicately balanced power structure between East and West will come toppling down . . .

THE ENEMY

Wealthy, respectable George Ashton flees for his life after an acid attack on his daughter. Who is his enemy? Only Malcolm Jaggard, his future son-in-law, can guess, after seeing Ashton's top secret government file. In a desperate manhunt, Jaggard pits himself against the KGB and stalks Ashton to the silent, wintry forests of Sweden. But his search for the enemy has barely begun . . .

'Bagley has become a master of the genre – a thriller writer of intelligence and originality.' *Sunday Times*

978-0-00-730475-2

DESMOND BAGLEY

'Compulsively readable.' *Guardian*

FLYAWAY

Why is Max Stafford, security consultant, beaten up in his own office? What is the secret of the famous 1930s aircraft, the Lockheed Lodestar? And why has accountant Paul Bilson disappeared in North Africa? The journey to the Sahara desert becomes a race to save Paul Bilson, a race to find the buried aircraft, and – above all – a race to return alive . . .

WINDFALL

When a legacy of £40 million is left to a small college in Kenya, investigations begin about the true identities of the heirs – the South African, Dirk Hendriks, and his namesake, Henry Hendrix from California. Suspicion that Hendrix is an impostor leads Max Stafford to the Rift Valley, where a violent reaction to his arrival points to a sinister and far-reaching conspiracy far beyond mere greed . . .

'From word one, you're off. Bagley's one of the best.'
The Times

978-0-00-730476-9

DESMOND BAGLEY

'The best adventure stories I have read for years.'

Daily Mirror

THE GOLDEN KEEL

When the Allies invaded southern Italy in 1943, Mussolini's personal treasure was moved north to safety under heavily armed guard. It was never seen again. Now, an expedition plans to unearth the treasure and smuggle it out of Italy. But their reckless mission is being followed – by enemies who are as powerful and ruthless as they are deadly . . .

THE VIVERO LETTER

Jeremy Wheale's well-ordered life is blasted apart when his brother is murdered. The killer was after a family heirloom – an antique gold tray – which sets Wheale on a trail from Devon to the tropical rainforest of Yucatan. There he joins the hunt for a lost Mayan city. But in the dense cover of the jungle a band of vicious convict mercenaries are waiting to strike . . .

'Bagley has no equal at this sort of thing.'

Sunday Mirror

978-0-00-730477-6

DESMOND BAGLEY

'Tense, heroic, chastening . . . a thumping good story.'
Sunday Express

THE SNOW TIGER

Fifty-four people died in the avalanche that ripped apart a small New Zealand mining town. But the enquiry which follows unleashes more destructive power than the snowfall. As the survivors tell their stories, they reveal a community so divided that all warnings of danger went unheeded. At the centre of the storm is Ian Ballard, whose life depends upon being able to clear his name . . .

NIGHT OF ERROR

When Mark Trevelyan dies on a journey to a remote Pacific atoll, the verdict that it was natural causes doesn't convince his brother, Mike. The series of violent attacks that follows only adds to his suspicions. Just two clues – a notebook in code and a lump of rock – are enough to trigger off a hazardous expedition, and a violent confrontation far from civilization . . .

'The detail is immaculately researched – the action has the skill to grab your heart or your bowels.' *Daily Mirror*

978-0-00-730481-3

DESMOND BAGLEY

'Bagley in top form.' *Evening Standard*

THE SPOILERS

When film tycoon Robert Hellier loses his daughter to heroin, he declares war on the drug pedlars, the faceless overlords whose greed supplies the world with its deadly pleasures. London drug specialist Nicholas Warren is called upon to organise an expedition to the Middle East to track down and destroy them – but with a hundred million dollars' worth of heroin at stake, Warren knows he will have to use methods as deadly as his prey . . .

JUGGERNAUT

It is no ordinary juggernaut. Longer than a football pitch, weighing 550 tons, and moving at just five miles per hour, its job – and that of troubleshooter Neil Mannix – is to move a giant transformer across an oil-rich African state. But when Nyala erupts in civil war, Mannix's juggernaut is at the centre of the conflict – a target of ambush and threat, with no way to run and nowhere to hide . . .

'Bagley is a master story-teller.' *Daily Mirror*

978-0-00-730480-6